# MENDING FENCES

## PATRICIA YAGER DELAGRANGE

ALAMEDA, CALIFORNIA

Digital ISBN: 9781954395015
Print ISBN: 9781954395008

I dedicate this book to Susan and Kathy, and I know they will understand why. You both have supported me in my writing career. You both have ridden the roller coaster with me that makes up a writer's journey. I love you both for listening to me when I was happy and commiserating with me when I was sad. You embody the true meaning of being a friend. I love you both.

# Chapter One

Patti and her sister Kathy exited the limousine and walked toward the double doors of Alameda's Greer Mortuary. Patti's ponytail swung side to side in the light spring breeze coming off San Francisco Bay, the air whispering through the trees that lined the walkway leading to the entrance.

She grasped the brass door handle, paused, and turned to Kathy. "You ready for this?"

Kathy shook her head. Tears filled her eyes, then slowly dripped down her cheeks. "I know it sounds stupid, but I never thought we'd be doing this."

Patti pursed her lips, then nodded. "Surreal, isn't it?" She opened the door wide and was struck by the scent of lavender wafting in the air. She momentarily closed her eyes in thanks. A week ago, when Patti had met with Mr. Greer, she'd told him lavender was her mother's favorite flower. She was so happy he'd been kind enough to remember.

She recalled the very last conversation she'd had with her mom. "Patti? Patticake?" she'd said, her voice raspy and dry from drinking so little water in the last few days before she passed away.

"I'm here, Mom."

"I made it," her mom had whispered.

"You made it? Made what, Mom?"

"To your birthday." She coughed, and the rattling sound cut through Patti's head like fingernails on a chalkboard. "Happy birthday, my dear, sweet Patticake."

It was Wednesday, March twenty-ninth. Patti's birthday was February fifth. Mom had once again gotten confused about time. Patti had leaned over her mom and kissed her on her smooth, cold cheek. "I love you, Mom. Forever and a day."

"Don't forget… lavender. Don't… forget me," her mom had said. Then her eyelids shut halfway, remained that way for several seconds, then closed.

"I won't, Mom," Patti had said. "Mom? Mom? Mom?" But her beloved mom had nodded her head slowly twice, smiling. She never opened her eyes again.

Patti gave herself a virtual shake, willing the memories away… for now. She linked arms with Kathy, and they walked toward the wide-open chapel doors, their footsteps muffled on the plush, red carpet.

Kathy hesitated at the mortuary's chapel doorway. "I can't do this."

Patti grasped her sister's hand and squeezed. "You'll be okay, Kath," she whispered. "We'll both be okay."

Patti's heart rapped an uneven beat as they made their way past pew after crowded pew. Her ears tingled with the undercurrent of whispers. *Just a few more steps before we reach the open casket.*

Slowly, Patti stretched out her hand toward the edge of the coffin and curled her fingers over the white satin. She glanced at her sister. Kathy's eyes were closed, and she was whispering under her breath.

"Kathy?" Patti said. "What're you doing?"

Kathy inhaled deeply through her nose, releasing it in a long breath. "Please don't let Mom look like a porcelain doll in a box. Please, please, please."

Patti glanced down at her mom. Again, Mr. Greer had done as she'd asked. Rose-red lipstick tinted the half smile on her mom's lips, and her hair was just as she'd always styled it. She looked as if she'd sit up at any moment and shout, "Surprise!"

"She looks exactly like Mom, Kathy."

Kathy turned to face her sister, eyes squinted tightly shut, their noses almost touching. "I can't look at her."

Patti's eyes burned. She'd cried so much in the last few days, she didn't understand how her body could possibly produce any more fluid. She felt completely drained. Patti grasped her sister's shoulders. "Kathy, she looks exactly as she used to, before hospice came into the picture."

A glimmer of a smile stretched across Kathy's face, and she opened her eyes. "She looked so good last year, didn't she?"

Patti nodded. "That's how she looks now, Kath."

"I'm glad I came up at the end," Kathy said, her voice wobbling.

"You got to say goodbye. And that's such a blessing."

"But it killed me to see her lying there, sick and feeble. She was always so full of life." Kathy's voice hitched. "I loved her so much."

"You kissed her. She smiled back at you. She knew who you were. Remember that. Hold tight to the memories. And we have so many good memories, Kath. All those years at the ranch. Birthdays, Christmas. Easter."

Kathy gripped Patti's hand, hard. "I'll regret it if I don't look her in the face and tell her I love her one last time, before they…" She drew in a deep breath. "Before they—"

Patti reached up and tucked a shock of strawberry-blonde hair behind her sister's ear, looked into her eyes. "And to dust we shall return." She paused. "I've got your back. I'm right here."

Kathy intertwined their fingers. "Don't leave me." She faced forward and slowly looked down into the casket. "Oh. My. God," she mumbled. "She's dead."

Patti squeezed her sister's hand tighter. "I know." She hadn't thought her mom would die this soon either. Or was that only wishful thinking? How about flat-out denial?

Yes, Mom had had Stage Four ovarian cancer, but she'd gone through fourteen rounds of chemotherapy over the past ten years. Patti had been sure that after her mom had endured months of vomiting, losing her hair, not eating, and feeling like crap, all those toxic chemicals would have made a difference. Well, they hadn't. The CA-125 tumor marker had kept shooting up and up, until the future was too obvious to ignore.

"The cancer's metastasized," Dr. Cecchi had told her. "Gone to her lungs, bones, her brain. She might live three months, but that's being generous," he'd added. *Damn him and his prognosis.*

Then, everything had gone to hell in a hand basket, as her dad used to say.

*And now here we are, teetering at the edge of Mom's coffin, holding on for dear life. Unlike Mom, who wasn't able to hold on to her life at all.* Patti tried hard to stifle a sob, covering her lips with her fingers.

"We're orphans," Kathy whispered, not taking her eyes off her mother's face. "We don't have a mother anymore."

Patti drew in a deep breath and was silent for several seconds. "We're not orphans. There's still Dad."

"Really, Patti?"

Patti sniffed and swiped at her tears. "He's here, you know."

"You mean in town, or in the funeral home right now?"

"Here. Now. In the back."

"But what's he doing here?"

Patti sighed. "They were married for more than thirty years."

"But I haven't spoken to him in a decade." Kathy shook her head. "I can't handle this. I have to get out of here."

"Listen to me, Kathy. Mom wouldn't want that. She still loved Dad even though they weren't married any longer. They remained friends. Honor that."

Kathy sidestepped to the right, reached the pew located next to the casket, and knelt down, clasping her hands on the padded railing. "Is there some way I can leave without talking to him? A secret side door? I just want to go back to your house."

Patti stood next to her sister and rested a hand on her shoulder. "Are you forgetting we still have to go to the cemetery?"

Kathy bowed her head, leaning her forehead on her clutched hands. "Ugh. I don't know what I was thinking. Of course I'm going to the cemetery."

"Remember when you, Mom, and I walked through the Piedmont Cemetery? That one in Oakland? It's so gorgeous, and the gravestones date back to the early 1800s. It was so peaceful. Mom loved it there."

Kathy nodded.

"Just talk to Dad, Kath. Get it over with."

"*He's* coming to the cemetery, too?"

"I would imagine so."

Kathy shoved herself upward. "Promise you'll stay right next to me."

"Forever and a day."

Kathy swiped at her moist cheeks with a hankie. "You've been saying that since we were kids."

"And I'll say it till the day I die."

"Don't talk about dying," Kathy hissed. "I'm teetering on the edge as it is."

"I'm not dying. In fact, I'm not going anywhere. You can't get rid of me that easily."

Kathy's lips quirked up at the edges. "Not for lack of trying."

"Where would we be without the sarcasm?" Patti reached out and hugged her sister. "He's in the last row to your left," she whispered in her ear. "Time to face the music."

"I noticed someone just started playing music. You know how I *love* organ music." Kathy dabbed at her eyes with her damp hankie.

"I hate organ music as much as you, but it comes with the funeral territory," Patti said. "Did you expect Jimi Hendrix?"

Kathy smiled for the first time in weeks.

Smiling had faded, along with laughing, and then departed along with their mom. "Can you at least *try* to be nice to him?" Patti said. "Mom would have wanted that."

"Why should I?" Kathy huffed.

"Underneath all that indignant behavior, you're just a big softy."

"*Big* being the operative word."

"You look just fine the way you are."

"If I could just lose the last, what, forty pounds?"

"Don't exaggerate." Patti reached for Kathy's hand, and the two sisters turned to face the back of the room.

Kathy gripped Patti's hand as they walked down the center aisle. "He already left," she said under her breath. "What did I expect? He left her ten years ago, too."

Patti tugged on her sister's hand, and Kathy turned toward her. Patti lifted her chin slightly.

Kathy followed her sister's gaze. "My God. He looks like he's eighty years old."

"Eighty-three, to be exact."

"Last time I saw him, he had at least *some* hair. And he had a pot belly back then, too."

"That was before the divorce."

Kathy turned to Patti. "Which one?"

Patti elbowed her sister in the side. "His thirty-two-year-old mistress-turned-wife-for-ten-seconds really took him to the cleaners."

"Serves him right for divorcing Mom in the middle of her first round of chemo," Kathy muttered.

"Well, he lost a bundle. I guess karma's a bitch. But, hey, I never met her. Did you?"

Kathy shook her head. "Wasn't interested."

Bill Michaels stepped out of the pew and stood in front of his daughters. Opening his arms wide, he smiled. "How's my Katydid?"

Kathy lifted an eyebrow. "I'm no longer your Katydid."

He dropped his arms to his sides, frowning. "Still mad at me?"

Patti leaned in and gave her dad a quick hug. "How're you doing, Dad?"

He switched his gaze to Patti and nodded. "Not too bad. Gettin' older."

"Aren't we all? Where's Helen, and Sharon?"

"Something came up at the ranch. They'll be here soon."

Patti looked at him askance. "But *both* of them are coming, right?"

"Of course they're both coming. Why would you even ask?"

Patti glanced to the side and pulled in her lips, then said, "Because Helen rarely came to see Mom when she was sick. So she might not bother now."

Kathy suddenly stepped out of their little circle. Her father grasped her forearm.

"Wait! Katy… uh, Kathy," he stuttered.

Kathy looked at his hand on her arm.

He instantly let go of her. "I'm sorry. I never meant to hurt your feelings."

Kathy lifted her eyes to meet his. "You're just now telling me you're sorry? Seriously? After ten years?"

"Just because I divorced your mother doesn't mean I don't love you."

Kathy's face flushed ruby red. "Not only did you leave Mom for someone younger than your own daughters, Dad. You left her when she needed you. She had cancer. What kind of man leaves his wife during a severe medical crisis?"

"Lower your voice, please," he said quietly.

"You shouldn't even be here." Kathy's tone grew angrier with each word.

Their father pursed his lips, looking as if he'd just sucked on a slice of lime. "Your mother and I were married for thirty years. I loved her," he whispered.

Kathy pulled back. "You loved her? Loving her didn't stop you from having affairs."

"I didn't have *affairs*, Kathy. I fell in love with another woman at a time when your mom and I were having problems. Our marriage had already deteriorated. We were talking about getting a divorce."

Kathy turned her gaze to the ceiling and sighed. "Do you think we're all stupid? Everyone—me, Patti, Helen, Sharon—we all knew about your little liaisons. Plural, Bill. You can't kid a kidder, as you always said."

Her father pointed his finger in her face, which only served to egg Kathy on even more. "There was only one other woman, Kathy."

"You *had* a woman—Mom. And she was a fantastic person. But she got cancer, so she was no longer perfect. Was that it?"

Bill shook his head. "You don't understand."

Kathy looked him in the eyes. "No, I do not."

"Why is it you think you can talk to me like this? What do you want to hear? That I fell in love with a younger woman who took all my money? Don't you think I already feel like a fool? And why do you insist on calling me Bill? You're my daughter. That'll never change, Kathy. I love you."

"I don't know if I love *you* anymore. When you ditched Mom in the middle of chemo, Dad, it was the worst time of her life. What if someone did the same thing to you? And did you ever think how difficult it was for her to leave her job? Working as a psychologist was her passion, and she had to quit so she could be treated for cancer." She whipped around and ran out of the room, tripped over the doorjamb leading to the parking lot, and fell flat on her face.

Patti ran after her, grasped her sister around the stomach, and pulled her to her feet.

Kathy gasped. "Wha-what're you doing?"

"I couldn't take being in there either. Let's wait in the limo."

Kathy swiped at her tears with a hankie, then looked at it and groaned. "Do you have a Kleenex?"

Patti drew a tissue from her purse and stuffed it in her sister's hand. "Let's get outta here."

They walked toward the limo, which was parked at the side of the funeral home's front doors. The driver opened the rear door and stepped aside.

Kathy slid into the backseat, and Patti followed her.

They both snuggled into the thick cushiony leather. Patti sighed. Kathy followed with a sigh of her own.

"I'm surprised Charlie didn't come up for the funeral," Patti said.

"If you want to see him so bad, you could come visit me."

Patti's eyebrows drew together. "What the hell are you talking about? It's not like San Diego is that far away. I haven't visited you because I couldn't get any time off work."

Kathy bent her head and pinched the bridge of her nose with her thumb and index finger. "I'm sorry. I'm sorry." She looked at her sister. "I'm being a bitch because I'm pissed off that Dad's here."

Or maybe because Kathy had never gotten over the fact Charlie was in love with Patti first. But that was so long ago, and Patti was going to do everything she could to dissuade Kathy from her misconstrued belief that he was still in love with Patti. Patti was definitely not in love with him.

After their parents' divorce, Kathy had moved away from the ranch to take a job in San Diego. There she discovered Charlie had a yacht business in La Jolla. He and Kathy had met for coffee, and Patti was happy they had found each other. Though it had been somewhat of a surprise… Had Patti's heart pinged with a tinge of jealousy when she heard about her sister's new romance? Of course not. As her dad always said, that boat had already sailed. What an appropriate pun, given Charlie's entrepreneurial interest.

Kathy leaned her head back and shut her eyes. "I'm emotionally exhausted." She flicked open one eye. "Wake me when we reach the cemetery?"

Patti settled into the seat and stared out the side window. "I'm not in love with your boyfriend, Kath." She turned to her sister, and their eyes locked. "And he's not in love with me."

Kathy sat in silence for a moment, a moment too long for Patti. Finally, Kathy looked into her sister's eyes and said, "I think I know that in my head. But my heart's a different thing altogether."

"For God's sake, the thing with Charlie was way back in high school. I swear to God, I don't even think about him any longer. And you've seemed so content since you've been with him. I'm happy for you. For both of you."

Kathy rested her head back. "I'm sorry. I love you, Patticake."

Patti stared at her sister's face, which for the first time in months looked almost serene. "I love you, too, Katydid."

# Chapter Two

Patti was glad when the limo pulled onto the curved drive of the cemetery. The last thing she wanted to do was walk down memory lane. Or rather, fall into a pit of intimate recollections about her first love. Not only had that boat already sailed, that train had departed the station a very long time ago. She was not interested in boarding that boat or train again.

Their mother had chosen to be buried in a crypt, so the service was to take place in front of the mausoleum within the hour. As Patti and Kathy exited the limousine, a yellow cab pulled up behind them.

Their sister Helen stepped out, wearing a skin-tight, black spandex dress. Her straight brown bob swayed beneath her chin as she swished it this way and that, glancing around for anyone who'd notice. *How can they not?* Patti and Kathy exchanged a look. Patti held in the sarcastic comments running through her head, though she found it hard to swallow the words burbling just behind her tonsils. *This is Mom's funeral, and I should not be dissing Helen.*

Next to exit from the cab were Sharon's long legs, followed by the rest of her statuesque body, as she unfolded herself and stepped out onto the pavement. Her blonde hair fluttered in the subtle breeze, and when she saw Patti and Kathy, she smiled and waved.

"*Sharon* looks great," Patti said to Kathy out of the side of her mouth.

"Yes, she does," Kathy whispered, then, "Helen hasn't changed one bit in ten years."

"You mean she dresses like she's eighteen, but she's not?" Patti shoved her shoulders back, expanding her chest underneath her black silk top. She could always outdo Helen in that particular area, but in a classy way. Helen was just pure hussy, right down to the slit in the middle of her dress that almost reached her crotch.

*Stop it!*

Helen leaned in to give both Patti and Kathy quick air kisses on both cheeks. Not to show any particular affection, but rather to give the impression she was schooled in the European way of greeting. Their oldest sister, Sharon, followed by giving Patti and Kathy solid hugs and real kisses on the cheek.

Patti and Kathy had spent many a night trashing Helen's character and behavior when they all lived under the same roof at the ranch in Northern California. And later on as well. They loved her because she was their sister, and they felt a certain filial obligation. And at times she manifested a hilarious sense of humor.

But that sense of humor had always been directed at someone in a cutting, biting way. For example, Helen was great at putting people down in a comedic fashion. Underneath it all, it was not difficult to admit the fact their sister was a two-faced bitch. She treated everyone but her relatives with kindness, fake as it was. The moment someone left a room, Helen's talons slid out and poked them in the ass. As for her family, Helen didn't wait for them to exit the room, and it was not fun being the brunt of her sharp tongue.

*But, hey, maybe she's changed.*

Patti remembered her mom analyzing the hell out of Helen's behavior to help Patti, Kathy, and Sharon understand her. But living with Helen had been difficult. Being the target of Helen's constant put-downs and insults had been exhausting, whether their mom's analyzing made sense or not.

"It's good to see you," Patti said to Helen, trying very hard to swallow any sarcasm that might slip into her tone.

"Oh, really?" Helen said.

"We're late because one of the horses was foaling. We had to stay," Sharon added.

Sharon had always been the peacemaker of the family. She'd read more psychology books than Kathy read romance novels, and Kathy never went anywhere without a book in her hand. Sharon had followed in their mother's footsteps in her desire to understand people and their emotional problems, so they were never surprised at anything Sharon said that touched on the human psychological condition.

"I understand," Patti said, tamping down her irritation. Just seeing Helen was enough to bring out the worst in Patti. And she hated the fact Helen had the power to do that. But Patti really didn't want to make waves at her mother's funeral. And maybe, just maybe, a miracle had occurred, and Helen had morphed into a kind person. "You can't plan an animal's birth. I totally get that, Helen."

Helen pulled the hem of her skirt down about an eighth of an inch and copped a quick glance at Patti. "Let's get this thing over with."

"Wouldn't want to put you out any," Patti muttered, knowing she was being pissy.

Kathy dug her elbow into Patti's side. "Stop it."

But in her head, Patti couldn't help herself. Helen had always been the most self-centered individual on the planet. And that obviously had not changed. She had come to visit their mother twice in ten years, and now she acted like this one-time funeral was putting her out?

"Sorry," Patti said. "I'm going to get through this day peacefully, the way Mom would have wanted. We're family."

Helen glared at her for several seconds, then walked away.

Like a group of balloons, Patti, Kathy, and Sharon seemed to deflate.

"How *do* you live with her?" Patti asked.

Sharon sighed. "I understand her."

Patti smiled. "Don't tell me. You understand why she is the way she is from reading *Psychology Today* magazines, right?"

Sharon stepped between Kathy and Patti and locked arms with each of them. "Actually, it was a class I took in college. I love psychology. The mind fascinates me."

Kathy chuckled. "Like mother, like daughter."

Patti leaned closer to Sharon. "You're a freaking saint."

"No, I'm not," Sharon said. "She's my sister, Patti. She has issues."

Patti and Kathy stared at Sharon, mouths slightly agape.

"She's insecure," Sharon explained. "Helen feels unaccepted by almost everyone she's ever known. But deep down, I believe she thinks she's not worthy of love. So she lashes out as a defense mechanism, and by doing so, she receives the exact rejection she believes she was going to receive in the first place, the rejection she feels deep down that she deserves."

"That's a new and interesting take on it," Patti said. "But I understand what you're trying to say. However, there are only so many concessions I can make for the fact she's my sister and she has issues before I just lose it. She pushes the envelope with her asshat behavior."

"Asshat behavior? That's a refreshing adjective." Kathy chuckled. "Helen makes absolutely no effort at all to be a friend or a sister. You know what I mean?"

Patti nodded. "It's her attitude. She so rubs me the wrong way. Always has."

"I guess she always will," Kathy added.

"I understand where you two are coming from," Sharon said. "We're all three so different."

Patti looked from Sharon to Kathy and back. "I think for Kathy and me, it's like we can never let down our guard when we're around her. We're always braced for Helen's next snarky onslaught."

"And for me," Kathy said, "Dad causes the same reaction. The whole thing with Mom just… I don't know if I'll ever get over that."

Patti turned to Kathy. "You're the sweetest person I know, but when it comes to Dad, you turn into a snarling hyena."

Sharon looked at Kathy. "Holding grudges and allowing negative thoughts to simmer inside causes anxiety and depression. Forgiveness is the only way to truly let go of the bad and allow the good to come in."

Kathy tilted her head and smiled at Sharon. "You're right, Saint Sharon." She reached out and hugged her.

"Well, Sharon," Patti added, "your advice about not holding grudges and learning to forgive Dad includes our behavior toward Helen, too. I promise I'll be good." She looked skyward. "I'll do it for you, Mom," she whispered, eyes glistening with unshed tears.

Sharon pressed her lips together and looked from Patti to Kathy and back. "I've been crying for days."

Patti nodded. "Me, too, Share. I miss Mom so much it hurts. Talking smack about Helen definitely turns my attention away from the overwhelming grief I feel over Mom's death."

Kathy let out a sigh. "I always thought it was so special that Mom and I were friends. Not just mother and daughter, you know?"

Sharon smiled. "Mom always encouraged my love for psychology. And she taught me so much about people."

"She was a great mom, wasn't she?" Kathy said.

Patti rubbed Kathy's back. "She was indeed."

"Her death leaves a huge hole in all our lives," Sharon added.

Helen's shrill voice cut through the peace of the cemetery.

Sharon, Kathy, and Patti turned their heads in Helen's direction.

Their sister stood, hands on her hips, about fifteen feet away. "I said, where's Dad?"

Patti hitched her chin up in the direction of the entrance to the mausoleum.

Helen turned. "Hey, Dad!" she shouted, waving.

"For God's sake, Helen, would you keep it down?" Kathy pleaded.

Helen shifted her eyes in Kathy's direction. "Who died and made you my mother?"

"You haven't had anything to do with your *mother* in ten years," Patti erupted.

If looks could kill, Patti's funeral would have been the next one for the family to attend.

"Don't start, Patticake," Helen replied. "I rarely get time off, because I'm always working on the ranch. With Dad."

"Dad had time to visit Mom, *Helena*," Patti answered.

"Stop it," Sharon demanded.

Patti sucked in her lips. *Here I go again.* Helen made it so difficult for Patti to be nice to her.

Their parents had watched a Greek play put on at the local theater every month during their mom's pregnancy with their youngest child. So when the time came to name their last child, they selected the name Helena, after their favorite Greek goddess.

Eternal ribbings and jokes abounded the moment Kathy and Patti met their baby sister. With each passing year, Helen despised her name more and more. Thus, the name "Helena" always found its way into any argument between the sisters at the moment when it was likely to cause maximum damage.

The tension had grown so thick, Patti could practically feel it in her bones. She took a huge breath, then said, "I'm sorry, Helen. I shouldn't have said that." She paused, and Helen remained silent. Of course, Helen would never apologize. *I'll be the better person—again.* "Can we all try our best to get along today? For Mom? I know I'm really stressed out about all this, and I apologize for being snarky, Helen."

Silence.

The four women walked stiffly in a line toward the cluster of chairs at the side of the mausoleum. Patti followed in Helen's perfume-infused wake. Kathy and Sharon brought up the rear.

About fifty people sat in rows of black folding chairs in front of a raised dais. After the four sisters took their seats, the monsignor from their mother's church stepped up to the podium, cleared his throat, and tapped the microphone with his finger.

"Good morning." He looked toward the sky and squinted. "Actually, good afternoon. I'm Monsignor Wolford from St. Joseph Basilica in Alameda."

Several of the guests nodded, mumbling quiet greetings.

"I met Barbara Michaels after she moved to this area. She was one of my favorite parishioners." He paused. "Barbara liked to run things, as some of you might remember." He smiled.

A chuckle ran through the small crowd.

"You can say that again," Bill said, laughing loud enough to be heard.

Several people turned to see who had spoken. Realizing the remark had come from Barbara's ex-husband, Barbara's friends gave him dirty looks.

Patti wasn't pleased about what had happened ten years ago either. But she'd tried to make peace with the fact her father had divorced her mother for a younger woman. Granted, his timing sucked, but he was her father. Though when wife number two, Carolanne, dumped him several months later, Patti had to admit she didn't feel one bit sorry for him. And she'd chosen to stay clear of him for most of the past ten years. But if she were honest with herself, she'd have to admit she'd missed him.

Bill had a terrific sense of humor. He could make anyone laugh. And he loved parties and family gatherings. His smile was so real and so "Bill," everyone gravitated toward him as if he were a human magnet. But after the divorce, almost all of their parents' friends aligned with Barbara. Those who remained attached to Bill were his buddies from the olden days—guys who had been in the Marines with Bill and others who were his childhood pals.

Feeling particularly sorry for her dad at the moment, Patti made a promise to herself. She would mend fences between Kathy and her dad, hoping to help them both.

When it came to Kathy's low self-esteem, Patti had some

thoughts on the cause, although she was by no means a qualified therapist.

Kathy had moved to San Diego after their parents' divorce. Because of the distance alone, Kathy hadn't been as close to their mom as her three sisters had been. And she hadn't been the one their mother turned to when she was depressed while going through years of cancer treatments.

Helen and Sharon were close to each other and to their dad by virtue of the fact they'd continued to live together at the ranch. Although Kathy and Patti had been close, their relationship had dwindled to occasional phone calls and no visits due to Patti's demanding job. Add to that the fact Kathy was in a relationship with a man who'd once been in love with Patti. In that regard, Kathy felt she was Charlie's second choice of the Michaels sisters.

Bottom line: Patti didn't think Kathy felt like "number one" to anyone in her life.

Patti's mind wandered. When she was a teenager, being around Charlie had always made her heart pump harder, at least until she found out a specific part of his anatomy was literally pumping another girl. She'd never forgive him for what he'd done to her way back when. Though he'd readily admitted his one-time mistake, as he'd called it, he'd never even said he was sorry. She wondered if he'd truly changed. Kathy sure thought so.

Now that Patti thought about it, Kathy hadn't answered her question: What was the reason for Charlie's absence today?

She turned her gaze back to the monsignor, kicking thoughts and memories of Charlie Seevers to the curb.

The monsignor continued. "Barbara loved to help out at church, for which I will always be grateful. And she did it with an enviable amount of energy and gusto. Even though she had a thriving business as a psychologist, she always found the time to help out when our parish needed someone to step up to the plate. But I'm not here to give a sermon. As some of you know, I can be a bit long-winded." Another chuckle from the crowd. "I simply want to say thank you, Barbara," he glanced upward, "for everything you did for the choir, for the high school, for the altar boys… and girls. Yes, altar girls." He gave a low, rumbling laugh. "I'll make this brief, as I said." Another few titters from the audience. "I'll end this with a short story."

He took a deep breath and scanned the intimate group of mourners. "Several years back, two never-identified thieves broke into our high school and stole fifty desktop computers. Some of the students brought in their own computers from home and shared with their classmates. But most had to do without and try to get their work done by using the public computers at the local library, with its meager supply and limited hours.

"About a week after the theft occurred, Barbara was in my office, counting the donations for Sunday. I walked into the room, and she handed me an envelope. 'For new computers.' Then she paused. 'I never gave this to you.' Then she looked me in the eye and said, 'And don't mess with me, Robert.' She called me by my first name, but only when no one else was around.

"Until now I have never told anyone this story, but I feel it's fitting, given the fact that she isn't around to berate me for opening my fat mouth about her extraordinary good deed." He laughed. "Barbara Michaels was one of the most generous ladies I've ever met, not only with her time but with her money and her kindness."

He nodded and stepped down from the dais. He took a few steps, then returned to the podium. "If anyone would like to say a few words about Barbara, please feel free to do so now. Otherwise, let us take a few quiet moments to remember her and hold her in our thoughts."

Patti turned to Kathy. Kathy shrugged and shook her head. Sharon didn't move. Helen glanced back at Patti and Kathy and lifted one eyebrow. Patti frowned. What was Helen's problem?

Silence reigned for several seconds before Bill stood and walked to the podium.

Kathy lifted her rear end off the chair, and Patti grabbed her arm and pulled her back down in her seat.

"Don't you dare," Patti whispered.

"What the hell is he going to say?" Kathy whispered out of the side of her mouth.

"It'll be fine, Kath. He's not going to talk about how he left her and married some freaking bimbo who dumped him for someone more her age. He's not foolish enough to mention it. Ever. Certainly not here. He loved Mom." She looked Kathy in the eyes. "Remember, you said you'd try. Give Dad a chance, Kath."

Kathy looked at the ground and sighed. "I'll *try* to try. It's really hard."

"Shield your sword," Patti advised.

Kathy shook her head. "You never change."

"Whatever. Now, name that movie."

Kathy shook her head again. "Duh. *Gladiator*." She settled back in her chair.

Bill stood at the podium and straightened his shoulders, then glanced around at all the faces in the small crowd and cleared his throat. "I loved Barbara. I always have. I know many of you think that sounds like a bunch of bull, I mean, a bunch of hoo-ha. You think I'm not telling the truth here. But for many years, Barbara and I were soul mates." He paused and swallowed, actually looking as if he was going to shed a tear.

"But we changed. Both of us changed. And, believe me—or not—we were planning our divorce long before she got cancer. Yes, I remarried, and Barbara never did. But she and I kept in touch. We remained friends. She was a good woman." He locked eyes with Kathy, and then Patti, and added, "Barbara said many times that her dying wish was for our family to mend fences. She never wanted our divorce to split us down the middle." He coughed. "I hope we can find it in our hearts to make her wish come true. Wherever she is, believe me, she still wants that to happen." He returned to his seat between Helen and Sharon.

Several minutes passed. Patti suddenly stood and walked to the podium. She tapped the microphone, then cleared her throat.

"As most of you know, I'm Patti—the third daughter—after Sharon and Kathy. Helen's the baby." Patti looked up and smiled directly at Helen, whose lips, miracle of miracles, actually quirked upward a little in response. "Mom was my best friend, and I already miss her. After she moved to the San Francisco Bay Area, she and I were together during her radiation and chemotherapy, which brought us closer than we'd ever been. We got a ton of time to talk and laugh and reminisce about our family's past.

"Mom was truly a special human being. As a psychologist, she cared what happened to her clients. In her heart she wanted to help them feel better about themselves and their lives. It meant the world to her to hear one of her clients tell her, 'Thank you, Barbara.' Her job meant everything to Mom. Which is why it was so devastating to her to quit her practice." She could feel tears forming and stopped, shut her eyes for a second, and took a deep breath.

She smiled. "I don't want to talk your leg off like Monsignor Wolford." Everyone laughed. Patti met the monsignor's eyes. "Just kidding, Monsignor. Anyway, I just wanted to put it out there for Mom to know." Patti looked up at the sky. "And Dad and my three sisters as well." She glanced at the four of them in turn. "I think we are all well aware Mom and Dad always cared for each other. Always. Whether they were married or not, there was a bond there. Though they were divorced, I think it was hard for us girls to face that reality. Dad is a good man." She shrugged. "Mom wouldn't have loved him if he weren't. And Mom would want us girls to get along. So I'm going to try harder, Mom. I promise."

She paused and wiped a tear from her cheek. "You know how much I love movies, Mom. You and I watched a ton of them in the last few months we had together. So, you'll understand that I'm not going to say goodbye to you. As John said in the movie *John* Q, 'See you later.' And as Juba said in *Gladiator*, 'I will see you again. But not yet. Not yet.'"

Patti returned to her seat, and several minutes of silence passed before Monsignor Wolford blessed Barbara's casket once again, and the ceremony ended. The placement of the coffin inside the mausoleum vault was reserved for family only.

Patti, her sisters, and their father followed Monsignor Wolford inside, where six men employed by the funeral parlor lifted the casket and slid it inside the vault. Monsignor once again said a few final words, then shook each of their hands and departed.

Together, the small family of five walked down the steps. Bill turned to his daughters, who stood in silence, forming a half circle next to the limousine. "I'd like to invite you two girls to come to the ranch," he told Patti and Kathy. "It would be good for us to be under one roof again. Maybe this weekend? We can go for a trail ride." He faced Kathy. "Maximus is still alive and kicking, Katydid. He was always your favorite."

Kathy chewed on her bottom lip with her top teeth—a habit she'd formed during her childhood when she was stressed. She'd always been an extremely sensitive kid who had grown into an überstressed adult, worrying about anything and everything.

When Kathy's eyebrows bunched together, Patti surmised her sister's answer was an unequivocal no. Not a good sign. Patti wanted Kathy to get back the relationship she once had with their dad. A short visit to the ranch with all its distractions and beauty would do wonders for talking and regaining the feeling of family they'd enjoyed in the past.

"I'll think about it," Kathy mumbled.

Patti held in a grin and let out a sigh. This was progress.

Kathy turned and shot into the backseat of the limousine as if she were escaping a fire.

"Yes!" Dad cried, glancing up at the sky for a few seconds. He turned to Patti. "And you?"

Was it just stubbornness that had kept Patti from renewing the friendship she had with her father for so many years, or was she truly still pissed off at him? Yes, they'd met a couple of times, when he was in the Bay Area, and they'd talked about Barbara and her health problems. But Patti hadn't visited Fabulous Friesians Ranch in Northern California for ten years. Was she willing to let him go to his grave without telling him she still truly cared, that she loved him just as much as she had since she was a child? *We're family.*

"It's only a three-hour drive from here, Patti," he said, reading her thoughts.

"Okay. I'll make sure Kathy comes, too. I think we'll have a good time." She glanced at Helen and Sharon, flanking their father like two armed guards. Was she imagining it, or was the expression on Helen's face one of barely concealed anger? Or was it irritation? Why?

Sharon smiled, but that didn't surprise Patti. Sharon would see this as a perfect opportunity to put some of her psychology education to work.

Patti had been angry with her dad for ten years, yet she hated this continuing conflict. Up until now, she'd been civil to him. Kathy could barely contain her irritation and confrontational remarks. Patti had acted the same way with Helen. The time had come to make peace between all of them.

All the girls despised how their father had treated their mother. But Sharon had said she owed it to him to help at the ranch. Otherwise, who else would? Helen left home as well. But as soon as Fabulous Friesians began making money, Helen suddenly went home and rallied to his side. Now both Sharon and Helen worked and lived with their father at the ranch in Quincy. Northern California was a gorgeous place to live, so it wasn't as if living there had been a horrible decision.

However, in Patti's opinion, Helen's change of allegiance was all about Helen's future inheritance. It had nothing to do with letting bygones be bygones and forgiving their father's deplorable behavior, nor did it have anything to do with helping him run the ranch. The bottom line for Helen? It was all about the money.

# Chapter Three

Sitting on the comfy couch in Patti's cottage in Alameda, across the bay from San Francisco, Kathy stuffed a handful of buttered popcorn in her mouth, but that didn't stop her from talking. "Why don't you move down to San Diego, and we can be roommates?"

Patti leaned across the couch in her comfortably furnished front room and fisted her own clump of popcorn. She leaned her head back and poured the handful of greasy puffs into her mouth, chewed, swallowed, then reached for her Diet Coke. "I love my cottage. This whole little island, actually. *And* I can still work in San Francisco."

"But you just lost your job."

"Oops." Patti took another sip of her drink. "Forgot about that."

"No, you didn't. Why not move in with me until you find a new job? It's the perfect opportunity. You stayed here in Alameda because Mom was sick, and she needed someone to take care of her." Kathy grabbed another handful of popcorn. "This is the perfect time to move." She paused, chomping on the kernels. "Or did you want to stay closer to Dad in Quincy?"

"I thought you and Charlie practically lived together down there," Patti said.

Kathy bit at her bottom lip.

"Uh-oh. Problems in paradise?"

Kathy shook her head. "It hasn't exactly been paradise for a while."

"I wondered why he didn't come to Mom's funeral. I thought you two were going to get married someday."

"He and I haven't talked about getting married in literally months. You know how you're all in love during the blush of a new relationship? You meet somebody and fall madly in lust, then the initial heat simmers down?"

"Is the flame already extinguished for you two?"

Kathy grimaced. "Not on my part, no. He still lights my wick, if you know what I mean."

Patti put up her hand. "TMI. Please don't talk to me about your sex life."

Kathy turned her eyes on her sister. "You, of all people, know what it's like to be with him."

Patti rolled her eyes. "We were so young, Kathy. You know how it is when you're a teenager. Sex is new and, to our parents, totally unacceptable behavior. Which only makes it that much more fun. You and Charlie are not teenagers."

Kathy paused. "I know. And I get it. But it sure cooled awfully fast."

"Lots of relationships run hot and cold, depending on all kinds of factors. One of you is tired or doesn't feel good or is overworked or stressed. You can't expect to go at it like rabbits for twenty years."

Kathy reached for more popcorn. "I'd settle for being a rabbit for *one* year. Dang! It's probably all the weight I've gained in the last couple of months. I sit at a computer all day. I'm developing secretary's spread."

"You're an attractive woman, Kathy. No, you're not built like some skinny-ass *Vogue* model. Most women aren't. I mean, yuck! The anorexic look, in my opinion, is so not sexy. I would hope Charlie has matured a little. Gotten a little deeper. Most guys do." She shrugged. "Then again, some don't."

Kathy chewed while staring at the ceiling. "I think he's pulling away. I've thought that for a while now."

"What does he say? Or haven't you brought it up?"

"I've asked him if anything's wrong. He denies it. Says he's just worried about his company's financial stability."

"How big is his yacht company?"

"I think they have more than five to ten custom-built yachts, depending on the time of year," Kathy explained. "They sell them and also rent them. To very wealthy people who are either businessmen or retired old geezers. They want to go out in the ocean while they're on vacation or here on business or while they're still alive. It's really expensive to rent a yacht. And buying one? My God. You're talking millions of dollars."

"And his business isn't doing well financially?"

"See, that's the thing. That's not true. I ran into Charlie's friend at Starbucks. He's the accountant for Charlie's business. I asked him how things were going, and he told me the company's finally turned a corner. They're in the black now for the first time. So Charlie lied when he said he's stressed about the company's financial stability. I think it's just the standard line he uses when he doesn't want to tell me what's really bothering him. And anyway, it doesn't jive with the fact he told me he's looking for a house in La Jolla. The one he owns now is okay, but if he's looking in La Jolla, he's gotta be making some serious money."

"Maybe you're making something out of nothing, Kath."

"Playing devil's advocate, are we?"

Patti pursed her lips, then sighed. "Owning a company can be stressful, no doubt about it. And stress can work all kinds of mischief on one's sex life. It takes too much effort. Some people just want to sleep. They become inactive, like human slugs. It may have absolutely nothing to do with you."

Kathy blinked, and several tears trickled down her cheeks.

Patti reached out and grasped one of her sister's hands. "Sweetie, you know how Mom would always say. 'Kathy? You're making a mountain out of a molehill'?"

Kathy looked into Patti's eyes. "I think he's seeing someone else. You know how you just *know* know?"

"Well, yeah, I know what you're saying. I remember back in the day." Patti paused. "I definitely *knew* knew, as you say."

Kathy nodded. "That's what I mean. Something's up. And it's not his yacht business."

"Charlie's a good-lookin' dude. And if he's a successful businessman on top of that, well, he's quite a catch, as Dad would say." She shrugged. "But so are you, Kathy. Plus, when this whole thing started between the two of you, you told me he'd changed."

Kathy swiped at her tears. "I thought he had. But maybe once a player, always a player?"

Patti lifted one eyebrow. "It's certainly possible. You told me he was committed to your relationship. He played around on me, but he was, what, eighteen years old? And the star quarterback of the football team? I figured it was just youth."

Kathy rubbed her finger round and round the edge of her Diet Coke. "This is where it gets to be too much information for you to handle. You know, the intimate parts of our relationship? But I don't have anyone else to talk to."

Patti wiped her fingers with a napkin, dabbed the butter off her lips, folded her legs underneath her, and sat up straight, facing her sister. "I'll listen to whatever you want to share with me. I'm a big girl. I can handle it."

Kathy cleared her throat. "In the last month, we've made love once. Once! And it was the day before I flew up here. Every time I want to have sex, he makes up some excuse. He's exhausted. He's stressed. Just like you said. But I don't buy it. And I don't like being lied to."

Patti shook her head and switched her gaze to the window behind Kathy's head. "I remember feeling that way when he and I were together. He did the exact same thing to me. We stopped having what he called 'nooners.' He told me final exams were driving him crazy, that his parents would disown him if he didn't get into some killer university. So he didn't have time to fool around, he said. He had to get home and study." She laughed under her breath. "Yeah, right."

"This is so embarrassing."

"Why? Because maybe he's a two-timing liar and always has been? That's no reflection on you."

"For whatever reason, he's going to dump me. I'm completely humiliated."

"Dump him, then," Patti urged. "You'll feel different being the dumper versus the dumpee. You'll be in control. Feel less helpless. I know I did."

"So when you dumped him, you walked away with a big smile on your face?"

Patti smirked. "Not exactly." She cleared her throat. "Don't ever tell anyone I told you this."

Kathy shook her head and crossed her heart. "Never."

"Okay." Patti sighed. "After I dumped Charlie, he was really pissed off. He didn't deny he'd had sex with that other chick, but he wanted to try to make a go of our relationship, said he was sorry, he'd never do it again, yada, yada. Why can't we put it behind us, and shit like that, he said. His ego was so huge, he couldn't believe I really wasn't interested. He was relentless. He kept pursuing me and pursuing me. I got sick of it. He wouldn't give up. He refused to accept the fact that someone would dump him.

"So I walked away from our last argument, and as soon as I was out of sight, I ran to the men's locker room and opened his locker. He used the same combination for everything, the dumbass. Anyway, so I took a pair of scissors and cut all his football gear into the tiniest pieces. It was hysterical. It looked like confetti."

Kathy covered her mouth, stifling a laugh. "Charlie obviously knew you'd done it, right?"

Patti shrugged. "He never said anything to me. I would have denied it anyway. I think that's considered destruction of personal property or whatever." She grinned. "But he knew, all right. How could he not?"

"God, I hope I don't ever get on your bad side, Patti."

"I *do* have a temper. If somebody does something to me or someone I love, I get really pissed off."

"Revenge is your drug of choice?" Kathy said.

Patti shrugged. "I've always felt sorry for the underdog, and I don't feel right sitting on the sidelines, watching others get hurt. And I don't like getting screwed over when I don't deserve it."

Kathy waved her hand back and forth. "Let's drop the subject of Charlie for now. I'll deal with him when I return home." She slapped her hands on her knees. "So. Will you move to San Diego or not? Puh-lease?"

"Well, you're right on one major point. I don't have a job anymore."

"And there are always jobs for professional photographers in San Diego and La Jolla. La Jolla is only about twenty minutes away from my house, and it's where a lot of rich people live. I'm not sure what you want to do, but they're constantly filming movies in the area, so there are a gazillion actresses and actors and models who need to have their portfolios done by a professional." Kathy sat up and leaned closer to Patti's face. "Come on. Just do it."

Patti smiled. "I promise to think about it."

"Yes!" Kathy shouted, then covered her mouth with both hands.

"Don't worry. My neighbors are hundreds of feet away. Even if someone did call the cops, I wouldn't mind *that* one bit. Cops in Alameda are super-hunks."

Kathy leaned back into the pillows. "Then why aren't you dating one?"

"Been there, done that."

"And what is that supposed to mean?"

"His hours were so janky—"

"Janky? What the hell? Is that some sort of Urban Dictionary word I'm not familiar with?"

Patti laughed. "Well, you *do* live in SoCal."

Kathy closed her eyes and took a breath, then opened them. "No one says SoCal. If you live with me, you have to promise never to say that. Ever."

"It's what we in the Bay Area call Southern California, Kathy. As I was saying, the guy's hours just totally did not jive with mine. He'd get off work and need to sleep just when I was leaving my job and wanting to play."

Kathy nodded. "I get it. No policemen. I understand."

"Well, they don't all have that shift, but John did." Patti shrugged. "It just didn't work out."

"So, you promise to at least think about moving to, quote unquote, SoCal, to live with me and look for a new job?"

Patti stood and lifted her arms toward the ceiling, yawning. "I promise to think about it."

"You don't have any real ties here any longer."

"I worked for that company for five years, Kath. I'm still reeling."

"They'll regret it. And you'll find a better job."

"I don't think Cassey, the owner, will regret letting me go. She hired too many photographers. Someone had to leave. We were all good. So when one of the photographers who was Cassey's lover left the company, Cassey turned her eyes on me." Patti shrugged. "I'm not gay, so she dumped my ass."

Kathy's jaw dropped. "You mean to tell me, if you'd had sex with your boss she would have kept you on?"

Patti nodded. "Yup. That's exactly what I'm saying."

"And you couldn't have sued her for sexual harassment or something?"

"I wasn't going to waste thousands of dollars to hire an attorney for something based on office gossip. I can't prove anything." She paused. "Granted, I was angry. Very angry. I thought of doing something."

"You mean like what you did to Charlie?"

Patti shrugged. "For a second, I entertained the thought of getting back at her for letting me go for no reason. She was wrong to fire me. I was going to show *her* what it felt like to be screwed over, you know? But she said she'd give me a good recommendation, so I couldn't take the chance, if I'd retaliated in some way. Though I really, really wanted to." She sighed. "But, onward and upward, Christian soldiers, as Sister Catherine Teresa used to tell us."

"All this talk of sex and stuff… don't you sometimes wonder how we turned out pretty okay, what with all the things the nuns told us to scare us into being good Christian soldiers when we were in high school?"

"You mean like, 'If you sit on a boy's lap, you might get pregnant'?"

Kathy let out a deep belly laugh, doubling over, gasping. "Oh, my God! I would have gotten pregnant a million times, right?"

Patti joined her, chuckling hysterically, slumping back down on the couch. "Remember Sister Delfina?"

Kathy tilted her head. "The one who used to measure the length of our skirts every morning with a ruler?"

Patti pointed in her direction. "That's the one. I dreamed of grabbing that ruler out of her hand and whacking her over the head with it."

Kathy laughed out loud.

Patti grinned. "Actually, *she's* the one who was totally whacked." She stood up again. "I gotta get some sleep."

"Thanks for the laugh, Sis. Love you."

"And I love you. See you tomorrow." Patti walked to the stairs, stifling a yawn.

"Think about San Diego," Kathy called out.

"You got it," Patti shouted back as she headed to her bedroom.

Patti didn't want Kathy to be unhappy with Charlie. But if he was cheating on her and the two went their separate ways, Patti could move in with Kathy. Patti wouldn't have to deal with seeing the two of them together, wondering if Charlie was screwing someone else behind her sister's back.

What was it with some guys having such difficulty being sexually monogamous? Charlie was no longer a teenage football hero. He was thirty years old. Acting like that in high school was one thing. No one expected to marry their childhood sweetheart.

But he was a grown man. By now he should have matured, maybe even be looking for a solid relationship, with a family life and a few kids. If not, he could at least be up front about it. Lots of women weren't looking for security and wouldn't mind dating a player. But Kathy wasn't one of them, and Charlie damn well knew it. What a creepazoid!

But, hey, if she wanted to move to SoCal with her sister, she'd have to put all that aside. Charlie was no longer her problem. Her sister would have to make her own decisions about her relationship. Too bad Kathy was the one who now had to deal with his wandering eye. And Kathy, of all people, didn't deserve to be jacked around by some gigolo.

*If you're cheating on my sister, Charlie, I'll kick your butt from here to Oregon.*

Patti's mind shifted to her mom. Sadly, she was gone, and it was time to get on with her life. Of course, it would take Patti a while to get used to her not being emotionally available for her.

During her mom's fight against cancer, Patti had stuck by her side every single time the cancer returned. Her mom had been so sick for so long. Patti knew that for at least the last two years she had been suffering and wanted all of it to be over.

But being the fighter she was, her mom had signed up for one experimental treatment after another to try to beat that freaking disease. When no one else was around, her mom would say to her, "You know, Patti, cancer's my bitch. I'm gonna beat the crap out of her one day." Then they'd both laugh. Her mom never used so-called bad words. To hear the b-word come out of her mom's mouth had startled Patti.

Patti thought about her options, her future without her mom. She needed to either stay in the Bay Area and look for another job, or move to San Diego and look for a job.

She climbed into bed, shut her eyes, and tried to fall asleep.

First, she had to figure out how to talk Kathy into visiting the ranch. The weekend was approaching—a perfect time for a short vacation.

She finally fell asleep, dreaming of riding one of her dad's Friesian horses through the meadow, her blonde hair floating behind her in the wind as she raced with her sisters across the hills.

Maybe they could be a family again. For the first time since her mom had passed, joy stirred in Patti's heart.

# Chapter Four

Kathy had called Charlie's cell phone after she'd gone to bed the night before. He hadn't answered. Typical. In the initial stages of their relationship, they had talked on the phone four or five times a day. Then it had dwindled to two times, then once a day, then sometimes they'd go an entire day without speaking. And he'd always blamed it on work.

She'd believed him. He sent her flowers unexpectedly, complimented her on her hair or makeup, or clothes. But perhaps that was guilt talking. He could be having sex with two women!

She jumped out of bed, took a quick shower, then went to the kitchen. She'd fix Patti a cup of her favorite Peet's Ethiopian blend, and they could talk about why Patti should move to San Diego. Or maybe she should lie low, not pressure her.

Patti was the type of person who would do just the opposite of what someone wanted her to do, because she hated being told what to do. She was very strong-willed, just like their dad. Kathy recalled when Patti was in high school. Patti loved their father, but she couldn't wait to be out from under his dictatorial thumb. Having been in the Marines, their father had been the one to make them toe the line, as he called it. And Patti didn't always like toeing her father's line. Or anyone else's line, other than her own, for that matter. She wanted to walk her own line, thank you very much.

Kathy understood that. Patti and their father had strong personalities. Just not the same type of personality. Patti could be a hothead, whereas their father remained cool in almost every situation, but in Patti's case, sometimes logic flew right out the window. She'd get so mad, she couldn't think straight, which got her into trouble at times. But Patti definitely was the type of person who would watch your back in times of trouble. She was always there for the ones she loved.

Kathy's bottom lip trembled. Even though she was missing her mom, never dreaming she wouldn't always be around, all these thoughts about her father made her miss him more than she'd ever thought possible. *And no one lives forever.* Which was why Kathy wanted to be happy for the limited time she had on this earth. No one knew when they'd be hit by the Big C, and then whammo! Gone forever. Just when she had plans to do something fun or spectacular.

*Or make amends with someone I've been carrying a grudge against for ten years!*

"Good morning," Patti chirped. She rubbed Kathy's back, then shoved her face in front of her sister's. "Are you crying?"

Kathy nodded and wiped her nose with another of her hankies.

"Allergies," Kathy responded. A convenient excuse to carry a handkerchief to dry her eyes. Handy, too, when she was missing her dead mother, as well as her estranged father, along with her boyfriend, who she was sure was cheating on her. It was only a matter of time before Charlie would blow her off, if his current silence wasn't indication enough that he'd already let her go. But if not, she could picture it. "Kathy, can we talk?" Ugh… she was sick to death speculating about his faithfulness.

"Or is it Charlie?" Patti said.

Kathy poured her sister a cup of coffee, handed her the cup, then sat at the table with her own mug. "Mostly Charlie. Maybe I should do like Richard Gere in that movie *Unfaithful.*"

Patti took a sip and leaned back in her chair. "Hire a private investigator to follow Charlie around? Or murder Charlie by bopping him over the head with a snow globe?"

Kathy laughed and choked on a sip of coffee.

Patti stood and patted her on the back until she stopped coughing. "Sorry, Sis."

Kathy dabbed at her mouth with a napkin. "You've always had a way with words. You could always make me laugh." She paused and took another sip. "After I moved to San Diego and ran into Charlie, we were friends before we were lovers. But I've heard enough stories at the office to make me jaded. Women are always talking about how they never dreamed their boyfriends would cheat on them. And I've met some of their boyfriends, too. They were stand-up guys."

"I told you, maybe he's going through some personal stuff that has nothing to do with your relationship. It's possible, right?"

"But I'm his girlfriend, Patti. He should be able to talk to me about anything." Kathy let out a breath. "It's just so frustrating."

"Want me to try?"

Kathy squinted at her sister. "You're kidding, right?"

"He and I used to be close. It was a long time ago, but maybe he'll talk to me about what's bothering him."

"And just maybe he'd make a move on you, too."

Patti laughed. "Remember, I dumped him." She put up her index finger. "And never looked back."

"Because you found out he was cheating on you. God! Is history repeating itself or what?"

"He cheated on me with some rich bitch cheerleader. But I never fit in with the crowd he hung out with anyway. It was awkward."

"You never were the cheerleader type. You didn't even like football."

"But I went to all his games. I was a freaking bookworm, though."

"But a beautiful bookworm. Which is why he went for you in the first place. I am so not the studious type. Nor am I beautiful."

Patti slapped at her sister. "Yes, you are beautiful. Your self-esteem could use a forklift to jack it up to where it should be. You know, it doesn't really matter what he was like back then. I think I could get a feel for what he's like now if I spent more than a few minutes talking to him. You know, see if I think he's changed at all. Maybe over coffee or something?"

Kathy smirked. "And if you got a, uh, feel for him, that'd prove to me he can't be trusted?"

"Good God, Kathy. Not *that* kind of feel, and you know it." Patti leaned toward her sister, looking her in the eye. "If you're seriously insinuating I'd be remotely interested in him, you're crazy. Been there, done that, Kathy. I'd never try to steal your boyfriend. You *know* that. I'd be on a mission to save you from him, if he's still having problems in the fidelity department."

Kathy chewed on her bottom lip. "Okay. Why not?"

Patti smiled. "So I can plan a visit to San Diego and incorporate a little tête-à-tête in Starbucks with him?"

"Forget about a visit. Why don't you plan on a tête-à-tête after you move in with me?"

Patti rolled her eyes. "I never said I was moving to San Diego. I said I'd think about it."

"How long is it going to take you to make up your mind? You'd love it down there."

Patti lifted her shoulder. "Who wouldn't?"

"My point exactly. Great beaches. Great weather. Great job market."

Patti huffed. "You *had* to mention that."

"It's true. I'm telling you, you should go for it. Nothing's tying you here any longer. What're you always saying to me? Just do it."

The landline rang, startling them both.

"Who has a landline?" Kathy asked.

"I know, right? It comes with the Internet and TV. An Xfinity package deal. Whatever." Patti looked down at the phone. "It's Dad."

Kathy stood and poured another cup of coffee. "Aren't you going to answer it?"

Patti picked up the phone. "Hi, Dad." She raised her eyebrows at Kathy. "This weekend? Yeah, I think we can do that."

Kathy chewed her bottom lip while staring at her sister.

"Hold on." Patti covered the phone with her palm. "It's a perfect time to try to mend fences."

Kathy glanced at the floor and shook her head. "Is this a good time to be doing that?" She looked at her sister. "Right after Mom's funeral? When everybody's all stressed out and depressed?"

"He's the only father you've got, Sis. Don't throw away this opportunity."

Kathy had given a lot of thought to what Sharon had told her about holding grudges, how allowing negative thoughts to simmer inside caused anxiety and depression. That forgiveness was the only way to truly let go of the bad and allow the good to come in. Sound advice, for sure.

But could she ever look at her father again with the admiration and love she'd had for him when she was a child? He totally burst her bubble when he divorced her mom, in the middle of her first round of chemotherapy, fighting for her life. Then remarrying so soon after the divorce was final? Geez. What a jerk!

But as everyone said, that was a long time ago. Just as she hoped had happened with Charlie—people changed, grew, regretted their past actions. But had her father? Had Charlie?

There was only one way to find out. Kathy nodded. "I'll go," she mouthed.

Patti did a little happy dance with her feet, then uncovered the phone. "Dad? We'll both be there Friday night, maybe Saturday morning. I'll let you know." Patti smiled, listening to whatever their father was saying.

Kathy could only imagine his surprise. She was sure he hadn't been expecting her to change her mind and spend an entire weekend at the ranch.

Patti ended the call and smiled. "What made you change your mind?"

Kathy shrugged. "Who else?"

"Sharon," they said in unison.

"So her psychobabble *does* make sense to you?" Patti asked.

"The alternative is depressing."

"You mean having no parent in your life?"

Kathy looked into her coffee, swirling it around with the spoon. "I loved him once." She shrugged. "I still love him. But I hate him."

"I know. I sometimes feel the same way. But not as much now."

"You seem way more accepting than I am, though. At least you've seen him a couple of times since the divorce. What changed for you?"

Patti poured a bit more hot coffee into her mug and took a sip. "Sharon makes a lot of sense to me, too. I don't want to spend the rest of my life being mad at Dad. It seems like such a waste of time. I saw a *Lifetime* movie a while back."

"You still watch those?"

"Hooked on 'em. Always have been."

"And?"

"It was about this woman who at the age of sixty-something finally talks to her mom after, like, thirty or forty years of silence between them, when her mom's on her deathbed. Come to find out, the real reason for their strained relationship was all a misunderstanding."

"What's there to misunderstand about what Dad did to Mom?"

"Marriage is something neither of us knows squat about, Kath. Maybe something happened between them that we don't know, something that's too personal to share with us daughters."

"I don't think so, Patti."

Patti added a spoonful of sugar and cream to her coffee and stirred. "You never know. But I'd sure like to find out if there's some hidden secret we've never been privy to."

Kathy didn't think that was the case, but she didn't want to be bullheaded. "I'll keep an open mind."

Patti grasped her sister's hand and squeezed. "That's all I'm asking."

# Chapter Five

They originally decided to leave Friday night for the ranch, which was located on the outskirts of Quincy, a small city in Northern California of around two thousand people. But Patti didn't relish driving three or more hours in the dark, and at the end, she'd be navigating her way along narrow, winding roads.

So on Saturday morning at seven a.m., she hauled Kathy's butt into her SUV, planning to drive straight through and make it to Fabulous Friesians in time for lunch. They'd been driving for almost three hours and were now smack-dab in the middle of Gold Country (also known as the Mother Lode Country)—a historic area primarily on the western slope of the Sierra Nevada mountains.

"I'm nervous," Kathy told her, while fiddling with the radio, trying to find a station without static.

Patti pushed her sister's hand away. "I'll plug in my iPhone, and we can listen to some real music."

"What, rap? I'll pass."

"Come on, Kath. Drake. Chris Brown. Chance the Rapper. Anderson Paak. Does that make me weird or something?"

"At your age? I thought you would have elevated your musical sensibilities by now."

Patti chuckled. "You mean I should be listening to classical music?"

"The only real music, in my opinion."

"Whatever."

Kathy tsked. "Let's compromise. We'll plug in my iPhone and start with a little Rachmaninoff."

Patti jabbed in her charging cord and scrolled through her playlist. "Drake first."

Kathy sighed, then laughed out loud. "You know what's funny?

You and I have never once in all our years had a knockdown, drag-out fight, have we?"

"You're pretty even-tempered, Kath. Except when it comes to Dad. Then you morph into a real—"

"Bitch? You're right. I won't argue with you on that. But you're the same way with Helen. The only thing in my life I can say I am royally, unequivocally angry about is how Dad treated Mom. With Helen, well…"

"Helen is just… Helen. What can we say? Helen just pushes my buttons—all of them. Normally neither of us likes confrontation."

Kathy's eyes widened.

"Wha-at?" Patti said, making the word two syllables.

"For someone who doesn't like confrontation, you can sure be in-your-face with someone you're pissed off at."

Patti touched her chest, smiling. "Me? Really?"

"Look at the way you were with Helen at the funeral," Kathy said, raising an eyebrow.

"She deserved it."

"Still." Kathy paused. "We were at our mother's funeral, Patti. And you still couldn't keep the sarcasm out of your tone, along with the subtle remarks."

"All right, all right." Patti blew out a breath. "When I'm angry, I can sometimes be snarky and—"

"Fly off the handle?" Kathy interjected. "Do things you regret later? That's the way you were in high school. Think maybe it's time to do something about that? Go to an anger-management class maybe?"

Patti shrugged. "Give me a break. We were all stressed out that day. I'm not the only one who showed my fangs."

She took the next exit and glided to the stop sign. "Hey, Siri. I need driving directions to Fabulous Friesians Ranch in Quincy, California, please."

She turned to Kathy. "I haven't been home in ten years. Dad and I have visited one another a couple times since then, but only when he was in San Francisco. He told me he'd renovated the main house and outbuildings since we moved away."

"We probably won't recognize the property," Kathy said.

"I can't wait to see what he's done to the farm."

"I really don't think it's considered a farm anymore, Patti."

"You're right. It's a *ranch*. Fabulous Friesians *Ranch*. This'll be fun."

Kathy smiled. "I haven't been on a horse since I left here. At the time, Maximus weighed more than fourteen hundred pounds." She let out a sigh. "I miss those huge, black horses."

"Me, too. They're such sweethearts. So… mellow."

"I hope we have a good time," Kathy said, anxiety evident in her voice.

"As long as Helen doesn't act like a total beyotch," Patti added.

"If she gets on a jag about why I haven't talked to Dad in ten years, I swear, Patti, I'll—"

"Don't even go there," Patti interrupted. "Helen's not one to talk. In the last ten years, *she* hardly visited Mom when she was so sick. Dad's having this family-come-ta-meetin' in order to bring us all together, not to argue. I'll try my best this time, when Helen's around. And remember, Sharon'll be there."

Kathy laughed. "The peacemaker. She can be a bit over the top, though."

"She's had more therapy than anyone I know."

Kathy tapped the dashboard. "Which practically gives her a PhD."

"She's Mom's clone," Patti said. "And that's not a bad thing. And you'll love riding Maximus again."

"Yeah, he must be about thirteen or fourteen by now. A good age. He'll have mellowed even more than he already was." Kathy chuckled. "If that's possible."

"He's the reason Dad branched out into breeding," Patti said. "That turned out to be the best business decision he ever made."

Kathy laughed. "Who'd have thought selling stallion sperm could be so lucrative? Or buying a second ranch in Holland?" She pulled the charging cord out of Patti's iPhone and inserted it into her own. Refrains of classical music filled the car. "Don't you think this is more appropriate for our entrance?"

Patti slowed down to let someone pass. "Dad told me the place got totally run-down after his second divorce."

Kathy gazed out her window at the farms lining the rural highway. "It's lucky Mom moved before that happened. She didn't have to see it like that. That would have been depressing. She loved living on the farm."

Patti glanced at her sister. "I know. But Dad made all his money back and then some after branching out. And you're right. That ranch in Holland was another great business decision." She pointed to a narrow, paved road that led off to the right and had a curved sign overhead that read, "Fabulous Friesians" in black, connecting horseshoes. "Look. Just like in the movies."

She turned down that lane. "As I recall, we're only about a mile away now."

Kathy rubbed her abdomen. "My stomach's in knots. Is it too late to change my mind?"

Patti wrapped her fingers around Kathy's forearm. "Chill, sister. Dad made it clear this is to be a casual get-together, a vacation. Let's have some fun."

They drove for about five minutes at a slow pace, the road flanked by an impeccable white fence.

Suddenly, Fabulous Friesians Ranch appeared on the horizon.

"Whoa," Patti said under her breath.

"It's gorgeous," Kathy added. "And look at the barn. Talk about Martha Stewart."

Patti slowed the SUV to a crawl. "She owns Friesians too, right? I read about that in her magazine."

"Well, I can understand why," Kathy said. "They're the most beautiful horses ever." She hitched her chin. "They know we've arrived."

Patti smiled at the welcome sight before them. "Dad. Sharon. And, oh… look… at… Helen."

Kathy leaned forward, eyes squinted. "Oh, my goodness! Are you kidding me?"

"Her shorts barely cover her ass."

Kathy shook her head. "I guess if I had an ass like hers, I might wave it in the breeze, too."

"Sorry." Patti rubbed her temples. "Apologies for losing it there. Let's agree not be catty from here on out, Kath. I won't talk shit about Helen, and you won't talk shit about Dad." She turned to look at her sister. "You down with this?"

"Yes. I understand. And I'll try. As best I can."

Patti laughed out loud. "You're funny."

They rolled to a stop in front of the two-story house painted blue-gray with white trim. The wraparound porch, with a cushioned swing and comfy-looking chairs, invited visitors. A widow's walk ran from one side of the top floor to the other, with French doors marking three bedrooms that faced the front of the house. The windows sparkled in the bright afternoon sunshine.

Hugs were shared among the five of them. Smiles graced everyone's faces. Patti thought Dad looked happy.

"Welcome to Fabulous Friesians, girls," he said.

Patti looked up at the second floor of the house, then turned toward the stables and other outbuildings. "It's absolutely beautiful, Dad."

"Thank you, Patti." He glanced at Sharon and Helen. "We do our best."

Kathy looked straight at her father. "It really is so gorgeous, Dad," she said, then turned toward Sharon and Helen. "You all did a great job. It's no longer a farm. I can see why it's called a ranch, as you said, Helen."

"Our legacy," Helen said seriously.

Patti could read the undercurrent in those two words. Helen obviously expected that she and Sharon would get more of their father's inheritance than Kathy and Patti. Patti didn't have a problem with that. But she found it extremely inappropriate to imply such thinking today.

Yes, her father was in his twilight years, but whatever he decided was fair would be okay with both Patti and Kathy—they'd talked about it. But leave it to Helen to bring up their inheritance in front of their father when they'd just arrived.

"So when's lunch?" Patti asked her dad. "I'm starving."

He gestured toward the front door. "Sharon fixed lunch, so let's get to it."

Patti and Kathy followed their father and two sisters through the front door. They entered the dining room, which was to the left of the foyer. An antique, highly polished mahogany dining table, big enough to seat twelve people, stood atop a dark blue Pakistani rug. Five place settings glistened beneath the chandelier's lights.

Patti and Kathy used the restroom before taking their seats at the table. Their father sat at the head of the table, the bay window behind him giving them a perfect view of the impeccable stables and rolling hills beyond.

"Business is good?" Kathy asked.

Helen took a bite of steak and chewed. "Very good. We've sold three horses in the past week alone." She moved her fork around, mixing the gravy and mashed potatoes. "Dad's a very rich man."

Of course Helen would bring up finances. Patti nodded and shoved her cut-up steak pieces from one side of the plate to the other. She refused to be goaded into having any conversation about their inheritance. With her silence she hoped it would be glaringly obvious she wouldn't engage in such a discussion.

"Well, I can't wait to see the horses," Kathy said, nudging Patti with her knee.

"You said something about taking a ride, Dad?" Patti said.

"Some clients are coming by after lunch to look at the horses, then we can have dinner together. Maybe tomorrow we can all saddle up and take a ride around the property." He glanced in Kathy's direction. "Just like we used to, Katydid."

Kathy nodded. "I'd like that."

Patti could see her sister was uncomfortable around their dad. She just hoped these two days at the ranch could break the ice between them. Kathy would regret it if her dad died and they never got back on track. And Patti planned to do her best to mend the broken fence between Kathy and her father.

"You can ride Maximus, Kathy. Right, Dad?" Patti said.

He nodded, wiped his lips with a starched white napkin, then smiled. "Just like old times."

Kathy stared at her plate.

"Aren't you hungry, Kathy?" Sharon said.

Kathy glanced across the table at Sharon. "Oh, you know. Mom's funeral and everything. I'm just tired. We got up really early this morning to get on the road. We wanted to miss the traffic."

"When you're both finished, I can show you to your new rooms," Helen said, leaning back in her chair, arms folded under her breasts. All four girls were well endowed, just like their mother, but Helen flaunted every good feature she was born with, whether it was her boobs or her booty.

Sharon had told Patti many times over the years that she was certain Helen's behavior indicated a deep inferiority complex. At times, Patti felt sorry for Helen, but then Helen would act like, well, Helen, and Patti's sympathy would go right out the window.

As the youngest daughter, Sharon had explained, Helen had taken the divorce harder than the rest of them. She'd been in her late teens at the time and had taken their parents' break-up personally. Sharon concluded that Helen felt abandoned by both her parents, hence her lack of self-esteem.

"Can we have our old rooms?" Kathy asked.

Helen dabbed at the corners of her mouth with her napkin. "Actually, no. We changed things up a bit during the renovation."

Patti stood, trying not to let her face show the resentment she felt. Helen seemed to get off on showing she had the upper hand in any and all situations. "Let's get our suitcases out of the car, Kathy."

Kathy followed Patti, who was mumbling her way to the SUV. "I don't know how I'll make it through an entire weekend with her."

Kathy smirked. "You can't possibly be talking about Helen."

Patti gave her a dirty look. "Who else?"

"I feel your pain," Kathy said.

"You still seem pretty uncomfortable with Dad," Patti added.

"It'll take me some time," Kathy replied. "But he's been nothing if not totally gracious."

Patti huffed. "What I don't like is feeling like a guest in what used to be our own home. Any hope I ever had that Helen would change has been thrown out the window. She constantly brings up money and our, quote unquote, legacy. Bugs the crap outta me. But, hey, Dad appears to be doing well."

"If we have a chance to talk to Sharon alone, we might get the real tale of our inheritance," Kathy added.

"The point is, I don't really care," Patti said. "And neither do you."

"You're right. I really don't, Patti. But I'm hoping Helen hasn't done anything janky, as you call it."

Kathy laughed out loud. "Don't get your hopes up, Sis."

Scowling, Kathy grabbed her suitcase, turned, and headed up the steps, where Helen held the front door open with her foot. Once inside, Helen walked ahead of them up the wide, curved stairway to the second floor.

Patti rolled her eyes at Kathy and pointed at Helen's backside, where Helen's butt cheeks practically jiggled in their faces.

Kathy covered her mouth with her hand, giggling, then slapped Patti's arm.

Patti's old bedroom, which faced the front of the house, was now Helen's. Kathy's room, which had been next to Patti's, was now Sharon's. Patti and Kathy would be staying in the bedrooms that faced the back of the property, with views of the small lake behind the house.

"Sharon and I wanted to be able to see who comes onto the property," Helen said.

"Understandable," Kathy replied.

Patti said nothing.

"Satisfied with your room, Kath?" Helen said with a smile that looked more like a smirk.

Kathy turned to her younger sister. "It's gorgeous, Helen. Thank you. Now I'd like to take a short nap."

"Those stairs are a bit of exercise, aren't they?" Helen said.

"I'm not as young as I used to be," Kathy replied.

"Nor as thin," Helen added.

Kathy turned to Helen, her mouth half open, eyes wide.

Patti walked in a beeline toward Helen, who was standing in the doorway of Kathy's room. Patti knew the look on her face would intimidate most humans, and as she approached her snarky sister, she backed up. Patti stood so close to her, their noses almost touched. Patti was practically breathing fire out of her mouth and nose, her exhales quick and loud, as if she'd been running a marathon.

Helen's eyes bulged, her lips curling inward, then she turned and rushed down the stairs. For a second, Patti entertained the idea of following her, then thought of her promise to Kathy to curb her temper.

Patti turned and smiled at Kathy, walked into her room, and shut the door behind her. She lay flat on top of the bed, arms stretched across a quilt her mother had made for her sixteenth birthday. She balled her hands into fists, digging her nails into her palms. It had taken every bit of fortitude in her body to refrain from pushing Helen to the floor and sitting on top of her.

But she'd made a promise to Kathy, and she was going to keep that promise. For now.

*But, dammit, Helen's such a bitch.*

However, Patti knew getting physical with Helen tonight would put a real damper on their stay at the ranch. "So don't go there," she whispered to herself.

She sighed, trying to calm herself, and looked around the room. No matter what bedroom she slept in, this house had always been home.

Patti wondered if, when they left Sunday, she'd feel the same way.

# Chapter Six

Just as Patti felt herself slide into that halfway zone between wakefulness and sleep, someone knocked on the door. She sat up. "Come in."

Sharon peeked her head around the edge of the door and smiled. "How're you doing?"

Patti scooted backward into the soft down pillows and patted the side of the bed. "Join me. It's been a while since we've had any alone time, just the two of us."

Sharon lay on her side at the bottom of the bed, leaning her head onto the palm of her hand. "This is nice. Really nice. Sister time. I love it."

"How's Dad doing? How's his heart?"

"After his heart attack five or so years back, he doesn't eat as much red meat, and he's still active. He's on blood pressure medication, and I make sure he takes a walk with me after dinner. Keeps me in shape as well."

Patti smiled. "You've always been in great shape, Share. And your hair looks so cute in a ponytail. You ought to wear it that way all the time."

"I do unless I'm going somewhere special. For Mom's funeral, I went to the beauty parlor. Oh, my goodness, that woman put so much hair spray on it, Hurricane Katrina couldn't have messed it up. But it was too late to do anything about it. I was really embarrassed."

Patti chuckled. "You're still a blonde. Which makes you stand out in a crowd. You're pretty no matter how much lacquer Marlene sprays on your hair. You *were* talking about Marlene, right?"

Sharon nodded.

"So she's still alive."

Sharon laughed out loud. "She owns Scissors and Curls now. Runs it like a tyrant, too."

Several seconds passed in silence. Patti hadn't talked to Sharon one-on-one in ages, and after so many years, it was a bit awkward. They'd never been as close as she and Kathy, maybe due to the five-year gap in age. Sharon was the oldest, then Kathy, then Patti, and Helen was the baby.

"With all your psych background, do you have any tips on how to get this family back on track?" Patti asked her.

"You know I do." Sharon sat up and crossed her legs. "I think we should have a family meeting. The four of us and Dad. To talk about the will."

Patti's eyes almost popped out of their sockets. "We can't do that. I mean, Dad would never allow it. He's always kept that information tightly fisted inside his head. And in his attorney's office, of course. He always said we'll know when the time comes. When he's dead. Sheesh, I don't care about his damn money any more than I think you or Kathy do. Am I right?"

Sharon nodded. "You missed someone."

Patti rolled her eyes. "I can't imagine what a meeting would be like if Helen were there. We all know she's obsessed with finding out how much she's going to inherit. That's never changed." She shrugged. "Dad will not talk about his will, Share, and you know it."

Sharon traced her finger along an embroidered rose on the comforter. "I think Dad changed his will."

"So? He can do whatever he wants with his money."

Sharon glanced up. "Of course he can. But I think Helen may have somehow coerced him into changing it. To benefit her more than the rest of us. And, no, I don't love Dad for his money. That's not why I'm living here on the ranch.

"I love working with the horses. You know that, Patti. But Helen? She never enjoyed riding that much. And she hated getting dirty. Heck, I used to be the same way when I was younger. But horses and keeping clean are diametrically opposed realities."

Patti sat up on the bed. "What do you mean, Helen wanted Dad to change the will for her benefit?"

"One evening when they thought I was asleep, I came downstairs. It was really late. I think it was one in the morning or something. I wanted a glass of milk. Soothes my stomach every time I eat too much beef. Anyway, I heard Helen say something about how she'd promise to live here and take over in exchange for owning seventy-five percent of the ranch." Sharon shrugged. "But I never heard Dad's answer. The stair tread creaked just about that time, and I ran back up to my bedroom. I didn't want them to know I was eavesdropping."

"I know Dad wants the ranch to stay in the family," Patti said. "I never thought about the fact that, obviously, someone would have to live here. He never asked *me*. Then again, I haven't been on the best of terms with him since the divorce. You and Helen have, though."

Sharon's bottom lip trembled, and Patti placed a hand on her sister's shoulder.

"He never asked me either, Patti. That's the thing. It was something Helen offered. To stay and live here on the ranch after he passes away, I mean. But I don't know what happened that night. They were still talking when I ran back upstairs."

"I cannot believe he would talk with her about anything that had to do with the will. I'd expect him to tell her it was none of her damn business." Patti shook her head. "I don't see Dad being coerced into anything. By Helen or you or me or anybody."

"He and Helen are pretty close. She cooks for him, cleans for him, does his wash. But I'm the one who takes care of the horses. Not to seem self-centered, but really? Taking care of the Friesians is what this ranch is all about. I train them. I exercise them. I ride them.

"Helen's learning the selling side of the business, so she spends a lot of time with Daddy, one-on-one. If Helen could get away with not grooming them or working them in the arena, she'd do her best to make up some plausible excuse. She's done it for years."

Patti stared into her sister's eyes. "Then you'd like to live here and get seventy-five percent of the ranch?"

Sharon shook her head. "Absolutely not. I help Daddy out because I want to. I work the horses because I want to. Helen does it for what she'll get out of it in the end."

Patti's stomach twisted into a big knotted ball, and she set her arm across her abdomen. "I hate that about her. She's always been a selfish bitch. Why is that?"

"She's the sun, and we're the tiny planets revolving around her glorious light," Sharon whispered. A lone tear escaped and ran down her cheek.

"Why the tears?"

"I hate that I'm talking about her like this. It's not nice. I don't want to be two-faced, and that's how I feel right now."

Patti intertwined her fingers with Sharon's. "You're not two-faced. You're one of the kindest people I know, Sharon. Always trying to make peace in the family. You have a good heart." She squeezed Sharon's hand. "You're just speaking the truth, and you shouldn't feel bad about that."

She paused, caught Sharon's gaze. "What're we going to do? Dad's as stubborn as they come. He won't yield to any pressure from us. That's why I don't think Helen could talk him into anything he didn't want in the first place. But I don't think she should come to this meeting with us to talk to Dad, do you?"

"Absolutely not." Sharon puckered her lips, then seemed to relax. "The one and only time I heard Daddy discuss a family secret, especially when he could be heard, was when he drank too much."

"Dad could always hold his liquor, so this comes as a surprise."

Sharon scooted next to Patti and lay back into the pillows. "Once, when Mom was alive, they were sitting on the front porch. Dad was drinking whisky and—"

"He always drank whisky. He never acted drunk to me."

"Wait," she whispered. "Regular everyday whisky, yes. But this was Johnnie Walker Blue Label King George V Edition."

Patti gasped, then covered her mouth. "Even I know that's one of the most expensive whiskies around."

Sharon nodded. "Comes in a crystal decanter. Seven hundred dollars a bottle."

Patti let out a low whistle. "You're kidding me, right?"

"Nope. And that night he drank, oh, I would say at least five shots, I'm guessing, based on what I saw was left in the bottle. All by himself. Mom never drank whisky." She paused, staring at the ceiling. "He was literally slurring his words, and when he stood up to come inside, he about fell over. Mom had to grab on to his arm, and he couldn't even walk up the stairs to bed. He slept on the sofa in the front room."

"What was the family secret?"

Sharon patted her sister's knee. "You'll never guess. *I* didn't believe it."

Patti leaned her face closer to Sharon's. "Out with it, will ya? I'm dyin' here."

"Okay, okay. But before I tell you, I have to be honest at last, but I've known this for years—they made me promise not to ever tell anyone. But now that Mom is gone, and we need to know if Helen's up to no good regarding Daddy's will, I'm breaking my promise."

"Okay, Share, I get that. You kept your word and kept a secret. I'd have done the same thing."

"But I should have said something earlier." Sharon started to cry and covered her face with her hands.

"Sharon, you're scaring me. You promised them. You were being honorable. I admire you for not blabbing to the rest of us."

Sharon swiped at her tears with her fingers and shook her head. "I feel so horrible for keeping this secret."

"Will you just tell me? I can't make sense of any of this if you won't tell me what you overheard."

"If I'd told you why they got a divorce, you and Kathy wouldn't have been on the outs with Daddy. Helen was never angry at Daddy over the divorce, 'cause all she cared about was the money anyway. But you and Kathy were close to Daddy."

"Will you just say it?" Patti cried.

"Shh," Sharon whispered. She took a deep breath, letting it out loudly and slowly, then locked eyes with Patti. "The reason Daddy divorced Mom was because Mom was a lesbian."

# Chapter Seven

Patti grabbed one of the extra bed pillows and buried her face in it. Sharon rubbed Patti's back in circles, while her sister cried, then sobbed, then hiccupped. Gradually, her cries lessened to a few whimpers.

Patti sat up straight, grabbed a tissue from the box Sharon handed her, and dabbed at the tears covering her cheeks. "All these years," she said under her breath.

"I know. That's why I feel so bad. But I promised Mom and Daddy I wouldn't tell any of you. Mom actually brought out the family Bible and made me swear. Then your and Kathy's relationship with Daddy deteriorated, and I knew it was because you thought Daddy was an ass for leaving Mom when she was so sick, for hooking up with what's-her-face."

"Carolanne the Bimbo?"

Sharon smiled. "Yes, Carolanne the Bimbo."

Patti stared across the room. "For ten years, I thought he was such a freaking lowlife, abandoning Mom in the middle of her chemo treatments, marrying that gold digger."

"It's my fault you and Daddy had a falling-out. And I'm so sorry, Patti."

"You did what you were supposed to do, Sharon. You promised our parents to keep your mouth shut."

"Daddy didn't want anyone to think less of Mom. He loved her. He still loves her. He wanted to preserve the memories we all had of our time with Mom. He didn't want to tarnish them in any way, you know?"

"Yes, I *do* know." She looked her sister in the eyes. "The funny thing is, I marched in the LGBTQ parade in San Francisco years ago. So did Kathy. I live in the San Francisco Bay Area. I have friends who are gay. It wouldn't have mattered to me."

Sharon sucked in her lips and shook her head. "They didn't know. Hell, *I* didn't know. And Kathy'd be cool about it, too?"

Patti nodded. "I can't imagine what it must have been like for Mom—holding on to that secret for years."

"Now I feel even worse, knowing this could all have been avoided. You and Kathy and I would have accepted Mom. There was absolutely no reason for her to hide the truth from us," Sharon said.

Patti screwed up her lips.

"Why the face?" Sharon asked.

Patti looked in Sharon's eyes. "Maybe Dad and Mom knew how the three of us would react, and it was *Helen's* reaction they were worried about."

Sharon cocked her head. "That's a possibility. I'd like the three of us to talk more about this, but if you don't mind, first I'd like to tell Kathy about Mom. By myself."

"Of course." Patti covered Sharon's hand with her own. "Not to be redundant, but again, this is not your fault. I don't blame you. Dad and Mom made a decision that, unfortunately, blew up in Dad's face."

"I don't want Daddy to know I told you about Mom. He'd never trust me again. But Helen going behind our backs about changing the will makes me very uncomfortable."

"I agree. I don't want to cause a problem between you and Dad, so there's no need to tell him you told us about Mom. But Helen trying to coerce Dad into changing the will? God, that makes me angry! What can we do?"

"Hmm." Sharon blew out a breath. "Tonight after dinner Helen has an acting class in downtown Quincy, then she and a couple of her classmates usually go to the local bar and have a drink, dance, that sort of thing."

"You and Kathy and I could *try* to talk to Dad about whether Helen asked him to change the will," Patti said. "If he talked to her, why wouldn't he talk to us?"

"Exactly." Sharon folded her hands in her lap, then looked at her sister. "I was thinking that while Helen's whooping it up, you and Kathy and I will break out the Jack Daniel's."

Patti chuckled. "I'm assuming there's some of the seven-hundred-dollar whisky left?"

"In Daddy's liquor cabinet," Sharon said. "In his office. We can all toast to getting the family together for the first time in years. That's certainly cause for a celebration, right?"

Patti nodded. "Yes. But I don't want to get Dad sloshed or anything like that."

"No, I wouldn't feel comfortable doing that. I'm just saying the really good whisky tends to make Daddy mellow. I don't want him to get plastered or anything. But if Dad, Kathy, you, and I have a little after-dinner drink, that might be enough to get Daddy to give us the information we need about Helen."

Patti lifted an eyebrow. "Mellow enough to talk about the will, though?"

Sharon shrugged. "If not, then there's nothing else we can do."

"You're right," Patti said. "It's not as if there's some magic truth serum we can give him."

"I'd like to give it a try, though," Sharon said. "If it doesn't work, at least we can have some fun tonight with our father without Helen jabbing at us about one thing or another." She jumped off the bed, leaned down, and hugged Patti. "Thanks for not making me feel like a total shit about not telling you about Mom."

"You don't have to feel bad, Share. If we find out Helen's scheming behind our backs regarding our inheritance, she's the one who should feel like shit."

"But she doesn't, and she wouldn't, Patti."

"How can you stand to live with her?"

Sharon folded her arms under her chest and stared out the bedroom window. "You know, she can be hysterically funny, and I enjoy living with her, most of the time anyway. But she has this other side, which comes out when I least expect it. Like Jekyll and Hyde, Patti. Usually, I can't even figure out why that side of her manifests itself. It can be that someone disagrees with her and she wants to prove to them that they're wrong and she's right. She won't compromise. She'll never, ever say she's sorry about anything. She's never to blame. Essentially, in her mind, she does nothing wrong, ever.

"And, oh, Patti," Sharon took a deep breath, "she'll plot these revengeful things to do to people to get back at them if they've dared to cross her. She'll rant and rave to me about this stuff as if it's totally normal, you know? And it's not, Patti. It most definitely is not what

I'd consider normal behavior. I've often thought, based on my research, that she has borderline personality disorder, or she's bipolar. Due to that aspect of her personality, I wouldn't put it past her to do something behind our backs. But if she didn't do any such thing, I'll feel bad saying these things about her behind her back."

Patti stood and hugged her sister tightly. She pulled back and looked into Sharon's eyes. "I don't consider what you're telling me necessarily talking shit behind Helen's back, Share. You're simply relaying information about our sister that you think I should know. And if Helen's up to something, it's not right, and we have to rectify it. If she were alive, Mom wouldn't want any of the sisters messing around with Dad's head about the will. And I don't believe Dad would do anything like what you're suggesting Helen wants. Which is why I don't believe he would go along with it."

"But maybe somehow Helen knows about Mom," Sharon said.

Patti closed her eyes for a few seconds, then said, "And she's holding it over Dad's head?"

Sharon covered her lips with her fingertips. "Maybe she's blackmailing Daddy."

Patti nodded. "Threatening to tell us about Mom being a lesbian in order to get more money?"

"It's possible, Patti."

"But unlike you, who has a ton of integrity, we all know money holds a helluva lot of weight in Helen's heart." Patti smiled. "Thank God you're not like her."

Sharon's eyes glistened. "I'd never do such a thing."

"I know that. Kathy does, too."

Sharon walked to the door and grasped the knob. "I'll come back after I'm finished talking to Kathy. Then we three can talk. Okay?"

"I'm going to lie down for a bit. All of this has taken its toll, and it's only Saturday afternoon."

Sharon closed the door behind her, and Patti stared at the ceiling. If only she'd known. But regret wouldn't do anything but make her feel worse, so she tossed it aside and focused on tonight's plan. She fell asleep and dreamed of flying crystal decanters pouring golden liquid over her and her sisters' heads.

# Chapter Eight

Kathy was so angry, she couldn't settle down. She wanted to throw something, but knew that wouldn't solve a darn thing. Helen was, uh, Helen. She'd been that way her entire life, so why was it bothering Kathy so much now?

She flicked off her shoes with her toes, then flung herself back onto the bed, letting out a loud sigh. "Why do you have to be so mean?" she said out loud.

*Helen's prettier than me. Thinner than me. Smarter than me. Ugh. I hate her guts.* Helen's litany of jabs and double-entendre compliments and put-downs toward Kathy was legion. And Kathy knew that she herself was a pussy—never sticking up for herself, acting like a freaking doormat as Helen walked over her as if Kathy was a piece of dog crap on the sole of Helen's shoe. Occasionally, Kathy would say something back to Helen, but usually not. It just wasn't worth it and never made a damn bit of difference. But that was the past, when they were all living under the same roof. *This* roof, as a matter of fact.

After their parents' divorce, their mom moved to downtown Quincy. Dad hadn't once asked Kathy if she wanted to live at the ranch—the "farm" then. By that time, the girls were old enough to move out on their own.

Sharon announced she wasn't going anywhere. She was staying to help Dad with the horses. Helen moved to Los Angeles for a short time to pursue an acting career and returned penniless, just in time to take advantage of Fabulous Friesians' burgeoning financial status. Kathy moved to San Francisco before taking a job in San Diego, and Patti went to the Institute of Photography in San Francisco.

Back then, their parents weren't making money. Fabulous Friesians was just getting on its feet, still in its formative stages. Then

Dad began selling Friesian donor sperm to other owners of the breed, who used the sperm to impregnate their mares. That part of the business brought in tons of money, but the business had flourished when he turned it into a place for people to buy a Friesian directly from Holland.

Dad purchased a ranch in the Netherlands that he visited once a year and brought young Friesians with varying levels of training back to the ranch. Most had won awards in various levels of dressage in Holland. By the time they arrived in the United States, the horses were ready to be sold to experienced riders.

Kathy loved riding horses and adored the Friesian breed. However, she would have turned her dad down had he asked her to stay. She had other plans. But it still felt like a knife jabbed sideways in her gut that he had never asked.

When she argued with him over the timing of the divorce, it resulted in a stalemate. He would not change his mind. Then, soon after, when he married Carolanne the Bimbo, well, that had been way over the top. Kathy believed everyone had a line that, when crossed, would inevitably cause a rift between two individuals. And her father had definitely crossed over to the dark side. Kathy couldn't say his name without seething. How must her mother have felt? Certainly abandoned. Definitely like a rag doll tossed aside for the newer Barbie model.

The knock on the bedroom door startled Kathy out of her reverie. "Come in."

Sharon peeked around the door and smiled. "Can I talk to you for a second?"

As much as Kathy got tired of hearing psychological platitudes about their family dynamics from her sister, Sharon's heart was always in the right place. She meant well. Kathy grinned. "Come, sit. Maybe you can lift me out of this funk."

Sharon settled in, across from Kathy at the foot of the bed, and tilted her head. "What's bothering you?" She held her hand out like it was a stop sign. "Don't answer that. Helen?"

Kathy laughed. "How'd you guess?"

"I just left Patti's room. We had a long discussion about what's going to happen tonight after dinner when Helen goes to her acting class."

Kathy rubbed her hands together. "Ooh, sounds intriguing."

"Believe me, it is."

Kathy dropped back into the pile of pillows at the head of the bed and crossed her hands behind her neck. "I'm listening."

Sharon launched into her tale of Helen's possible machinations to wangle control of their inheritance and ended with the real reason behind their parents' divorce.

Kathy lifted her head off the pillows as if in slow motion. "Mom was gay?"

Sharon nodded.

"So Mom's the one who wanted the divorce?"

Sharon nodded again.

Kathy turned onto her side, facing away from her sister, and closed her eyes. Tears rolled down her cheeks. "All these years," she said and hiccuped, "I've been pissed off at Dad. And he was just covering for Mom. He sacrificed his relationship with me and Patti for Mom." She coughed and continued to sob.

Sharon put a hand on her sister's leg and patted it. "Patti said the same thing. And I'm so sorry for not speaking up. I hope you understand."

Kathy sat up and swiped at her tears with a hankie. "I don't blame you. I really don't. Seems to me you were placed in a very difficult position for ten years."

"And our plan for tonight? You feel comfortable being a part of it?" Sharon said.

Kathy nodded slowly once, twice, then again. "Yes. Yes, I do. What about Patti? She agreed to do this?"

"She did. She's resting right now. We're hoping Daddy feels mellow enough to talk with us about the will and what happens to the ranch after he's gone. Maybe somehow Helen found out about Mom and threatened to tell us unless Daddy changed the will." She shrugged. "It's possible. Daddy was aware that I already knew about Mom, but Helen didn't know that, of course. And I, for one, am going to make sure she doesn't get away with this, no matter what reason she gave Daddy that changed his mind. It's not the money, though. It's the principle of the matter."

"I agree with you." Kathy chewed at her bottom lip.

"You look nervous. If you don't want to participate, I'll understand, and I'm sure Patti will, too."

Kathy waved her hand. "No, no. It's nothing like that. It's just upsetting that Helen would do such a thing. And sickening that we have to go behind her back to find out the truth. It's like something from a *Lifetime* movie."

Sharon laughed, then covered her mouth. "I'm sorry. It's not funny. But I think I saw a *Lifetime* movie that could have been about this scenario, I swear."

"We'll have to Google it and sit down and watch it together sometime."

Sharon stood and grasped the doorknob. "Let's go wake up Patti and talk before dinner."

When they got to Patti's room, Patti sat next to Kathy at the head of the bed, grabbed a pillow, and stuffed it in her lap. "So, Kathy, Sharon told you about Mom."

Kathy nodded. "It was a surprise. And a disappointment."

Sharon's eyebrows shot up. "You're disappointed to discover Mom was gay?"

Kathy slapped at Sharon's knee. "No, silly. I don't care about that. What I'm disappointed about is the fact she didn't feel comfortable telling us about it."

"I agree," Patti said. "I guess I just *assumed* Mom knew how we felt." She turned to Kathy. "Had you ever talked to Mom about gay rights and marching in San Francisco and stuff?"

"I don't think so." She shrugged. "When I look back at my time with Mom, I don't know that the subject ever came up. It's not like I knew there was a reason to discuss it."

"Yeah," Patti added, "we used to go out together, Mom and I, and we'd shop and go to lunch but—" She stopped.

"What is it?" Sharon asked.

Patti tilted her head. "I did discuss with her the fact my boss was gay, and because I wouldn't have sex with her, she fired me. I was really angry, and Mom knew it. She might have taken that as a negative reaction to my boss being gay."

"I wonder when Mom discovered she was gay," Kathy said.

Patti rolled her eyes. "Well, I'm sure she didn't suddenly wake up after giving birth to four girls and say, 'Hey, Bill, ya know what? I'm feeling gay today.'"

"No, I'm sure that's not how that conversation went down," Sharon said.

"I know that," Kathy replied. "I just wonder when and how she went about telling Dad."

"Inquiring minds want to know," Patti added.

"I'd really like to know how Helen feels about gays," Sharon said.

"I don't know, because I've never had a real down-to-earth discussion with Helen in my whole life," Patti said.

Kathy stared at her folded hands.

Patti reached out and grasped Kathy's forearm. "What's wrong?"

Kathy let out a breath. "I remember back in high school, there was this girl who was super shy. She wore her hair really short and always dressed in jeans with cuffs at the bottom and checked, flannel, button-down shirts, which made her look flat as a board. I knew she was gay. Everyone did. Helen asked me once if I saw the, quote unquote, butch bitch standing on the periphery of the school yard. I knew who she was talking about and told her that, yes, I'd spoken to Cisco. That was the girl's name. Helen asked if she'd ever hit on me. I told her of course not.

"Anyway, Cisco knew I wasn't gay, because I'd spoken to her about a gay-rights rally that was going on in San Francisco, and I told her my boyfriend at the time and I were going, so she knew I was straight. Anyway, I told Helen that story, and she said something like, 'Lucky you. Otherwise, I'm sure Cisco would have jumped your bones if you were alone with her.' I told Helen she was crazy to have that kind of attitude toward gay people, and she called me naïve and stupid and walked away.

"It's just so sad," Kathy continued. "Mom was damned if she did and damned if she didn't. If Mom had come out of the closet, knowing Helen was anti-gay and we three were pro-gay, not only would Helen have probably disowned Mom, Mom knew we three wouldn't be too happy with Helen's attitude toward our mother, thus causing even more family upheaval."

"You," Patti pointed at Sharon, "always got along well with Helen, so it was more the dissension between Kathy and Helen and me and Helen that would have escalated."

Sharon nodded. "Mom wouldn't have wanted to cause more of a rift than already existed between us girls."

"And if Mom kept her secret to herself," Patti said, "besides telling Dad, hence the divorce, then Mom could have had a good relationship with all her girls and not caused more dissension among us."

"So," Sharon agreed, "Mom and Dad must have agreed to have the burden placed on Dad's head. We'd all think he was a two-timing creep, having affairs behind Mom's back. Thus keeping Mom being a lesbian firmly in the proverbial closet."

"Mom was very stubborn," Patti said. "She usually got her way when she felt strongly about something. She could convince Dad of anything." Patti chuckled. "Maybe he was scared of her."

"You're probably right." Kathy smiled. "You took after someone, right, Patti?"

They all laughed out loud.

"I could see the discussion between Mom and Dad happening just like that," Kathy said. "Mom could back Dad into a corner with her logic and unrelenting reasonableness."

"Sounds realistic to me," Sharon agreed. "Poor Mom."

"And poor Dad," Patti added. "Agreeing to be the scapegoat for their divorce. How sad is that?"

Tears rolled down Kathy's cheeks. "Poor Dad. And poor Mom."

"I know, right?" Patti said. "Makes me want to start crying all over again. I wish Mom had felt comfortable telling me. It would have brought us closer, if anything, though she and I were always close. Which is why this hurts so much, her not feeling she could be open with me.

Sharon nodded, twisting the ring on her finger. "Sad, don't you think, that people can't accept the fact this is a free country? A free world. And we can love whomever we want to love."

Patti leaned over, placing her hand on Sharon's knee. "One of my favorite signs at the rally I went to said, 'Love is love.' That pretty much sums up how I feel."

"Me, too," Kathy added.

"Yeah," Sharon said.

Patti sniffed away her tears. "A friend of mine once said, 'Who you sleep with is none of my business.' I thought that was *so* true."

"Yeah," Sharon said again, yet there was something strange about her response.

"What's wrong, Share?" Kathy said.

Sharon's head popped up. "Oh, nothing. Just thinking about this family's dynamics."

"Pretty damn dysfunctional, wouldn't you say?" Patti said.

Sharon shrugged. "I don't know. No more dysfunctional than anyone else's family, I'll bet."

"True dat," Kathy added, then laughed. "Coining one of Patti's favorite phrases."

Patti snickered. "For having gone to college, I still seem to talk as if I'm not very educated sometimes, don't I?"

Sharon and Kathy joined in the laughter.

"Where *is* Helen?" Patti said.

"Downstairs?" Sharon said.

"No, I think she's in her room," Kathy said.

"Think she feels left out?" Patti asked.

"I don't know that she'd really care all that much," Sharon said. "She's very much caught up in her own little world." She shrugged. "I love Helen, but she's so—"

"Helen," Kathy and Patti chimed in.

"There have been so many times I'd like to beat the crap out of her," Patti added. "But it wouldn't change anything. Helen is so—"

"Helen," Kathy and Sharon said again.

The three women hooked pinkie fingers, scooching together to form a circle.

"We three musketeers are as one," Patti sang, to the tune of the Christmas song *We Three Kings*.

"Bearing boobs, we've traveled so far," Kathy and Sharon continued in tune.

They fell back on the bed, faced the ceiling, and laughed.

Patti slowly sat up.

Sharon and Kathy looked at her face and bolted upright.

"What is it, Patti?" Kathy said.

"Are you feeling ill?" Sharon asked.

Patti shook her head. "It's something you said, Sharon. When we were talking. Before you went to Kathy's room."

"Go on," Sharon prodded.

"We were talking about Helen, and you said she'll plot these vengeful things to get back at people, usually when someone's disagreed with her. You said it's not what you'd consider normal behavior. You think she has a borderline personality disorder, or she's bipolar."

Sharon nodded. "That's all correct."

"Don't you agree, Patti?" Kathy said.

"Do you think I'm bipolar, or have some borderline personality disorder, too?"

Sharon pulled her head back. "Why would you say something like that?"

"Where's this coming from, Patti?" Kathy said.

Patti rolled her eyes. "It's not as if you two didn't grow up with me. You know darn well I have a temper. I've gotten angry enough at someone and gone totally ballistic."

Sharon tsk-tsked. "Getting physical or getting into fights and screaming bloody murder… those are totally different things than what I'm referring to with regard to Helen, Patti. She becomes consumed, and I mean totally consumed, with plotting revenge against anyone who's simply disagreed with her. She needs to prove that they're wrong and she's right. And what they said or did isn't necessarily *against* her. They might have simply said something *in front of her* and not actually *to her*, you know?

"Helen just has to be right, and anyone who doesn't *see* that she's right… oh, my, they're doomed. She can be devious and underhanded and sneaky. She plots and plans. I've seen it with my own eyes. It's deviant behavior, in my estimation. Which isn't professional, because I'm not a therapist. I've always analyzed it away. But I realize now that I was wrong to do that."

Kathy laid her hand on Patti's forearm. "You're not devious or underhanded or sneaky. I have to admit, I wasn't aware you'd gotten into that many fights when we lived together under this roof."

"Where's this coming from, Patti?" Sharon said.

Patti huffed. "Maybe I didn't get into actual fistfights, but yes, I got physical at times," she said in a tone so low she wasn't sure if her two sisters even heard the words.

"What do you mean then?" Sharon said, eyes wide.

Patti eased back into the pillows with a guilty look on her face. "Neither of you will deny I can be a bit of a hothead."

"I've seen you get angry, not at me, though, and yes, it was a little scary," Sharon said.

"I've seen it, too," Kathy added. "But it was never directed at me." Kathy chuckled. "Thank goodness."

"Well," Patti shrugged, "there have been times when someone has had to hold me back, and thank God, I didn't get physical, because I can't say I'd have won many of those battles." She paused.

"Give us an example," Kathy said.

Sharon nodded her agreement. "Please do."

"Okay." Patti sighed. "Let me think. Here's one that's, shall we say, close to home." She cleared her throat. "Once, I think I was in high school, Helen made a derogatory remark about how Sharon never had a boyfriend because she had her head in psychology books day and night. I told her to shut the hell up. That whether Helen knew it or not, Sharon always had Helen's back. I called Helen an effing slut-bag."

"You didn't!" Sharon said. "We weren't allowed to swear, remember?"

"I knew that," Patti said. "But Helen shouldn't have been talking shit behind your back, Sharon. You were always so nice to her, for God's sake. Anyway, so Helen told me if anyone was a slut-bag, it was me, then she called me a ho-bag. I saw red, man. I took my right hand, grabbed Helen's right hand, pulled her into me while curling her arm in front of her stomach, and squeezed so hard she couldn't breathe. Then with my lips near her ear, I whispered, 'Talk shit about Sharon behind her back again, and I'll mess you up, and you know I can do it.' Then I let her go. She slumped to the floor, and I walked away."

Sharon and Kathy shook their heads, mouths half open.

"You're a badass," Kathy said.

Patti lay back on the bed again and faced the ceiling. "I am, aren't I?"

"Wow," Sharon added. "I recall you took martial arts classes in high school, right?"

"Yep," Patti said.

"You *are* a badass," Sharon said.

The women's laughter echoed off the walls of the room.

"So do I have some sort of personality disorder, Share?"

"Maybe you have anger issues," Kathy answered.

"That may be true," Sharon added.

"Am I bipolar?" Patti asked, sitting up.

Sharon reached out and placed her hand on Patti's forearm. "Please don't take what I said about Helen as having anything to do with you. Maybe you need to learn to control your temper, Patti. I didn't know about the incident with Helen, nor about most of the other incidents, if there were that many."

"There weren't *that* many," Patti said.

"Do you have other stories you'd like to share tonight?" Sharon said.

"Not at the current moment," Patti answered.

Sharon chuckled. "Oh, boy."

"Ditto," Kathy muttered.

Patti laughed out loud, and her sisters joined her.

# Chapter Nine

Bill held up his full-to-the-brim shot glass of whisky and glanced around the table at his three daughters. "To our family."

Kathy, Patti, and Sharon picked up their glasses, tipping them toward the middle of the table. "To our family," they said in unison.

"Too bad Helen couldn't join us," he said.

"She didn't feel she should skip class," Sharon explained. "Tonight they're meeting up early to run through the play they're putting on next month."

"We'll all go riding together tomorrow, Dad," Patti added.

Their plan hinged on Helen's absence, and so far everything was going according to plan. Sharon had suggested Dad break out the Johnnie Walker, since it had been over ten years since they'd all eaten at the same table together.

The conversation flowed smoothly. Patti talked about getting fired from her job. Kathy told them about the people she worked with at the computer firm and the creation of her own computer game. Sharon and their dad spoke about last night's clients, who were deciding which Friesian they wanted to buy.

Their father had just finished his first shot of whisky when he leaned back in his chair and let out a great sigh. "This is the life, girls," he whispered. He closed his eyes for several seconds and smiled.

Sharon shared a look with her two sisters and nodded.

Patti rolled her eyes, and Kathy stifled a giggle.

As serious as this interaction was meant to be, seeing their father just a little bit tipsy was an atypical event.

"Daddy, what are your plans for the ranch after you're gone?" Sharon asked.

Patti's eyes widened. *Isn't that a bit too direct? Then again, Dad is either going to tell us the truth or not, and this is a unique opportunity to find out.*

Their father lifted his gaze to Sharon. "Why would you ask that question?"

His eyes roamed to Kathy. "Are you three ganging up on me tonight? And if so, why now?"

Kathy smiled. She'd always been closer to her father than to her mother. Mom and Patti had been best friends.

Sharon, well, Sharon's affinity for analyzing her family's every move had kept her a bit distanced from them, though she seemed to be mellowing with age, like an expensive whisky. Everyone knew she meant well, and she had a kind heart. Patti's discussion with Sharon that afternoon had been one of the best they'd ever had.

"Yeah, Dad," Kathy answered. "We're all ganging up on you." She chuckled.

He glanced from Kathy to Patti to Sharon. "What exactly would you like to know, girls?"

Patti smiled at Kathy and gave her the okay sign with her fingers.

"What's going to happen to the ranch when you're no longer here?" Kathy said.

"What are your plans?" Patti asked. "Do you want one of us to run the ranch or all of us as a family or what?"

He laughed. "Helen offered—" he began, then screwed up his lips and looked toward the ceiling.

"Helen offered what, Daddy?" Sharon said.

"What did Helen offer to do for you, Dad?" Patti added.

He looked at each daughter in turn, then said, "Helen offered to run the ranch after I'm gone in exchange for—" He chuckled, took another sip of his drink.

Silence permeated the room. The only noise audible were the crickets chirping outside the windows.

"Helen wants to run the ranch after you... uh... aren't here, in exchange for what, Daddy?" Sharon asked.

"In exchange for seventy-five percent ownership of the ranch." He shook his head. "You three have to promise not to tell her anything about this little discussion."

"Don't tell her what, Dad?" Patti asked.

"Daddy, what is it you don't want us to tell her?" Sharon repeated.

"I never changed the damn will."

"So Helen didn't try to blackmail you into changing the will?" Sharon asked, sounding surprised.

He pulled his head back sharply. "What leverage would Helen have to blackmail *me*?"

Sharon shrugged. "I don't know, Daddy. I just wouldn't put it past her."

"It's sad, but unfortunately I can understand why you'd ask the question. But I'd never let that happen. The will's the same as Mom and I always wanted." He paused. "But I think *Helen* thinks I changed it. Mom would kill me if I ever changed the will in favor of one daughter over another." He laughed out loud. "If she could, that is."

"So you *did not* change the will?" Sharon prodded.

"Nope." He swept his hand in a half circle. "All you girls own the ranch. Lock, stock, and barrel, as my daddy used to say. Even Steven, all the way. Each of you gets the same amount."

"But Helen *thinks* you changed the will so that she'd get more than the rest of us?" Patti asked.

He nodded, took another sip of whisky. "Yup. Always been the selfish one of you girls. Your mom and I talked about my will before she died. Even though we were divorced and it's my money, you're *our* children. And we wanted all of you girls to get the same amount. I'm not gonna go behind her back now that she's gone and doesn't have a say." He shook his head slowly, side to side. "Wouldn't be right."

Patti stood. "I am so not accustomed to drinking whisky. Let me clear away the dishes, then I'm going to go to bed. Would you mind, Dad?" She bent over and kissed him on the cheek.

"Not at all, honey. That whisky always puts me to sleep, too." He smiled.

"I'll help you, Patti. I think I'll hit the hay, too," Sharon said.

"Me, three," Kathy added.

"You girls have sweet dreams. I'm going to sit her for awhile and enjoy this fine whisky," he said.

The three sisters did the dishes and cleaned up the kitchen, then they filed out of the room and up the stairs.

"Helen is not my favorite person right now," Sharon mumbled when they reached the second floor. "I wanted to be wrong about her."

Patti felt sorry for her older sister, but was also surprised. Normally, Sharon would mention a litany of reasons to explain Helen's behavior, which only sounded like excuses to Patti. Helen was the youngest daughter. Helen never felt truly loved because their parents abandoned her by getting divorced. Helen felt she was entitled to more of the ranch than her sisters because she'd been working there for the last ten years. Yada, yada, yada.

Patti walked into her room, turned on the light, and gestured for her sisters to follow her, then closed the door behind them. The three women sat on the bed.

"Well, that makes me feel better. How about you guys?" Patti said.

"I was so worried Helen had coerced Daddy into changing his will," Sharon said. "But do I feel better? No. I am so very disappointed in Helen," she said, her chin trembling.

"I am, too, Share," Kathy agreed, rubbing Sharon's back.

"It makes me feel good to know our father's an upstanding guy," Patti added. "Not only did he not want us to think ill of our mother because she was gay, he wasn't about to be manipulated by Helen into changing the will that he and Mom agreed to years ago. That's an honorable thing to do, especially since it's all his money, and he didn't have to keep his word to Mom. But he *did* honor his promise to her."

Tears flowed down Kathy's cheeks. "All these years, I thought such bad things about him. I thought he was lower than pond scum." She held her head in her hands and stared down at the comforter.

"Don't beat yourself up about it, Kath," Patti said. "I felt the same way."

"Yeah, but you talked to him a bunch of times over the last ten years," Kathy said. "You were willing to forgive him."

"I didn't talk to him that often, Kath. He always had to come to see me. I refused all his invitations to visit the ranch. And my forgiving him in my heart took a long time."

"I know, but—"

"You can make up for all those years now, Kathy. You, too, Patti," Sharon said. "You can start again. Call him. Visit him. Invite him to San Diego. And Alameda. You can make this right again."

Kathy and Patti nodded.

"Tomorrow's a new day," Sharon said. "We'll go for a trail ride. All five of us."

"If Dad's not too tired," Patti chimed in.

"Oh, he'll be just fine. He only had one shot," Sharon said. "Though, obviously, he's getting older. He probably can't hold his liquor as well as he could years ago."

Patti smiled. "It's been one helluva long day."

"What're we going to do about Helen?" Kathy asked. "Just go on as if none of this happened?"

"Stop worrying, Kathy. Dad didn't change the will, and that's the most important part. We can forgive and forget," Sharon answered. "Well, I can try to forgive, but I'm not sure about the forget part."

"She doesn't even know we had this conversation with Dad," Patti said.

"Patience really and truly is a virtue, girls," Sharon said. "Her time will come."

Patti laughed lightly. "At the reading of the will?"

Kathy nodded. "That sounds about right."

"It'll be the worst surprise she's ever gotten," Patti added.

"I wonder how the will really is set up," Sharon said. "Will we have to sell the ranch and divvy up the profits, or can one of us buy the others out and work the ranch? How does that work?"

"Hopefully, we won't have to deal with that for years," Patti said.

"Yeah," Kathy added, "I need time to get to know Dad before he passes away."

Patti laid her hand on Kathy's arm. "I feel the same way."

"I don't really care about the darn will," Sharon said. "It just intrigues me. How ever Mom and Daddy set up the will, I'm sure he had excellent guidance from Mr. Harrington, who's very well-thought-of in this community." She stood. "I'm heading off to bed, you two."

Kathy followed her and waved to Patti on her way out.

Patti felt as if she'd gone back fifteen years to when they were all under one roof. She lay back on the comforter and stared at the ceiling. She promised herself she would not regret all that had happened before tonight and her anger toward her father.

Tomorrow held the possibility of a better and different future. And she was determined to make the most of it.

# Chapter Ten

"Dad's not feeling up to riding today," Helen said. "I went in his room to wake him up for breakfast like I always do, and God, his entire bedroom reeks of booze." She looked from one sister to the next, glowering. "What the hell went on here last night?"

Sharon glanced up from the newspaper spread on the table next to her bowl of cereal and banana. "We had dinner. He had one shot of his favorite whisky."

"The Blue Label?"

Sharon nodded, then went back to reading.

"Seems to me he got plastered," Helen said. "You shouldn't have let that happen. If he doesn't want to go riding, he must have been sloshed."

Kathy sipped her coffee while watching Helen work herself into a snit. "We had a relaxing family dinner, Helen. We made sure he only had one shot of whisky. Perhaps one shot affects him more now that he's older, or maybe, after we went to bed, he drank some more. You know as well as the rest of us, you can't tell Dad what to do nor what to drink or eat."

"Maybe *you* can't, Kathy," Helen snarled. "Then again, why should he listen to you? You haven't been around for ten years."

Kathy held her tongue, not wanting to get into an argument. Helen would never change, so why bother? To think her youngest sister believed their father had revised his will to practically give the ranch to her because of everything she'd done for him over the last ten years! What a selfish bitch.

Instead of realizing she'd had free room and board for all these years, and most likely a small salary as well, Helen had stayed at the ranch for one reason only—to cement her future and guarantee herself a beautiful place to live for the rest of her life on the profits from a thriving family business.

All the sisters knew that if Helen had her way, she'd be the only person in their dad's will, because of everything she'd done for their parents throughout her life. How arrogant!

Patti had been taking care of their mother since she'd been diagnosed with cancer. She'd taken their mother to all her chemotherapy and radiation appointments. Patti hadn't asked for money. Sharon had worked at the ranch a little longer than Helen, but Helen still thought Sharon didn't deserve to receive as much as she? If anyone should receive less than the rest of the sisters, Kathy and Patti both felt they didn't deserve as much as Sharon and Helen.

But was that what an inheritance was all about?

Kathy walked out and went upstairs to change into riding clothes, leaving Helen standing in the middle of the kitchen. When Kathy glanced back to see if Helen would follow her, she saw she hadn't budged, arms akimbo, glaring at Kathy's departing backside.

"Oh, don't worry. I'll stay here and take care of Dad while you all have a nice ride," Helen yelled, then mumbled, "Fat-ass."

Patti slammed her mug down on the table and stood. "What the hell did you call her?"

Helen turned to Patti, lifting an eyebrow. "Someone has to tell her the truth. It's not healthy to be that heavy at her age."

Kathy scurried down the stairs, and Helen turned toward Kathy.

Patti grabbed Helen's upper arm and swung her around to face her. "Do you remember in high school when you made a remark about Sharon?"

Helen let out a bored-looking sigh. "Yes, Patti. So what?"

A deep blush crawled up Patti's neck into her face. "So what?" She paused. "So what?" she shouted into Helen's face, squeezing Helen's arm even harder. "I've taken martial arts most of my life. I could drop you to the floor right now."

Kathy placed her hand on Patti's back. "I don't need you to fight my battles, Patti."

Patti ignored her sister and said in a monotone, not taking her eyes off Helen's face, "Someone needs to put you in your place, Helen. And I think I'm just the person to do it."

"Patti, don't," Kathy whispered.

Patti tightened her grip on her sister's arm, and Helen inhaled suddenly.

Helen's arm shook beneath Patti's grasp.

"You think you're better than all of us, don't you?" Patti said between clenched teeth.

Helen met Patti's gaze and remained silent.

Patti slid her hand down to Helen's forearm, then slowly twisted Helen's arm behind her back, at the same time bringing Helen's back against Patti's chest.

Helen gasped. "You're hurting me, you bitch."

"I wanna hear you say you're sorry to Kathy."

"Patti, don't," Kathy said again.

"Be quiet, Kathy." Patti tightened her arm wrapped around Helen's stomach. "I can't hear you," Patti whispered in Helen's ear. "Say it, or I swear I'll break your arm."

"You wouldn't do that," Helen said between gritted teeth.

Patti slowly pulled Helen's arm up several inches higher against her back.

"Ow! Stop! What the hell's wrong with you?" Helen shouted.

"Say it," Patti whispered a second time against Helen's ear.

"Okay," Helen yelled. "I'm sorry."

"You're sorry for what?" Patti said, yanking her sister's arm up another inch.

"I'm sorry I called Kathy a fat-ass," Helen yelled.

"Tell *her* that," Patti said through gritted teeth.

"I'm sorry I called you a fat-ass, Kathy," Helen mumbled.

Patti suddenly let go and pushed Helen away from her.

Helen stumbled, caught herself, then turned to face Patti. "You're crazy, you know that?" She paused. "Crazy," she shouted at Patti, then turned and ran up the stairs.

Kathy let out a huge breath. "I can't believe you just did that."

Patti smirked, her gaze focused on the vacant stairs. "She had it coming." She laughed. "In fact, her time *will* come. At the reading of the will." She paused. "E-ven-tually," she whispered, very slowly.

Kathy walked in front of Patti and stood, facing her. "You truly are a badass." She chuckled. "And a bit nutso, too."

Patti shifted her eyes to her sister's, as if coming out of a fugue state. "Thank you."

"It's probably best if Helen stays here and watches Dad while we ride today," Kathy said.

"It'll definitely be more fun without her. She thinks she's the only one who's concerned about him anyway." Patti shook her head. "It's sad. I don't think Helen will ever change."

Kathy sighed. "Doesn't she know how much her behavior alienates the rest of us? What does she want from us, besides all the money we'd inherit, that is?"

"For us to get down on our knees in respect for Saint Helena the Wonderful. To thank her for everything she's sacrificed for our father."

"Well, no way is that ever going to happen," Kathy replied.

"I am so pissed off at her for what she tried to pull over on us. Let her stay here and sulk the entire day. With *her* father."

"Let's go," Kathy said in a monotone. "This is too dysfunctional for me."

Moments later, the three sisters met on the porch and walked to the barn together.

"Fresh air," Kathy said, taking in a big breath. "Everything looks so different. The dark green color with the white trim on the stables makes the place just sparkle. I can't wait to see Maximus again."

Sharon slid her arm through Kathy's and leaned in. "I'm sure he'll recognize you."

Kathy frowned. "You think so? After all these years?"

"Of course," Sharon answered. "Don't you agree, Patti?"

Patti smiled and came around to the other side of Kathy and grabbed hold of her hand. "This'll be fun. Just the three of us. We got to spend some quality time with Dad last night, and now it's sister time."

Sharon and Kathy chuckled.

"Someone's missing," Kathy added.

"Screw Helen," Sharon said, then looked at her two sisters, who burst out laughing.

Kathy came to a dead stop and stared at Sharon. "Well, I'll be damned. So now it's three against one."

"I know, right? I think I might faint," Patti said.

"Wha-at?" Sharon made the word several syllables.

"You know darn well what," Kathy said, catching Patti's eye. "You never talk like that about Helen."

Sharon glanced at Patti, then turned to Kathy. "Maybe I've

grown some backbone over my years of living with our baby sister. She can be so self-centered. I've wanted to tell her that so many times, but I always tried to make sense of her behavior based on psychological analysis and cut her some slack. I think in some way I thought Mom would be proud of me for treating Helen as any therapist might, you know? But now that I know she tried to sway Dad to change the will, I could... I could just—"

"Strangle her?" Patti finished.

The look of confusion or surprise or whatever on Sharon's face made Patti giggle. Kathy joined her, and they both bent over, holding their stomachs.

Patti was the first to quiet down, then she took hold of Sharon's hand. "You've changed, Sharon. I like the new you."

"Me, too," Kathy added. "You should have been there today when Patti used her martial arts moves on our baby sister."

"What the hell?" Sharon gasped.

Patti waved her hand back and forth. "Let's forget about Helen and have some fun. We can talk about my little tête-à-tête with Helen some other time."

"It was way more than a little tête-à-tête," Kathy added.

"You can tell me later." Sharon smiled. "Let's forget about the negative. Focus on the positive." She looked from Patti to Kathy. "I'm glad the three of us are together today. I love the both of you so much."

Patti pulled the three of them in for a group hug before they entered the barn, where twelve black heads turned in their direction.

"There you are," Kathy whispered as she walked to the third horse on the left side. She stopped in front of his stall and looked up into his dark brown eyes. "It's me, Maximus. Remember me?"

He stretched his long neck over the side of the stall and nudged Kathy's shoulder. She reached up on tiptoe and stroked his forelock and mane, nuzzling her face against his. "I've missed you, big guy."

Sharon strode up next to her, holding the saddle, girth, and bridle. "Put him in the crossties and saddle him up."

"If I remember how," Kathy said with a smile.

"It'll all come back to you," Patti said. "Who do you think I should ride, Sharon?"

Sharon introduced Patti to another beautiful Friesian. "This is

Sterling. He flew here from Daddy's ranch in Leeuwarden. He's more than sixteen hands, which is taller than most Friesians. Plus, he weighs more than fourteen hundred pounds. He's built very much like Maximus, actually."

"You're a big guy, Sterling." Patti stroked Sterling's velvety nose. "I wonder what they think while they're in the planes flying to the States. It must be really weird."

Sharon led Sterling out of his stall. "Daddy has a vet who flies back with them, and they're mildly sedated, because it's a very stressful experience for a horse. The flight is a little over six hours to San Francisco, then they have to trailer them here, which takes more than three hours. That's a long time."

Sharon brought out Diamond, one of her favorites, and they tacked up the horses.

"The mounting block is outside, next to the old oak tree," Sharon said. "Remember to use it. Less stress on the horses' backs."

They led the horses out the barn doors, then each took a turn climbing onto them. Within moments, they were trotting through the pasture toward the trail leading into the hills.

"I thought I would have forgotten how to post the trot, but I'm feeling pretty confident," Patti said as she nudged Sterling forward with her heels. "Springtime in Quincy. I love it."

Kathy rode up beside her. "Too bad I've got to go back to work."

Sharon joined them, looking like she'd lost her best friend. "You're leaving me alone with Helen?"

"You live with her, Share. Nothing's changed," Kathy said.

"I know, but *I've* changed," Sharon answered, brows furrowed. "Don't you two feel, I don't know, betrayed?"

"Of course I feel betrayed, and if I were you," Patti said, "I certainly wouldn't be able to live under the same roof with her."

"Me neither," Kathy concurred. "I'd never expected you to stay here and work with Dad if you wanted to move out on your own, Sharon."

Patti pulled Sterling in front of Maximus and Diamond, turned, and halted her horse. "If and when the time comes that Dad needs help, we can deal with it, together, as sisters. Nothing says Helen or you, Sharon, has to be the caregiver."

"What will we do?" Sharon asked.

Patti glanced at Kathy, then faced Sharon. "It's something we should talk about. All of us. Dad's not poor. We could hire a caregiver. Whatever we decide. Together."

"I have to catch a flight early tomorrow morning from Oakland International, so Patti and I have to leave soon," Kathy explained.

"We don't have to talk about this today," Patti added.

"You're right," Sharon added. "We can talk about it at our next family get-together. Dad has to be a part of the discussion anyway."

"You're totally right," Patti agreed. "The perfect excuse for our return visit to the ranch. Now, let's drop all this serious stuff and ride." She nudged Sterling up to a canter.

Kathy and Sharon hooted and hollered, following right behind her.

# Chapter Eleven

Patti yawned as they pulled into the gas station. "I should have fueled up before we left Quincy, but I was eager to get on the road. You need to get some sleep before you catch your flight tomorrow morning, Kath."

Kathy pushed open the car door. "Thanks for driving. We can trade places if you want. I can handle the next hour. Want a coffee?"

Patti grabbed the nozzle and pumped the gas. "No, thanks. You drive for an hour, and I'll take a catnap."

Kathy slid into the driver's seat. "What's the difference between a nap and a catnap anyway?"

Patti pursed her lips. "Hmm. Ever notice how cats tend to fall asleep, wake up shortly thereafter, and then doze off again? I think that's what it refers to."

Kathy drove away from the gas pump. "I've never had a cat or a dog, so—"

"Me neither. But I hope to one of these days." Patti cleared her throat. "I've made my decision. I'll move to San Diego and look for a new job."

Kathy whipped her head to the side, then pulled the SUV to the edge of the road. "You're kidding me, right?"

Patti shook her head. "Nope." She motioned for Kathy to get moving. "Don't be so shocked."

Kathy pulled back onto the road and pressed down on the accelerator to enter the freeway. "You could have knocked me over with a feather, as Mom would say."

Patti grabbed her purse, rummaging around inside.

"What're you looking for?" Kathy asked.

"My cell phone. I want to look at the classified ads. See if there are any places in San Diego or La Jolla that might be interested in hiring an unemployed photographer. How close did you say those two cities are?"

"Well, from San Diego to La Jolla, probably about a twenty-minute drive."

"And La Jolla's smaller, right?"

Kathy nodded. "La Jolla has about fifty thousand people. It's north of San Diego, which has about one and a half million." Kathy slapped the dashboard. "I just thought of something."

Patti located her phone, then quickly dropped it back into her purse. "Talk to me."

Kathy chewed at her bottom lip, tipping off Patti that she was nervous about something.

"What is it, Kath? You're stressing again."

Kathy tapped on the steering wheel with both hands. "All right. This is going to sound weird, but…"

"Spit it out, will ya?"

"Okay. Okay. Remember Robert Blakely?"

Patti's insides tightened at the name of the only man she'd ever thought of as husband material. They'd met at the Institute of Photography in San Francisco five years ago. After three years, their relationship had foundered when he'd moved to the San Diego area to pursue a career as a teacher at the Institute's satellite campus in La Jolla.

Six weeks after his departure, he'd phoned to tell her it would be detrimental to continue their relationship. That was it. No explanation or reason, other than he didn't want to pursue a long-distance romance. She'd been heartbroken.

"What does he have to do with my moving down there?"

"He might have connections. I'm sure he knows people who know people. He'd probably help you find a job."

Patti's face grew hot, whether from the memory of their last lovemaking session or anger at herself for still missing him. "No, thank you."

"Patti, it's been, like, two years or more since you two broke up."

"And it still hurts. I don't want to ever see his face."

"I saw him once at Starbucks. He asked about you."

"You never told me that."

Kathy blew out a breath. "And I would never have mentioned his name, except I think he could give you quite an advantage over others in your search for a really good job."

"What did he say?"

"Not much. He was engaged."

"How nice. I'm happy for him."

"Doesn't sound like it. I know *I* wouldn't be. He's a jerk for breaking up with you over the phone. But you hadn't been dating for *that* long, right?"

"We dated for three years, for God's sake. I was in love with him. I thought he felt the same way," Patti said, raising her voice.

"I understand. Using the phone to end a relationship is—"

"Shitty?" Patti interjected.

"Well, that, too. It's also easier. You can say what you have to say and hang up, obviously forestalling any elongated crying jags or arguments and such."

"It's not right. It made me feel like I didn't mean much to him. Like I wasn't important. It was humiliating, actually. So, to see him face-to-face would be, I don't know, kind of embarrassing. If *I* contact *him*, he might think I want to get back together or something."

"Robert's probably married by now, Patti. He'll know you know he's in a relationship, because I told him I'd have to pass that bit of information along to you. Therefore, he'll understand you're not trying to rekindle something between the two of you. You're simply looking to find a good job."

"You make it sound so easy."

Kathy glanced at her sister. "You can make it as complicated or as easy as you like." She raised her eyebrows. "Name the movie."

"Robert Redford. *The Horse Whisperer*," Patti replied.

Kathy chuckled. "Dang, you're good."

Patti waved her hand. "Back to what we were talking about. You're telling me this discussion with Robert would be easy? Says the woman who wants me to find out if her boyfriend has another chick on the side."

Kathy laughed. "Point taken. But it's been years since you and he were together. You have no ties to him any longer. He'll either help you, or he won't. You don't even have to see him. This can all be done on the phone or by text or e-mail."

Patti searched inside her purse for a piece of chewing gum and offered the pack to her sister, who shook her head. "I thought you said there were tons of opportunities in the San Diego area for professional photographers."

"Yes, I said that. And I believe there are. But I see Robert's picture in the local newspaper often. He's a professional photographer himself. He does more than teach at the Institute in La Jolla. I'm telling you, he knows people."

Patti nodded. If she could save herself from having to work her way up to the top, which she'd already done for the last four years, she should grasp this possible chance at a future position. "I'll do it."

Kathy raised her hands in the air and clapped them.

"Keep your hands on the wheel, Sis. And don't get all 'I told you so' about it. It makes professional sense to pursue this, and I will. I don't want to have to work for minimum wage. I'm past that."

"I'll give you his business card after you move your stuff into my condo."

Patti stared out the side window, chewing and snapping her gum. Robert Blakely. She'd never thought she'd see him again. He lived almost five hundred miles away. Eight hours' driving time. When she made her decision to move in with Kathy, she hadn't even thought about the fact he might still be living in the San Diego area. For all she knew, he'd moved away or even moved back to the San Francisco Bay Area. She simply didn't think of him at all anymore. Well, she tried not to. It only brought back memories she'd rather forget.

They reached Patti's cottage in Alameda a little before midnight. They were both tired and went straight to bed. Patti planned to give her sister a ride to Oakland International Airport at seven in the morning.

On the short, twenty-minute drive the following morning, they talked about what furniture Patti should sell and which pieces she should bring with her. She planned to return her SUV to the dealership, since she leased it, and rent a U-Haul to carry most of her belongings. She could accomplish all the packing in a few weeks, hopefully, and leave right afterward, arriving in early May.

She had no job, so her to-do list was a short one. Though the money she had in savings was significant, she didn't relish using it for living expenses. Now that she'd made the decision to move in with her sister, she was eager to get to San Diego and find a new job.

Traffic was heavy around the airport terminal, and Kathy didn't want to be late boarding. Patti parked in front of Terminal Two, raced around to unload her sister's suitcases, then hugged her. "I'll call you."

Kathy yelled as she rushed through the automatic doors, "I want you down there by May at the latest, girlfriend."

Patti waved again, then scrambled into the driver's seat. She zoomed away from the curb, heading back to Alameda. Back home. For the next few weeks anyway. Then it was *San Diego, here I come.*

When she arrived home, Patti phoned Sharon to tell her about the big move. Helen answered the phone but was understandably brusque, explaining she was too busy to talk, because she had a meeting with a few clients. Patti was happier talking to Sharon anyway.

"I'm excited for you, Patti," Sharon said. "I hope it all works out."

"Kathy and I get along so well, it's the perfect fit as far as a roommate goes. I just hope I can find a good-paying job."

"If Kathy's right about that Blakely guy, maybe he'll solve all your employment worries."

Patti had finally told Sharon about her personal connection to Robert. She rarely talked on the phone with Sharon, so Patti's relationship with Robert was news to her sister. "I hope he can help me." She paused, then continued. "You know, Share, I wanted to say something."

"What's up? You sound like you're about to cry. You okay?"

"I wanted to thank you for not hating me for distancing myself from Dad… and you for all these years."

"Oh, honey," Sharon said, "I never took it personally. It was never about you and me. You have your own relationship with Dad, and I wasn't going to come between the two of you. I believed all along the both of you would work it out. I know it seemed as if he was behaving like a chump when he and Mom divorced."

"He did. But now I know why," Patti said. "It just proves no one can really know what goes on inside anyone else's relationship unless they're part of it. We're the daughters. Mom and Dad were married. Now that I know what was going on between the two of them, it all makes sense. But the timing sucked."

"It did indeed."

"Anyway, Share, thanks for welcoming both me and Kathy to the ranch after Mom's funeral."

"Fabulous Friesians will always be your home, Patti. It might look different after all the renovations, but it's still our family home. I hope you know that."

"Thanks. You have a good heart. By the way, Kathy told me you were upset about what happened between Helen and me."

Several seconds passed before Sharon spoke. "I understand your frustration and anger toward our baby sister, Patti. Kathy and I both feel that way as well. It's just…"

"I need to learn not to respond to her snarky remarks."

"You get so angry, Patti. I worry about you. Some day you're going to say the wrong thing to the wrong person and—"

"Helen pushes my buttons," Patti interrupted. "There are times when I can't help myself."

"We don't want you to do something you'll regret. You can understand Kathy and my concern."

"And I love you two for that. Thank you. But don't worry. I'll try to keep my hotheadedness in check. It almost seems impossible that Helen's even our sister. She can be such a douchebag. Maybe she's adopted."

Sharon laughed. "On that note."

"I'll call you when I get settled in," Patti said. "Love you."

"And I love you, too, Patticake."

Patti hung up the phone, making a promise to keep more in touch with her older sister. It took two to make any relationship work, and Patti was determined to have a better connection with Sharon in the future.

She planned to be ready to depart Alameda in a little less than a month, arriving in San Diego after the first week of May. She'd have to meet with a realtor and arrange for the agent to find a lessee for her cottage, oversee any repairs and problems, and collect the rent, hopefully for a reasonable fee. Then she'd load up a U-Haul and head for her new home, a smile on her face.

# Chapter Twelve

Kathy arrived at San Diego International Airport and looked around for Charlie. He'd told her that he'd pick her up when she returned home from her mother's funeral. She'd texted him last night to confirm her arrival time, but he hadn't replied. She stood at the curb, flanked by her two suitcases, tapping her foot, wondering where the heck he was. She grabbed her phone and sent him another text, then waited fifteen more minutes before hailing a cab.

When she arrived home, she slumped on the couch, remote in hand, and turned on the television. *Why would he tell me he'd pick me up, then not show?* She seethed. Was this another way of hinting their relationship had changed? Why couldn't he say it to her face? She jumped off the couch, walked into the kitchen, and swung the freezer door open.

"Yay! I didn't eat it all before I left." She pulled out the pint of Ben & Jerry's ice cream, grabbed a spoon, and jammed it into the middle of the open container. "Chocolate Cherry Garcia. Mmmmm." She sauntered back to the front room.

She wasn't looking forward to returning to work the next day. Still sad about her mother's passing, she dreaded the thought of staring at a computer screen at Techno Inc. for hours, where she'd spent the last eight years. Being ignored by Charlie was really doing a number on her, too, stressing her out to the max. Living in a state of limbo grated on her nerves.

During her morning and afternoon breaks, she worked on creating a video game she hoped to sell one day. She'd taken a class at San Diego Community College in computer video creation a while back and loved it.

She wondered if and when Charlie would get in touch with her. If he wanted out, this was not the mature way of breaking up with a woman. It reminded her of high school. She decided to send him one last text, and if he didn't respond, she'd consider their relationship over and done with.

Patti called to see if she'd arrived home safely, and Kathy explained her dilemma. "I don't know what to make of him. What do you think I should do?"

"I'll be down there soon. If you still haven't heard from him, I could try to intervene. If you still want me to."

"I'll play it by ear. When you get here, I'll have made my decision, depending on what he does or doesn't do. I just can't believe the way he's acting. Why has he suddenly frozen me out of his life? I deserve an explanation, don't you think?"

"Of course you do, Kath. One would hope he'd grown up. Or that he had the balls to confront you to your face. What a chickenshit." She paused. "Just playing the devil's advocate again, but maybe something happened. A car accident? Maybe he's in the hospital, and no one knew about you?"

"Of course anything's possible, Patti. It's also possible I could grow a horn out of the middle of my head and become a unicorn."

Patti howled. "Maximus would really fall in love with you then, huh?"

"All kinds of people know Charlie and I have been together. Someone would have called me if he was in the hospital." She sighed. "I gotta go. I have to get a good night's sleep."

"Lucky you," Patti said. "You're gainfully employed."

"You will be, too, soon enough. Just get your butt down here."

Now Kathy found herself staring at the clock on the wall at work, begging the big hand to make it to twelve. The little hand was already at five, and quitting time was almost here.

She still hadn't heard from Charlie and refused to get in touch with him. She looked at the calendar. Her mom had passed away on Wednesday, March twenty-ninth. The funeral was on Wednesday, April fifth. She and Patti had gone to the ranch on Saturday, April eighth, and gotten home on Sunday evening, April ninth. It was Monday, May eighth, and Patti would arrive that evening. She'd given Charlie more than enough time to reach out to her.

*But do I really want Patti to run interference for me?* What was the point? Charlie obviously was no longer interested and had picked the perfect time to pull out of the game while Kathy was in Quincy. Pussy! But it still bugged the crap out of her. She wanted, no, she needed to know *why*.

She bolted out of the office at five o'clock, excited for Patti's arrival. Later, when she heard the knock on the door, Kathy raced to answer it. Patti stood on the front step with a big smile on her face and the U-Haul parked in the driveway.

"Welcome home!" Kathy said and enveloped her sister in a big hug.

"It feels funny, calling this home, you know? I'm such a *NorCal* girl. Do you think I'll fit in here, in *SoCal*?"

Kathy imitated her sister and rolled her eyes. "Don't you dare say that to anyone. You'll stick out like a girl wearing a bikini in Alaska."

Patti laughed out loud. "I'm just trying to rattle your cage, Kath. I won't say it in public."

Kathy took her sister's suitcases and headed upstairs. "Your room's ready. I made up the queen bed and cleaned the bathroom. We can order pizza, if you're up for it. I figured you'd want to just relax tonight. I have to go to work tomorrow, so I can't stay up too late."

Patti followed her up the stairs, then sat on the edge of the bed and kicked her shoes off. "I'm tired. Pizza sounds delicious. You're always talking about Petroccini's. I'd love to try it. My treat."

"No way! You're unemployed. I'll buy the pizza, and I've got Cokes in the refrigerator. Or you can have sparkling water." Kathy turned and headed downstairs. "Whenever you want me to call for the pizza, just tell me."

"I'll be down soon. I want to at least put my clothes away."

Twenty minutes later, Patti joined her sister on the couch. "Still haven't heard from Charlie, eh?"

Kathy shrugged.

"You look pissed off."

Kathy nodded.

"Man, I'd be royally ticked off, too." Patti placed a hand on her sister's arm. "What can I do? Anything?"

"I could arrange to accidentally run into him at Starbucks, if I was that interested. But it's obvious things are over. There's no need to bop me over the head with a shovel in order for me to understand what's going on here."

"I just don't get it, Kath. I'm dying to know what's going on, and I'm not even his girlfriend."

Kathy laughed. "Apparently, neither am I." She picked up the remote and turned on the TV. "Let's just drop it."

"Which Starbucks?"

Kathy searched through the guide, looking for something to watch. She glanced at her sister. "Huh?"

"I said, which Starbucks? I don't think this is doing you any good at all. The not knowing. You can't move on with your life until you have some sort of closure. You love him, don't you?"

"Past tense, Patti. I loved him, yes. But this is not what I'd expect from someone I thought was equally enamored with me."

"Aren't you just a little bit intrigued? You're telling me you're willing to just let this drop and totally forget about it? Just go on with your life as if nothing ever happened between the two of you?"

Kathy shrugged. "There's a part of me that wants to hear why he chose to disappear off my radar. But the other part is saying 'screw him.' If he doesn't have the guts to man up and face me, tell me we're finished, then he's not the man I thought I loved. There's absolutely and unequivocally no sane reason for him to simply fall off the grid. So, no, I don't want to hear from him. Nothing he'd tell me could excuse his behavior. I'm moving on with my life. Starting today."

Patti settled into the couch cushions and put her feet on the ottoman. "I feel you. I really do. And it's your choice, not mine. Let's watch a movie."

Kathy grabbed a blanket and covered her legs and feet. "I'll call for the pizza, and we can have girls' night before the reality of life hits us tomorrow, when I return to work and you look for a job." She tapped her forehead. "And I don't want to forget to give you Robert's info. Remind me before I leave in the morning, if you're awake."

"Oh, I'll be awake. I'm eager to get going on my job search. But for now, what about *The Curious Case of Benjamin Button*?"

Kathy chuckled. "Brad Pitt's a total fox, but I was thinking more on the lines of *Fast & Furious 6*. I love Paul Walker. Though I'll probably cry just looking at him."

"I know. His death was so tragic. I'm a big fan of Vin Diesel."

Kathy pushed her sister's knee. "I never knew you liked bald guys."

"I never met a young bald guy. The only men I know who don't have any hair are old geezers." Patti flicked her eyebrows up and down. "It's all about the muscles."

Kathy tilted her head back and stared at the ceiling. "I'm picturing you with Vin Diesel. You have such thick hair. When you have it in a ponytail like you do right now, it's like a big poof ball on the top of your head." She chuckled. "The two of you would be an awesome pair."

Patti pressed the On Demand button on the remote and selected *Fast & Furious 6*. "Order the pizza, and let's watch these two good-lookin' dudes. Forget about our problems for one night."

Kathy scrunched back into the pile of throw pillows. "You're on. I'll completely forget I've been dumped by your old boyfriend, and you will not think about finding a job right away so you can pay your half of the rent."

Patti nudged her sister's leg with her foot. "I have savings, you know. I'm not worried yet. I can pay my half of the rent right now. No need for you to carry me."

"I was just kidding." Kathy found her cell phone and scrolled through her contacts. "Half veggie for you. Half pineapple and pepperoni for me."

Patti stuck her finger halfway into her mouth. "Pineapple and pepperoni? Gag me."

Kathy kicked Patti's foot away and smiled. "This'll be fun, living together."

"Like old times. Minus the fighting with Helen."

Kathy nodded. "Minus Sharon's analyzing every single movie character's motivation for wanting to risk his or her life just to drive fast cars."

# Chapter Thirteen

Patti slept in and missed seeing Kathy before her sister left for work. It felt so good to get a few hours' extra sleep in a comfortable bed with plenty of comforters at the foot of the bed if she needed one. She was perennially cold, always needing a blanket, even when there had been a heat wave in the Bay Area.

She expected she would be much warmer living in San Diego—another plus to moving here. Whereas it was in the mid-sixties in Alameda in May, the weather forecast for today in San Diego was seventy-seven degrees. She looked forward to finding not only a job, but spending quality time with Kathy, who'd left the Bay Area soon after their parents' divorce.

After a quick breakfast of yogurt and a banana, she took a shuttle to the nearest mall, which Kathy told her had a Starbucks.

Latte in hand, she sat at a small table in the corner with an unadulterated view of the front door. People in suits and ties and expensive purses and briefcases crowded the café. When a man dressed in perfectly ironed khaki shorts, a white Izod shirt, and brown Top-Siders sauntered in with his own mug, her stomach dropped to somewhere below her intestines.

When he smiled at the barista and waved as he walked in, Charlie's light tan set off his white teeth. Patti remembered when she was the recipient of that killer smile. Then she recalled the anger she'd felt at herself for letting him crawl into her heart in the first place, and she clenched her teeth so hard her jaw popped.

He'd been her first love. Her last love, Robert, had hurt her in a different way when he decided to end their relationship. Robert hadn't been a player.

She recalled the outrage she felt when she found out Charlie was screwing around behind her back. If he was doing the same thing to Kathy, she'd like to kick him where it would hurt the most.

She was not prepared for this. Kathy hadn't told her *which* Starbucks Charlie frequented. San Diego was a large city. What were the odds this was the Starbucks Kathy had been referring to? *Crap!* She wasn't sure if she should make her presence known, or wait until some other day to talk to him. But if he noticed her, she'd be forced to open the discussion about Kathy, and now her fury had ramped up to the point where she'd have trouble not screaming at him in front of all the people enjoying their morning coffee. She hadn't realized she was carrying around so much animosity toward him. Maybe she could make an immediate escape out the back door.

She turned her head to the side and feigned interest in the passersby in the mall, holding her breath. "Please don't see me," she whispered. But she felt a shift in the air and intrinsically knew someone was standing next to her.

"Patti?"

She'd recognize that voice anywhere. Long ago, she'd heard it many times, when they'd play hooky from school and lie in bed at his house while his mom and dad were at work. Their lovemaking had forever stayed in her mind as the best part of their relationship. They'd been madly in love. Until he no longer was. *Once a jerk, always a jerk, even though that was so long ago. But after what he's putting Kathy through, apparently he hasn't changed.*

She turned her head and leaned back to look into his face. "What are you doing here?"

He pulled his head back and frowned. "Shouldn't that be *my* line?"

She took a deep breath. "You were always good at one-liners."

He took a seat, scooting the chair out of the way of other customers, nearer to hers.

She looked him in the eyes. "Oh, by all means, please join me."

"Don't mind if I do. I'm my own boss. What brings you to our beautiful beach city?"

"I lost my job. Well, I didn't lose it. It didn't actually go missing. Someone else took my place. I was fired. But anyway," she rambled, "Kathy convinced me to move down here with her." She shrugged. "I had nothing important keeping me in Alameda, so I packed up and drove down here in a U-Haul." She ran out of breath and sat back in her chair, reached for her coffee cup, and took a sip.

"Whoa. I didn't know. And Kathy didn't mention it either."

"She would have told you if she'd heard from you when she got back."

He took several gulps of coffee, set the cup on the table, then stared at the brew. "About that…"

"Yeah, about that. You were always so direct when I knew you in high school. Granted, that was a long time ago. But when I asked you a question, you'd be brutally honest with your answers. I ought to know, because when I confronted you about screwing that chick behind my back, you straight up admitted it, no hemming and hawing, no BS. So, what's up with you and my sister?"

He took another sip, not meeting her eyes, shifting his gaze out the window. "It's a little hard to explain. I—"

"You don't need to tell *me*, Charlie. You need to meet with your *girlfriend*, my *sister*, and explain what's going on to *her*."

He nodded, then faced her. "I know. I know. I've been putting it off. Plus, we've been swamped at the shop."

"Swamped? I hope that's just the wrong word choice, since you're in the boat business."

He smiled, and she recalled when that smile meant something to her. But right now, seeing his gleaming white teeth, she wanted to throw her cup of coffee in his face and watch it drip all over his nice white shirt. She shivered, trying to rein in all the negative feelings bubbling just beneath the surface.

"Cold?" Their eyes locked. "Or do you feel what I'm feeling?"

"The air conditioning in here is turned up way too high," Patti answered.

He shook his head, his eyes never leaving hers. "I'm not talking about the AC, Patti, and you know it."

She had assumed she was imagining the subtle vibes emanating from Charlie when he'd sat down too close to her. Maybe she'd misinterpreted the way he looked so intensely at her.

Now, she knew exactly what vibe she'd felt. He wanted *her*.

She stood.

He grabbed her hand.

She looked him in the face. "Maybe you're feeling something, Charlie, but nothing's coming from *me*. And if you think so, you're hallucinating."

"But that's why I couldn't talk to Kathy. I didn't know what to say. How would I explain I'm still in love with her older sister?"

She yanked her hand out of his grasp. "Since high school, Charlie? Really? You're the one who two-timed me way back then." She moved her face closer to his. "I dumped your ass, if you recall. And you've been in a relationship with my sister for almost a year now. Get over yourself, because I have no feelings whatsoever for you."

"Haven't you ever heard what they say about your first love?"

"You're out of your mind. Yes, you humiliated me back then, and you broke my heart. But I'm no longer that girl. Why don't you grow up?" She picked up her purse and draped the strap over her shoulder. "Don't confuse our teenage sexual relationship with a mature love relationship. Which is what I thought you had with my sister."

"My insides never went all to mush when I was with Kathy."

"You're full of shit, Charlie. It's been years since I kicked your butt to the curb. But get this one thing straight. I would never have anything to do with *you*," she said, pointing a finger in his face. "You were, or are, my sister's boyfriend. We will never have a future—ever. You were a player in high school, and from what I can surmise now, you're still a player." She picked up her cup and turned to throw it in the nearest trash bin. "Grow a pair, Charlie, and go talk to Kathy."

Again, she sensed his presence, and within seconds, his hand grasped her forearm.

"Can we please talk?"

She turned to look him in the eyes. "What you need to do is talk to my *sister*. Not me. You owe her that. Have you not changed since freaking high school? Still two-timing? The girl you're with is never enough? The grass is always greener on the other side? Excuse me, but I have more important things to do than waste my breath on a piece of shit like you."

He leaned in and whispered in her ear, "You'll regret dumping my ass, as you call it, in high school." He squeezed her arm until she gasped. "And you'll regret treating me like a piece of shit today, too." He released her.

She pulled away and rubbed her arm up and down. "Don't ever threaten me again. You are seriously wasting your breath." She rushed out the door, hoping beyond hope he wouldn't follow her. She made it to the corner and refused to look back. She absolutely could not believe he was coming on to her after all these years. *I guess a tiger really doesn't ever change its stripes.*

She was so pissed, she took the shuttle back to Kathy's condo, let herself in, and scrambled upstairs to her bedroom. She slammed the door behind her. Her sister deserved an explanation, but it looked like she'd never get one from Charlie. The chickenshit coward.

Yes, she and Charlie had been a couple back in high school. But sex had been the biggest part of their youthful relationship. And the qualities that had meant the most to her? Fidelity. Trust. Those two had absolutely gone missing. Which was why she'd dumped him.

Kathy had actually asked if it was okay with Patti if she dated him, not wanting to alienate her favorite sister. And, naturally, Patti had been fine with it, hoping, and assuming, Charlie had changed his ways and his wandering eye after so many years.

Well, his eyes were still wandering. But in the wrong direction. Aimed at her. He obviously hadn't changed. And he'd two-time Kathy in a nanosecond if Patti were to give him the green light. What an unbelievable bastard! He wanted a repeat performance of their past relationship, but she sure didn't. She'd never forget what it felt like to be cheated on.

And now Kathy was getting the same treatment.

*He's such an ass.*

# Chapter Fourteen

Kathy arrived home after work and found Patti in front of the TV, remote in hand, tears running down her face. She rushed inside, plunked the grocery bags on the kitchen counter, then returned to the front room and sat next to her sister. "What's wrong?"

Patti wiped her eyes and shook her head. She wasn't about to tell her sister what was upsetting her. She'd already decided to say nothing about her talk with Charlie. There was no way Kathy would find out about it, unless Kathy saw Charlie and he mentioned it to her.

Patti sniffed and decided on a good story. "I was just remembering Mom. I used to visit her every day at the senior center and then in the hospital during her last days. It just suddenly hit me. She's really gone. And we can't even visit her at the mausoleum, because it's too far away."

Kathy patted her sister on the knee. "You were the closest to her, especially since you lived right there. I called her often, but at the end, sometimes she didn't know who I was when I phoned. She recognized me when I said goodbye, though." She shrugged. "I couldn't quit my job to be there for her, and I feel guilty about that."

Patti grasped her sister's hand and squeezed. "Do not do that to yourself. No way could you move all the way from San Diego to the San Francisco Bay Area to be with Mom. I was already living right there in Alameda. Helen and Sharon were almost four hours north in Quincy at the ranch with Dad, so they couldn't help out. You moved here for your job. Sharon visited Mom when she could, and Helen came once, or twice. I don't remember. You visited her more often than they did, Kathy."

"Really? You're not just trying to make me feel better?"

Patti smiled. "No, I wouldn't do that. I'm being honest with you. Sometimes, Mom confused me with Helen, which made me crazy.

But in the end, she recognized all of us. She didn't call me Helen when she took her last breath, and believe me, that would have made me feel awful."

Kathy chuckled. "I think you should be compensated in Dad's will for helping her out all those years. Taking her to her chemo and radiation and doctor appointments. Driving her everywhere. It's common knowledge they drew up a will together, and Dad said he wasn't changing anything, even if Mom passed away before he did."

"Well, following that logic, Sharon and Helen should be compensated for helping Dad at the ranch for all these years."

Kathy shook her head. "Not exactly. They're getting free room and board and probably a salary. If they'd been living in the Bay Area, they would have had to pay a ton of money every month for an apartment and food."

"I did it because I wanted to, Kath. And Sharon helps out Dad because she wants to. We don't know if either of them is getting paid a salary, but I'll bet if they are, it's because Helen bitched about it and somehow convinced Dad it was in his best interests, or some bullshit."

"Okay, let's not talk about this anymore. I'm sorry I said anything."

Patti smiled through her tears. "I'll be okay. It was just one of those moments. You caught me when you walked in the door."

"I have my moments, too, Patti. In the shower when I have time to think, or at work when I see the picture of Mom on my desk." She paused. "Hey, did you talk to Robert today?"

Patti grabbed a tissue and wiped her nose. "No, I spent my day getting my room organized, took a run, watched some daytime TV."

"Good for you, taking a day off. You deserve it. We've all been through the wringer, as Mom used to say." Kathy paused. "What the hell does that mean, anyway, through the wringer? What's up with that?"

Patti laughed for the first time that day. "Just a phrase whose literal meaning is based on the word wringer, with a w. It was a device that pressed water out of clothes that had been washed."

"Oh, you mean that thing Mom had in the basement that was her mother's? It had, like, a stack of rolling pins, and you fed the clothes through the rollers to squeeze the water out?"

Patti nodded while Kathy explained. "You got it. Now what were we talking about?"

Kathy tapped her finger on her lips. "Oh, yeah, all of us have had a hard few months, what with Mom getting sicker, then dying, then our little family reunion with Dad and Helen's machinations to try to take the ranch out from under us." She leaned back and stared at the ceiling. "I'm depressing myself with all this stuff." She looked at her sister. "Did you see Robert's contact information I left for you on the counter in the kitchen?"

"Yeah, thanks. But today I just wasn't feeling up to it. Maybe tomorrow."

"There's always tomorrow, right? I'm a proponent of that platitude. And what's the other one? If at first you don't succeed, try, try again?"

"Oh, you're just full of catchy and rather cliché phrases for living life, aren't you?"

Kathy stood and began putting the groceries away. "I wish Charlie had formally broken up with me, then I'd have closure. I still feel like I'm waiting. Like he'll show up one of these days. It's driving me insane."

Patti's stomach clenched. "I don't know what to tell you, Kath. You have to just move on with your life. He's obviously got other plans that don't include you. If you can't hear it straight from the horse's mouth, though in his case, I'd call it the horse's ass," she chuckled, "that he doesn't want to be in a relationship with you any longer, you'll have to pull on your big-girl panties and move forward. I mean, at this point, you really don't have to hear him say the actual words. He's saying them right now with his silence, whether you hear the words or not, right?"

Kathy put the milk away and closed the refrigerator door. "Wow. Please don't mince words. Tell me how you really feel about my situation." Her bottom lip trembled.

Patti realized she'd been too harsh and way too candid, given the way Kathy felt about Charlie. She had to remember her sister wasn't privy to what had happened with him at Starbucks today.

Patti stood and confronted her sister. "I'm sorry. I came on way too strong just now. I guess it's just me being protective. I don't want to see you hurt any more than you already are with him ignoring you.

The damage is done. I want you to move on. Instead of trying to find *me* a boyfriend, why don't we concentrate on looking for someone new for *you*?"

Kathy nodded, sniffed, then grabbed a can of green beans and looked at the label. "Green bean casserole sounds good."

"With cream of mushroom soup and dried onion rings on top?"

"I'll fix that for dinner. What else would you like?"

Patti came around the counter and helped her sister. "I'm going to text Robert. See if he can meet up with me tomorrow so we can talk."

"Sounds like a good plan. I think he's your best bet. He must know a lot of people."

Patti put the dirty dishes in the dishwasher, then joined her sister in the front room. She grabbed her cell phone off the coffee table. "I'm telling Robert I moved in with you after Mom died, and I want to know if we can talk sometime about job prospects." She pressed the send button. "Now I just wait."

"It's so cool you have a career doing something you really love. I wish I had that."

Patti's brow furrowed. "I thought you liked working at Techno. You love computers. My memories of you in high school are you sitting on your bed with your computer on your lap every single afternoon and after dinner. That's how I'll always remember you."

"I was such a nerd. *Am* a nerd, I should say."

"Not in a dorky way, though. You were cute as a bug with your red hair and bright blue eyes. You had tons of friends, so, no, not a nerd like lots of people think. You were, are, just really smart. So what is it about your job you don't like?"

Kathy paused. "Remember that class I told you about that I took several years ago at the community college? Video game development and design?"

Patti nodded.

"I absolutely loved that class. I've been designing my own game during my coffee and lunch breaks at work and also here at home."

"That's so cool. What kind of game?"

Kathy held up a finger and ran upstairs, returning with her computer. "Let me show you." She pulled up a screen with a pastel blue background and paths leading in every direction with men and women of all ages running to and fro. "See these paths? Think of them as similar to the Yellow Brick Road in *Wizard of Oz*, okay?"

Patti nodded.

"But instead of Dorothy and the Scarecrow and the Lion, it's the person who's playing the game and anyone else the player selects to travel with them on whichever path the player chooses. They head down the path, and there are various obstacles they have to go through and exercises they have to perform at each level. But it gets harder and harder to navigate the barriers and things until they reach the end."

"You mean, like, they reach Heaven or Oz or whatever?"

Kathy nodded. "Exactly. Except for the fact that, along the way, the path may divert them to somewhere that's more like hell, but they won't know it until they get there, only to realize they're at a whole other level of playing, where they have to continue to maneuver their way through to get to where they really want to go." She paused. "I'm nowhere near finished, and that's about the easiest way I can explain the game. It's much more complex. More of an adult-type video game because of some of the violence involved and the blood and gore and stuff."

Patti patted her sister on the back. "I'm so proud of you. You're amazing."

Kathy smirked. "I'm not amazing. Do you know how many video games are out there? And the ones that are really popular have huge companies backing them with a slew of young developers sitting in high-rise buildings creating this stuff." She slumped back on the couch. "And I only have me, myself, and I. I don't know how I'm ever going to get this off the ground and into the hands of the public."

"I believe in following your dreams." Patti pointed to the computer. "And this is your dream. It's coming true right here, right now. You're working on it, and when it's done, you'll do your research, find out how you can market it. You can *do* this. I know you can."

"Thanks. Maybe I needed to hear that, because the more I get into this and the more time I spend on it, the more I realize I just may have a talent for this. One of the guys I work with? His name's Mark. All he does is play video games when he's not at Techno. I showed him my game, and he was captivated. He said he wasn't trying to kiss up to me either. He really meant it. So." She shrugged. "Maybe I've got something here."

"Congratulations on following your passion." Patti yawned. "Excuse me. I'm still getting used to the time change."

"Get outta here." Kathy shoved Patti's back. "It's Pacific Standard Time, no matter how far north or south you travel in California, you nutbar."

Patti grinned. "Nutbar? Where the hell do you find your expressions?"

Kathy raised an eyebrow. "Just because I'm not wittily snarky like you doesn't mean I can't get my point across."

Patti stood. "Well, tomorrow's another day in paradise."

"You going to look up Robert if you don't hear back from him?"

Patti stretched her hands above her head. "Yup." She yawned. "That's why I have to go to bed. Tomorrow could be a very stressful day."

Kathy nodded. "Don't overthink things. It's not like the two of you had a knockdown, drag-out fight when you broke up. It was amicable, right?"

Patti nodded.

"Then go have coffee with him or lunch or something and talk. He may be just the person who'll find you a really good job."

## Chapter Fifteen

When Patti woke up the next morning, she found a text from Robert on her cell phone.

*Wow! Welcome 2 the dark side. Would love 2 c u. La Jolla Photography and Media Group, 63344 Prospect Blvd. 10 a.m. today?*

"I thought he worked at the Institute," she mumbled. She texted she'd meet him at ten and jumped in the shower.

After applying her makeup with a light hand and dabbing on a bit of pink lipstick, she rushed to her closet to pick out an outfit. She slapped each dress hanger to the side. She had nothing appropriate for a casual meeting in eighty-degree weather. After perusing her entire closet, she discovered a sleeveless, pale pink dress, tags still hanging from the side, with a scoop neck and a light green, hand-painted vine climbing from the hem to the bodice. "Perfect," she whispered as she removed the tags and slid the smooth rayon fabric over her head. It fit her to a tee. She jammed her feet into a pair of Manolo Blahnik, off-white, five-inch heels and was out the door in a flash.

She took an Uber to La Jolla since Kathy'd said it was almost twenty minutes from San Diego, plus she didn't want to risk mussing up her dress on the bus, and arrived at 9:55. Upon exiting the car, she leaned back and gazed up at the thirty-story, all-glass black building, its windows sparkling in the sun. A man dressed in a red suit with black trim opened the front door for her with a morning greeting.

Her heels clicked across the marble floor as she headed to the reception desk and asked for the location of the café. She took the elevator to the top floor, exiting into a lavish restaurant with a 360-degree view of the beaches of La Jolla and the mountains to the east.

Her mouth must have dropped open as she took in the gorgeous views, because when she felt a hand at her back, she jumped.

"Isn't it beautiful?"

Robert.

She turned and stared into his deep brown eyes. Damn. He was as good-looking as ever, like someone out of a movie. Suave as DiCaprio but with dark brown hair, mustache, and a goatee like Robert Downey Jr.'s, he exuded sexuality just standing in front of her with a smile on his face. Straight teeth with a teensy gap between the two front ones added to his unique cachet.

"Yes, it's beautiful. How are you, Robert?"

He kissed her on the cheek and perused her from her heels to the tips of her blonde bangs hovering above her eyes. "You're as pretty as ever, Patti. How do you do it?"

"Livin' the dream," she said, then laughed.

He crooked his arm. "Shall we? Our table awaits us."

They were shown to a corner table, and both placed their starched white napkins in their laps before their eyes met across the slim expanse of the dining table.

"So how can I help you?" he asked.

Her eyes widened, and she took a sip of water. "You always were direct, Robert. Something I admire."

"We haven't spoken in years, so I assume this has nothing to do with our relationship, because we don't have one."

"As you wanted it. I honored your request, didn't I? Never called you. No cards, letters, texts, e-mails. Definitely no stalking."

He nodded. "Thank you for that."

"Kathy told me you work at the Institute. I guess she's behind the times."

He stared into her eyes. "I took this position only two months ago. I'm in charge of acquiring the photographic art for wealthy clients and their businesses, as well as for galleries and upscale stores in the San Diego and La Jolla areas. The commissions are quite handsome."

"I'm impressed. That must mean a lot of money. Does your wife work as well?"

"Why are you so sure I'm married?"

She shrugged. "Kathy told me you were engaged."

"I'm single."

She chuckled. "Oh, really? Not ready to be committed yet? I was sure you had some beauty queen hanging on your arm two seconds after you dumped me… or maybe before that."

He shook his head. "I was always faithful. I waited until we ended our relationship before dating again."

"How kind of you to wait those two seconds, then."

He turned toward the window, his expression serious. "My fiancée passed away."

She covered her lips with her fingers. "I'm so sorry. Sometimes my sarcasm comes back to bite me."

Their eyes met. "It's okay. She was killed by a drunk driver." He glanced down and moved his water glass several inches. "Along with our child."

"Robert, I am so incredibly sorry. That must have been devastating for you."

He looked her in the eyes. "More devastating for her. She dreamed of being a mom."

"Wow. You must be heartbroken."

"I was. What about you? Married?"

"No. I've dated a few guys since you moved away."

"I loved you, Patti."

"Then why did you sever all ties with me? We could have at least *tried* to have a long-distance relationship." She took a sip of water. "You broke my heart, Robert."

"I saw what being apart did to my parents. Their marriage was a total sham. My dad was gone six out of seven days a week, and when he was home, he and Mom fought like cats and dogs." He paused. "That's not the type of future I wanted for us."

"You never told me that about your parents. Is there a reason you didn't share that bit of family history during our last conversation?"

"You would have tried to talk me into continuing a long-distance relationship or offered to move down here with me."

"Would that have been so terrible? If I'd moved down here?"

He sighed. "See what I mean? That's what I'm talking about. We weren't at the place in our relationship to consider moving five hundred miles from home. We weren't engaged or anything close."

"I guess you didn't love me as much as I loved you, then."

"I *did* love you, but the timing was all wrong. I was very focused on finding my career path and wasn't ready for marriage yet. A fantastic job popped up that brought me here. It was the right thing to do, my moving here."

She sighed. "All in the past, Robert. Unfortunate, but nothing can be undone or rectified." She reached for the menu.

"Today is not the past, Patti. We only can live in the now. And you're here. Now."

She slid the menu onto the table. "You're right."

"Can we start again? Forget the past? See where it goes now?"

"Robert, as my dad always said, that ship sailed a long time ago."

"I still have feelings for you. I did when I left the Bay Area. That was never the point. Our relationship was in its beginning stage. It was too early for a deep commitment like living together."

Patti took in a deep cleansing breath, letting it out as she picked up the menu again. "Okay. All right. I understand what you're saying." She shrugged. "In my opinion, dating exclusively for three years is significant. Obviously, you disagree. Perhaps I was more committed than I let on." She sat up straighter, pulling her shoulders back. "Today, I'm here to talk to you about photographer positions in this area. My sister Kathy figured I might be able to pick your brain, make use of your connections. But I'll understand if you don't feel comfortable doing that."

"You don't have any residual feelings for me?"

She sighed. "I haven't been in love with anyone since you and I were together, but that's not to say I've been pining over the loss of you for the last two years, no."

"That's not what I asked. Do you still feel something for me?"

She slapped the menu down on the table and looked him in the eyes. "It's not something I've thought about. Can't you understand that? After you left, I was devastated. You no longer wanted me. It took months and months for me to rebuild my self-esteem."

"And now? Do you have your self-esteem back?"

"I think so, yes. I'm here, aren't I? I felt comfortable enough looking you up, wanting to pick your brain. I need a job, Robert. That's all I want from you. And if you don't want to help me, just say so. It's the only reason I'm sitting here."

"So you were never serious about any of the men you dated after we parted ways?"

She laughed out loud. "Oh, is that what you want to call your dumping my ass? Parting ways? By the way, you owed me better than that, Robert." She thumped her chest with her hand. "I deserved better."

"I just explained why I left."

Patti rolled her eyes. "Yeah, today you did. But back then all you said, *on the phone*, I might add, was you didn't want to have a long-distance relationship. Not much of an explanation, if you ask me."

A slight grin graced his perfectly shaped mouth. "Seems to me your self-esteem is alive and kicking up a storm." His expression turned serious. "You haven't answered my question. As we're sitting here, across this tiny table from each other, you feel nothing?"

"No, I don't have any residual feelings for you, okay? I've been very busy building my career in the Bay Area."

"Then why are you looking for a job here?"

She shrugged. "I got fired." She sighed again. "All right. I wouldn't sleep with my female boss, so she let me go."

He tilted his head. "Your *female* boss?"

"It's 2017. Yes, my female boss." She motioned with her hand as if swatting away a fly. "Whatever. That has nothing to do with now. I'm here. Living with Kathy. And I need a job. I just wondered if you could help me find a suitable employer. Someone who's interested in hiring a professional photographer. I'd like not to have to start at the bottom and work my way up."

He nodded and opened his menu. "Let me think about it, will you?"

She let out a sigh. "God!"

He glanced up. "What's wrong?"

"Why would you even talk about having feelings for me, Robert? Aren't you still mourning your fiancée and baby?"

"There's only one you, Patti. Connie was never you."

She squinted at him. "Were you looking to replace me with a clone or something? I'm sorry, Robert, but that's weird."

"That's not what I meant. I loved Connie, but we didn't get engaged until after I found out she was having my child. It was the right thing to do." He reached out and placed his hand over hers. "But the love I felt for her was just… different than what I felt for you."

She closed her eyes and took a deep breath, then opened them. "Thank you for sharing, but this is way too much for me to deal with right now." She slipped her hand out from under his. "Can we talk about the job market or something?"

He glanced at his Rolex watch. "It's past coffee-break time. Let's have lunch. The fettuccini here is delicious."

Relieved he was willing to change the subject, she tamped down the surprising emotions bubbling beneath the surface, engendered by Robert's unexpected announcement of his feelings for her, and resigned herself to enjoying a meal with a good friend. Plus, she needed a job.

# Chapter Sixteen

Kathy woke up that same morning and turned onto her side. Exhaustion screamed through her entire body, and she had a massive headache. She sat up and immediately felt something crawling up her throat, flew to the bathroom, and retched. No one enjoyed having the gastrointestinal flu, but she'd already taken a week off work to visit her mom and attend the funeral. This was the last thing she needed.

She notified her employer she was sick, then went back to bed, slept for three hours, and awoke starving. "Maybe it was something I ate," she mumbled as she entered the shower.

After eating a light breakfast of toast and tea, she felt completely normal and opened her computer to work on her video game. When Patti entered the apartment that afternoon, Kathy turned to her with a smile.

"How'd today go? Did you talk to Robert?"

Patti dumped her purse on the coffee table and sat on the couch. "Aren't you home early? It's barely three o'clock."

Kathy saved her work and closed her computer. "I was sick this morning. I threw up, called in sick to work, went back to bed, and slept for three hours, and now I'm fine."

"Sounds like food poisoning."

Kathy nodded. "Must have been. I ate breakfast and kept it down. Now I feel like eating a burger and fries."

"That would *not* be wise."

"Sure you don't wanna come with me to In-N-Out Burger?"

Patti laughed. "I really am not interested in watching you puke hamburger and greasy French fries when you get back home."

Suddenly, a hot flash burned through Kathy, from her toes to her forehead, and she broke out in a cold sweat.

"What's wrong? You look like you've seen Casper the ghost."

"I'll be right back." She ran upstairs to her bedroom, grabbed the calendar off the back of her bedroom door, and rushed down the stairs, plopping down on the couch. She turned the page back a month and slid her finger side to side, then turned the page back again. She chewed her bottom lip, shaking her head slowly.

"What's wrong with you? Did you forget your best friend's birthday?"

Kathy looked up at her sister and continued to shake her head, then leaned back on the cushions and closed her eyes.

"It can't be that bad, Kath. You can buy a nice gift, attach a card explaining your mom died and you've been out of town. I'm sure whoever it is will understand."

"This just can't be. No way could the universe let this happen," Kathy whispered.

Patti slowly moved over to her sister's side and gently took her hand in hers. "You're scaring me. Is something wrong?"

Kathy opened her eyes and leveled a gaze at her sister. "I think I'm pregnant."

Patti dropped Kathy's hand and opened her mouth, then closed it.

"You look like a fish gasping for air," Kathy said.

"I didn't know you were currently sexually active."

"I'm not. But what with Mom's being in hospice and her funeral, then the whole thing with Dad and Helen and the will, I forgot all about my period and dates and stuff." She pointed at the calendar. "Look. Look at the calendar, Patti. It's been almost two months since my last period."

Patti perused the last two months on the calendar, then stood, looking down at her sister. "Charlie."

Kathy closed her eyes again, tears streaming down her face. "What the hell am I going to do?"

Patti sat back down and brought her sister in for a hug. Kathy sobbed for several minutes before Patti let go and grabbed a tissue, stuffing it into her sister's palm.

"Let's not get ahead of ourselves. You have to do a pregnancy test before you start freaking out."

Kathy shook her head. "I know damn well I'm pregnant."

"Okay. Well..." Patti cleared her throat. "Do you believe in abortion?"

Kathy dabbed at her cheeks and blew her nose, grabbed another couple of tissues, and blew her nose again. She scooched back into the cushions and crossed her legs. "I believe in a woman's right to do what she wants with her own body, yes." She slapped her knees with her hands. "Dammit all to hell."

Patti nodded. "What're you gonna do if you *are* pregnant?"

"I don't owe that asshole a thing, Patti. He dumped me and ran. I've never heard from him. I sent him text after text until I was too embarrassed to send another. I was humiliating myself, so I stopped. He obviously doesn't want anything to do with me." Kathy leaned her face closer to her sister. "*You're* the one who told me to get on with my life. *You* said he told me without words that we were done. Don't you remember saying all that?"

Patti touched her sister's knee. "But if you're pregnant, it's not just *your* baby, Kathy. It's Charlie's son or daughter, too. Would you feel right not telling him?"

"If I chose to have an abortion, I wouldn't say anything to him, because it wouldn't make any difference. The baby would be gone, finito, over with. If I decided to keep the baby, then what? I suddenly owe Charlie an explanation? He doesn't want me in his life. And I don't want him in mine. Ipso facto, I'd be abiding by his wishes by not contacting him."

Patti nodded slowly. "Makes sense to me. I'm certainly glad to hear you've made up your mind about not wanting him in your life any longer. So if he were right here, right now, and if you were having his child, you're telling me you wouldn't own up to this baby? Or get married if he asked you and raise this child together? Tell me the truth, Kathy."

Kathy's head pounded, and she leaned over, holding her head in her hands. "When I got back from Mom's funeral, if he wasn't acting weird like he was before I left, then yes, I might be happy about having a baby with him. But remember I told you I felt there might be someone else in his life? That I was already losing him? I was right, wasn't I? I haven't heard from him, and I haven't seen him. He's cut me out of his life. He doesn't want me." She looked up at her sister. "So, if there's a baby, it's too late for him to be a part of my life. Or part of my baby's life either, if I'm pregnant."

The edges of Patti's lips lifted a small bit, and she sighed. "Personally, I'm glad to hear you say that. I don't believe he's changed since I knew him. He's proven that. To both of us." She was so glad Kathy had finally made her decision about Charlie. Now she wouldn't have to add more misery to her sister's situation by revealing what Charlie had said to her at Starbucks. It would only exacerbate Kathy's negative feelings about herself that he'd dumped her. Charlie wouldn't want to marry Kathy under normal circumstances, and if he decided to now, they'd probably end up divorced within a year anyway.

But that still didn't mean he wouldn't be interested in being a part of this child's life. *If Kathy's pregnant, is it fair to keep the baby a secret from its father?* That thought kept wiggling around in Patti's brain. She stood and paced back and forth. "Something's still bothering me. If you find out you're pregnant," she lifted a finger, "and if you decide to keep the baby, isn't it highly probable he'd find out?" She stopped and faced her sister. "What would you do then?"

Kathy let out a huge breath and closed her eyes, then opened them and looked Patti straight in the eyes. "Fact. If Charlie discovers I'm pregnant, enough time has passed that I can easily deny he's the father. Fact. Charlie does not want to be a part of my life. Fact. Therefore, I don't want him to be a part of my life either. Ergo, I don't want him to have anything to do with this hypothetical baby. I don't want to be around him." She stood and faced her sister, blinking back tears. "I would not want to spend the rest of my life with Charlie around, just so he could play Daddy." She paused. "I. Don't. Want. Him. Near. Me. Pregnant or not."

Kathy ran up the stairs, leaving Patti alone with her thoughts. Her sister had been very hurt by Charlie's cruel behavior toward her. Patti didn't blame Kathy for being angry. She recalled how angry *she* had been when she'd found out Charlie'd been cheating on her way back when. She'd wanted nothing more to do with him.

Then again, Patti hadn't been pregnant with Charlie's child. Didn't Charlie have a right to know if he was going to be a father? Give him the opportunity to step up to the plate? Give him the chance to do the right thing?

Hopefully, Kathy wasn't pregnant. But if she was, and maybe when she calmed down, she and Kathy could talk about this again. Then again, maybe not. It wasn't Patti's place to try to convince her sister to change her mind. Kathy was an adult with her own beliefs. *I have to accept that.*

# Chapter Seventeen

The next morning, Patti woke up and jogged to the nearest drugstore to buy a home pregnancy kit. When she returned, she walked up the stairs and heard Kathy groaning. She knocked on her sister's bedroom door, then popped her head in. "You all right in here?"

Kathy turned on her side, saw Patti, then jumped up and ran into the bathroom.

After the toilet flushed, Patti knocked on the door and opened it. While Kathy washed her hands, Patti placed the pregnancy kit on the sink.

Kathy screwed up her lips, then nodded. "I'm going to see a big fat pink X on that thing, aren't I?"

Patti shrugged. "Just thought you should rule out the stomach flu."

"You're right."

Patti closed the door and sat on Kathy's bed. Five minutes passed before the bathroom door opened.

Tears dripped off Kathy's chin, and Patti jumped off the bed and hugged her.

Patti resolved right then to do something for Kathy, anything to help her out. Lots of women went through pregnancy without a partner, and Patti would be there for her sister.

"Can I get you anything?" Patti said.

Kathy swiped at the tears. "I'll be fine. Maybe I should stock up on saltine crackers. Put them on the table at the side of my bed until I get through this phase."

"You don't have to do this alone, Kath."

"I have no choice, I *am* alone. I don't have a partner. Get that through your thick skull, Patti." Kathy sat on the side of the bed, head in her hands.

"I meant you don't have to do this alone because I'm here for you, Kath. I wasn't talking about Charlie."

Kathy turned her head to the side and looked at her sister. "I'm sorry. I thought you were referring to me telling him about this child. But still, I shouldn't have jumped down your throat." She tried to smile while she rocked back and forth, hugging her stomach. "Thanks for offering your help, Patti. Maybe I'm already what they call 'hormonal.' I'm freaking out. Having a kid is a big responsibility. *My* responsibility. And *my* decision to do it alone. And you're just trying to help me out, and I love you for that. Forgive me?"

Patti sat next to her sister and rubbed her back. "Stop apologizing. I love you. And I want what's best for you and the baby. I understand why you want Charlie out of your life, and I'm sorry if I seemed pushy about letting him have a chance to be a father. Just because I think you should consider that option doesn't make you wrong and me right. I'm the one who should be apologizing. And I'm sorry."

Kathy sat up straight and placed her hand on her sister's forearm. "Now that we know it's Charlie's child, the bastard, do you *still* think I should tell him?"

Patti let out a deep breath. "Children need two parents. That doesn't mean you and Charlie should get back together. Some real assholes turn out to be great fathers. Charlie's not totally bad. It's not like he's a child molester. I think he's a commitmentphobe. Hence, him dumping you and never showing his face around here again. The same goes for him screwing around on me behind my back. He can't seem to commit to one woman."

Kathy shut her eyes for a few seconds. "You've got a point."

"About which part?"

"Maybe he wouldn't be a bad father. Maybe I should give him a chance to prove himself."

"Just think about it, Kath. No one says you have to make a decision today."

Kathy nodded. "I don't want to be hasty. It's an important decision. And it should be a decision that's not driven by my emotions right now. But I can't get past the fact I hate his guts."

"How'd this happen anyway? Your getting pregnant, I mean."

Kathy chuckled. "Well, first you stick the—"

Patti swatted her sister's leg. "You know damn well what I'm talking about, silly. Didn't you use protection?"

"Of course we did. I have an IUD."

"Which isn't one hundred percent effective, I'm guessing."

Kathy held up her index finger. "Au contraire. The IUD can prevent unwanted pregnancy up to twenty times better than birth control pills, patches, and vaginal rings."

"Then what happened?"

"I have no idea. They can get displaced, but I checked mine once a month as my gynecologist suggested, and it was always there, in the right place." She shrugged. "Shit happens."

Patti put her arm around Kathy's shoulders. "I'm here for you, Kath. I'm not going anywhere. I'll do whatever you need me to do before, during, and after you have the baby. We'll work something out. We'll do this together."

Tears edged down Kathy's cheeks, and she smiled. "Thanks, Sis."

Patti walked to the doorway and turned. "I'm going to check my computer. See if Robert sent me an e-mail. He told me to give him some time to think about our meeting the other day."

Kathy took in a deep breath, then said, "I have to get to work, too. This morning-sickness stuff could last for months, and I have a job."

"I've never been pregnant, so I'm not much help in that department. The crackers sound like a good solution. Try that for a while. Maybe it'll work." She headed to her room and scanned her e-mails. She'd gotten several from Sharon since their reunion at the ranch. They were upbeat. Dad was doing fine. The horses were being sold at a fast pace. Helen was acting weird, according to Sharon. *Go figure.*

Patti always answered her sister's e-mails, keeping her up to date on her and Kathy's lives. Of course, she had no intention of revealing Kathy was pregnant. Now that she thought about it, Sharon might have some interesting thoughts on whether to tell Charlie about his child. Then again, Patti had no idea when or if Kathy would say anything to the family about this impending new addition to the Michaels clan. It wasn't Patti's place to do anything about Kathy's situation right now.

After showering and getting ready for the day, Patti dressed in shorts and a sleeveless blouse, slipped into sandals, and headed downstairs.

"Feeling better?" she said to her sister, who was sitting at the counter eating toast with butter and jam.

Kathy nodded. "The morning sickness doesn't seem to last that long, a few minutes or so, which is a blessing. I feel pretty normal now. I'll pick up a box of saltines on the way home. See you after work?"

Patti nodded. "I think I'll do some computer searches. See if I can find anything of interest on my own until I hear from Robert. I shouldn't count on him finding me a job. That would be way too simple. I should try to find employment on my own, too."

Kathy left for work, while Patti ate her breakfast. She exited the condo fifteen minutes later, headed for the beach area in La Jolla and a mall she'd never been to before. She'd get a coffee and a newspaper and look for a job. La Jolla was very, very upscale, and a job in that city would pay more than a job in San Diego. Conducting business by the water would make her feel better, too. She was so angry about Kathy's situation with that bastard Charlie, she needed to chill out.

She exited the shuttle in La Jolla and walked two blocks toward the beach area. She paused, looking right and left for a nearby Starbucks or Peet's.

And then she saw it. The big blue and white sign for Seevers' Yachts.

She walked along the boardwalk toward the impressive two-story building. If Kathy refused to confront him, Patti would. When she opened the front door, balloons and streamers hovered everywhere, decorating the interior with a lively kaleidoscope of colors. The inside of the building resembled a high-end warehouse, with boats of various sizes on display above sparkling linoleum floors. A gigantic sign pointing toward the back read, "Yachts."

A gorgeous blonde in a formfitting red dress and heels sauntered up to Patti with a wide smile. "May I help you?"

Patti felt like a country bumpkin next to this buxom blonde. She squared her shoulders and swiped her own blonde bangs from her eyes and smiled back. "I'm looking for Charlie. Is he here?"

The woman looked her up and down and screwed up her lips while doing so. "Is this business or personal, Miss… ?"

Patti stared her down and widened her smile. "Personal. Patti Michaels. I'm a friend of his from high school."

The woman turned and swayed her backside all the way to the front desk, picked up a phone, said a few words, then pointed toward the back. "Follow the yacht sign to the docks."

"Thank you." Patti walked through the back door, exiting into the bright sunshine onto a gigantic redwood deck. Men and women roamed casually among tables covered with silver trays and tureens of steaming food. A fountain graced the middle table with chocolate flowing over three tiers, a bowl of strawberries to the side.

She felt someone grasp her hand and turned. Charlie. "Patti, what are you doing here?" He pulled her in for a kiss on the cheek.

She grimaced. "So what's going on here?"

"It's my company's fifth anniversary. And that's a big celebration in this business." He tugged on her hand. "Let me give you a tour of one of my yachts."

"Okay." She nodded, pulling at her hand. But he wouldn't let go. "I'd like to talk to you for a minute alone, if that's possible."

He stared in her eyes and grinned. "I can make that happen. Come with me."

He held her hand tightly, pulling her along behind him, greeting people along the way, smiling, and waving at men and women dressed in very classy boating attire.

"Where are we going?" she asked.

He glanced back at her. "To the biggest, most beautiful yacht in the La Jolla marina."

"Oh-kay," she said, drawing out the word slowly as she tried to keep up with his fast pace.

He took a short set of wooden stairs in one leap, then turned to face her, his hand extended. "It's at the end of this dock. Let me help you."

She refused to give him her hand and walked up the stairs on her own.

In another fifty feet, he stopped and gestured at the biggest boat—yacht, rather—she'd ever seen.

She leaned back and looked up. "That's very large."

He grinned. "Follow me. I want to show you the inside. You won't believe how gorgeous it is."

"I know zilch about boats, Charlie."

"Yachts, Patti. There's a difference. And you don't have to know much in order to appreciate their beauty, darlin'."

She shook her head at the cutesy name he used to call her in high school. She did not consider this a social visit. Granted, it had been an impulsive move on her part—dropping by his workplace—but now she was on a mission. She'd told Charlie at Starbucks that he needed to talk to Kathy, and he hadn't. Kathy didn't deserve to be treated like a piece of dirt on the bottom of Charlie's Top-Siders. Kathy was just too sweet for her own good sometimes. Patti had no qualms about telling it like it was when it came to Charlie Seevers.

Once burned, very pissed off. Twice burned, angry as a hornet. That's just the way Patti rolled, as they said. She had a temper that, at times, did her more harm than good, and this was one of the times she was on fire.

She followed him up a short stairway to the main deck, then up to the fly bridge.

He stopped and pointed to the west. "Gorgeous view, right?"

"A perfect day for boating or yachting, or whatever the term is," she said.

He rested his hand on her shoulder. "Let me show you the front room."

She wiggled her shoulder, trying to shake his hand off. "A front room?"

"I told you, this is one of *the* biggest yachts around. Come on!"

They walked down a short flight of stairs to a large, mahogany-paneled room with a grand piano at one end and a curved bar at the other. A buttery-yellow couch in a half circle graced the center of the room, with a glass coffee table cut in a multi-edged design and etched carvings of swans and whales along the edges.

"This is, uh…" she began.

"I know, right?" He walked to the bar and stood behind it. He held up a sparkling crystal glass. "Drink?"

"It's a bit early for me."

He chuckled. "Seevers' Yachts is celebrating today. Do you know how many businesses like this go bankrupt within the first year?"

"Haven't a clue."

"All of 'em. But not mine. That's something I'm proud of."

She nodded. "Congratulations," she said in a monotone.

"Thank you. Now have a small flute of champagne with me."

"Okay, but make it very small. I've never been much of a drinker."

"I remember. In fact, there's not much I've forgotten about you."

She could feel a rush of revulsion gliding up her throat. *Man, does he have it coming.* "As I said, I wanted to talk to you about something."

"I'm surprised to see you after how mean you were to me at Starbucks." He sauntered toward the couch and sat down, legs spread wide, leaning back into the cushions. "I like that in a woman, though. A bit of spunk and fire. A real turn-on." With a flute of champagne in one hand, he gestured toward her with the flute in his other hand. "Join me in a toast?" He smiled. "To us."

She sat on the edge of the couch about three feet from him and grasped the top of the flute. He stared into her eyes before letting her take it from him.

Lowering her eyes, she took a small sip.

"Louis Roederer Cristal Brut, 2007," he said.

She cleared her throat. "You obviously have no clue why I'm here."

He smirked, never shifting his gaze from her face. "Us?"

She rolled her eyes. "No, Charlie. There is and will never be an 'us.' I'm here to talk to you about Kathy."

"Can we at least finish our champagne before we have to talk about your sister?"

"You dated my sister for more than a year, and she thought you were in love with her. You led her on, Charlie. And by the way you acted with me the other day, you were probably playing around behind her back."

He raised his glass and clinked it against hers. "To our renewed friendship."

She pulled back her hand and shook her head. "I'm not your friend."

He tipped his head back and drained his flute.

She wanted to get this over with, say what she came to say, so she drained her own glass in one long sip.

"I'm not in love with Kathy. Never was."

"So she was just someone you dated for almost an entire year and had sex with for the hell of it? You know damn well she's not that kind of woman. She's committed. She's serious about the men she goes out with, and there haven't been many others."

"That doesn't mean I'm the same way. She and I enjoyed each other's company. The sex was all right. We had fun doing the same things. Go ahead and ask her. It's all true."

Her lips and face tingled, then her vision blurred. She shut her eyes for several seconds and felt the glass fall through her fingers.

# Chapter Eighteen

Patti felt lips on her forehead. A soft kiss. Just one. Then a nudge to her knee. She opened her eyes. The light was so bright, she blinked several times.

"Hi, darlin'."

She glanced around, her eyesight blurry.

Charlie lay next to her, elbow cocked, his hand supporting his head, staring at her. The edge of the sheet lay just below his belly button. He pulled it aside, revealing his massive erection. "Ready for more after your little nap?"

It was as if she were awakening from a dream, her brain ever so slowly taking in her surroundings. She was lying on her back in bed. Outside the window, the sun's rays waned. It appeared to be almost sunset. She grasped the sheet, pulling it up to her chin. She could feel her nakedness, but remembered nothing after finishing the flute of champagne.

She cleared her throat, which was dry and scratchy. "What am I doing here? What are you doing here?" She sat up, pulling the sheet with her to cover her breasts. "What did you do?"

He grinned like a Cheshire cat. "As a matter of fact, this wasn't my idea. You were all over me. I saw no reason not to oblige you."

She shook her head and immediately wished she hadn't. Pain radiated from the base of her skull to the crown of her head. "You drugged me."

He frowned. "I most certainly did not. After your second glass of champagne, you jumped my bones." He chuckled. "You took me by surprise, Patti. In high school, you were shy and reserved, which turned me on, big-time. But today? You were like a tiger in heat, man. You were really into it, darlin'."

"You raped me," she whispered, seething inside with rage at his disgusting behavior.

"If anyone was raped, it was me, darlin'."

"I'm not on any birth control."

"Don't worry. You slid on the condom like a pro." He reached under the covers and stroked her thigh.

She kicked at him, then threw her legs over the side of the bed, dragging the sheet with her. "Where're my clothes?"

He pointed to a chair on the far side of the bedroom. Her shorts and blouse hung over the back of the chair, and her bra and panties lay on a glass table next to the chair. A tall, ornately etched glass vase stood on the table with a solitary rose in full bloom.

"You won't get away with this, Charlie." Her stomach roiled as if a snake were unfurling inside.

"Get away with what? We had consensual sex. You enjoyed it. We both had a good time. You took me by surprise, though, darlin'. But I wasn't about to turn down a nooner, if you know what I mean."

She stared him down for several seconds, fury seething in her gut. "The only good thing about this is, if I wasn't one hundred percent sure before, now I know for a fact Kathy's better off without you, you son of a bitch."

He crawled over to the side of the bed she'd vacated and stood, his engorged penis pressed flat against his belly, ejaculate dripping from its tip. "Why don't you join me again? Kind of like an aperitif," he said, grasping his elongated organ, rubbing slowly up and down.

"Oh, Jesus," she whispered, grabbing her clothes and covering her chest. She paused, grasped the vase with her free hand, then flung it across the room, aiming at his face. He ducked his head, and the vase whizzed past him, hitting the wall and smashing into pieces.

"You bitch," he said. "That vase was worth thousands of dollars."

She turned to her left, saw the bathroom, then rushed in, locked the door, and hastily dressed. When she exited, he was no longer there. She hoped he wouldn't force himself on her again, now that she was lucid and awake.

She ran out of the bedroom into the front room and thankfully remembered where the stairs were located. Exiting the yacht as fast as she could, she jumped down the stairs to the dock and ran across the deck through the warehouse to the front exit. The store appeared to be deserted. No Charlie, no receptionist. Empty.

Her legs felt heavy, and her head throbbed, but she continued to run, finally reaching the beach. She bent over and vomited in the sand.

The beach was deserted as well, not a soul in sight, and for that she was grateful. She glanced down and groaned: Her shoes were covered in yellow bile, her legs had been scraped from the prickly bushes edging the beach, and the buttons on her blouse were in the wrong holes. Luckily, she'd had the sense to grab her purse. Her cell phone chimed, notifying her of an incoming call.

Kathy.

She pressed "Remind Me Later" and plopped down on the cool sand. *I need to think. What am I going to do now? Should I report him to the police?*

If she went to the Emergency Room, they could test her blood for drugs, but she wouldn't be able to prove that he gave her the drugs. People took Ecstasy and other drugs these days like candy, especially if they wanted to have heightened sexual experiences. Performing a rape test would be a waste of time. Naturally, the sperm was Charlie's. *He said, she said.*

If the police interviewed the receptionist, she'd tell them Patti came looking for Charlie. If they talked to any of the guests at the yacht party, they'd say they saw her holding his hand, rushing down the docks toward the yacht. Probably to enjoy a "nooner." They would have looked like two consenting adults who'd known each other for years.

But she could go on record by reporting to the police that Charlie had raped her, so if he did the same thing to another unsuspecting woman, there would at least be *something* on file.

*What should I do?*

*Oh. My. God. What if Charlie lied about using a condom and I get pregnant?* She was pretty sure she could take the morning-after pill. She surely wouldn't want to have that man's child. But if one of her eggs was fertilized by Charlie's sperm, wasn't taking the morning-after pill just another form of abortion? And she didn't believe in abortion. At least not for herself, that was.

She reasoned there was no particular timeline when an embryo actually became a "human." In Patti's mind, a child was a human being once the egg was fertilized by the sperm. *Well, they can't force me to take the morning-after pill. And if I'm pregnant, then I'll deal with it.* God's will be done and all that, Mom used to say.

Taking deep breaths, one after the other, she tried to think straight. Her brain felt fuzzy, her thoughts erratic, going from one point to another. She needed to focus. Right here, right now. *What should I do? Who should I call?* She couldn't take the shuttle looking like this. *Should I tell Kathy what happened?*

She walked to the water's edge. She could at least clean the vomit off her feet and button up her blouse correctly, splash some cool water on her face. Within moments, she was more awake, but her insides hurt. God knew what Charlie had done to her while she was knocked out.

She could tell there had been no anal sex, for which she was enormously grateful, but her vagina felt as if she'd been scraped with a serrated knife. She'd never experienced what women termed "rough sex" and silently thanked God she hadn't been awake during the ordeal. She pitied rape victims. Being aware of what had just happened to her while she was *not* lucid was terrifying enough.

*Okay, it's time to decide, Patti. Go home or go to the ER? Which is it gonna be?*

She took an Uber and arrived at Scripps Memorial Hospital in La Jolla within minutes. She pushed herself out of the backseat and slogged her way toward the ER doors. She felt as if she were walking through mud, as if the sliding glass doors were a million miles away, and she'd never get there. Maybe the drug Charlie'd slipped into her drink had strange side effects. She guessed it would depend on which one he'd given her.

It seemed to take thirty minutes for Patti to walk to the registration counter. Her sense of time was totally off. Maybe it was just stress, but she knew she was fooling herself. It was due to whatever drug was in her system, which she found frightening.

A woman wearing green scrubs sat behind a computer, typing away, and when Patti reached the desk and opened her mouth to speak, she suddenly didn't know what to say. *What am I here for? Oh, right. Whoa!* Another side effect of the drug, she was sure of it.

"May I help you?" the woman, whose name tag read "Kristen" or "Kirsten" said.

Patti's vision was still a bit blurry, and it didn't matter what her name was anyway. Patti stared at the woman for several seconds, trying to think of how to explain what had happened.

"May I help you?" the woman said again.

Patti nodded and tried her best to focus on the woman's name tag, which had slowly come into focus. "Yes, Kristen, I hope you can." She paused. "I need—"

That was the last thing Patti remembered before waking up on a gurney, pale green curtains surrounding her on all sides. Within minutes, a young woman spread the curtain open, stepped toward Patti, and stood next to her.

"Hello. I'm Dr. Marsdale. How are you feeling?" She glanced at the chart. "Miss Michaels?"

Patti's mouth felt so dry, she swallowed several times before answering. "Yes. Patti Michaels. And I'm not feeling a hundred percent, Doctor."

Dr. Marsdale had a friendly smile and gently grasped Patti's wrist to take her pulse. "You weren't able to fill out the paperwork, so I'm not sure what you're here for, Ms. Michaels. You've been out for almost three hours. We did an EKG, which was normal, and we're running an IV drip because you looked a bit dehydrated. We noticed vomit on your shoes. We drew blood, which we sent to the lab. Initially, your blood work appears fine. Your vitals are stable. Can you tell me what happened?"

"I was talking to my sister's ex-boyfriend, and he'd just given me a flute of champagne. After I drank it, I blacked out. When I came to, I was in bed with him, and he'd raped me. I'm afraid he might have given me an STD, or I might have gotten pregnant."

Dr. Marsdale nodded. "I'll call Dr. Osborn, and she'll perform a Sexual Assault Kit test on you, with your permission, of course. We'll also call the police, so you can file a report. Again, with your permission."

"Yes. I'd like both. Will you be able to tell if I've been drugged?"

The doctor looked her in the eyes. "If it's within a certain number of hours, we usually can. What time did this happen to you?"

Patti closed her eyes and mentally went back over the day. "I would say sometime around noon, maybe. But when I woke up, the sun was already going down, so it was probably already seven or eight o'clock."

"You arrived here at nine thirty. It's now midnight. Most of the date-rape drugs stay in your system for at least twelve hours, so we're cutting it close, depending on exactly what drug he gave you." She paused. "To be honest, recently we've seen a few, not many, but a few women in the ER who have been slipped a new drug that just appeared on the market. It didn't show up in their blood within two or three hours of ingesting it. We're not even sure what the drug is called on the street. The police are looking into it, but as of now, they don't know much about it." She shook her head. "It's not showing up in their urine tests either."

Patti smirked. "Just my luck, right?"

She placed her hand on Patti's forearm. "Let's not jump to any conclusions until we know the facts. You said you're not feeling a hundred percent? Can you explain what you mean?"

"I had a bad headache, and I was really dizzy before I blacked out. My vision was blurry, too. My stomach just doesn't feel right, and I still have a bit of a headache. Otherwise, I don't feel too bad. I'd like to call my sister. It's late, and she'll be worried about me."

"I'll tell the nurse." She looked through the papers in the chart. "Will your sister be able to give you a ride home?"

"I can take an Uber."

"Okay. We'll notify the police. It might take them a while to get here, but they're usually extremely prompt, especially in this type of situation. First, Dr. Catherine Osborn, who is a sexual assault forensic examiner, will perform the exam for the Sexual Assault Kit. She'll be in as soon as I give her your chart. She'll ask you a lot of questions, and of course, the police will ask you a lot of the same questions. When you're finished, I'll sign the discharge papers, and you can go home. Does that sound good?"

Suddenly, Patti was overcome with emotion, and the tears began to flow. She never thought she'd be in the Emergency Room, getting ready to have an exam for being drugged and raped, even though it wasn't a date she'd actually been on. How disgusting! And what would she tell Kathy when she phoned? She didn't want to tell her the truth—that she'd gone behind Kathy's back and talked to Charlie. *Now look what happened. Serves me right for meddling where I don't belong.*

The doctor set her hand on Patti's forearm. "I'm sorry this happened to you, Ms. Michaels. We'll do our best to keep you comfortable while you're here. Dr. Osborn is a great physician. I think you'll like her. Why don't I get her? She'll be in as soon as I talk to her for a few moments."

Patti swiped at her tears. "Do you think I'll be here much longer?"

"It's hard to tell, Ms. Michaels. Your examination with Dr. Osborn could take an hour or more. Your interview with the police could take an equal amount of time."

Patti sat up slowly. "I don't feel dizzy anymore. And my headache's gone. I'm starving. Can I call my sister now? My cell phone's in my purse." She looked from side to side. "I don't know where it is."

"We have it. I'll tell the nurse to bring in the bag of your belongings. But depending on what you and Dr. Osborn talk about, we might need to send some of your clothing to the forensic lab. In that event, we'll give you something to wear home, so don't worry. Dr. Osborn will explain everything to you."

"Thank you."

The doctor smiled and left the room.

Patti let out a sigh and stared at the swirling design on the curtains. *What am I going to tell Kathy? I have about five minutes to make up a story.*

A nurse brought Patti a plastic bag with a drawstring and reiterated that Dr. Osborn would be in shortly.

Patti grabbed her cell phone out of the bag and held it tightly in her hand, closed her eyes, and focused on a plausible story. She dialed Kathy's cell phone, which her sister answered immediately.

"Patti, where the hell are you? I've been so worried, I—"

"I'm sorry," Patti interrupted. "I was feeling really stressed out, so I went to the beach, thinking I'd take a nap. I rented one of those beach chairs. The weather was so beautiful today. Anyway, when I woke up, it was later than I thought, so I went to the mall to get dinner. I met a classmate from the Institute in San Francisco. We got to talking and—"

"It's one in the morning."

"I know. I know. I lost track of time."

"Are you on the way home?"

"Actually, no. We're going to go out for a drink. We haven't seen each other in such a long time. It's so good to see her because we were close friends, but we lost touch. Anyway, I was feeling pretty down, what with Mom's passing away and all the stress from being at the ranch again, the crap with Helen, worrying about finding a job, freaked out about seeing Robert again. It's been really good seeing her, too."

"That's cool. I'm sorry if I came off as your mother or something. You're old enough to take care of yourself, and you don't have to report to me. I was just worried since you've never stayed out this late."

"I don't blame you. It was rude and insensitive that I didn't call you to at least tell you I'd be late coming home. So, please, go back to sleep. I'll see you tomorrow. I'll probably sleep in late. So you can stop worrying, Mom." She laughed.

"You'll take an Uber home?"

"Yeah. I'll be fine. I'm sorry to have woken you up, Kath. I love you. And thanks for caring."

"I love you, too. See you tomorrow."

Within moments, a beautiful woman who looked to be in her fifties entered the room and smiled at Patti. She instantly made Patti feel comfortable with her kind, quiet voice and gentle, understanding nature. She documented Patti's account of what happened and explained every step of the process. She collected DNA evidence, including semen, saliva, more blood and urine, fingernail scrapings, a hair sample, as well as Patti's clothes.

She asked if Patti wanted to take the morning-after pill, but when Patti declined, explaining she'd read about it and how it worked, Dr. Osborn said she didn't need to know why she didn't wish to take it. She just wanted to make sure Patti was aware it was available and how it worked. It was Patti's prerogative to accept it or decline. She then suggested Patti make an appointment with her gynecologist with regard to pregnancy testing if she was interested. Within an hour, Dr. Osborn left, and a female police officer entered the room shortly thereafter.

Sergeant Ann Kramer also treated Patti with respect and kindness. Patti explained what happened on the yacht, including the background between her and Charlie. Sergeant Kramer told Patti what would happen with the evidence that was collected by Dr.

Osborn. She explained the Combined DNA Index System, or CODIS—the national, state, and local databases managed by the FBI that allowed crime laboratory personnel across the country to compare DNA profiles from known criminal offenders with biological evidence from crime scenes.

"Usually, the results take between three and six months to process, though in some jurisdictions, it can take more than a year," Sergeant Kramer said.

"Wow," Patti said, "I had no idea I'd have to wait that long."

"Are you planning to take him to court?"

Patti shrugged. "It depends on what they find. If there's no proof I was drugged, then it would seem to be a 'he said, she said' case. His word against mine, you know?"

The sergeant nodded. "Unfortunately, I *do* know. Many times, there's just not enough proof for the District Attorney to charge the guy. And sometimes it boils down to who has the most money to spend on an attorney."

Patti pursed her lips, then said, "He definitely has more money than I do."

"With regard to the Sexual Assault Kit results..." The sergeant paused. "So let's just say, in La Jolla, due to certain higher-ups knowing other people of importance who are involved in the process... what would probably take months will most likely, and don't quote me here—"

Patti shook her head. "Don't worry about that."

"—you'll most likely have the results within a month. As they say around La Jolla, that's just how we roll." She smiled.

Patti returned the smile. "Thank you. Thank you so much, Sergeant Kramer."

The sergeant gave Patti her card, and within an hour, Patti was finished and walked out the door to wait for the Uber driver to take her home.

Patti was grateful that Kathy was asleep when she got home. She didn't want to have to make up another lie to explain why she was dressed in green scrubs the hospital had given her. Patti dumped her purse on the kitchen table so Kathy would know she'd arrived home safely, then she tiptoed up the stairs to her bedroom and quietly shut the door.

She stood in front of the bathroom mirror. Her mascara, smudged under her eyes from crying, made her look like a raccoon. Now that she was alone and safe inside the house, the thought of Charlie raping her punched her right in the gut. The picture of him on top of her while she lay in a drugged stupor underneath him was all too vivid. She gagged, then covered her mouth. "Stop it," she whispered.

After undressing, she rolled the scrubs into a ball and stuffed them in the garbage can next to the sink. Tears flowed down her cheeks. *How could he do that to me?* She'd known Charlie since high school. He'd dated her sister for a year. Yes, she'd known he was still interested in her, but she would never have thought he would stoop so low.

Out of the blue, another memory washed over her. *Kathy is carrying his child.* What kind of father would he be for the baby? If Kathy told Charlie he was the baby's daddy, the baby would have a father who had raped its auntie. *Oh, my God.* Her stomach spasmed, and she bent over the sink and retched. She brushed her teeth until they hurt, then stepped into the shower.

The hot spray eased the tension, but did nothing to quell the mental video running through her mind. Her last memory of Charlie handing her the flute of champagne, smiling, all along knowing damn well what he had in mind. Emotionally exhausted and physically stressed to the limit, she pulled on a pair of fleece shorts and a tank top and got into bed.

# Chapter Nineteen

The following day, Patti slept in, then grabbed her cell phone and called Kathy at work. "Just wanted to say hi since I got home so late."

"It must have been late, because I didn't hear anything. Guess I was exhausted, too. It's been quite a month, huh?"

"I know. I've never fallen asleep at the beach like that before. It felt good, though. My friend and I went to one of her favorite bars in La Jolla, and we talked forever."

"I'm glad you had a good time. How'd the job search go?"

"I looked through the paper, but I didn't find anything. I didn't get that far before I was too tired to continue. The beach was calling to me, so I decided to take the day off."

Kathy laughed. "I wish you'd asked me to go with you. I had the day from hell yesterday. Mark didn't show up, and I had to pick up the slack. Every time I looked out the window, I wished we didn't have such gorgeous views. Sometimes, I feel like screaming and running out the door."

"Next time I have the urge, I'll call, and you can play hooky."

"You're on, Sis. So nothing from Robert?"

"I haven't checked yet." She grabbed her computer—a much better bed partner than her previous one. "Stop it!" she said under her breath, berating herself for the negative thought process.

"Stop what?" Kathy said.

"Oh, sorry. My computer's running kind of slow." She opened her MacBook and scrolled through her e-mails. "Yes!"

"He sent you an e-mail?"

"Yes," Patti said. "It says, 'Thanks for having lunch with me. You probably thought I forgot about you. Been busy. Can we meet? Got something I think you'll like.'"

"That's great, Patti. If he wants to talk with you, it's probably about a job."

"I hope so," Patti said.

"Hey, you sound funny. Are you all right? You sound a little under the weather."

"I just need more sleep. That's what I get for staying out so late. Hey, I better get going. See you tonight, okay?" Patti hung up the phone and stared at the wall.

It was over and done with. She was alive. Hopefully, she hadn't gotten an STD. And she'd better not be pregnant. Best of all, she'd found out who the real Charlie Seevers was. Thank God, Kathy had decided not to have anything to do with him.

A cloud with an honest-to-God silver lining.


Robert had secured dinner reservations at the Catania Restaurant in La Jolla for several days from now, on Saturday evening. He'd sent Patti an e-mail that his schedule was so booked he couldn't take time for lunch or dinner during the week.

He explained his job entailed a great deal of public relations with clients, constantly schmoozing over meals. Patti wondered if that was the real reason he selected one of the most expensive restaurants in the area for discussing a potential job opportunity for her.

On Friday evening, Kathy stood next to her sister while Patti perused the clothes on the hangers in her closet. "What're you going to wear? The Catania's a very upscale place."

Patti slid her fingers over the tops of the hangers as if playing the piano. "I haven't a clue. All my really nice dresses are for winter. I don't have anything appropriate for dining in warm weather. I mean, it's almost the end of May, and it's already warm."

"It's usually in the seventies, but this week's been hotter than usual."

Patti turned to her sister. "Unfortunately, the truth is written all over these hangers. No matter how many times I go through this closet, the perfect outfit is not going to miraculously appear before my eyes. I should have looked through my clothes earlier."

Kathy threw herself on the bed and watched Patti's facial expressions. "Shopping spree," she shouted. "The mall's open until nine. Meet you in the garage," she yelled as she ran into her bedroom to change clothes.

They drove the short distance to the Westfield Horton Plaza, and once there, headed to Macy's, where Patti could buy both a dress and shoes. It took only an hour for her to find the perfect outfit.

Patti walked out of the dressing room and stood in front of Kathy, who was thumbing through a magazine. Patti turned left then right, sliding her hands down the sides of the black, formfitting sheath. "So?"

"You look mah-velous," Kathy said. "You'll take it."

Patti glanced at Kathy in the mirror. "I'm making too much of this. It is not a date."

"After you told me what he said at lunch, I have a feeling you're the only one thinking of this as a business meeting."

"Actually, he was irritating. He kept asking me the same question over and over."

"Well, what's the answer?"

She whipped her head around and locked eyes with her sister. "What's the answer to what?"

Kathy let out a loud breath. "Do… you… still… have… feelings… for… him?"

Patti threw her hands up in the air. "Oh, my God. You, too?" She stomped into the dressing room and slammed the door.

"No need to get angry." Kathy chuckled. "It's actually a very simple question, Sis. Right now, today, how do you feel about Robert Blakely?"

No sound emanated from the dressing room, and Kathy waited. And waited. Several minutes passed before Patti exited with the little black dress draped over her arm.

"You are so freaking irritating, Kath."

Kathy grinned. "You can shut me up by telling me the truth. It's not like I'm going to run home and send him an e-mail telling him what you said." She tapped her temple with her index finger. "I'll keep all information you reveal right here. So own it, Patti. What's in your heart?"

Patti plopped down in the chair across from her sister and sighed. "He's so damn good-looking."

"Answer the question."

"I love his directness. I always have. Sometimes it comes across as almost rude, but I love the truthfulness of the man. He's honest." She shrugged. "Guess I find that appealing."

"So the answer to my question is?" Kathy said, raising her brows.

Patti closed her eyes and sighed again, then opened them. "Okay. My heart danced in my chest when I saw him. Satisfied?"

Kathy wiggled her eyebrows up and down. "I'm not the one who needs to be satisfied."

"Will you stop that thing with your eyebrows? You remind me of Groucho Marx."

Kathy stared her down, unblinking.

Patti jumped off the chair, turned on her heel, and rushed to the cash register, mumbling to herself.

"If you have something to say, I'm right here," Kathy said, trailing behind her sister.

"I already told you what you want to know. You can be as exasperating as Robert, you know that? You're relentless."

"I just want you to face the truth about this dinner with him. As Dad would say, don't kid yourself, buster. I don't want you to be blindsided by whatever it is Robert has planned for your future."

"I hope he doesn't have anything on his agenda besides giving me the name of someone who wants to hire me."

"That's what you say now. Wait till after your romantic dinner at the Catania."

Patti slapped down her credit card. "I refuse to fuel your already raging fire of determination to make this meeting something it's not."

Kathy laughed out loud. "Keep telling yourself that, buster."

Patti grabbed her shopping bag and walked off in a huff. "Let's go home and eat some ice cream. I've worked up an appetite spending my money."

Robert and Patti agreed to meet at the restaurant, and Patti borrowed Kathy's car. The valet greeted her at the entrance with a smile, and the hostess took her to the table where Robert stood and kissed her on both cheeks.

"Glad you could make it," he said as he took his seat.

She put her napkin in her lap. "I should be thanking *you*." She looked into his eyes. "I appreciate your taking the time to look into job prospects for me."

He gestured toward the window. "Can you believe this view?"

She smiled. "It's pretty awesome. The view at the top of the building where you work is also amazing."

He picked up the menu. "I think you'll love the food. Italian used to be your favorite."

"Still is." She opened her menu. "It's going to be hard to select a dish."

"I've heard the lobster gnocchi is excellent."

"Wild Alaskan salmon with risotto? Hmm."

"No matter what you pick, you'll love it. I promise."

"You eat here often, then?"

He nodded. "I've dined here several times with clients. They expect a high-priced dinner cooked by a well-known chef, so yes, this is my restaurant of choice if I want to impress someone."

She laughed. "You're trying to impress *me*? Why?"

Their waiter sauntered slowly by the table, and Robert nodded. The young man took their orders and left them alone.

"You ordered champagne, Robert. Are we celebrating something?"

His smile brought back memories of when they'd dated, and she swallowed, remembering all the times they'd gone out to dinner, then gone back to her place. He'd spend the night. Her favorite part was waking up in his arms, though he was an attentive sexual partner, always thinking of her needs before his own. Her stomach flip-flopped. She remembered the last time she was in bed with a man. Charlie's face appeared before her eyes. For a second, she thought she might vomit, but the ill feeling passed quickly.

The waiter brought a bottle of champagne, which he uncorked at their table, then poured the bubbly liquid into crystal flutes.

Robert picked up his glass and waited for Patti to do the same. He tipped his flute in her direction, and they clinked glasses.

Just as Charlie had done on the yacht. *Oh, my God.*

She glanced past Robert's head, completely caught up in a mental reverie of the night Charlie raped her. She shivered.

Robert turned around to see what she was staring at, then looked at her face. "What's wrong?" He waited several seconds, then asked, "Patti?"

His voice calling her name shook her out of her daze, and she refocused on his face. "Sorry. I was just remembering something."

"You looked afraid. And you shivered. Are you cold? I can get you—"

She mentally berated herself for returning to the scene on the yacht. She wanted to enjoy this evening, hoping something positive would come out of it. "No. No. I'm fine, Robert. Where were we?"

He held up his flute again. "I'm hoping to hire my new assistant this evening. *If* she's interested."

"Your new assistant? Is she joining us for dessert?"

He tipped his flute at her and grinned. "She's already arrived and is sitting across the table from me."

Her jaw dropped open.

"Surprised?" he asked.

She lowered her flute to the table, her hand grasping the stem to keep it from tipping over. "You're serious?"

"I told you I've been in this new position for almost two months. I've interviewed five men and five woman for the position. Not one of them is as qualified as you."

"I don't know what to say."

"Anything other than an affirmative will break my heart."

She swallowed. This would mean working with him closely. Did she want to spend five days a week at his company? She still found him attractive, but he'd left her two years ago. Granted, it wasn't for another woman, but did that matter? He'd broken her heart, and it had taken her until now to regain her self-esteem.

"You haven't said anything, Patti."

"Can I think about it?"

His demeanor changed, the smile wiped from his face. "The commissions are phenomenal. You'll almost be considered rich."

"I'm tempted, Robert, don't get me wrong. It's just—"

"I won't fire you if you won't date me. This is an opportunity that most candidates for the position would kill for."

She nodded, questions and thoughts whirling around in her brain like a twister. "Thank you. I mean it. I'm not saying no. This wasn't what I expected you to tell me. You can understand that, can't you? We were once in a relationship. Doesn't that make this a bit... unusual?"

"We had a relationship over two years ago, Patti. We are no longer attached."

"As I recall, when we had lunch together, you mentioned you still have feelings for me. That could make a working relationship very messy."

"I remember every word I said at lunch. I also recall you didn't do a very good job of convincing me you had absolutely no feelings for *me*."

She crossed and uncrossed her legs, took a sip of champagne, couldn't meet his eyes.

He reached across the table and grasped her hand. "I loved you, Patti. That never changed. As I said, our relationship was not at the point where I felt it appropriate to ask you to move down here with me. And we weren't ready for marriage either. I wasn't cheating on you. I told you the truth." He leaned back in his chair. "You used to tell me you loved the fact I'm always honest with you."

She nodded, not at all disliking the warmth of his hand holding hers. "Yes, that's true. And no, we weren't ready to get married."

"So you understand my logic? At least somewhat?"

She closed her eyes, sucked in a breath, then opened her eyes. "Okay."

"Okay, as in, you accept my job offer?"

"Okay, I see your point. I understand why you broke off our relationship. I wanted more, and you weren't ready. I get that."

"A-nd?" He lengthened the word into several syllables.

"And we're still friends."

"Yes, we are. Even after the relationship has ended," he added. "Look at us now. Sitting here together. Enjoying a wonderful evening out. What's messy about this?" He crooked one eyebrow upward. "I don't see why we couldn't work very amicably together, Patti."

She sighed. "You won't take no for an answer, will you?"

"I will not go down without a fight."

She shook her head. "Why am I not surprised?"

He grinned. "You know me too well."

Should she admit her feelings of déjà vu or the tingle in her lower abdomen when he smiled at her?

*Will I ever have another offer of this magnitude handed to me on a silver platter? Yes or no?* The money was very tempting. But was that the only thing tempting her?

No amount of extra time would stave off the inevitable truth.

She had to make a decision. She took in a deep breath. "I accept your offer."

He squeezed her hand, then let it go and picked up his flute, tipping it toward her again. "Another toast? To our new relationship? Working relationship, that is." He chuckled.

She waited several seconds. Had she just made the worst decision of her life? She picked up her glass and clinked it with his. "To our new *working* relationship."

Their waiter appeared at their table, holding their plates. They both kept quiet as he placed the dishes in front of them, waited for their thank-you, then left them with a quick, "Bon appétit."

# Chapter Twenty

The next day, the two sisters were sitting at the kitchen table, discussing Patti's dinner with Robert. Kathy clapped her hands. "I can't believe he offered you that position! That's great, Patti. You'll be rolling in money soon."

Patti walked away and threw herself onto the couch. "I slept well last night for the first time since I moved here. Maybe that's a sign I'm comfortable with my decision."

Kathy followed her, frowning. "Why wouldn't you be?" She sat across from her sister.

"Isn't it obvious? Is it really wise to be working with your ex-boyfriend? And I told you, he admitted still being in love with me. That combination does not make for a solid business relationship."

"Your breakup was amicable. You felt comfortable enough approaching him about a job in the first place. So it's obvious you two can conduct yourselves in a responsible manner when you're together. He didn't try anything, did he?"

"No. Though I know it's only a matter of time."

"If you're truly not interested in getting back together, then nothing will become of this. You're just friends. Or, here's an idea. How about friends with benefits? You could try that."

Patti rolled her eyes. "I'm not into that. I'm interested in having a relationship, getting married, having a kid."

Kathy smirked. "Me, too. But look what happened to me."

"How's the morning sickness?"

"Not so bad. I eat two saltine crackers before I get out of bed, and it works. By the time I'm showered and dressed, I'm ready to eat breakfast, and it stays down."

"I'm glad that part seems to be over. Now when can we go baby shopping?"

Kathy held out her hand like it was a stop sign. "Not ready for that yet. I'm still trying to wrap my head around this whole baby thing."

"Have you decided yet? About keeping the baby, I mean."

Kathy nodded. "I'm not having an abortion, and I don't want to put my baby up for adoption. Keeping this baby is my only alternative."

Patti grinned. "I'm happy for you, Kath. And as I said, I'll help out in any way I can."

"I'll get six weeks' maternity leave, which is great. I haven't thought about what I'm going to do after that."

"Nannies are probably very expensive in this area."

"You don't even wanna know."

"We'll work something out. Have you told Sharon or Dad or, uh, Helen?"

"Oh, I'm sure Helen would have something sarcastic to say about a woman in her early thirties having an unplanned pregnancy. But she doesn't hold me up on a pedestal anyway, so after I tell her, I won't be falling very far in her eyes."

"You ever wonder if she finds it difficult being perfect?"

Kathy laughed out loud. "We are being so, so catty."

Patti laughed along with her. "Feels good sometimes, though, doesn't it? I mean, it's not like we're saying it to her face. If we did, she'd never believe it anyway. She's too self-absorbed."

Kathy stood. "She couldn't handle the truth," she said in a gruff voice. "Name that movie."

Patti grinned. "*A Few Good Men.* Jack Nicholson, Tom Cruise, Demi Moore."

"God, you're good. I have to make an appointment with my ob-gyn. Wanna go with me?"

"Hell, yeah, I want to go with you. Just tell me the date and time and we'll go together."

Kathy smiled. "I'll call as soon as I can. Hey, I've got stuff to do, so I better get my butt in gear." She stood. "What's up with you today?"

"Robert said he'd e-mail me a job description, along with information about his clients. That ought to keep me busy for days."

"When do you start?"

"This Monday." She stood and poured herself a cup of coffee. "I'm already anticipating my first paycheck two weeks after that. So after June, I can stop dipping into my savings." She sipped her coffee. "I have a lot of reading to do, so I better get to it." She stared out the window. "I guess if something romantic does end up happening and we break up, the worst thing that can happen is I have to find another job."

Kathy tilted her head. "Don't go there. It's way too soon to be conjuring up scenarios that most likely will never come to fruition."

"I think I'm being realistic as well as prepared. Oooh, this job will do wonders for my career. I'd like not to screw it up."

"Have a little faith. Suck it up and act like the level-headed adult I know you are. You can do this. And from what he told you, so can he. You're not a couple of teenagers. Plenty of married couples get divorced and continue to not only be friends, but they don't sever their working relationship."

Patti nodded slowly, still staring out the window. "I keep going back and forth about my decision, but I really want the job. It's like a dream come true."

"I think you made the right decision. Don't go looking for trouble. And as you said, if you start becoming romantically involved, you *could* resign and get a job somewhere else. After working with Robert, you'll be a highly marketable commodity. Someone else would hire you, just like that." She snapped her fingers.

"I hadn't thought of that."

She resolved to follow Kathy's advice and not go looking for trouble. Weighing the pros and cons, she concluded she'd have no problem working with Robert. They always got along well and had been great friends. That was definitely a pro.

If they hooked up again, she could get another job, just in case. Or she could stay, and if it ended badly, look for another job then. Either way, having this job on her résumé was a coup. She could definitely do this.

Monday arrived, and a kaleidoscope of butterflies took up residence in Patti's stomach. She didn't know if she was just nervous, or if she was suffering from PTSD after what happened with Charlie. Or it could be that, thank God, her period had started, and her stomach never felt normal on the first day. *Now I don't have to worry about any future Seevers child. Booyah!* Or was she anxious about seeing Robert again? Perhaps afraid she wouldn't be able to succeed in such a high-pressure position?

The Weather Channel said it would be in the mid-seventies, so she dressed in a lightweight peach suit with a cream-colored silk blouse and heels, grabbed her black leather briefcase, and took the shuttle to La Jolla. A car most definitely was on her list of things to buy. She couldn't count on public transit and guessed she'd need a nice car to impress clients.

She arrived at the office at eight a.m. and found Robert already at his desk on the phone. He waved at her to take a seat.

Five minutes later, he hung up the phone and let out a deep breath. "New client." He grinned. "In fact, your first client."

Patti raised her eyebrows. "I'm not prepared to take on a client yet, Robert. I thought I'd be following you around for at least a month, before I go out on my own."

He tapped a pen on his desk. "In a perfect world, that's how I'd want it done. But I have too many clients. That's why I need an assistant. Trial by fire."

"Well, you don't want to lose clients. And that's what might happen if you set me loose with someone I don't know, who might be looking for something I'm not familiar with, and—"

He put up his hand. "Stop. I know what your job entailed before this. I think you're ready to take this on. You're extraordinarily familiar with the world of photography. You have a great eye for what looks good and where. Honestly, the job entails listening. Plain and simple.

"You have lunch or dinner with the client, and you listen to him or her. She gets to know you. You get to know her. You talk about what's happening in photography, what's in, what's popular, what's eclectic or eccentric. She takes you to the office building or her home or wherever, and then it's all up to you. Not that difficult."

She took in a deep breath. "And if I have questions, I just call you?"

He nodded.

"And if you're too busy to take my call?"

"Look. Most of the time, I'll be able to schedule both of us with the client. It's just that there are going to be unexpected times when I can't be in two places at once, or I have to leave in the middle of a meeting. You'll do just fine, Patti. I wouldn't have hired you if I didn't think you could handle this job." He shrugged. "And if you can't get in touch with me? Bullshit them." He stared into her eyes. "This is very much a PR job. You do a lot of schmoozing. You're a beautiful woman with excellent verbal and social skills. You won't find this difficult, I promise."

She smiled. "I can do this, right?"

He leaned back in his leather chair. "Never doubted it."

"You sound like Kathy. She was giving me pep talks all weekend."

"How is she, by the way?"

She shifted her gaze out the window, then back to him. "Between you and me?"

He nodded.

"She's pregnant."

"Tell her congratulations for me."

"With her *ex*-boyfriend's child."

"Ex? Are they going to get back together?"

"Not gonna happen," she said with more anger than she should have exhibited.

"Why do you say that?"

Realizing she'd already said too much, she made a waving motion with her hand. "I'm sorry. I shouldn't have said anything to begin with. Forget I told you."

"Or you could explain what you're talking about."

She stood. "Not now. I can't believe I even said as much as I did. It's not my place to talk about my sister's pregnancy or love life. I apologize for opening my big, fat mouth."

"Maybe another time, then. Let's get on the road." He pushed back his chair. "You know, you'll have to get yourself a car one of these days."

"I was just thinking about that. What with all the entertaining I'll be doing, I'll want something nice. What do you have?"

"Mercedes E-Class Cabriolet."

"I don't know anything about cars, Robert. If it's a Mercedes, it's probably expensive."

He shrugged. "Seventy grand."

She gasped. "I am so not in that league. I was thinking something along the lines of a nice used BMW?"

"You can certainly start with that." He smiled. "Believe me, you'll soon be able to afford a really nice car."

They took the elevator to the underground garage, and upon exiting, Robert clicked the key fob. They followed the chirping sound to a dark red Mercedes convertible. He opened the passenger door for her.

She slid into the cream leather seat. "I could get used to this."

"Suits you. Beautiful car. Beautiful woman."

She ignored him and asked, "Where are we headed?"

He settled himself into the driver's seat and turned toward her. "Maxwell Galbraith. Forty years old. Started his own dot-com company five years ago. Opened a satellite office in La Jolla. Totally into impressing his über-wealthy clientele. Overinflated ego perhaps, but you almost can't blame him. He's a very, very successful man." He raised his eyebrows. "Not married." He grinned.

She met him, eye to eye. "And that would interest me because?"

"He'll see you're not wearing a wedding ring."

"Robert, this is my job. I am not looking to hook up with anyone. This is strictly business."

"As long as I know you're not looking outside the office for a husband."

"Outside the office?"

He laid his hand on her forearm. "Just saying. You won't have to look far for romance in your life. You should be able to see what's right under your pretty little nose." He tapped the tip of her nose and smiled.

She swatted his hand. "Stop it, Robert. For God's sake, this is my first day on the job, and you're already making sexual innuendos about the two of us."

He turned the key in the ignition, and the car roared to life. After he pressed another button, the top quietly slid backward into its own compartment like a folding fan.

"You're always thanking me for being honest and direct," he said. "I don't think those are bad qualities. Would you rather I wait a specified amount of time before showing my hand?"

She let out a loud huff. "I don't know what I want or don't want right now. But I do know that we have an appointment, and I'm nervous enough about that. Don't add to my stress level, will you? Just be my friend, please."

He slammed down on the gas pedal and peeled out of the parking space, headed toward the exit, screeching to a halt upon reaching the sidewalk. He glanced at her and nodded. "I can be your friend." He pulled out of the garage, gunned the engine, and they flew down the street. "For now."

Her head slapped against the headrest when he accelerated, the warm, fresh coastal air filling her lungs. She shut her eyes and tried to relax, knowing she was in for one helluva ride.

In more ways than one.

# Chapter Twenty-One

Several weeks later, Kathy sat at her desk at work, staring at her computer, where the newest addition to the video game she'd created hovered on the screen. It was her fifteen-minute break, and she'd just completed Level 20. It appeared to work perfectly. She'd always shown Charlie every step of her progress in creating this game. In fact, he'd been helpful with his ideas.

He'd been on her mind constantly. She missed him, no doubt about it. As much as she vociferously denied it to Patti, she wanted, no, she needed to know what happened between them and why. Why had he dumped her and never explained?

When she last spent time with him, right before her mother's death, he'd been loving and comforting. She'd been impressed by his attentiveness and concern for her. They'd made love before she'd gotten on the plane, headed for San Francisco. He'd held her hand in the airport, draped his arm around her shoulders. And when it was time for him to say goodbye, he'd kissed her passionately, with greater fervor than she'd felt in months.

What went wrong? Was it something she said or did? She kept returning to that day over and over and over in her mind and could not think of one thing that could have set him off or made him angry. She'd never obsessed about anything like this in her life.

But he'd been less romantic the weeks *before* her mom had died. She'd chalked it up to work, and he'd admitted he was worried about the financial state of his business. He'd forgotten that only a week before he'd told her he was selling, leasing, and renting so many yachts he couldn't keep up with the demand. And the lie was verified when she ran into his accountant. Something was up.

And suddenly she realized *not* knowing was killing her. She wasn't being honest with Patti or herself, saying she didn't care any longer, that she didn't need to know. That was an out-and-out lie. She might not want to admit it to Patti, but…

*Come on, Kathy. You damn well ought to admit it to yourself.*

She had to find out his reason for dumping her, so she could stop thinking about him and what part she might have played in his leaving her. But she didn't want to call him or text him or leave him a message. He wouldn't call or text her back, and she knew it. She needed him to tell her to her face the reason he'd dumped her so ungraciously and cruelly.

She must have gotten pregnant the last time she and Charlie had sex, the day before she flew up to see her mom, the day before her mom died. It was now June. She was carrying a baby. A baby the two of them had created. They'd once spoken of what it would be like to have children and how many each of them wanted. She yearned for a passel of kids. He wanted one boy and one girl and, if not, two kids was his limit. That conversation had been about six months after they started dating.

Looking back, it was the blooming of their relationship, the best of times. They'd just made love and had lain in bed on their sides, staring into each other's eyes, talking about having kids. He'd tickled her afterward, making her laugh so hard she could hardly breathe, and he had to stop.

She'd been worrying about not telling him about the baby. She'd watched enough *Lifetime* movies to know that keeping this type of secret inevitably backfired. The guy always found out when he saw his ex-girlfriend with a baby. He'd do the math, figure out the child was his, demand a DNA test, then insist on being a part of the child's life. Also, sometimes the couple got back together, forging a stronger relationship through the shared custody of the child.

*Is it worth taking a chance by not telling him about the baby?* If he found out, well, she'd tell him that when she hadn't heard from him, she'd started dating and had hooked up with another guy. He'd accept that explanation. He didn't want to be with her, so he'd swallow the lie she'd tell him.

If, for some unknown reason, he pressed the issue and wanted a DNA test, she'd make sure he knew she didn't want child support or his help. If he insisted on being involved in the child's life, she'd deal with it.

But wait. If there was a possibility he'd want to be a part of this child's life, was it fair to keep the truth from him? If they were to trade places, wouldn't she want to know? Well, of course she would.

*Then have I already decided what I'm going to do?*

Her coffee break ended, and she finished up her work for the day, rushed to her car, and drove home to shower and change. She hadn't seen Charlie in almost two months and wanted to look good, if only to prove how well she was doing without him in her life. She didn't need him.

She dressed in a cotton, above-the-knee, sky-blue dress that showed off her now very expanded chest, slathered on her favorite scented cream as well as the matching perfume. Turning from side to side in the mirror, she was ready to go and looked pretty darn good. "Well, for a pregnant woman," whispered her nasty little inner voice.

"Nope," she said to her reflection. "You look good, period."

She ran her hands up and down the sides of the dress to smooth out the wrinkles, smooched her lips in the mirror to make sure her lipstick was set, blinked her mascaraed eyes, then grabbed her purse and left, heading to Charlie's house. She'd show *him* how well she was doing without him around.

The sun was just starting to set, and the orange and yellow glow above the ocean was, as always in this area, absolutely spectacular. She found a parking spot, took a deep breath, and exited her vehicle.

"Well, here goes nothing. Or something, depending on how you look at it," she whispered and walked, head held high, chest out, up the path leading to the porch.

She inhaled deeply through her nose and knocked on the oversized front door of his 1910 Craftsman house. His yacht business had just started booming this year, and he'd told her he was looking to move from San Diego to La Jolla and buy a really nice house. Kathy loved old houses like this one and hoped someday to sell her condo and buy a similar one in San Diego.

She waited for what seemed like forever, then she heard footsteps, and suddenly the door swung open.

"Kathy!"

She couldn't tell whether he was just surprised to see her, or unhappy she was standing on his doorstep, because he wasn't smiling.

"Hi, Charlie." She waited for him to invite her in. However, he stood there with his hand on the back of the door, not opening it wide enough to allow her to walk past him.

"What…" he began, his mouth half open.

"What am I doing here?" she said.

He nodded.

"May I come in?"

He didn't answer, and she counted the seconds. Ten seconds. *Is it really that difficult to decide whether to let me come in and talk to you?*

He shuffled back several steps and opened the door wide, gesturing her inside.

She walked into the foyer and turned toward him, waiting for him to invite her into the front room. He stood motionless and speechless. *What the hell is going on?*

"Can we talk?" she said.

He nodded.

So far, he'd said her name once and the word *what*, and it was pissing her off. He was treating her as if she were the enemy or a religious proselytizer handing out pamphlets.

Realizing she'd have to take control of the situation, she walked deliberately into the front room and took a seat in the chair across from the couch.

He followed her and sat on the sofa, looking like a guest in his own home.

She folded her hands in her lap and crossed her legs. He'd always said her shapely calves turned him on, so she uncrossed them. "What's going on with you, Charlie?"

"I think that's fairly obvious."

"Not to me it isn't."

He glanced away from her, looking as uncomfortable as hell. "We're no longer together. I don't know what you want me to say."

She leaned back into the cushion, deliberately trying to look at ease. Which she wasn't. In fact, she felt like throwing up, but refused to let her nerves make a fool of her. "I want you to tell me why I never heard from you when I returned from my mom's funeral."

He finally looked her in the eyes. "We both know things hadn't been right between us."

"I didn't know that, Charlie. When I asked you if anything was wrong, you said you were worried about your business. Financial problems or whatnot. I ran into your accountant soon after, and he said the company has finally moved into the black."

"I didn't know what else to tell you." He shrugged. "We were growing apart."

She laughed. "You're full of crap. We were not growing apart. There's a reason for everything, and I want to know what it was. Come on, help me out here."

"I hope you *have* moved on, Kathy."

"I don't see that that's any of your business, but no, I haven't. You?"

"I've been busy with the business. Don't have a lot of time for socializing."

"You didn't have the balls to confront me? Tell me you wanted out? You just dump me, don't answer my texts or phone messages. The only thing I didn't do was come to your business, demanding an explanation. Consider yourself lucky I arrived on your doorstep at home instead."

He nodded. "Thank you for that. You're always very thoughtful."

She frowned. "And so were you, Charlie. You owe me an explanation, don'tcha think?"

His eyes shifted left to right, and he settled back into the couch. "I could have ended it in a nicer way, yeah."

"A nicer way?" She leaned forward, looking him in the eyes. "I didn't even know it was ended until I couldn't reach you. I had no other explanation for not hearing from someone I'd been dating and sleeping with for more than a year."

"Looking at it from your perspective, I see your point."

"My perspective? We'd been together for way more than a few days or weeks. We'd talked about how many kids each of us wanted to have. We fantasized about what our favorite house would look like."

She could feel the tears coming and tried so hard to not let them pour down her cheeks, but it was impossible. She swiped at her face with her fingertips and cleared her throat. "I loved you, Charlie. And you loved me. Doesn't that mean anything to you? Don't you think you should tell me why you don't want me in your life any longer? What the hell is wrong with you?"

He screwed up his lips, as if this was a most distasteful subject. "I'm sorry. I should have done things differently. But it's still over. Let's not rehash the whys and wherefores now."

"We can't rehash something that we never discussed in the first place. That 're' indicates doing something over again, and we never talked about any problems between us. Ever. I thought everything was fine."

"Well, it wasn't."

"Well, duh. I guess I'm savvy enough to have figured that out on my own by now, right? With no help from you."

He looked at her with boredom written all over his face, and she seethed. Her stomach clenched into a concrete knot, and she truly felt like puking. Silence reigned. She could hear the *click-click* of the grandfather clock, the tweets of the birds in the trees outside the windows.

"So, that's it? 'See ya later, Kathy, it's been a pleasure'?"

"What do you want me to say? Can't you just accept the fact that, for me, it's over? I don't want to do this anymore. You're a nice person and all, but I don't love you, okay?"

What was she supposed to say now? "I thought you *did* love me." That sounded so pitiful, she wanted to run away and hide.

Her classical ringtone sounded, and she grabbed it out of her purse. Sharon was phoning her? She pressed "Remind Me Later" and put it back.

"I came here for several reasons, Charlie. I needed to know why you walked away, and you've told me. I get it. You don't love me anymore. Okay." She thought about the baby growing inside her. The fact that in a few months she wouldn't be able to hide her pregnancy. That she and Charlie lived in the same city and might run into each other. She opened her mouth and blurted, "I'm not finished talking."

He let out a deep sigh and focused on something across the room. "Can we get this over with, please?"

"I wasn't going to say anything, but Patti told me—"

He smirked. "I knew there was a reason you came here. She told you, didn't she?"

"Told me what? What're you talking about?"

He stood so quickly, the couch slid back about a foot. "She deserved everything she got. You know why?" He slowly walked toward her and stood directly in front of her. "No one dumps me, you got that? Nobody walks away from Charlie Seevers."

Her mouth dropped open. "You're still holding a grudge about something that happened in high school?" She frowned. "And what do you mean, 'she deserved everything she got'? You're not making sense."

He squinted at her. "She told you what happened."

"When?"

He raked his hand through his hair. "Wait a minute. What the hell is going on here? You said Patti talked to you. Oh, never mind. Look. She walked away from me. I walked away from you. Get over it."

"So it was a revenge thing, breaking up with me? She screwed you over, so you screwed me over? I didn't know you were so vindictive."

Her phone rang again. When she looked down, she saw Sharon had sent a text.

*Found Dad unconscious on kitchen floor. At the hospital now. Call me ASAP.*

"Oh, my God," Kathy whispered, then jumped up. "I have to leave."

He turned and walked to the foyer, opened the door, and gestured her outside.

As she passed, she stopped in front of him and looked him in the eyes. "Now that I know what kind of person you really are, I realize you don't deserve to know what I wanted to share with you. I'm done here."

He grinned. "You're a little late, Kathy. I dumped your ass months ago. As I said, no one walks out on me, least of all you. But your sister paid for what she did to me back in high school. It might have been years ago, but Charlie Seevers never forgets."

She shook her head, trying to figure out his skewed logic. "I don't have any idea what you're talking about, and I don't want to know. You're one sick piece of shit." She rushed out the front door to her car and drove as fast as she could back to her condo.

# Chapter Twenty-Two

Kathy pulled into the driveway with a squeal of brakes, slammed the car door, and ran into the house with her cell phone stuck to her hand. She'd tried to get in touch with Patti several times during the short trip home, but refused to leave a voice mail that would totally freak out her sister.

Her cell phone chimed, and she answered it. "Patti, where have you been? I've been trying to call you."

Patti laughed. "There's such a thing as voice mail."

"Sharon found Dad passed out on the kitchen floor."

"What? How do you know? What happened? Oh, my God, I'm coming home right away."

"I'll call Sharon, then make reservations for the earliest flight out."

"Thanks, Kath. I'll be home in a few minutes."

Kathy ended the call and immediately phoned Sharon. "What's going on? Patti and I are flying out tonight."

"I found Daddy collapsed on the kitchen floor this morning and," her voice hitched, "I called 911. He's in the hospital. Quincy General. The EMTs didn't tell me anything. I don't know what to do. I feel so helpless."

"I'm sure I can get us a flight out this afternoon. I'll text you our arrival time. We'll rent a car and should be there by this evening. How's Helen holding up?"

Sharon paused before answering. "She's in LA. At an acting seminar. She always makes him breakfast, right? This morning, I slept in, then found Daddy on the kitchen floor. Helen blames me. Told me if I'd made his breakfast like she does every day, Daddy wouldn't have been making his own breakfast in the first place. That he wouldn't have been lying on the floor for God knows how long.

That I would have been able to call 911 sooner. She called me a lazy shit for sleeping in."

"Oh, Sharon, stop listening to her. Helen's so focused on Helen there's no room for empathizing with anyone else. It's always about her. She acts like she's the only person in this family who's ever loved Dad. His life is her sole responsibility. Patti and I know how much you do around the ranch. Just ignore her."

Sharon sobbed. "She's impossible to ignore. She totally gets in my face about everything. She was yelling at me on the phone."

"You don't deserve that, and you know it, Share. Listen to some of the advice and counsel you give us all the time, will you? Don't take anything Helen says to heart. Promise me that."

"Okay," she mumbled. "I'll see you when you get here."

"Text me if there's any change or new information."

When Patti arrived, they packed and drove directly to San Diego International Airport. After a stop along the way, their flight was scheduled to land in Reno, Nevada, at seven o'clock that evening. They then had to take a small plane to the airfield near Quincy and rent a car, giving them time, hopefully, to see their father and talk to the doctor.

Neither of them spoke much during the three-hour flight. Patti had work to do on her computer. Kathy mulled over the bizarre conversation she'd had with Charlie. He'd made absolutely no sense. Patti had dumped him, so he'd dumped Kathy? And to top it off, somehow in his mind, Patti had paid for what she'd done to him? How? What was he referring to?

Kathy had gone to his house to ask him why he'd dumped her. Then she'd suddenly decided to do what some people would call "the right thing" and admit to being pregnant. But then, after listening to him rant about his revenge and how he didn't love her anymore, she was glad she hadn't said anything. He'd sounded so hateful. It blew her away to discover the depth of his grudge and his mean-spiritedness.

Thankfully, she'd found out who the real Charlie Seevers was. Now she definitely would never tell him she was carrying his child. Most important, she didn't want her baby to have *him* as a father. Thank God she'd gone to talk to him. Otherwise, she would never have known what a horrible person he was. He didn't care about anyone but himself, making him a bad candidate to be a parent.

And, dammit, she'd been so stressed after finding out she was pregnant, and trying to figure out what to do about Charlie, that'd she'd put off making an appointment with her gynecologist. She typed in a reminder on her phone for several days from now and leaned her head back.

She fell into a light sleep moments before landing, and Patti startled her when she tapped her on the arm. "We're here already?"

Patti nodded. "You were snoring. You know, all this stress is not good for you and the baby."

"I know. And don't say anything to Dad about it. He'll worry about me being a single mom, and he doesn't need the stress while he's in the hospital. I'll tell Sharon later when she and I can be alone."

"And Helen?"

"Ugh. I can't deal with her right now. I didn't even tell you what she said to Sharon. Helen blames her for not getting up early to fix Dad breakfast. She told Sharon that if she'd woken up early like Helen always does, none of this would have happened. In reality, it's no one's fault. Something must have been wrong if Dad collapsed suddenly. Maybe finding him earlier would have made a difference. Who knows? The doctors will probably explain all that to us when we get there. Anyway, I hate it when people play the blame game. God! It does no one any good at all." She slapped her hands on her legs. "I absolutely hate that our family is so dysfunctional."

Patti turned and hugged her sister, as awkward as that was in their tightly packed seats. "We are pretty dysfunctional. Or should I say, one of us makes the rest of us feel as if we have a dysfunctional family."

Kathy pulled away, grabbed the hankie in her pocket, and wiped her nose. "Helen makes all of us crazy."

"She's one person, Kathy. I don't think you and Sharon and I are dysfunctional. We get along. You and Dad are talking now, and that's great, isn't it? And I'm looking forward to visiting the ranch more often, now that we've finally found out the real truth behind Mom and Dad's divorce. The whole thing with Helen going behind our backs to try to get Dad to change the will really blindsided me. But that's all about her, Kathy. We're not as screwed up as you might think."

Kathy nodded, sniffing and swiping at the tears on her cheeks. "I'm sorry I used the term dysfunctional. I agree with you. Now that we know more about their divorce, we've cleared the air. I've been thinking of visiting the ranch, too, but time got away from me, what with work and finding out I'm pregnant. Plus, I hate the negative vibes I always get from Helen. It's enough to keep me away."

"We shouldn't let her do that to either of us," Patti argued. "You and I will regret it if we let her win that battle. Let's try to make the best of it. We'll never change her. Helen is Helen. Let's just work around her."

Kathy nodded, took a deep, shuddering breath, and smiled. "It's all these hormones, I swear. I've never been pregnant before."

"Neither have I. So, hey, can't help ya there, kiddo."

They both shared a laugh as the plane made its descent, landing right on time. They took a small plane to Gansner Field Airport, one mile north of the center of Quincy, and rented a new Toyota Corolla.

Patti offered to drive. Kathy was an emotional mess, saying over and over she wanted to have a better relationship with her father before he passed away.

Patti slid behind the wheel, drove down the frontage road, and headed to the outskirts of Quincy toward the ranch. They reached a crossroads with a four-way stop. Patti slowed to a stop and started to turn right.

She heard Kathy suck in a breath and glanced at her sister. Kathy's mouth opened in an O shape just as Patti felt an intense impact at the left rear side of the car. At that exact moment, she heard the side airbag burst open and smashed into her arm, ribs, and face. Everything went black.

Patti opened her eyes to semidarkness and an insistent beeping above her head. Someone held her right hand, and she turned in that direction. Her neck muscles cramped, and she gasped.

"You're going to be okay, Patti. Stay still now."

Sharon's voice.

Patti wiggled her fingers and toes, then scooched her butt to the side. No aches or pains so far. She let out a sigh.

Sharon hovered over the hospital bed, looking down. "Patti?"

"What happened?"

"A truck ran the stop sign and almost T-boned your car. It smashed the rear on the driver's side."

"Kathy's okay?"

"Her neck's a little sore, and her face is bruised from when the airbag deployed, but thank God, she and the baby are just fine."

Patti stared into Sharon's eyes. "She told you."

Sharon nodded. "I can't wait to have a little niece or nephew, so I can teach her or him how to ride." She smiled. "How long have you known?"

"Not long. What did she say?"

"I know all about Charlie. We had a long talk."

"Helen knows, too?"

"She's still at that acting seminar in LA."

Patti closed her eyes for a moment, exhausted. "I'm so glad Kathy and the baby are okay. Do I have any broken bones, internal injuries?"

Sharon shook her head. "The information I have is from the nurse. She said you'll probably be released tomorrow if the doctor wants you under observation overnight."

"How's Dad?"

"He's going to be fine. He stood up too quickly, I guess, and blacked out. Hit his head on the kitchen floor and has a pretty good gash above his eyebrow. He's lucky. I swear I thought it was another heart attack."

Patti smiled. "So we probably didn't need to fly up here. But I'm glad we did. Kathy and I both want to spend more time with the family. Dad's not getting any younger."

"Patricia Michaels?"

Patti and Sharon turned toward the door.

"I'm Dr. Rubens." He stuck out his arm and shook Sharon's hand. "You must be the sister who lives near here."

"Sharon," she said. "Nice to meet you, Doctor. Should I leave while you talk to Patti?"

Dr. Rubens walked to the head of the bed and looked into Patti's face. "Whatever Patricia wants."

"It's Patti, Doctor," Patti said.

He grinned. "Should Sharon leave?"

"She can stay. In case there's something you want me to

remember, it would be better for two sets of ears to hear it. My mind is sort of fuzzy right now."

"That's understandable. Any time an airbag deploys is cause for alarm. Sometimes, they do more damage than you'd expect." He paused, opened her chart, and read it for several seconds.

"We did an MRI to make sure there were no internal injuries. There were none. And the scans suggest you're approximately four weeks pregnant, but the baby looks viable. No problems there."

"Baby?" Patti's voice came out barely audible.

"You're pregnant?" Sharon said at the same time.

Dr. Rubens glanced from Patti to Sharon, then focused on Patti. "You didn't know?"

"Oh, my God," Patti whispered, then burst into tears.

# Chapter Twenty-Three

Patti's quiet tears turned into uncontrollable sobs, and Dr. Rubens said a few words to Sharon, then left the room at a quick clip.

Sharon grasped Patti's hand and squeezed. "Seems as if the baby's an unpleasant surprise."

Patti turned her head from side to side while tears continued to flow. This could not be happening. "I got tested for an STD, but I didn't take a pregnancy test. Then I had my period."

"What are you talking about, Patti?" Sharon said.

"This is impossible."

"Well, having sex at times will produce an unwanted child, but it's far from impossible," Sharon added.

"I can't be having his baby." She slapped her fist on the bed. "I won't."

"Honey, you can always have an abortion if you don't want this man's child."

Patti took in a huge, shuddering breath and let it out super slowly. "But it's not the baby's fault I was rape—"

"You were raped?" Sharon's jaw dropped. "You never told us that. When the hell did that happen? My God!"

The tears began to flow again, and Patti shut her eyes. "Can we talk about this later when we all get to the ranch? Don't say anything about it."

Sharon patted her sister's arm. "Of course. Rest. Get some sleep. It's almost eleven o'clock anyway. Past your bedtime." She smiled, bent down, and kissed Patti's forehead. "We'll work all this out. Sleep tight."

"I hope the bedbugs don't bite," Patti added.

Sharon closed the door behind her, and Patti stared at the wall. Every hour, a nurse came in to check her vitals, so she wasn't able to sleep much, leaving her plenty of time to think.

Charlie had raped her several days after she moved to San Diego, so maybe May fifteenth, sixteenth, seventeenth? The test for STDs had already come back negative. It was almost mid-June, and she was going to give Sergeant Kramer a call soon to find out about the drug test and DNA comparison with the CODIS databases. Because she'd had her period, she'd assumed she wasn't pregnant. Well, she knew it wasn't impossible to have a period but still be pregnant. Obviously, she was one of the small number of women that happened to. *Damn!*

She'd convinced herself that she was okay, despite what Charlie had done to her. Kathy wasn't interested in having anything to do with him, and now Patti knew her sister had made the right decision after all.

She was enjoying working with Robert so much that the trauma was easier to put behind her. She was actually happy and hadn't felt many residual emotional effects of the rape for a couple of weeks. She wondered if she'd have a delayed reaction at some point. Maybe she was in denial. She knew that being raped had an emotional and mental impact on her.

Yet she wasn't depressed. She didn't feel like killing herself. Was she angry? Hell, yeah, she was angry. She constantly fantasized about how she'd torture Charlie, if she could get away with it. Scared? Well, a bit fearful in an unidentifiable way, which she was sure would dissipate over time. She'd read that rape victims usually knew their rapist. *Well, that's sure true in my case.*

She'd have to tell Kathy about Charlie now that she was pregnant with his child. She had no idea what her sister's reaction would be. They were both pregnant with Charlie's babies. This was an absolute nightmare, like something that'd be on the cover of the *National Enquirer*.

How would Kathy take this news? Would it affect their relationship? *Will Kathy hate me? Oh, why did I have to stick my nose into Kathy's business where it didn't belong?* She hated having regrets, and she sure had a shitload of them now.

What would she tell Robert? She hadn't called him yet to tell him about her father. She'd do that when she arrived at the ranch. It was too late now. She would phone him tomorrow.

Helen would have had a field day with Patti's news, as Mom used to say. Helen wouldn't pass up the opportunity to berate Patti about her apparent lackadaisical use of birth control, her choice of boyfriends, her immaturity, and on and on. Plus, there would be no way to hide the fact from Helen once Patti gave birth.

She should probably admit to everything while she was at the ranch. Explain it all to Kathy first, then the rest of the family afterward.

The next time she looked at the huge clock hanging on the wall across from her bed, it was six thirty, and the morning sun's light yellow rays seeped through the blinds.

She, her father, and Kathy were scheduled to be released around noon. After they signed the release papers, they were taken downstairs in wheelchairs. It had been a short hospital stay for the three of them ,and this was the first they'd seen one another since entering the hospital.

Patti reached out and grasped Kathy's outstretched hand. They smiled at each other, then waved at their father, who was coming up behind them.

"I never thought we'd ever meet here," he said, chuckling.

"Me neither," Patti said.

"That's for sure," Kathy added.

"Okay, you three," Sharon interjected. "I brought Daddy's SUV. Hop in and get ready for an uneventful ride to the ranch."

"You don't have to make fun," Patti said. "The accident wasn't my fault."

"Just trying to inject a little black humor," Sharon said.

One at a time, they climbed into the SUV and hooked their seat belts, as if in slow motion. They each had their particular aches and pains. Their father had a large white bandage covering ten stitches above his eyebrow, and his sprained right arm was in a sling. Kathy had pulled the muscles in her neck and was wearing a temporary neck brace. Patti's neck also hurt, and her range of motion was severely restricted.

But they were alive, all three of them.

Sharon settled into the driver's seat, glanced in the rearview mirror, and laughed. "I feel like a tour guide with a van full of patients." She pulled away from the curb. "Mental patients," she added with a grin.

Patti laughed. "I'm the only one without any medical paraphernalia hanging all over me."

Kathy shifted the neck brace back and forth. "And this thing isn't going to last long. It's irritating the heck out of my skin."

"Well, I'm not complaining," Bill said. "I'm alive. I didn't have another heart attack. I *am* getting old. Or I should say, I'm getting old*er*. Lucky to be able to even have this discussion with my three beautiful daughters."

"Yes, Dad, where *is* Helen?" Kathy said.

"I thought I told you, she's at an acting seminar," Sharon said.

"That's right. Sorry. My head's still not in the game," Kathy answered.

"I would think she would have made an appropriate excuse and come home," Patti said with a sarcastic tone in her voice.

"She was really looking forward to that seminar," Bill said. "It cost her a thousand bucks to attend. She probably couldn't get her money back."

"Would that have been the end of the world?" Patti asked.

"It's only money," Kathy said.

"I've said it before, Dad. Helen can be self-centered at times," Sharon added.

"At times?" Patti said. "You gotta be kidding me, Sharon. More like always."

"Girls, girls," Bill said. "Stop all this. She's not here to defend herself, and that's hardly fair."

Sharon pulled up to the ranch, parked, then opened the back door. She reached in. "Here, Dad, let me help you."

He held on to her arm and ducked his head, stepping out of the car. "Thank you, hon." He stood and looked into her eyes. "I really appreciate all you do around here, you know? I know Helen isn't the only daughter looking after me."

"Sharon does a lot around the ranch," Kathy interjected. "To coin one of your favorite expressions, Dad, Helen's always tooting her own horn. It isn't fair."

He turned to Kathy and Patti. "I'm well aware of Helen's faults. But her heart is in a good place."

"Her heart is wherever the money is," Patti said.

"Enough of that!" he shouted, then looked at the ground. "I'm sorry for yelling, but let's not get into this right now."

Sharon patted her father on the back, frowning at Patti. "Let's get you to bed, Daddy. You can take a short nap before dinner."

He nodded and allowed her to lead him into the house, up the stairs, and into his bedroom.

Sharon came down, puffing out a deep breath. "I've tried to talk to Daddy about Helen a thousand times, Patti, but whenever I say anything that even hints at her not being the perfect daughter, he just changes the subject or pooh-poohs everything I say. He can be so darn stubborn."

"I'm sorry," Patti answered. "I didn't mean to upset him, especially today when he's not feeling well. I shouldn't have opened my mouth."

Sharon smiled. "We all said things we shouldn't have." She shrugged. "It's pretty much a useless endeavor to try to convince him that Helen has some really serious issues." She shrugged. "But you know what? He's the same way about both of you when Helen says mean things. He sticks up for both of you."

"Well, I'll be damned," Patti said under her breath.

"Who knew?" Kathy added.

"Don't look so down, Sharon," Patti added. "You know damn well he sticks up for you, too, when you're not there to defend yourself."

"I hope so," Sharon mumbled.

"I don't want to upset him after this nightmare," Kathy said, "but I want to tell him about this pregnancy before I fly back home. What do you think?"

"It depends on how long you're staying, Kathy," Sharon said. She glanced at Patti, and they shared an understanding look. Telling their father about Patti's child was not going to happen soon.

Kathy turned to Patti. "We didn't talk about it. After all, we thought he might have had a heart attack or a stroke or something, so…"

"I have to call Robert," Patti said, "before I make any decisions about staying. What about your work, Kath?"

"I'll talk to my boss. I have plenty of sick leave," Kathy said.

"Won't you want to use that for maternity leave?" Sharon asked.

"That's above and beyond my regular sick leave, so I'm not worried about that."

"What are you going to do after you have the baby?" Sharon said. "Go back to work? Hire a nanny?"

Kathy shook her head. "I haven't planned that far ahead. I can't afford the mortgage on the condo and the bills and a nanny on my salary."

Patti draped her arm over Kathy's shoulders. "I have some ideas about that, so don't worry your pretty little head, as Dad would say."

Kathy's eyebrows furrowed. "What're you talking about?"

"I don't know exactly," Patti said. "We could each trade off working from home to avoid hiring a nanny. We'll talk about it later. We have plenty of time to deal with the birth of your child and what's going to happen afterward, trust me," Patti said.

Kathy's eyes shifted from Patti to Sharon, then she shrugged and walked up the stairs. "I'm going to follow Dad's example and take a nap."

Patti rubbed her neck, hoping to massage the ache away. "Sounds like a good idea to me, too. Later, Sharon."

Sharon stood at the bottom of the stairs, shaking her head. "Sleep tight, you two. You've had a hard couple of days."

# Chapter Twenty-Four

Patti woke up to the sound of her father humming. She stepped out of her bedroom and listened.

Kathy popped her head out of her room and smiled at Patti. "This is like taking a walk down memory lane, I swear."

"You mean his singing, or rather, humming in the bathtub?"

Kathy nodded. "It's kinda cute."

"At his age, a lot of people would say they don't have anything to hum about. So, hey, I like it."

Just then, their father opened the bathroom door and looked at his daughters. "Feelin' okay, you two?"

"Neck's a bit sore, Dad, but I'm on the mend," Patti said.

"Me, too," Kathy added. "I took off that damn neck brace. It was driving me crazy. How's your head and arm, Dad?"

"Feelin' fit as a fiddle this mornin', thank you. Arm's a bit stiff. Hey, Sharon," he shouted. "When's supper?"

Patti rushed down the stairs. "I wanted to help her out with dinner. Hopefully, she hasn't done all the work already."

Kathy followed. "You're right. We're not guests here. We should carry our weight. That's what you always said when we were young, Dad," she yelled as she hurried downstairs.

Bill took his time joining them. When he reached the front room, he sat in his favorite chair and rested the back of his head on the small cushion at the top.

Thirty minutes later, Kathy sat down gently on the couch across from him, so as not to jog her neck muscles. She waited for her two sisters to join them, and they settled back into the cushions. "Dad, I have something I'd like to tell you, but if you're too tired, I can wait until another day."

"I was bored just spending one night in that dadgum hospital.

Not used to sitting around a lot." He gestured with his hand for her to go ahead. "I'd love to talk. Go on."

Kathy cleared her throat. "You remember Charlie, right? He used to be Patti's boyfriend in high school."

"Sure do. Came over here a couple of times." He glanced at Patti. "Your sister didn't bring him around here much, but that's pretty typical of teenage girls and all. Afraid their daddy is gonna scare 'em away or something. But he seemed like a nice enough guy. Polite. What does that have to do with you, hon?"

"After I moved to San Diego, I bumped into him, and we started dating."

"Oh, I get it. So, you two getting hitched?"

Kathy swallowed and shook her head. "No. That's never going to happen."

"Oh, yeah? Why's that?"

"The thing is, after Mom's funeral, I never heard from him again. I was pretty broken up."

His almost completely white eyebrows bunched together. "Doesn't sound like an upstanding young man to me. Shoulda stepped up to the plate and spoken up like a man. Told you what all was wrong."

"That's what I thought, too." She coughed, looked at her two sisters, then back at her father. "Yesterday… was it yesterday? Oh, my God, it seems like days ago, what with rushing to get here, then the accident, then spending the night in the hospital. Anyway, I went to see him yesterday."

Patti sucked in a breath. "You *what*? You didn't tell me that. What the hell did you do that for?"

Kathy tilted her head. "I was obsessing about it. I know I acted as if I was finished with him and good riddance, but I needed to know why I never heard from him. It was bugging the crap out of me. You told me that when you confronted him way back in high school about his screwing that girl behind your back, he gave you an honest answer. I wanted the same thing. An answer to why he did it. Why he just left me."

"But the last time we talked, you said you didn't want to confront him. You washed your hands of him. Remember?" Patti said.

"Whatever. I changed my mind, okay?"

"Let's not get into that now," Patti replied. "Go on with your story."

Their father held his hand out like it was a stop sign. "Wait just a minute here. That's why he stopped comin' round here, Patti? Because you broke it off with him for going out with another girl?"

Patti took in a deep breath. "Yes, Dad, that was the reason. I couldn't trust him."

"Hold on," Kathy interrupted, focusing on her dad's face. "Look, Dad, I thought he'd changed. He seemed like a nice guy, upstanding citizen, and all that. I was in love with him, and I thought he loved me, too. But come to find out, after all these years, he's carried a grudge because Patti dumped him." She glanced at Patti. "I'm serious. When I went and talked to him, he told me, 'No one dumps Charlie Seevers.' So he dumped me. Kind of like a revenge thing. Oh, and he no longer was in love with me."

"So you and he are broken up, then," her father said. "I'm sorry to hear it, hon, but there's plenty of fish in the sea. You're a cute, smart girl. You'll find somebody else in no time."

Kathy blushed. "Thanks, Dad. But the truth is, I was just about to tell him…"

"Go ahead, Kathy," Sharon urged. "Daddy's heard more surprising things than what you have to tell him."

Their father glanced at each of his daughters. "What's going on here? Tell me what?"

"I'm pregnant, Dad," Kathy finally blurted. "With Charlie's baby."

Bill leaned forward and clasped his hands between his knees. "Are you okay, hon?"

Kathy's lower lip quivered. "Yes, I'm just fine, Dad."

"Did you tell him about the baby?" he asked.

"After what he said to me and how he acted? I don't want him to be a part of my life or my baby's life. He's an uncaring bastard. Sorry about that, but I don't think there's a better word."

"When's the baby due?" he asked.

Kathy looked down. "I must have gotten pregnant at the end of March, but I haven't been to the doctor—"

"We're already into June, Kathy," Sharon interrupted.

Kathy shrugged. "I know, but I didn't realize until after Patti moved to San Diego in May, Sharon. The minute I get back home, I'm setting up an appointment. I already set a reminder on my phone."

Her father stared down at his hands. "So you're a little over two months pregnant."

"I'm sorry, Dad," Kathy continued. "I wanted you to know, and I wanted to tell you to your face. Please don't hate me. I don't think I could stand for us to go another ten years not talking to one another."

He turned his face upward and met her gaze eye to eye. "I think what I have to do is call my attorney. Change the will."

"Oh, Daddy, that's not right," Sharon said. "You can't cut Kathy out of the will just because—"

"Who said anything about cutting her out of the will? Do you think your mother would want me to do that?"

Sharon heaved a sigh. "Of course not, Daddy, but—"

"What I was going to say," he interjected, "is that I want to set up a trust fund for my grandson's, or granddaughter's, education. It's the right thing to do. I'm gonna be a grandpa!" He grinned.

Kathy shot off the couch, then cringed when her neck muscles spasmed. She stopped, rubbed her neck, then knelt in front of her father, clasping his uninjured hand. "Oh, Dad. I love you." Tears flowed down her cheeks.

He squeezed her fingers. "Your mom would've wanted this. And I want this, too. She never got to see any grandkids, but it looks like I'll get to, and I'm thrilled."

"Oh, really." Helen came around the doorway and entered the room.

Patti, Sharon, and Kathy watched as Helen walked up to their father and kissed him on the forehead. "You aren't going to change the will so some bastard kid can have the money you worked so hard for all of your life, are you?" She gestured at Kathy. "She's not even married to the guy. The kid won't even have a frickin' father."

He grasped the arms of his chair and pushed himself to a standing position, turned, and faced Helen dead-on. "One thing you keep forgetting, my dear Helen, is that no one tells me what to do. Your mom never tried, and I didn't push her around either. We were both strong-willed people. She and I agreed on my will, and in honor of what she and I both wanted for our children, it's never been changed. It doesn't matter that she and I were divorced. We still cared about each other, and we both loved all you girls. Equally. And I am never going to change the will to make it other than what I know your mom and I wanted."

Helen's eyes looked as if they'd bulge out of her head. It was obvious she assumed their father had changed the will when she'd talked to him about taking over the ranch when he died. This must have surprised the hell out of her.

Helen's mouth dropped open. "Then the will is the same as always?"

He nodded.

"Okay, then, why change it now? What if I have a baby or… or Sharon? What then?"

He shrugged. "Guess it was stupid that me and your mom never thought of that. But I can rectify it now. I'm still alive, you know. I can do whatever I want with my money. But I won't ever do something that your mother wouldn't agree with, that's for sure." He plopped down in his chair. "And that's exactly what I'm going to do. I'll consult my attorney on how best to deal with this situation in the event any of you have children, not just Kathy. So don't worry, Helen, your future kids will be taken care of as well."

Sharon, Kathy, and Patti smiled at their father. Helen glared at her three sisters, then stomped out of the room.

They let out a collective breath, but within seconds Helen returned.

"You know what? If I'm going to work my ass off to keep this ranch going both now and after you die, but you don't think it's fair to compensate me for that, then I'm outta here. I can make it in LA as an actress. I *will* make it in LA." She faced Kathy. "I'll show your little bastard." She turned toward her father. "What if I never have kids? You said I'd be compensated for working my butt off on this ranch. Instead, you'll compensate your daughter for being stupid and getting knocked up. You'll dole out money for some illegitimate kid, but not give me what you owe me. You lied to me."

He glanced in her direction. "You've got that wrong, Helen. You told me how you wanted me to change the will your mom and I set up, and I said I'd think on it." He paused. "And I did. Then I talked to my attorney, and he and I discussed your mom's and my wishes, and

I decided not to change anything. It just wouldn't be right. All of you will get the same amount of money, Helen."

"But it's right that she gets knocked up and has a bastard kid, so in the end I get less money? And I'll get even less money if I'm the only one who doesn't have kids? Even though I've been slaving to make this ranch the best damn Friesian stables in California? You *are* changing the will. Just not for *me*. You won't change it to accommodate my taking over and working it so it prospers after you're gone. How is that fair?"

"No one asked you to live your life here on the ranch," her father said. "You told me that was what you wanted to do. That was *your* decision. Heck, for all I know, Patti or Sharon or Kathy will want to work on the ranch after I die. All you're in it for is the money.

"Helen, I love this ranch. And I love my horses. I do this not for the money, but for the enjoyment I see on people's faces when they buy their first Friesian. The tears of joy running down their cheeks when they ride him for the first time. Their life's dream coming true because I made it so." He shook his head. "It's in my blood, Helen. But I think the only thing in your blood is a desire to make more and more money. That isn't what this ranch is built on, honey. And it shouldn't be the sole reason you're working here. That just ain't right."

Helen raked her hands through her hair. "So that's it? You're going to change the will for whatever bastard comes into this family and screw me, right?"

He got out of his chair again and stood in front of her, practically nose to nose. "Don't ever call my grandchild a bastard, do you understand me? Because if you do that again, you will find yourself locked out of this house. I plan to make provisions in my will for your children, too, Helen. If you have any. And if you don't, my attorney will take care of how the will is written. How he'll do that, I don't know right now. You'll just have to trust me on that. And it won't matter if my grandkids have fathers or not. They will still be a part of the Michaels family. And that's what's important to me." He walked around her toward the doorway. "And don't worry about working the ranch when I'm gone. It's just not in your blood."

Sharon joined her father. "I'll do it, Daddy."

He grasped Sharon's hand. "I always knew you would. Never doubted it."

Helen rushed out of the room and clomped up the stairs.

They all looked at each other in silence, wondering what the hell had just happened.

"This is all my fault," Kathy whispered.

"That's bullshit," Patti said.

"I concur," Sharon added.

"Don't be ridiculous, Katydid," Bill said. "This has nothing to do with you or my future grandchild. This is about Helen. I guessed she was like this, but she hadn't shown me her hand before, if you know what I mean. Life's a poker game, you know?" He walked through the doorway. "And Helen just folded."

# Chapter Twenty-Five

Later that day, Sharon discovered her father sitting in an ancient rocking chair on the front porch. "Are you okay, Daddy?"

"Just resting, honey. Don't worry 'bout me."

She sat across from him on the swing and kicked it into a slow rocking motion with her toes. "I hope you don't think I wanted any of this to happen."

"You mean about Kathy being pregnant?"

She chuckled. "No, Daddy. I really had nothing to do with that, silly. But I feel sorry for her. The way Charlie treated her is despicable. And Helen is being so mean-spirited about Kathy's situation."

"Yes, she is." He rocked back and forth, staring at the sunset. "If I could lay my hands on that guy, I'd choke the life outta him."

"Get in line, Dad," Patti said, settling next to her sister on the swing.

"Behind me, all of you," Kathy added, joining her two sisters and scooching into the corner next to Patti.

"So his reasoning behind having a relationship with you was all about getting revenge for me dumping him back in high school?" Patti said.

Kathy shrugged. "I think so, yeah. That's what he said. Oh, and he also said, 'Your sister paid for what she did to me back in high school.' I have no idea what he meant by that. Do you?"

Patti swallowed, but kept her face expressionless. She was not going to tell Kathy in front of Sharon and her father, right here, right now, that Charlie had raped her. "I have no idea. The guy's crazy, Kath."

"Talk about holding a grudge," Sharon added. "The man has a self-esteem problem with a whole lot of control issues mixed in."

"How do you figure?" her father asked, smiling at Patti and Kathy.

Sharon grinned. "Over the years, I've seen all your faces go blank when I start psychoanalyzing." She laughed out loud, which caused her sisters then her dad to join in. "Seriously. You think I never saw the looks on your faces when I'd get on my soapbox? I'm not going to lecture you this time. But," she held up a finger, "Charlie's statement that 'nobody dumps Charlie Seevers' shows classic narcissistic tendencies. On top of that, if he felt good about himself, he wouldn't be so ticked off that you dumped him, Patti."

Bill nodded slowly. "Sounds logical to me, Sharon." He pointed at her. "And I'm proud of you knowing all that psychology stuff. You're a very smart woman. Wonder where you got that from?" He grinned.

"Mom," the girls chimed in at once, then burst out laughing.

"I guess Mom's passion for psychology is in my genes," Sharon added.

"Then none of us should be surprised." He chuckled, then pushed himself up out of the chair. "I'm starved."

"I came out here to tell you dinner's ready," Kathy said.

"We have several clients scheduled for tomorrow afternoon, Daddy," Sharon said. "Should I reschedule?"

He waved his hand in the air. "Nah. You can handle them."

Sharon's eyebrows scrunched together. "Me? All by myself?"

He opened the screen door and turned back to face her. "You're perfectly capable, Sharon. You're my daughter."

"Could I join her?" Kathy asked. "I'd like to see how it's done."

Sharon grinned and clapped her hands. "I'd love that. It would be fun to have you there, Kathy."

"Great idea," their father added. "That way, if Sharon and I ever need your help, Katydid, you'll know a little bit about the business."

"Yeah, Kathy," Patti added. "You never know when Dad and Sharon might need us, and you and I don't remember much about the breed. It's been ten years since I've sat around and talked, quote unquote, horse. It would be a great time to reacquaint myself with their history and such."

"I'm up for that, too," Kathy added. "I just don't want anyone to think I want to run the ranch someday."

Bill nodded. "I understand." He glanced at Sharon. "We both understand. Sharon could take my place when I'm gone."

"Stop talking like that, Daddy. You're not going anywhere," Sharon said.

"I have a great idea," Patti cried. "Why didn't I think about this before now?"

"What is it?" her father asked.

"I'm a photographer. I could take some beautiful photos of the horses."

Sharon beamed. "And I could upload them onto our website. Great idea, Patti."

Kathy put her arm around Patti's shoulders. "Maybe I could incorporate Friesians into my video game."

"What video game?" her father said.

"Let's go inside and eat. I'll tell you over dinner," Kathy said.

Their father walked into the house, and Kathy followed him. Sharon and Patti hung back.

"I thought you were going to tell Daddy about your being pregnant, too."

Patti shook her head. "I got pregnant in mid-May, so I can't be more than a month along. I'm not in any hurry to give Dad a freaking heart attack."

"But it was a golden opportunity to get the truth on the table. Kathy's announcement could have segued into an announcement of your own. Daddy is obviously happy about having a grandchild, Patti."

Patti looked down then up into Sharon's eyes. "It's complicated, Share. More complicated than you can imagine." When Sharon found out the baby's father was Charlie, she was going to lose it.

Sharon grasped Patti's forearm. "Would you feel comfortable telling me about it?"

Patti nodded. "Yes, I will. Just not at this very moment. How about after dinner? Come into my bedroom, and we'll talk."

Their father sat at the head of the dining table, while the sisters ferried dishes from the kitchen. When everyone was seated, their father clasped his hands and glanced around the table, then bowed his head. His daughters followed his example.

"Dear Lord," he began, "bless this meal prepared by my

daughters' loving hands. Thank you for bringing us all together under the same roof to partake of this food. Forgive Helen her selfish ways. Help her to open her mind to other people's lives and situations. We are all so grateful that Kathy and Patti walked away from the car accident with only minor injuries. And I'm grateful I didn't have a heart attack, Dear Lord. Thank you for that, too. And I'll end this by saying a huge thank-you," he opened one eye and looked around at his daughters, then closed it, "for my first grandchild, who'll be arriving sometime next year. Amen."

"Amen," his daughters chimed together.

They passed dishes around—steaming vegetable lasagna, green beans, fresh garden salad, hot French bread.

"So," Kathy said, "it's been more than ten years since I've been around the horses. Can you explain a little about the breed again, so I'm not totally in the dark tomorrow when your clients arrive?"

Their father pointed at Sharon. "You're up, hon."

Sharon leaned forward in her chair and steepled her hands in front of her, fingertips touching her lips. "Okay, here goes. After listening to Daddy over the years, I know quite a bit about the breed, but certainly not as much as he does. Daddy, why don't you pretend to be a client and ask me a few typical questions?"

He nodded. "Can do, sweetheart."

"Okay." She cleared her throat. "Welcome to Fabulous Friesians." She smiled, glancing from her sisters to her father. "Our twelve Friesian horses—I think we have twelve now, right, Daddy?"

He nodded.

"Anyway, our twelve Friesian horses all flew here from Holland."

"They actually sprouted wings and flew here from Holland? Wow!" he said.

"Daddy! Stop."

"Just sayin'," he added.

Patti and Kathy chuckled.

Sharon rolled her eyes. "Okay. Our twelve Friesian horses were flown here from Holland—"

"When you say Holland, is that the same thing as the Netherlands?" he said.

"You really are making this hard for her, Dad," Patti said.

"I know, right? Cut her a break," Kathy agreed.

"These are the questions I get all the time, girls. Sharon's got to be prepared for everything if I'm not standing right next to her."

Sharon closed her eyes and launched into a seemingly well-prepared lesson about the Friesians, starting with their history in the Netherlands during the Middle Ages, when they were used in battle by knights in armor, to their near extinction, and finally, their return to popularity in both arena and trail work.

Sharon glanced at her father.

He smiled and clapped. "Good job, honey."

"You know, the trait I love the most about them is their personality," Kathy said.

"That's where they shine," Bill added. "They're gentle and docile and carry themselves with great presence." A slow grin formed at the edges of his lips. "You're better at this than Helen is, Sharon."

"Why do you say that?" Patti asked.

"Because Helen gets irritated by the constant questions. She expects clients who come here to already know about the breed, when in reality they often have seen one and love the look, but know next to nothing about them, whether they're appropriate for the type of riding they want to do and all that.

"But you, Sharon, have great patience. And empathy for people who want to know more about the breed, but might be hesitant to ask. You make it seem like you enjoy teaching them. That's a good quality." He pointed at her and winked. "You're good at this, honey."

Sharon's grin went from ear to ear. "Thanks, Daddy. It'll be fun to be included in this part of the transaction."

"What did you do before now?" Kathy asked.

"She's the one who shows the clients what it looks like to ride a Friesian in the arena. Your sister's an excellent equestrian."

Sharon blushed. "I love riding. Not competing, but simply riding."

He shoved himself up from his chair. "Now this old guy had better get to bed. I'm tired."

"Thanks for the lesson, Share," Kathy said.

"Yeah, I feel the same way," Patti said. "It's been years, and I'd forgotten so much."

"Thank you all. Let me settle you into bed, Daddy. I'll get you a glass of warm milk, if you like."

He laughed. "You treat me too well. I might just get used to all this pampering."

"You deserve it after everything you've done for us throughout the years, Daddy," Sharon added.

Patti and Kathy kissed their father on the cheek. "Night, Dad," they chimed in together.

He walked up the stairs a little slower than usual, and Patti frowned.

"What's wrong?" Kathy asked.

"He seems to be slowing down a bit from the last time we were here," Patti said.

"He just had a terrible fall, hit his head, and landed in the hospital. And he's past eighty now. He's still recovering," Kathy said.

Patti nodded. "I guess you're right. Gotta cut him some slack. I'm glad they didn't find anything wrong with him."

"I know. He just needs to be careful when he stands up so he doesn't get dizzy."

"You going to bed, or are you up to having a little conversation, Kath?"

"Sure. I'll be there in a moment," she said, then headed to her bedroom.

"Sharon?" Patti said.

Sharon turned and glanced at Patti.

"Come join us."

Sharon nodded.

# Chapter Twenty-Six

Kathy grabbed a fat, down pillow from her room and settled herself at the foot of Patti's bed, snuggling the pillow in her lap. Sharon followed soon after and sat in a rocking chair at the side of the bed. Patti sat cross-legged, leaning her back against the headboard.

"What's up?" Kathy said. "I know we've all been through a big ordeal, what with Dad's fall and the three of us in the hospital. I feel like I've been through the wringer. And your finding Dad on the floor must have been terrifying, Sharon."

She nodded. "I totally freaked out, seeing him lying there. I thought for sure he was going to die." Her bottom lip trembled.

Patti nodded slowly. She felt like a freaking bobblehead doll in the back window of a car. "I haven't been totally upfront with either of you about something." She turned to Kathy. "And I don't want you to be mad at me. I did what I did with the best intentions in mind. I wanted to help you out, but then it turned into—"

Kathy leaned over and grabbed her sister's hand and squeezed. "You do not have to go on and on with the prologue, okay? Just spit it out."

Patti covered her face with her hands and groaned, then dropped her hands into her lap, took a deep breath, then turned to Sharon. "I'm directing my explanation to Kathy, Sharon, but you'll understand why in a moment."

"I have no problem with anything that's going on here, Patti." Sharon gestured to Patti. "Go ahead. I'm here to listen, and I'll support you, no matter what."

Patti smiled, then looked at Kathy. "Knowing Charlie since he and I were together in high school, I couldn't believe he just ended your relationship without a word. It seemed so out of character to me. He wasn't like that when he and I were going out. Yes, I dumped him because I found out he was a player, but communication-wise, he was good at telling me about his feelings. And he readily admitted he cheated on me, so his behavior with you wasn't typical, in my opinion anyway." She took another deep breath. "Remember about a month ago, that night I phoned you and told you I'd met an old friend from the Institute?"

Kathy nodded.

"Well, I was headed to the beach, but on the way there, I looked over and saw Seevers' Yachts. Suddenly, I thought, okay, I'm going to go talk to him. I wasn't going to tell him about you being pregnant, or anything like that. I just got a bee in my bonnet, as Dad would say, and I walked over to see if he was in his office."

"You didn't," Kathy whispered, a look of horror on her face.

Patti tapped her sister's forearm. "No, wait, please. Let me finish, and I hope you'll understand. Trust me, okay?"

"Okay," Kathy said.

Patti continued. "He was happy to see me. He took me on a tour of one of his yachts, and we were sitting in the front room on this huge yacht way far away from the actual shop."

"I know the one you're talking about. It's gorgeous."

Patti tried to level her breathing, so nervous she was almost hyperventilating, not wanting Kathy to hate her for what happened. "He broke out a bottle of champagne and poured me a flute, and I told him he probably knew why I wanted to talk to him. I said you two had been dating for over a year, and I thought you guys were in love. He said… he said that…"

"He never was in love with me, was he?" Kathy interjected.

"Yeah, that's what he said, then that's all I can remember."

Kathy leaned forward, pressing her chest against the pillow in her lap. "What do you mean, that's all you can remember?"

"Literally, my lips started to tingle, and I blacked out."

"But why would…" Kathy covered her mouth with her hand. "He drugged you?"

Tears flowed down Patti's cheeks, dripping onto the comforter. She nodded. "I woke up several hours later in bed, naked. I could feel we'd had sex."

"That son of a bitch," Kathy said, eyes bright with unshed tears.

Sharon stood and sat down next to Patti and held her hand. "You poor thing. What a horrific experience. And you've been holding this inside you for the last month?"

Patti nodded.

Kathy's face was beet red, and she kept shaking her head. "I cannot believe he could stoop so incredibly low. But after his behavior yesterday when I was at his house, this doesn't come as a total surprise, Patti."

Patti fought back the tears. "He denied drugging me. He said I had raped *him*. That I was all over him after my second glass of champagne. I didn't have a second glass of champagne, and I did not rape him."

Kathy moved next to her sister and enveloped her in a hug. "Oh, my God. This is absolutely sickening. He accused you of raping *him*?" She pulled back to look into Patti's face. "Thank you for telling me this."

"I wasn't going to say anything."

"But why?"

"You told me you were through with him. That you didn't want anything more to do with him. You were finished with that asshat. And I shouldn't have meddled in something that was none of my business. And I'm sorry. I should have honored your decision and kept my nose out of it." Patti glanced down, then met Kathy's gaze straight on. "But now that we know what he's really like, who would want their child to have anything to do with a father who's a rapist?"

"I understand," Kathy said. "And I agree. I did tell you I wanted nothing more to do with him, and I wanted to raise this child on my own. I'm sick to my stomach that he did this to you, but now that I know what happened, I appreciate that you told me. And I feel good about my decision not to tell him about the baby. When I went to talk to him. I thought I'd give him a chance to make his own mind up about whether to be part of his child's life." Kathy looked at the ceiling for a few seconds. "Thank God I didn't say anything." She gently caressed her abdomen. "I know your intentions were good. You wanted to help me. I get that."

"So you don't hate me?" Patti swiped at the tears on her cheeks.

Sharon leaned over and rubbed Patti's back. "Of course Kathy doesn't hate you. You do know it wasn't your fault, don't you? He's the guilty party here, not you."

"She's right," Kathy added. "I love you. And… and…" She closed her eyes and shook her head.

"What? What're you trying to say?" Patti said.

Kathy glanced up at Patti, her face blotchy and flushed. "Right now, I am so angry, I want to kill him. Literally get a gun and shoot him."

Sharon sat on the bed between her sisters and crossed her legs, so the three of them formed a circle. She turned to Kathy. "You don't want to do anything that will ruin your life forever." Then she turned to Patti. "And neither do you."

Patti nodded. "I understand, Share. I truly believed I was handling the aftermath of the rape pretty well. But I realize that holding this inside me is making me literally sick. Last week, every time I'd see him in my mind's eye, I'd start feeling nauseous." She shrugged. "I guess I was in denial for weeks. But now, if I start obsessing about what happened, I'll throw up. Right in the middle of the day. It's not morning sickness either. And I dream of ways to get back at him for raping me, and for the way he treated you, Kathy." She huffed. "Mom would have had a field day with this, wouldn't she, Share?"

Sharon smiled. "She would indeed."

"Charlie shouldn't be able to get away with this," Kathy added. "In fact, isn't there something we can do? Report him to the police?"

"That's why I was gone for so long that night, Kath. I went to the ER in La Jolla and had a Sexual Assault Kit examination and talked to the police as well."

"Oh, my goodness," Sharon said. "You went through that ordeal all alone? All by yourself with no support from anyone?"

"Yes," Patti said, her voice quivering. "And the thing is, Charlie said it was consensual. That I came on to him, and we'd been drinking, and on and on. He knew damn well it would be a 'he said, she said' kind of a thing. My word against his. The receptionist at Seevers' Yachts greeted me, and I told her I wanted to talk to Charlie. Then when he saw me, he grabbed my hand and led me to that yacht. I'm sure it all looked really, really chummy. Anyone could have thought we were boyfriend and girlfriend."

Kathy grasped her sister's arm. "What if we could figure out some way to force him to admit the truth? Record his owning up to the fact he raped you? There's gotta be a way."

"If we literally forced him to admit what he did, it could be construed as coercion, Kathy," Patti said.

Kathy chewed at her bottom lip. "I was thinking more of something along the lines of… for example, he tells someone what happened that day, and he's being recorded, but he doesn't know it."

Patti shook her head. "Not admissible in court, I'm afraid. Not unless the person knows they're being recorded."

"Damn," Sharon said.

"Shoot," Kathy added.

"I got the results from the test for STDs, and it came back negative, thank God."

"What about a DNA test?" Sharon said.

Patti sighed. "Sergeant Kramer told me what would happen with the evidence. She explained that there's this database called CODIS- the Combined DNA Index System. It's the national, state, and local databases managed by the FBI that allows crime laboratory personnel across the country to compare DNA profiles from known criminal offenders with biological evidence from crime scenes. That takes more time to get the results back. And I'm still waiting for the results of what drugs they found in my blood, too. So, depending on all that, ideally I'd like to get an attorney and take him to court."

Kathy chewed at her lip for a few seconds then said, "For date rape?"

Patti shrugged. "Actually, date rape is a bit of a misnomer. It refers to rape committed by someone who's known to the victim, not necessarily someone the victim is on a date with."

"So you obviously didn't take the morning-after pill?" Sharon said.

Patti shook her head. "I know there are those that say the morning-after pill is not a form of abortion, but I disagree. I read all about the morning-after pill. It does three things: It temporarily stops the release of an egg from the ovary, prevents fertilization, or prevents a fertilized egg from attaching to the uterus. If my egg has met Charlie's sperm and been fertilized, well… in my mind, that constitutes a human being." She looked from Sharon to Kathy, then down at her folded hands. "I'm sorry if I'm offending either of you with my explanation, but that's what I believe."

Sharon patted Patti's forearm. "Makes sense to me, Patti. It's a woman's body and her choice regarding what to do with the baby growing inside of her."

Kathy nodded. "I agree with Sharon. It's my body and my life, and I didn't want an abortion. End of story."

Sharon smiled. "Or just the beginning."

"You know what makes me really sick? He told me I relished putting the condom on. Can you believe that?"

Kathy frowned. "He refused to ever use a condom when we were together. He said it covered his manhood and reduced his pleasure."

"Oh, brother," Sharon added. "Now I've heard everything."

Patti shut her eyes and burrowed into the down pillows at her back. "There's more."

Kathy's eyes grew wide. "You're kidding me. More? What could be worse than being raped?" She paused. "Did he sodomize you?"

Patti shook her head, glanced at Sharon.

Sharon smiled at Patti. "It's okay. Finish your story."

Patti shut her eyes for a few seconds, then looked directly at Kathy. "After our accident, the doctor came in to talk to me. He said I'm in good shape and… and so is…"

Kathy leaned closer to her sister. "And?"

"He said… he told me…" She swallowed. "That my baby is fine, too."

Kathy's face fell, and her eyes glazed over.

"I really didn't think I was pregnant, Kath, because I had a period soon after Charlie raped me."

Kathy covered her mouth with both hands, eyes bulging. She bolted out of the room.

The bathroom door slammed, and Patti and Sharon looked at each other.

"She's upset," Sharon said.

"She should be. Can you imagine finding out your ex-boyfriend raped your sister? This conversation is freaking surreal, unbelievable, and makes me want to puke, which is probably what Kathy's doing right now."

"That's what it sounds like," Sharon said.

The toilet flushed, then a few moments later, Kathy returned to the bedroom, sat between Patti and Sharon, and grasped their hands.

"I am so, so sorry he did that to you, Patti." She paused. "You're obviously not having an abortion."

Patti let out a long breath. "Not only do I not believe in it, but it's not this baby's fault she or he was conceived by rape. I'm keeping it." She paused, faced Kathy, eye to eye. "Do you hate me?"

Kathy closed her eyes for a moment, shaking her head. "Of course I don't hate you. This isn't your fault, and actually you and I are in the same position. We're each carrying a baby whose father is a total shithead. I agree, it's not the children's fault. But neither of the babies will be subjected to his twisted influence, because we can raise the babies as we choose without that bastard. In fact, he'll never know, right?"

"I'm not telling him." Patti paused, raised an eyebrow.

"What is it?" Sharon asked.

"What're you thinking?" Kathy said.

Patti sat up straight. "A plan."

Kathy's eyebrows drew together. "What? Kidnap him and make him confess?"

Patti grinned.

Kathy covered her mouth with her hand. "You're not serious."

"Kidnap him? No. Force him to confess? Yes, Kathy, I *am* serious about that part. That's exactly what I want. I think if we put our heads together, we can come up with a plan that won't put us in jail."

"Neither of you can afford to get caught by the police," Sharon said. "You'll both have children who will need you."

"You're absolutely right," Patti answered. "But deep down inside me, in my gut, I think he should pay for what he did to me. Not to diminish what he did to you, Kathy, because you know how I feel about that, but drugging me and then raping me?"

"That's a crime," Kathy added.

"For which he should do jail time," Sharon said.

"For which he'll probably never do jail time," Patti responded. "The sperm the doctor collected in the examination will come back as Charlie's. And to everyone around, it looked like he was my boyfriend. So, even if some sort of date-rape drug was in my blood, lots of couples use those drugs to enhance sexual experiences. I really think it's going to come down to my word against his. The DA isn't going to press charges, and no attorney is going to take my case."

Sharon grasped Patti's hand and squeezed. "But you have to try. The legal way, I mean. Revenge could put you right into jail… pregnant."

"She's right, Patti," Kathy added.

Patti looked down and shook her head.

"What?" Sharon and Kathy said at the same time.

"Revenge is a dish best served cold," Patti whispered.

"And just what does *that* mean?" Kathy asked.

"Well," Patti continued, "it's an old phrase that means revenge that's delayed and executed after the heat of anger has dissipated, is more satisfying than revenge taken as an immediate act of rage."

Kathy sighed. "So I'll ask you again. What does that mean, Patti?"

"My immediate feelings of rage have cooled down already." She looked from Kathy to Sharon and grinned. "Soon enough, Charlie Seevers will get what he deserves." She lay her head down on a pillow and curled into a fetal position.

Kathy and Sharon shared a look.

Kathy was the first to lean to the side and stuff her pillow under her head. "I don't think I'm going to like what you have planned."

Sharon lay on her back and brought her legs up. "My thoughts exactly."

# Chapter Twenty-Seven

Kathy opened her eyes and watched Patti sleep. She couldn't recall the last time they'd slept in the same bed. Probably when they were teenagers under this same roof. She turned onto her back, expecting to see Sharon, but she must have left sometime after Kathy'd fallen asleep. She stretched her arms above her head, the rays of early morning sun streaking across the bed. Her neck felt almost normal. She turned left then right without any cramping.

Patti mumbled something in her sleep, then her eyes popped open. "Whoa. You're still here."

"I guess Sharon left. I never woke up. Usually, I get up once during the night to pee, but this bed is so comfortable. I had a great sleep, and my neck's almost fine."

"Yeah, I feel pretty good, too. I have to think about getting back home. I called Robert, and he was very understanding. I was kind of surprised, being that I'm a newbie at the job."

"I never met him, but you've always said he treated you well."

Patti shifted onto her side and faced her sister. "He did. Until he left for San Diego and dumped my ass. But it wasn't like we fought about it or anything."

"He loved you?"

"He said he did, but he didn't feel our relationship was at the point where asking me to move down there with him was appropriate, and we surely weren't ready to get married. He thought it best to just cut ties completely."

"Makes sense, but that doesn't mean you weren't hurt."

"I *was* hurt. Terribly. He didn't even want to discuss it with me. I had absolutely no say in the matter. And I thought he was the one."

"And now?" Kathy said.

"We've had one lunch and one dinner together, and I just started working with him. We haven't been together long enough for me to tell what I'm feeling yet."

"You said 'yet.' That must mean something."

Patti sat up and leaned back on the pillow. "I don't know. I'm a mess, really. So many things have happened. Mom dies. I come here to the ranch and find out she was a lesbian. We discover Helen's conspiring behind our backs. I'm suddenly on good terms with Dad. I move to San Diego. Charlie drugs me and rapes me. We get in a car accident. I discover *I'm* pregnant with Charlie's kid. Helen shows her true colors to all of us, Dad included, after she calls the child you're carrying a bastard, and she leaves the ranch, and God knows what's going to happen with her. Now… drum roll… if I find out I can't take Charlie to court, I want you to help me exact revenge on him for raping me." She paused. "My mind is literally whirling so fast, I feel dizzy."

Kathy raised her eyebrows. "I really don't feel comfortable with this revenge thing, Patti. Did you dream up a plan for getting back at Charlie while you were sleeping? One that will not land us in jail, that is."

Patti scrubbed her face with both hands. "I don't know. On top of being emotional because I'm pregnant, it scares the crap out of me that I'm going to be a single mother. I feel so angry he did this to me. I don't regret deciding to keep the baby, but dammit, Charlie should have to pay for what he did. And it's never gonna happen the legal way, because I can't prove a damn thing. The DNA test will show it's Charlie's sperm, but so what? We had sex. And unless Charlie's a serial rapist, his DNA's not going to be found in the CODIS system anyway.

"And even if they find a drug in my system, that doesn't necessarily mean Charlie's the one who drugged me. It'll look like I took the drug so we could have extraordinary sex on that yacht. I need to think seriously about this, Kathy. Of course, I don't want to get caught. I want to pull it off without any hitches. I just want to hear him admit the truth. That's enough revenge for me, the bastard."

Kathy swung her feet onto the floor, stood, and faced her sister. "Then we're on the same page. Let's wait to see what the rape kit shows first, and if it's not enough for the DA to file charges against him, and therefore useless for you to hire an attorney, then… I'm good with planning a strategy that includes his admission of guilt. Not that I wouldn't like to chop off a certain part of his body."

Patti grinned. "When I was in the ER, I was thinking, am I the only woman he's ever done this to? Drugged and raped, I mean. I doubt it. I don't think rapists do that just once. He pulled it off perfectly. But now, his DNA will be in the CODIS system. I tried to do the right thing for any future woman who he rapes. I don't want any other woman to have to go through what I went through. It's just not right, Kath."

Kathy rubbed her eyes and yawned. "I completely agree. You weren't the first, and you probably won't be the last."

"In my mind, that's even more reason to exact some type of revenge, if I can't take him to court, that is. He should think twice about doing it again, and I'm hoping I can scare the crap out of him to the point he never does."

Kathy high-fived her sister. "Stop saying 'I this' and 'I that.' It's 'we' now. I'm in this with you, Patti."

"Really?"

Kathy nodded. "Yep. So both of us have to think long and hard about a way to pull it off, so we don't get caught. No hurry. As you said—what was that expression? Revenge is a dish best served cold? So we wait. And plan. Hey, I better call work. I told them I'd probably only be gone a couple of days. Sharon's here. All is well. I think we can probably leave soon."

Patti jumped out of bed. "Yep. I've got to shower, then make breakfast for everyone."

"What are you going to fix? All I ever see you eat is yogurt and granola in the morning."

"I'm full of surprises." Patti walked out of the room. "See you downstairs in a bit."

Two hours later, the breakfast dishes were in the dishwasher, their father was taking a nap in the front room in his rocking chair, and Patti and Kathy were packed and ready for their afternoon flight.

"Too bad the clients canceled," Patti said.

"I was looking forward to watching Sharon outdo Helen in front of Dad," Kathy added.

"I'll have to take pictures next time."

Patti and Kathy walked into the front room and stood in front of their father.

"He looks so peaceful," Patti whispered.

"I'm so glad he didn't have another heart attack or a stroke," Kathy said.

Patti winked at her sister. "Actually, I was kind of hoping he had, then we would have our money sooner."

Their father opened his eyes. "You're so full of you-know-what, Patti. I was never asleep. Just resting."

Kathy laughed. "We knew that." She glanced at Patti. "Didn't you?"

Patti nudged her sister in the ribs with her elbow. "Of course I knew he wasn't asleep. I think you have me mixed up with Helen."

Their father pushed himself out of the rocker and stood in front of them. "I'm feeling like my old self today. Fit as a fiddle."

"You have to take it easy, Dad," Patti said. "The doctor will tell you when you can resume your duties."

"I think I know how I feel, missy," he argued.

"Back to your old sassy self," Kathy said.

"Don't call me old," he replied.

Kathy reached out, and they embraced in a long hug. She kissed him on the cheek. "I'm sorry this happened to you, Dad, but I'm happy we could all be together like this."

"Twice. You were here in April, and now you're back again in June." He smiled. "I'll have to go to the hospital more often, if that's what it takes."

Patti reached for him and gave him a big hug. "I love you, Dad," she whispered in his ear. "And no more talk of hospitals. You stay out of those places, you hear me?"

"Yes, sweetheart. Anything you say."

Sharon appeared in the doorway. "Ready to go? Your luggage is in the SUV."

Their father followed them to the front door and waved as they drove away.

"He's feeling just fine," Sharon said, glancing at him in the rearview mirror as he closed the door. "I hope he takes it easy."

"I hope so, too," Patti added. "I'm glad I didn't tell him about what Charlie did and me being pregnant, though. It's just too much. I'm stressed out about it. He would have gone ballistic, which would be bad for his heart. Do you agree with me?"

"I do," Sharon said. "If you're only about a month pregnant, you can wait and tell him later, Patti."

"I agree," Kathy said. "And you know, from what we saw at the dinner table last night, you can handle his clients, Sharon. That should really help reduce his stress level."

"Good point, Kath," Patti added. "Too bad those people canceled today. I was looking forward to watching you do your thing, Share. Thanks for taking us to the airport."

The drive to the airport took only a few minutes, and before long, the two sisters were on the little puddle jumper for the first leg of their flight home. They arrived at Kathy's condo in the early evening.

Patti bent down and picked up the package lying next to the doormat. "I can actually say it feels good to be home." She walked through the front door. "It took me a while, but I'm beginning to love San Diego."

Kathy dropped her suitcase on the floor and stretched. "I knew you'd fall in love with this place. Who's the package for?"

Patti glanced down at the box and smiled. "Me."

Kathy peered around her sister's shoulder. "From the ranch? What?"

"Mailed it to myself."

Kathy's eyebrows drew together. "When did you have time to do that?"

"FedEx picked it up off the porch at the ranch yesterday. I still have an account with them at work. Had it sent here overnight."

"You got up after we all fell asleep?"

"Yep," Patti said. "Right after Sharon went to her bedroom. It wasn't that late. We fell asleep pretty darn early. You were out like a light."

Kathy shook her head. "I don't understand."

"Why you were out like a light?"

Kathy crooked her arm, cupping her hip with her palm. "Don't treat me like I'm stupid. Why did you mail something to yourself from the ranch, Patti?"

"I couldn't very well bring it with me on the plane."

"What the heck are you talking about?"

Patti grabbed scissors and cut through the miles of clear packing tape, then tore open the brown paper, revealing a small box.

"What is it?" Kathy said.

Patti put up her hand like it was a stop sign. "In due time, my dear, all will be revealed."

Kathy stood next to Patti, watching her open the box, then gasped. "Are you crazy?"

Patti pulled out a .357 Magnum and a small box of ammunition. She stretched out her arm as straight as an arrow and pointed the gun at the far wall. "You will tell us the truth, Charlie," she whispered.

Kathy shuffled backward until her legs met the couch, and she plopped down. "It's illegal to send a gun in the mail, isn't it?"

"I have no idea. I didn't declare that it was a gun when I filled out the form. I took a chance, I know. But I thought it was pretty unlikely anything would happen."

Kathy shook her head. "You never said anything about killing anyone."

Her sister flicked her eyebrows up. "I have no intention of harming anybody, Kathy."

"Wait a minute, Patti. I thought you agreed with me to take the time to think about any plan for revenge. That's what we talked about. Did you forget what we said?"

"No, I did not forget. But I've been thinking about something ever since it happened." Patti shrugged. "If I don't end up using it, then I have a gun for home protection."

Kathy gestured toward the gun. "Where the hell did you get that? Wait! Isn't that Dad's gun?"

Patti nodded. "Yessiree." She pointed it again at the wall. "I have a gun, and I'm not afraid to use it."

"Wasn't that from some movie?"

"I'm not sure which one, though," Patti replied. "I must be slipping."

"What do you plan to do with it?"

"That's for me—and you, if you decide to join me—to figure out." She dropped the gun into the box, closed it, then carried it to the stairs and walked halfway to the second floor. "As I said, all in due time, Sister. I promised to take my time to think about a plan, and I intend to do just that."

Kathy stared at the television without seeing it. "You're not going to harm anybody, right?"

Patti walked back down a few steps and sat on the stairs. "I promise you I am not going to hurt anyone. But you have to admit, a gun is pretty darn scary. How else are we going to make Charlie admit to anything, unless we hire some goons to do it for us?"

"That gun is registered to Dad, though, isn't it?"

"Actually, Dad told me years ago he got this particular gun illegally from a friend of his. The ranch is out in the middle of nowhere, and he didn't feel safe without one. It's not registered. Believe me, he won't miss it anyway. He acquired quite a few guns over the years. Plus, I have no intention of shooting anyone, so stop worrying your pretty little head about it, as Dad would say."

"Now you even *sound* like Dad. Good God, Patti. I think you've gone off the deep end." Kathy chewed on her bottom lip. "Seriously, if it involves a gun, what you've dreamed up for Charlie is a crime."

Patti joined her sister on the couch and nestled in the corner. "You're right. But I have not gone off the deep end. You're the one who was so pissed off and started all this talk about exacting revenge. I kept thinking about how he shouldn't be able to get away with raping me. He just shouldn't, Kath. I'm willing to take the chance I could get caught, but I doubt I will.

"And you don't have to be involved at all. I'm serious. I'm not trying to guilt-trip you into accompanying me in this endeavor. I don't expect you to do anything you feel uncomfortable with. And if you want me to promise you that it'll go the way I plan, and you won't get caught, then I'm sorry. I can't do that."

Patti leaned over and tapped Kathy on the knee. "I saw this movie once where this guy murdered this woman's little girl. So she got a gun, broke into his house, and waited for him to come home. And when he arrived, she surprised him and forced him to sit in a chair while she tied him up. She made him tell her why he murdered her daughter. And when he was finished, she shot him in the knees, then the arms, then ended it all with a bullet to his stomach. Believe me, I'm sure he wanted to die by then. She walked out, and no one could prove she'd done anything."

"So she got away with it?"

Patti nodded. "Yup."

"But what she did was a crime, Patti. And your plan involves a gun and who knows what else, and if Charlie reports us to the police, we could go to jail."

Patti nodded slowly. "Which is why you are under no obligation to join me. Though I intend to walk away from this leaving no evidence proving we did anything wrong."

"And you're not going to fire that thing, right?"

"I'm not planning to, no." Patti grinned. "I just want to see him squirm."

"But you already told the police about Charlie, and they're going to investigate him if they find his DNA from the Sexual Assault Kit, right?"

Patti rolled her eyes. "No, Kathy. They'll investigate him if they find his DNA is a match with any other rape that's in CODIS. Otherwise, like I said, during an investigation, they'll interview people who saw us that day and we looked like we were a couple."

Kathy nodded. "I get it. But won't they *know* it was you if you exact *any* revenge on him? I mean, it would be so obvious, right? I can't believe you, Patti. Do you actually have any concrete ideas about how you'd pull this off?"

Patti stood and walked into the kitchen. "I haven't a clue. I'm tired. I think I'll go to bed." She stopped at the bottom of the stairs with a Coke in her hand. "Think about a plan, Kathy. I'll need your input."

"As long as no one is hurt with that thing, I'll think about it. But I'm not promising anything yet," Kathy stated.

"Sometimes, I do my best thinking when I'm asleep. You oughta try it sometime. Tell yourself before you close your eyes tonight that you want to come up with a plan to put the fear of God in Charlie's soul." She paused. "And not get caught in the process," she added, grinning.

Kathy frowned. Some of her best ideas for the video games she created came to her in very vivid dreams. But this plan? She stared out the bay window for several seconds before grabbing a bottle of water, then headed off to bed with her computer.

# Chapter Twenty-Eight

Patti arrived at work the next morning at seven thirty, before Robert came in, giving her plenty of time to settle in, get a cup of coffee, and look through the client files. She'd just read through the first one when Robert entered their shared office.

"Good morning. How's your dad doing? You said on the phone it wasn't another heart attack or a stroke, but that you'd explain later."

"He's doing great. He had a drop in blood pressure when he stood up too quickly, which caused him to black out, like a head rush. He hit his head on the kitchen floor. How are things here? I'm sorry I had to leave you so suddenly without any notice. I apologize. Not a good way to start off our working relationship."

He bent down and kissed her forehead. "All is forgiven. It's family. I understand and support that."

She was more than a bit surprised that he kissed her. Thankfully, it wasn't on the lips, or she would have had a helluva time focusing on work. But even then, it was an unexpected gesture that she wasn't sure she was all that comfortable with. She'd just started working with him. What was next?

He grabbed a file off his desk and settled into his leather chair, leaning back while perusing the information. "We have a new client we're meeting today." He looked at his watch. "For lunch, actually. If he takes us on, his office will open in about eight or nine months. It will be the largest deal I've ever handled. That *we* will handle, that is. Exciting."

Patti did the math. Although she had yet to set up an appointment with a gynecologist, she surmised this deal would come to fruition around Christmas or early next year—about the time she would give birth.

"No comments?" he said, tilting his head. "This is something most people in your position would die for. What's wrong?"

She snapped out of her preoccupation with how best to handle the situation and focused her attention on him. "Sorry. It's just, I want to be up front with you. I've told you many times this job means a lot to me. I appreciate the fact you offered it to me, since we haven't been in touch in several years."

"Where is all this headed, Patti? It sounds like there's a 'but' coming."

She inhaled a deep breath and plunged into what she hoped wouldn't be an abyss, but rather, an opening for an honest discussion about her future at the La Jolla Photography and Media Group.

"I'm pregnant, Robert."

His brows scrunched together. "You're what?"

She sighed. "I didn't take this job knowing I was pregnant, so I wasn't trying to deceive you. I just found out when I was in the hospital after the accident."

He worked his lips back and forth for several seconds, still frowning. "I wasn't aware you were dating anyone. You neglected to mention that."

"Actually, I'm not seeing anyone, Robert. And haven't seen anyone seriously since you and I broke up two years ago."

He stared her down. "Immaculate conception, then?"

She pursed her lips. "No, not exactly."

He still had a confused expression on his face. She owed him the truth if they were friends and, in the future, perhaps something more.

"My sister Kathy had been dating someone for the last year or so. After my mom's funeral, he never contacted Kathy again. And she had absolutely no idea why." She paused. "You'll keep what I'm telling you in strict confidence, right? She never said it was okay for me to tell you."

"You can trust me. You know I'm not into gossiping. This is strictly a confidential conversation."

"Thank you." She grabbed a pen from her desk and fiddled with it. "She found out shortly after returning from Mom's funeral that she was pregnant with his child. But she had no intention of ever contacting him, because he obviously didn't want anything to do with her." She sighed. "I took it upon myself to go to his business, because

I wanted to talk to him. For Kathy's sake. She deserved to know why he left her so suddenly after they'd been together for a year. She was devastated and obsessing about it."

She leaned forward, elbows on her desk. "As an aside, I dated this guy when I was in high school. I thought he was a nice guy. Polite, good conversationalist, kind. Long story short, I discovered back then that he was a player, so I dumped him. Typical teenage stuff. Anyway, I went to see him at his business in La Jolla. We sat down to have a glass of champagne on one of his yachts, and he drugged me. I woke up several hours later in his bed."

Her lip trembled, tears imminent. "He raped me. But he denied it. Said *I* was the one who wanted to have sex. That it was consensual. The bastard even said I raped *him*." Tears flowed down her cheeks, and she swiped them away with her fingertips. "He also said he wore a condom." She shrugged. "Now here I am, pregnant with his child, with a new job, and I'll need to go on maternity leave about the same time as this possible future client you're telling me about will need us the most." She stared into his eyes. "Maybe I'm not the best candidate for this position. I want to give you the option of letting me go now. It might be best for the company."

He hadn't said one word during her explanation. He'd met her gaze eye to eye, expressionless, and hadn't interrupted her once. He was silent for almost a minute before she stood. "Maybe I should grab my briefcase and leave. I can see you're upset. And I don't blame you."

He reached out his hand. "Please, sit down."

She opened her mouth to protest, then plopped back down in her chair. It would only be polite to listen to what he had to say.

"I have no intention of letting you go. You're an asset to this company, and I have big plans for both of us here at La Jolla Photography." He sighed. "I'm assuming you reported this bastard to the police. Had a rape-kit exam. Hired an attorney."

Patti stared at the pen in her hands and twisted it round and round. "Yes, I went to the ER, and yes, the doctor did a Sexual Assault Kit examination. Thankfully, the first results showed he didn't give me an STD. The DNA and drug results could be finished any day now. In fact, I plan on calling the sergeant soon to follow up."

"Will they be able to charge him with rape based on the DNA and drug results?"

"Probably not. They'll see if his DNA has a match with other known rapists in what's called the CODIS system but—." She shrugged. "With regard to the drug he gave me in my drink, to those around us, I'm sure we looked like an ordinary couple. Ordinary couples have sex. Ordinary couples sometimes use drugs to enhance their sexual experiences. So if there's no match in CODIS, I don't think the DA will charge him."

"If I could get my hands around this guy's neck, I'm afraid I'd kill him. What's his name?"

"I don't think it would be a good idea for me to tell you."

"I'm not going to kill him. That would be foolish, and you know I'm not that type of person."

"I didn't think I was a vengeful person either, and I don't want you involved in my mess," she said.

"Meaning what?"

Patti stood, leaned on the desk with her fists, and looked Robert in the eyes. "I'd be willing to bet my next paycheck that the DA and any experienced attorney is going to tell me I don't have a chance in hell of winning a case against this guy, Robert. Like I said, we looked like we were a couple. He said we had consensual sex. He denies drugging me. He can still say we both wanted to have really great sex, so we took whatever drug they find in my system. There were no bruises. He didn't beat me up or anything."

She waved her hand back and forth. "Whatever, okay? If it comes down to the sergeant or an attorney telling me I won't win in court, then yes, I'm going to exact my own revenge on the bastard." She sighed. "But no way am I involving anyone else in this."

"But we're friends, Patti. And you're also my employee. And most of all, I care about what happens to you. This is a terrible thing you're going through. You shouldn't have to go through it alone either. And he shouldn't get away scot-free."

"My thinking exactly. Which is why I don't want you to have to lie about anything if the police ever got involved."

"What the hell are you going to do? You're carrying a child. You ought not to get involved in anything illegal. You're smarter than that."

She laughed under her breath. "You'd think so, wouldn't you? But revenge can be a very addicting drug. There's an appealing flavor to it that I've come to enjoy."

"You cannot do anything that might get you in trouble."

"I refuse to say anything more, Robert, on the grounds that it may incriminate you in the future, and I refuse to put you in a precarious position."

"Then you do plan on doing something illegal. Otherwise, you'd let me in on this. You're obviously not thinking along the lines of TPing his house. It must be much bigger than that."

She pursed her lips. "I can't say any more. Now, about my future here—"

"I'm not letting you go, Patti. But I do want to talk to you about this plan of yours."

"I have Kathy to discuss it with, Robert."

"Oh, that's just great." He smirked. "Another hormonal woman on the loose."

She let out an audible breath. "That's rather condescending, Robert."

He shut his eyes for a few seconds, then said, "I'm sorry. I shouldn't have said that. It was inappropriate. I'm just angry."

"Anyway, we're getting ahead of ourselves here. I don't have the final results of the assault-kit tests."

He walked around to her side of the desk and stood inches away, his eyes meeting hers. "I think you should see a counselor, Patti. You've been raped. Don't tell me they didn't give you tons of information and names of therapists to talk to about this. Perhaps if you talk about this with a psychologist, or someone else who's qualified to deal with this matter, you'll change your mind about seeking revenge."

Patti shrugged. "Yes, the doctor and the sergeant I spoke to advised me to see someone, but I chose not to. I'm fine, Robert. And if it comes down to my not being able to take this guy to court and win, then I'm afraid I can't let this go."

He grasped Patti by the shoulders and stared her down. "Please, do this for me. No, sorry, I mean do it for yourself. See a therapist. Please, Patti. Then, if you still feel like exacting revenge on this guy, I'll help you. I insist."

She dropped down into the chair, leaned her elbows on the armrests, and steepled her fingers, placing them under her chin. "Okay. I'll see a therapist." She looked up at him. "But if it doesn't help, which I'm sure it won't, then I'll do what I have to do. If it's necessary to do something outside the legal system, then so be it."

"I'm hoping therapy will wipe the need for revenge out of your head."

Patti shrugged. "I doubt it."

"I want to be there for you, Patti. Whatever you decide to do, I want to help."

"You can be so stubborn, Robert."

"And so can you. You said you'll see a therapist. That's a good thing. But if it doesn't change your mind, promise me that if you find out that proceeding with legal action is a waste of time, you'll tell me what you plan to do, so I can help you."

She looked away for a few seconds, then faced him. "I'll think about it. But I'm not promising you anything. Understood?"

He squinted at her and nodded. "Okay."

# Chapter Twenty-Nine

Within a week, Patti was able to get an appointment to see the therapist whose name was on one of the business cards Dr. Osborn had given her. She took the shuttle and walked two blocks to the therapist's office located on a quiet cul-de-sac. She found the numbers 1716 on a pastel pink mailbox and glanced up at the Victorian-style house. If ever there was a house that exuded peace and tranquility, it was this one.

A mint-green picket fence surrounded a small front yard with a heavily laden lemon tree on one side and what looked like a fig tree on the other. Several flower boxes hung from the edges of the roof covering the front porch, where a chair swing swayed in the mild ocean breeze. In the middle of the oversized front door, below a brass knocker, hung a feathered dream catcher.

Patti knocked softly, and within seconds, the door opened wide. An older woman, possibly in her sixties, slender, with bobbed silver hair, smiled and stepped aside.

"Patti?"

"Sandra Mangolin?"

"Please, come inside."

Patti entered the foyer and followed Sandra into a high-ceilinged front room.

"Sit wherever you feel most comfortable." She pointed. "That couch faces the front garden. Most of my clients find the view outside enhances concentration and focus."

Patti took a seat on the old-fashioned, purple velvet couch lined with plump pillows, and Sandra sat across from her on the matching couch.

Patti cleared her throat. "Thank you for squeezing me in. I know your practice is full, so I appreciate it."

Sandra crossed her legs and leaned back, a legal tablet across her lap. "Have you ever been in therapy, Patti?"

Patti shook her head. "No. I never felt the need for it." She looked at her hands folded in her lap. "Frankly, I've always dealt with any issues I had on my own. I never needed any help."

"What's different now?"

Patti looked Sandra in the eyes. "A friend of mine suggested I talk with a therapist." She shrugged. "I promised him I'd give it a try."

"What issue is bothering you?"

"I was drugged and raped by my sister's ex-boyfriend who used to be my boyfriend in high school."

Sandra tilted her head and met Patti's gaze eye to eye. "I don't know of many women who wouldn't feel better reaching out for a little extra help dealing with something like that, Patti. Being raped is a serious issue."

"And I'm not trying to diminish its severity. But it happened. I'm not trying to deny that. It wasn't my fault I was raped, but I shouldn't have put myself in that position—alone on a yacht with a man I hadn't been in contact with in years. I knew Charlie when we were teenagers. But my sister Kathy told me he'd changed."

"What do you mean by 'changed'?"

"I broke up with him way back when, because he was having sex with some other girl behind my back, but that was typical of the guys at our high school. I believed my sister when she said he'd grown up and was an upstanding guy."

"Do you have any idea *why* he did what he did to you? Did he say anything that, in retrospect, could have been a warning sign, or did this come out of the blue?"

Patti stared out the window behind Sandra.

Sandra continued. "I ask this because often women neglect what I would term their gut feelings. Instead of following their gut, they think intellectually that the man would never do something like force them to have sex. They don't want to believe the man they're with could possibly assault them. They think they know him, and they ignore their gut feelings."

Patti nodded. "I bumped into him at Starbucks a while back, and he told me he still had feelings for me. I explained to him I absolutely did not feel anything for him, and there was no chance in hell we'd ever get back together. So, yeah, I knew he was interested. But I stated my position unequivocally to him at the time. I didn't mince words."

"So what led you to meet up with him?"

"I wanted to talk to him. Tell him my sister deserved to be told why he'd dumped her so suddenly. I wanted to ask him why he'd treated her like crap. He owns a yacht business, and when he took me on this yacht to show me around, he was relaxed and happy. I had absolutely no idea he intended to slip me some sort of roofie. One minute I was talking, and the next minute I woke up next to him, naked, in his bed."

Sandra scribbled on her notepad, then looked up. "What did you do then?"

"After he told me I was the one who'd initiated sex and raped *him*, I told him he was full of shit, and I got dressed and ran out of there as fast as I could."

"Did you go to the Emergency Room?"

"I did. I wanted an examination for being sexually assaulted, and they tested me for STDs, took all kinds of forensic evidence."

"Did you take the morning-after pill as well?"

Patti shook her head. "I know this may sound old-fashioned, but I don't believe in abortion or any drug that kills an embryo."

"That's not old-fashioned thinking, Patti. It's your belief, and there's nothing wrong with taking that stance on abortion and the morning-after pill."

"So you understand my point of view?"

"I'm here to listen to you, and yes, I understand. Your stand on abortion is valid and real. It doesn't matter what anyone else thinks." She paused. "So are you pregnant?"

"Yes, I am, but luckily I don't have an STD."

"And are you taking that man to court?"

"I'm still waiting for the police to get back to me to determine whether they find his DNA in the CODIS system, and also what drug he gave me." Patti shrugged. "It really will depend on whether I can win the case."

"Have you considered adoption, or do you plan to keep the child?"

Patti smiled. "Yes, I'm keeping my baby. And since my sister Kathy is pregnant, too, I have support. It'll be fun, actually."

"So, Patti, what brings you here? You obviously promised your friend you'd come and see me." Sandra smiled.

Patti stared at the bright yellow lemons hanging from the tree and thought they looked like oversized Easter eggs. "My friend thinks my need for revenge is unhealthy and dangerous." Her eyes met Sandra's. "What normal human being wouldn't want revenge for being raped? I don't believe I'm unusual because I want Charlie to pay for what he did to me."

"Of course you're not unusual," Sandra replied. "Wanting him to pay in some way for raping you is a normal reaction. But I'm sure what your friend is probably worried about is this. Is your need for revenge taking over your life? Is it all you think about to the point that it's impacting your daily activities in a negative way? Is it hindering you from entering into another relationship? Are you considering doing something that may ruin your life and the life of your child?"

Patti nodded slowly. "I get what you're saying, and no, it's not something I think about all the time. I have my work, and I love living with my sister Kathy. We've always gotten along, and it's great to be close to her again, like we were when we were younger. So, no, it's not impacting my life in any negative way. And I'm enjoying being around this male friend of mine again, who used to be my boyfriend years ago. To tell you the truth, I don't know if anything will happen between the two of us. But I like him a lot. I think I'm open to the possibility of having a relationship with him again."

"And the last point I mentioned? Are you considering doing something illegal or dangerous to you and your baby?"

Patti let out a sigh. "If I find out it's not worth taking this guy to court for drugging and raping me, what am I supposed to do? Just go on with my life as if it never happened? I don't think that would be right, Ms. Mangolin."

"Please, call me Sandra."

Patti nodded. "The thing is, Sandra, I went to *his* place of business. I asked to meet with *him*. I let *him* hold my hand, and I walked willingly to an empty yacht in front of hundreds of people. It looked like we were a couple. Even if a date-rape drug is found in my blood, lots of couples voluntarily take them for fun. I looked it up on the Internet, and some drugs pass through your system quickly, others not. So in the end, it may result in a case of 'he said, she said,' and I'd lose. This man is an upstanding citizen in the San Diego and La Jolla areas, for God's sake. I'm a newcomer who sought *him* out."

Sandra leaned forward. "So, Patti, if you're not able to take this man to court for drugging and raping you, what will you do?"

"I hate him," she shouted, then covered her mouth with her hand. "I'm so sorry," she whispered.

"Nothing to be sorry about. These walls are well insulated, and no one's around anyway." Sandra paused. "You're obviously very angry."

"You're damn right I'm angry. That son of a bitch raped me. I will not be a victim."

"Isn't there some way we can talk about this feeling of revenge that's consuming you? We can work on a healthy way for you to deal with your anger, reframe your thinking to deal with what happened to you in a constructive way. A way that doesn't ruin what sounds like a very bright future."

Patti laughed. "If what you're suggesting is for me to forgive him in my heart... since I'm the one who's suffering the negative consequences... then no, I can't forgive him."

Sandra nodded. "Patti, I think you and I can talk about your feelings and find a way for you to choose to relate and react to those feelings in a healthy manner."

Patti set her elbows on her knees and cupped her face in her hands. "I was watching a video the other day. This woman had survived one of Hitler's death camps. I think it was Auschwitz. She was one of Dr. Mengele's guinea pigs. He gave both her and her twin sister some drugs for one of his sick experiments. Later in her life, she looked him up, along with one of the guards whose job was to watch through a peephole while the Jews were gassed and write out death certificates when they were finally lying on the floor, dead.

"Do you know what she did? She decided the only thing she could do to rid herself of the bitterness and sadness in her life from that terrible situation was to forgive both Mengele and that prison guard. That was the only decision she could control, and she latched on to that and forgave them in her heart to be free of those toxic feelings."

Sandra lifted her eyebrows. "That's exactly what I'm referring to when I say that you can get to a healthy place, Patti."

Patti smiled. "I'm telling you that story because that is most definitely *not* something I can do. I don't forgive Charlie for what he did to me. I'll never forgive him. I'm not one of those people who believes forgiving him will make me all happy inside and free of any negative feelings having to do with the night he drugged and assaulted me." She shook her head slowly. "No fucking way will I ever forgive that bastard for what he did to me."

"You don't want to spend your life consumed with negative feelings, Patti. It's not good for your emotional health nor that of your child."

Tears dripped down Patti's cheeks. She'd thought about this before coming to see Sandra. She'd looked it up on the internet. If a psychotherapist determines that a patient poses a serious danger to another, the therapist must use reasonable care to protect the potential victim. Patti had to watch what she said or she'd be in serious trouble.

Patti took a deep breath. "Yes, I hate him. But will I actually do anything to harm him? No. I can promise you that. And I'm in no danger of harming myself either. I'm just really angry. If I can't take him to court and win, I'll make another appointment with you to deal with all these negative feelings."

Sandra leaned back into the cushions of the couch and looked Patti in the eyes. "I'm glad you're not planning on doing anything that will hurt you or your child's future or anyone else, Patti."

"I'm just venting."

"Of course you are. And that's perfectly natural, Patti. There's nothing wrong with that. It's only when you act on those feelings in a way that's harmful to you or someone else that you need to think very carefully about. You can learn to reroute those feelings into something that will make you a stronger individual. Believe me. I've seen it happen over and over again, right here in this room, Patti. You can do it, too."

"I know I can, Sandra. Verbalizing my feelings today has helped me get in touch with what I plan to do if I can't take this guy to court. I'll come back to see you." She stood. "Thank you for talking with me."

Sandra stood and reached out, taking Patti's hand in both of hers. "I hope it works out in your favor, Patti. But no matter what, I'm here for you. This is a safe place for you to air your thoughts and feelings, whatever they are. My clients who have been through a similar experience have all gotten through it, Patti. With help and guidance, so can you."

Patti squeezed Sandra's hand. "Good to hear. I've enjoyed talking to you, I really have."

Sandra nodded and walked to the foyer, then turned. "Good luck, Patti."

Patti grasped the front doorknob. "Thank you."

She walked to her car, deep in thought. She was glad Robert had suggested she talk to someone. The therapy session had helped to solidify her thoughts. Not in the way Robert had wanted, she was sure of that. And not in the way Sandra envisioned either. If it came down to exacting revenge, she had no intention of returning to chat with Sandra about her plan. And she surely would not ask Robert to be involved in any attempt to get back at Charlie. It would be selfish. It wasn't his business. Yes, he was her friend. A friend who could be more, if she was honest with herself. And friends didn't put their friends in harm's way.

*Shit. I have to call Sergeant Kramer right now and find out the results of the rape kit.*

# Chapter Thirty

When Patti came through the front door of the condo, Kathy was sitting on the couch with her computer in her lap.

"How's work? How's Robert?" Kathy smiled. "Maybe more importantly, how are you and Robert?"

Patti slumped down on the couch across from her sister. "I have to tell you something."

Kathy nodded. "Go ahead. I'm all ears."

"Last week, I told Robert all about Charlie."

Kathy's eyebrows shot up. "About me or about you?"

"Both." Patti looked at her sister, gauging her reaction. "He was talking to me about a possible client who will need us in about eight or nine months. I wanted to be honest with him about my situation, so I had to tell your story first, so I could explain my story about visiting Charlie and what happened. I know I should have asked for your permission first, but I didn't see any way around telling him the whole truth once I started."

Kathy shrugged. "It's okay. If it ever gets to the point where Robert comes over here, he's going to know I'm pregnant and ask me who the father is. I could always lie, but it's the twenty-first century. Lots of women are single mothers. How did he react when you told him about Charlie, uh, taking advantage of you?"

Patti rolled her eyes. "As awful as that experience was, Kath, you can call it what it is. He didn't take advantage of me. He raped me. He committed a crime. Straight and simple. I can handle dealing with the truth."

"I was just trying to be sensitive of your feelings. It can't be fun bringing up the subject."

Patti looked down and rubbed her abdomen. "I'm reminded of the incident almost every waking moment. My body's already changing.

My breasts are very sensitive, and I'm hungry all the time." She nodded at her sister. "What about you? How's the morning sickness?"

"Almost gone. I made an ob-gyn appointment for both of us. We can go together."

Patti smiled. "Thank you for doing that. One less thing on my to-do list."

"You didn't say anything to Robert about our plan, did you?" Kathy said.

"*Our* plan?"

Kathy nodded. "Yes, our plan. But only if you can't take Charlie to court."

"About that," Patti said.

"You got the results from the rape kit, didn't you?"

Patti's eyes burned with oncoming tears, and she blinked them away. She shook her head and took in a huge breath. "There was no match in the CODIS system. The drug results didn't show anything conclusive for any date-rape drugs either."

"What does that mean exactly? Were there other drugs in your system?"

Patti shook her head. "The sergeant explained to me that there are new drugs coming onto the street almost every week from overseas and Mexico and Colombia. The labs can't even keep up with them. Charlie could have gotten hold of some new drug off the Internet, or from friends who like to party."

"Are you going to contact an attorney?"

Patti closed her eyes for several seconds. "Why bother? I talked to the sergeant for a long time on the phone. She was so nice and informative. She's had a lot of experience with this, because the entire San Diego area is so close to the Mexican border, which gives rapists easier access to new kinds of date-rape drugs. She said the evidence would not give me a slam-dunk case against him by any means."

"Did they ever bring him in or talk to him?"

"When Sergeant Kramer left the ER that day, she went straight to Charlie's house. He didn't deny being with me or having sex with me. He also didn't deny that he'd gotten a drug from a friend who dealt in Ecstasy-type pills and such. He didn't recall the name of the drug. He said I took it willingly and that we had sex over and over during the hours I was with him on the yacht. He explained the connection we had in the past and then elaborated and said we also had a current connection because you were his girlfriend. He said I was jealous of your relationship with him, and I wanted him back."

"That freaking bastard," Kathy whispered.

"I know, right? He said I've been showing up at his house almost every day since then, begging him to get back with me."

"Oh, my God. What a lying asshole."

"Yup."

"I have a pair of handcuffs," Kathy said. "Maybe we can use them. Have you already concocted a plan?"

"Wait a minute. Why do you have a pair of handcuffs? Or do you feel uncomfortable telling me about your secret sex life?"

Kathy chuckled. "It's not what you're thinking. I got them from a cop friend of mine years ago for a Halloween party. I never gave them back to him. He moved out of the area. But I still have them. In the attic, I think."

"Handcuffs could fit into my plan. Then again, it's not like I've ever done this sort of thing. I've seen a couple of movies involving kidnapping and home invasions, though. Once the prisoners are wrapped up with duct tape, there's not much they can do. Or you can use tie wraps."

Kathy nodded slowly. "Okay."

"I don't plan for us to be there very long. And we won't leave him alone. I'm sure I'll think of other things we have to watch out for." She raised an eyebrow. "I was thinking maybe next week?"

Kathy's mouth dropped open. "That soon?"

"I see no reason to wait. We'll arrive at his door. He'll let us in, and—"

"And if he doesn't?" Kathy said.

"Then we do a home invasion." Patti paused. "Does he have security cameras?"

Kathy laughed. "He said the house he's planning on buying in La Jolla will certainly have them, but his current house? Nah." Kathy wagged a finger at her sister. "Wait! There's a double-hung window in his bedroom with a lock that's missing. All we do is slide it up, and voilà. We're in."

"So, if he won't let us in, we take him by surprise," Patti said.

"We'll surprise him no matter which way we get into his house, Patti. He won't be expecting us."

"You're right. Either way, we'll have the upper hand with the element of surprise. I think he'll let us come in the front door, though, if we play it right."

Kathy nodded. "What're we going to say to get him to let us in the house?"

"Hmmm." Patti shut her eyes for just a few seconds. "That we want to bury the hatchet. Start fresh. Wipe the slate clean."

Kathy laughed. "Kind of like, why can't we all just get along?"

"Something like that," Patti agreed. "Kathy, you do not have to accompany me on my mission of revenge. No pressure."

"I don't want to get caught."

"Well, I can't promise you that, Kathy. I don't know how this thing is really going to play out. In case something goes wrong, I don't want you to regret your participation."

Kathy was silent for a bit, then said, "I know that, but I want him to pay, too, Patti. If the DA doesn't have enough evidence to charge him, and if you can't take him to court, then we'll do this ourselves. I think the enormous satisfaction I'd get from listening to him beg would be worth it."

"If it comes down to that, you'd want him to beg?"

"I can hear him now. 'Please let me go, Kathy. I promise I'll do anything you want. Please don't hurt me.'"

Patti chuckled. "I can't picture it."

"Then what would you want out of it?"

"An admission of guilt. When you think about it, Charlie would never admit under oath to drugging and raping me. But in front of me while I'm holding a gun? He just might. I want him to admit we did not have consensual sex and that he drugged me and then raped me." She paused. "I'm afraid I'll have to scare the shit out of him in order to get that confession, however."

Kathy shook her head. "I agree with you that even if an attorney wanted to proceed with trying to prosecute him, Charlie would deny it until the day he died. But after seeing how he acted when I visited him last, so arrogant and self-centered and just plain mean, I can't picture him acquiescing just because we tie him up and point a gun at him either."

Patti frowned. "So you don't think I'd get him to confess to anything?"

"Let's say you threatened him with that gun. Do you really think he's going to believe you'd use it? I don't think so. He'd call your bluff. Then what would we do?"

"Start with a bullet to the leg?" Patti shrugged. "I don't know."

"A bullet to the leg? What if he bleeds out and dies? That would be murder, Patti. You said you weren't going to shoot that gun."

"I know. I know. I'm not going to fire the damn thing." Patti stood and paced back and forth in front of the bay window. "Maybe something more along the lines of torture."

"You can't be serious. Who do you think you are? Jack Bauer from *24*?"

Patti laughed out loud. "Not that type of gross stuff. But think about it, Kathy." She lifted her index finger in the air. "I buy lots, and I mean lots, of duct tape. We tape him to a chair, force him to sit there for as long as it takes. And we wait. Until we get what we want. We wait for him to break."

"You think he'll break? He's terribly stubborn. When he wants to get his way, he succeeds."

Patti tapped her finger to her lips. "But we'll have the upper hand. He'll feel as helpless as he made me feel when I woke up and realized he'd raped me. As helpless as you felt when you discovered you were pregnant and he'd already dumped you. Now you're going to be a single mom, and you'll have no help from him as a father for your baby. The word for having no help, Kathy, is helpless. And he did the same to me. I want him to feel as helpless as he's made us feel."

"Okay. So he feels helpless," Kathy retorted. "What if he refuses to confess to anything? You'd really risk shooting a .357 Magnum in his quiet neighborhood? I don't think so."

Patti laughed. "A silencer?"

Kathy huffed out a breath. "Are you serious?" She slapped the couch cushion. "You're not going to buy a silencer. And anyway, is there such a thing as a silencer for a .357 Magnum?"

"All right. All right." Patti stopped pacing and faced the window. "If I can't get a confession out of that bastard, I guess I'll have to settle for knowing we had the upper hand for the evening and made him feel helpless. That'll have to be enough for me. Although I *do* want more."

Kathy joined her sister near the window.

Patti turned to Kathy. "What're you thinking?"

"Something's stuck in the back of my mind." Kathy patted her head with her palm. "Something he told me once that… wait! Wait! I know what it is." She grinned. "He once told me that when he was a kid, his father took him hunting. He put a rifle in his hands and forced him into the woods and told him he had to bring home their supper for that evening."

Kathy started pacing, biting at her bottom lip. "It's coming back to me. Just a minute," she mumbled. "Charlie asked what was he supposed to shoot, and his dad said a rabbit. Charlie had a pet rabbit, and his father knew how he felt about that rabbit. Charlie named him Bun-Bun." She waved her hand back and forth. "So Charlie was thinking there was no way he'd be able to kill a rabbit, but his father forced him to aim and shoot." She paused.

"Did he do it? Did he kill the rabbit?"

Kathy stopped. "No, he did not. And he knew what the repercussions would be for his defiance, too."

"His father beat him?"

"To within an inch of his life, he told me. Charlie never forgave him. He said he felt so helpless. His father forced him to lie across his bed and whipped him with his belt. Charlie was helpless, humiliated, angry. And there wasn't a damn thing he could do." Kathy nodded slowly. "He told me he'd never touch a gun or a rifle ever again. He's scared to death of them. He dropped the gun and ran home. And when his father made it home, that's when the beating started. So for Charlie, guns bring up a lot of fearful memories." She shrugged. "So maybe your plan could work after all, Sis."

Patti gave Kathy a high five. "Tomorrow, I'm taking a drive out of this area to a hardware store I found on the Internet in the small town of San Jacinto. I'm going to pick up some duct tape, scissors, surgical-type gloves, and anything else I think we'll need."

Kathy hugged her sister. "I'm sorry it didn't work out the way you wanted as far as taking him to court." She pulled back and looked Patti in the eyes. "But I'm here for you. And I'll be right next to you when we go to Charlie's house."

Patti smiled. "I know you will. And I love you for voluteering. But if you want to change your mind, no hard feelings, okay?"

"No hard feelings." Kathy paused. "But I'm not changing my mind. Even though this whole thing scares the crap out of me."

Patti nodded. "I know."

# Chapter Thirty-One

After several days of lunches and dinners at fancy restaurants, Patti felt as if she'd gained at least twenty pounds. Kathy had scheduled an obstetrics appointment for both of them for the thirtieth of June, so they could accompany each other during their examinations. They'd both taken Friday morning off to take care of baby business.

"Kathy Michaels?" the nurse announced.

Patti followed her sister into the examination room. After taking Kathy's temperature and blood pressure and extracting two vials of blood, the nurse told them Dr. Holmer would be in in a few moments.

"How'd you find this doctor?" Patti asked.

"Someone at work recommended him. I've been seeing him since I moved here, so about eight or nine years."

"That's right. You moved down here shortly after Mom and Dad got divorced."

Kathy glanced around the room, then focused her attention on the poster of a woman's reproductive system. "It's always amazing to me how a baby can live in a sac in your belly for nine months, then suddenly its new home is the world."

Patti stared at the poster. "Amazing isn't the word I'd use." She stood directly in front of the picture. "Every time I think of giving birth, do you know what movie comes to mind?"

"I'm afraid to ask. My first guess would be *Nine Months* with Hugh Grant and Julianne Moore."

Patti laughed out loud. "That movie was so funny. Especially the part where Robin Williams plays the cameo scene as a Russian gynecologist. Totally makes me roll on the floor laughing."

Kathy howled, then covered her mouth. "Oh, my God. Remember that part where he says he'd worked as the head of obstruction, and then Hugh Grant says, 'Don't you mean obstetrics?' Man, Robin Williams was so funny!"

Patti felt her stomach clench. "He made me laugh so hard."

They heard a knock on the door, then Dr. Holmer's head popped in. "Good morning," he said, walking to the sink and washing his hands. He turned toward them, drying his hands with a paper towel. "Is this your birthing coach, Kathy?"

"My birthing coach and my sister, Doctor. In fact, she's your next appointment, and I'm going to be *her* birthing coach."

His eyebrows flew up into the deep brown wisp of bangs hanging in his eyes. "Both of you at the same time? That should be fun. Dual baby showers. Kids who get to play with each other. Built-in babysitters."

Kathy laughed. "As a matter of fact, both babies were fathered by the same man."

He sat on the leather stool and rolled closer to the table. "I don't know if I should even ask how that happened, ladies. Of course, it's none of my business."

Kathy's face turned slighter pinker than normal. "It's too long of a story to tell, Doctor, but we thought you should know. He was originally my sister's boyfriend way back in high school, then he and I became close this past year or so. His relationship with Patti's a bit more complicated, but…"

He stood. "It's okay. No need to share." He pulled a pair of sterile gloves on and helped Kathy lie back on the table. "I'm going to do a complete pelvic examination. While you're dressing, I'll take a look at your blood and urine. I'll meet you in my office across the hallway. Then we can talk. All right?"

Kathy nodded and stared at the mobile hanging from the ceiling. Blue whales, pink flamingos, white elephants, all slowing spinning in carousel fashion from the AC circulating through the room. She smiled. *I'm having a baby.*

Doctor Holmer finished the examination, then he left the room while she redressed. She and Patti walked across the hall to his office and waited. Within moments, he returned and sat behind his shiny mahogany desk.

He signed on to his computer. "Well, you're definitely pregnant." He looked up at Kathy and smiled. "Your due date is calculated by adding two hundred and eighty days, or forty weeks, to the first day of your last menstrual period. So when was that, Kathy?"

Kathy looked at Patti. "I remember looking at the calendar the day after you went out to lunch with Robert."

"That was at the end of May. After I met up with Charlie at the yacht."

Kathy nodded. "That's right. I remember now. Sorry, Dr. Holmer. I should have looked at the calendar before coming in. But I recall my last period was March fifteenth. I had sex for the last time the day before I flew up to Alameda, right before my mom died, so March twenty-eighth. That must have been when this child was conceived."

Dr. Holmer typed on his computer. "Okay, then. The first day of your last period was March fifteenth. Hold on a few seconds."

Kathy glanced at Patti and smiled. Her stomach was in knots with anticipation.

"Now remember," Dr. Holmer said, "this is only an estimate. Your baby is due around December twentieth."

Kathy clapped her hands. "Yay! A Christmas baby. What a great gift for myself. This is exciting." She turned to Patti. "I can't wait to find out when you're due."

Dr. Holmer cleared his throat. "You're young and in good health, Kathy, so I'd like to schedule prenatal visits once a month for weeks four to twenty-eight, then every two weeks for weeks twenty-eight to thirty-six. For weeks thirty-six to forty, once every week. You can schedule those with Megan on your way out." He leaned back. "Any questions before I go on to my next patient?" He glanced at Patti and winked.

Kathy shook her head. "Not at the moment, but I'll write down anything that comes to mind and ask you next time."

Megan appeared in the doorway.

"Patti, why don't you and Kathy follow Megan into the exam room, and I'll be there shortly?"

Within ten minutes, Dr. Holmer entered the room where Patti lay on the table. Following the examination, they once again met back in his office.

He smiled at both of them. "This feels like déjà vu." He sat up straight and glanced at his computer. "Now for you, Patti, given you said the first day of your last menstrual cycle was April eighteenth, correct?"

"Technically. yes. The last time I, uh, had sex," she said, glancing quickly in Kathy's direction, "was May fifteenth. A few days later I had a light period, which lasted for only two days, which isn't normal for me."

"We'll go with the April eighteenth date and, once again, this is an estimate, Patti, especially since you had a period in May. So, your due date would be January twenty-third."

"Thank you, Dr. Holmer. It will be a new year with a new baby. I'm psyched."

"Just like your sister here, you're in great health, Patti, and you can schedule your visits on your way out. Do you have anything you'd like to ask me?"

Patti inched closer to the doctor's desk. "Do people our age, I mean, we're both in our early thirties... do you find more complications than if we were both, say, in our early twenties?"

He chuckled. "Don't get me wrong. I'm not laughing at your question. This issue engenders great debate amongst obstetricians. I could sit here and quote statistics and cite results from hundreds of published papers by well-known doctors. The one thing I've found in my, what," he glanced at the ceiling, then looked at Patti, "more than thirty years of practice, is this..."

Elbows on the desk, he steepled his fingers. "Age and maturity do not always rise proportionally, and some women in their early forties may be healthier than their twenty-something counterparts, thanks to excellent lifestyle habits. Everything depends on the woman's health, energy, personality, and perspective on life. But no matter how old you are, there are steps you can take to boost your odds of having a healthy and happy experience.

"Have Megan give you a couple of pamphlets I've written, which I distribute to all my patients, no matter their age. Continue to stay healthy and active with a positive mind-set, and you and your child should enjoy a wonderful life together."

Kathy reached out and grasped her sister's hand. "This is all good news, Dr. Holmer. Thank you for seeing both of us today."

Patti leaned over and shook his hand. "Yes, thank you so much. I look forward to seeing you again, Dr. Holmer."

He stood, shook Kathy's hand, and followed them through the doorway, where they said their goodbyes. After scheduling a slew of appointments, they walked out into the typical lovely, breezy, and warm San Diego day.

Kathy stopped. "Wait! You never told me what movie reminds you of what it's like to be pregnant."

Patti glanced at her sister and laughed out loud. "You won't like it."

"Just tell me and get it over with."

"Okay," Patti said. "Ever seen the movie *Alien*?"

"Sigourney Weaver, right?"

Patti nodded. "Remember the part where the guy's eating and suddenly chokes so they lay him right smack-dab in the middle of the dinner table, and he's writhing around, making these horrible noises, and suddenly a miniature alien pops right out of his chest, splattering blood all over everyone around him?"

Kathy's eyes bulged. "That's what pregnancy means to you?"

Patti shrugged. "You asked."

Kathy shook her head, then grabbed her sister's arm. "Shall we celebrate with lunch?"

Patti looked at the time on her cell phone. "I have about two hours before I have to meet Robert at the office. We're having dinner with a new client today."

"Lucky you. You're becoming a font of information with regard to where to eat to impress around here."

Patti patted her abdomen. "If I don't watch it, I'll blow up like a freaking hot-air balloon before my little alien is due. Watching your weight is critical to having a healthy pregnancy, you know."

Kathy rubbed her stomach. "I could stand to lose ten pounds. What am I going to do to pull that off?"

"Listen to Dr. Holmer, and he'll keep you on a healthy path to giving birth. I like him a lot."

"I knew you would. He came highly recommended as one of the premier ob-gyns in the area, and his bedside manner is so upbeat. He really listens when you talk to him, unlike some doctors who can't wait until you stop talking so they can go on to the next patient."

Patti glanced up and down the street. "Where shall we eat? Do you have anything in mind?"

"I feel like a nice, healthy salad," Kathy answered. "How about Insalata Mista? It's just down the street."

Patti squeezed her sister's forearm. "You don't feel like any lettuce I've ever eaten."

Kathy nudged Patti with her elbow. "You've said that since we were teenagers. You're such a dork."

They hooked arms and walked down the street to the restaurant. Since it was only eleven thirty, they were seated immediately at a table overlooking the water.

Patti let out a huge sigh. "I'm glad we got our examinations out of the way. We're both healthy, and now we know our due dates. How fun is that?"

Kathy picked up her menu. "Yep. Hey, I'm starving to death."

Patti perused the menu, lips moving as she read the descriptions. "I'm going to have the salade Niçoise with a Diet Coke. How about you?"

Kathy slid her finger from side to side on the menu. "Caesar salad for me. I need the egg for protein." She glanced out the window, and the smile on her face fell.

Patti glanced out the window. "What is it?"

"Charlie," Kathy whispered.

"You're freaking kidding me. Entering this restaurant?"

Kathy nodded. "Is it too late to leave? We haven't ordered yet."

"There's no reason to make a getaway, Kath. We have no reason to hide from him. La Jolla's a small city. We're bound to run into him eventually."

"But today of all days? After receiving such good news about our babies?" Kathy lifted her rear end from the chair.

Patti motioned for her to sit down. "Don't you dare leave me here all alone."

"Then come with me," Kathy whispered through half-closed lips.

"I'm not going anywhere. And neither are you. We'll ignore him, and I'm sure he won't come by us on the off chance he even sees us anyway. We're in the farthest corner of the restaurant, and it's filling up. Stop worrying."

Just as she'd finished speaking, Charlie walked by, then suddenly stopped, turned around, and stood next to their table. "Well, if it isn't the Michaels sisters. How have you two been?"

Kathy clenched her jaw and glanced at her sister.

Patti looked up at Charlie, who was standing so close she could feel the heat of his body. She shivered involuntarily and felt like puking. Instead, she took a deep breath to calm down.

"You're shivering, Patti," he said. "They ought to turn down the air conditioning. Or are you just excited to see me?"

A wiggling rattlesnake seemed to writhe in Patti's stomach, and she swallowed to keep the bile from spewing out of her mouth. But she refused to let him have the upper hand. "Ever heard the expression a dog never shits where he eats? And since you've shit on both of us, Charlie, I'd suggest you leave this area before it's too late."

He laughed under his breath. "Too late for what, Patti? Before you have your way with me? Like last time?"

"Don't flatter yourself, asshole," Patti said. She waved him away.

"Got anything planned for the Fourth of July? It's coming up in four days. Maybe we can meet up after the parade."

"In your dreams," Patti replied. "Now get the hell away from us before I summon the owner, who just so happens to be a close friend of mine."

He chewed on the inside of his cheek, turned, and walked out of the restaurant.

Kathy let out a breath. "You know the owner?"

"Robert and I have eaten here many times. The owner's actually a friend of Robert's, not mine." She shrugged. "A little white lie never hurt anyone."

Kathy slumped in her chair and rested a hand on her abdomen. "He makes me sick to my stomach. He actually thought you'd want to meet up with him? The arrogant prick!"

Patti sat up straight. "Forget about him, Kath. I will not let him keep me away from eating my salade Niçoise."

The edges of Kathy's lips turned up. "Nor me my Caesar salad. You're right. I can't let him get to me either."

Patti tapped her finger on the white tablecloth. "Revenge will be very, very sweet, Sis. Concentrate on that."

"I know, but it still scares the crap out of me."

"Let's not go over that again. My plan is almost ready to hatch."

"Okay." Kathy chewed at her bottom lip. "You've been thinking about this since—"

"Mid-May." Patti leaned back in her chair. "So, hey, I've had almost two months to formulate a plan." She grinned. "This will be so much fun."

# Chapter Thirty-Two

Despite her initial determination to make Charlie quickly pay for his transgressions, it wasn't until the end of July before Patti turned her attention to the bastard. She'd underestimated the energy her new job would demand, and Kathy was avoiding the subject altogether. Patti was still thinking about it—oh, yes—but she knew she had to deliver on her job, so that's where she directed her attention—and energy.

She and Robert had lunch and dinner with clients three or four days a week. He always accommodated her eating preferences with his selection of restaurants. Since they were all very upscale, she was able to order dishes made to order for her new semi-vegetarian lifestyle. She'd decided to cut back on beef and ate mostly tofu, turkey, and roasted chicken. She wanted to lead as healthy a life as possible for her unborn child.

Thursdays and Fridays were particularly busy, due to clients flying in for the weekend. Robert came into the office an hour before their Friday lunch meeting, wearing a big smile and carrying a bouquet of orange roses.

He held out the generous arrangement of flowers and smiled. "Happy Friday."

She dropped her pen on the desk and sat back in her chair. "What are these for?"

"To celebrate the fact that our lunch client canceled. We now have three days off. You've been working your tail off for months, and I want to show you my sincere appreciation for your diligence and hard work."

Her insides warmed at his kind gesture. They'd become good friends since she started working at La Jolla Photography and Media, and she loved her work, enjoyed meeting new clients, and was often showered with expensive gifts when they completed their contracts.

Most customers were wealthy and spared nothing to show their gratitude for a job well done.

"Thank you, Robert. You didn't have to do this."

"No, I did not. But you and I have earned some time off. How would you like to come to my place? We can have lunch by the pool and relax. You can go home for a change not totally exhausted from working ten or twelve hours."

Patti waved her hand. "I enjoy it here, Robert. The work is almost entirely schmoozing, so I can hardly complain about eating at expensive restaurants and meeting millionaires. But I am really tired these days."

Robert stared into her eyes. "You're almost three months pregnant, right?"

Patti nodded. "About that far along, yes."

"You don't want to push yourself. If ever you need some time off, please tell me. I don't want this job to jeopardize you or your child's health."

"You're so kind, Robert." Patti smiled. "If only every boss were like you. You know, I love working here."

"I love working here, too, but that doesn't mean I don't get tired when Friday rolls around, especially since we often book meetings on the weekends as well. And I'm not expecting a child."

She hesitated for a moment, thoughts of the last time she was alone with a man swirling through her mind. But Robert wasn't Charlie. She knew that. But it was hard to dismiss the niggling feeling of distrust holding her back. She drew in a breath and stood. "Sitting by the pool sounds wonderful."

"And Marcella can pamper us with a special lunch. We can have a massage afterward if you wish." He cocked an eyebrow. "Sound good to you?"

"Don't tell me. Marcella is your maid?"

He nodded.

"And you have a masseuse?"

He nodded again. "Join me this afternoon?"

"I'd love to. Just let me get my purse."

"We'll take my car. Put the top down, cruise along the beach on our way, let our hair blow in the wind. I'll drive you back here to pick up your car later."

"You've got yourself a deal I can't pass up."

He closed and locked the office door and, with a hand lightly at her back, escorted her to his red convertible Mercedes in the underground garage.

They took off toward the ocean. Weather in late July was warm, hovering around seventy-seven degrees that day. Patti leaned her head back, enjoying the sun's rays on her face as the ocean breeze lifted her hair off her neck, cooling her off.

Robert maneuvered the convertible around a slight curve back toward the beach and down a cul-de-sac. At the end of the road stood a house with all-glass walls offering an unobstructed view of the Pacific Ocean.

She gasped. Yachts and sailboats skimmed the surface of the water beyond. "This is unreal."

"Welcome to my bachelor pad."

She smiled at him. "I'm sure you put it to good use."

He parked in the driveway and came around to open her door. "Au contraire. There have been two women whom I've invited to walk through my front door. My mother and my sister. You will be the third."

She gave him a withering look. "Now I know you're not being your typical direct self."

He covered his heart with his hand. "I'm being completely honest with you."

"Just your mother and your sister, huh?" She shook her head.

"I bought this house *after* Connie died."

She nodded. "Sorry. I didn't mean—"

"It's all right, Patti."

She walked down the pathway to the front door, and he followed. After pressing several buttons on a keypad, he opened the door and they entered the foyer.

It was cool inside the house, and she couldn't take her eyes away from the unadulterated view of the ocean. "I would get absolutely no work done if I was surrounded by this view." She turned to him. "Do you just get used to it or what?"

"I do a lot of my work at night when the view, though still spectacular, is not quite so distracting."

She nodded, following him past the sunken front room and

through more glass doors that led outside, where a spectacular dark blue pool sparkled under the afternoon sun.

"I've never seen a pool that color."

He took her hand and led her to the edge of the pool. "Salt water. Much more enjoyable than chlorinated and much better for you."

He chuckled and pulled her toward a table under a Cinzano umbrella. "Have a seat. After lunch, we can go for a light swim."

Patti rolled her eyes. "I don't have a bathing suit that would cover up this new belly of mine, Robert. My baby bump isn't that attractive," she said, taking a seat on one of the padded chairs.

He leaned down and kissed her on the forehead. "There's no way you could possibly be unattractive, Patti."

A rush of heat infused her face, and she pulled her hair up with her hands, waving air toward her neck. "You always were the flattering type."

"Does the truth bother you that much?" He sat in a chair on the other side of the table, legs stretched out in front of him.

"I have always admired the fact you tell the truth, even when you left me. That's only one of the reasons I despise Charlie so much. He dumped Kathy without word one. And when she did confront him, he said he didn't love her anymore, the coward."

"You haven't mentioned your plan for revenge in quite a while. Changed your mind?"

She shrugged. "Too busy. My mind's been on work most of the time, and I'm feeling the pregnancy more now. I get tired earlier and go to bed right after I get home from our dinners out."

"Have you decided when you want to actually fulfill this plan?"

She shook her head. It didn't really matter what she told him. She didn't plan for him to participate. He had a lot to lose if something went wrong, and he'd be an accessory to all her scheming. She'd always been a bit overconfident. Okay, a lot overconfident. However, she saw no way they'd ever get caught or be implicated. Still, she wasn't going to risk his career, too.

"Well, you will tell me so I can help you, right?" he said, staring at her, unblinking.

She nodded. "Sure. But don't worry about it. I'm in no hurry."

"Shall I have Marcella whip us up some lunch, then?"

"I'm starving," she said. "I'm eating for two, right? Though that's such a bunch of BS."

He stood. "I'm going to change out of my suit and tie. If you'd like, I can show you to one of the guest rooms, where there's a closet filled with various skirts and summer dresses in all sizes and colors. You might even find a bathing suit you feel comfortable wearing."

She tried to keep her mouth from dropping open. "And, uh, why would you have all these clothes for women? Says the man who told me he's had very few girlfriends."

He grinned. "I have a bedroom filled with men's attire as well. I entertain quite often."

She smiled. "You're richer than I thought you were. I'm impressed."

He chuckled. "Don't be. It's only money, and that's never been the guiding force in my life. Two years ago, I never dreamed I'd be living here."

"You've done well for yourself. You've earned it."

"And so will you, Patti. You'll be picking out your new home sooner than you think."

"Do you give out bonuses at La Jolla Photography?"

"Yes, we do. Your direct supervisor takes care of that." He grinned.

"Why, Robert, aren't you my direct supervisor?"

"I am."

She stood and looked him straight in the eye. "Am I getting a bonus, too?"

He took her hand and guided her into the house, then he turned to face her. "You most definitely are getting one. You've earned it."

"Thank you so much."

He continued toward the stairs, and she followed him up to the second floor, where doors lined one side, allowing a 180-degree view of the ocean along the hallway.

He stopped in front of one of the doors and gestured inside. "You should find everything you need or want in here. I'll wait for you on the patio."

She entered the spacious bedroom, walked to the window facing the street, and stood, transfixed. In the distance, white clouds skimmed the low-lying hills, which were dotted with homes that only the überwealthy could afford.

The closet beckoned. After she flipped a switch, the mirrored door slid open and a light flashed on, revealing a small room bursting with garments on hangers.

"Whoa! I could get used to this," she said under her breath. She found a flowing forest green and peach loose-fitting chemise with a scoop neck and thick, black velvet straps. She slid it off the hanger, turned to the inside mirrored door, and draped it over her chest, turning left then right. Gorgeous.

After stepping out of her clothes, she slipped the shimmery garment over her head. Not too tight, not too short. It skimmed lightly over her breasts, ending a few inches above her knees. Her intention was not to look seductive. This dress definitely had style and class. Shoes of all shapes and sizes lined the back wall. She selected a pair of black sandals, slid her feet into them, and turned to face the mirror.

"That'll do, pig," she said, mimicking one of her favorite movies, *Babe*.

She folded her clothes and set them on the bed, then left the room, heading downstairs to the patio.

Robert sat on a chaise lounge at the edge of the pool, sunglasses perched on his nose, glass in hand, staring at her above the black lenses.

She reached the chaise next to him and stood, blocking the sun. "This life suits you, Mr. Blakely."

His mouth dropped half open, and he cleared his throat. "Uh, you look…"

She glanced down at her outfit. "This dress feels as good on as it looked on the hanger."

He stood, took two steps, and stopped a couple of inches in front of her. "As I was trying to say, you look absolutely striking." He lifted a strand of hair from her neck, sliding it through his fingers. "I always thought you were beautiful, but in the last two years while I've been here… I don't know, you've blossomed, Patti." He took in a breath. "Magnifique!"

She lowered her eyes, overwhelmed by his compliments. He'd always been generous with his words, but also handed them out appropriately. After what had happened with Charlie, she felt almost shy, still a bit vulnerable, a tad frightened even, in this one-on-one situation. But Robert had done nothing to make her feel that way. She knew her feelings were completely normal after what she'd been through, and it wasn't Robert's fault. It was Charlie's.

*And Robert is not Charlie.*

He lifted her head with a finger under her chin. "You seem different."

With a diffident smile, she stared into his eyes. "Since Charlie, I *am* different, Robert. Something like that changes you."

"You're not afraid of me, are you?"

She shook her head. "I have no reason to be. We're friends."

"With a history," he whispered.

"But I do feel something inside that's like—"

"You *are* afraid of me, aren't you?"

She closed her eyes and sighed. "Being raped—" She opened her eyes and met his gaze. "I have this knot in my stomach. Like something's wrong. Or something bad is going to happen."

His breath feathered across her lips. "I'll never push myself on you. Never. You've got to know that, Patti."

"I *do* know." Memories of their lovemaking skimmed through her mind. She took a step back. "Yes, we have a history, but that ended when you left me."

He let out a breath. "I thought I explained that. And I've changed and grown as well. I don't feel like the same man you once knew. Leaving the Bay Area—and you—challenged me to find my place in the world. Here in San Diego, I've become the man I always wanted to be. Stronger, more confident than I ever felt when we were together before, comfortable in my own skin."

She nodded slowly. "It suits you."

"Mr. Blakely?"

They both turned their heads in the direction of the voice.

"Yes, Marcella?"

"Will you be having lunch on the terrace or next to the pool?"

"The terrace will be fine." He returned his gaze to Patti. "Ready for lunch?"

She stuffed down her thoughts of what it had been like with Robert in the past and nodded.

"Let's have a quiet, relaxing meal." Grasping her hand in his, he led her up to the terrace.

<h1 style="text-align:center">Chapter Thirty-Three</h1>

Patti dabbed her cloth napkin on her lips and leaned back in the chair. "If Marcella cooked my meals all the time, you'd see me on that program *My 600-lb Life*."

Robert pushed back his chair and stood. "I told her you're more the vegetarian type."

She rubbed her belly. "For now, I sometimes eat roasted chicken and turkey. Otherwise, no meat. Marcella's quinoa salad with mushrooms and brie—oh, my Lord. Delicious."

"I enjoyed it as well, though I love barbecued hamburgers. Sorry."

She stood and took a deep breath. "We could walk off all these calories."

He pulled her in for a hug, rubbing his chin on the top of her head. "It feels so good to hold you again."

She leaned into him, and her resistance tumbled like a stack of dominoes. She sighed.

"I don't know what you have underneath that gorgeous dress, but have you ever gone skinny-dipping in salt water?"

"Hmmm. No, I haven't. The beach was always too crowded."

"Thank goodness I have a private pool. And Marcella's off for the rest of the day."

"Does that closet of yours upstairs have any bathing suits?"

"If you'd feel more comfortable, yes, there are many to choose from." He gestured. "Be my guest." He raised an eyebrow. "It's not like I haven't seen you naked before."

A current of warmth ran up her legs into her belly. "Actually, I *am* wearing my bra and panties."

He grinned. "That's more material than the bathing suits in that closet, I assure you."

"I doubt you have any bathing suits appropriate for a pregnant woman." She grinned. "Am I right?"

"Uh, no, I guess not."

She rolled her eyes, then bending over, she grasped the edge of her dress and pulled it over her head, tossing it on the chair beside her. "Satisfied?"

He stepped back, taking a long gaze from her sandals to her scanty thong to her black lace bra, her breasts bursting over the edges, the skin over her baby bump soft and creamy. "Pregnancy becomes you."

"I feel good. I'm eating better than I ever have. The one thing I can't seem to fit in is exercise. You and I get home so late most nights, I'm too exhausted to even take a walk."

He reached out, taking hold of her hand, pulling her closer. "There's another type of exercise that they say burns approximately a hundred and forty-four calories in thirty minutes."

She pressed her other hand to her chest, her heart pounding hard and fast under her fingers. "I don't know if that's a good idea. We work together."

"I'd like to think we're both mature enough to act like adults. If it doesn't work out between us, we can do what we did before, revert to being friends only. It's worked well so far, hasn't it?"

She nodded, the attraction of everything Robert pulling her toward him.

Inch by inch, he lowered his lips to hers, touching them lightly at first, once, then again and again until she opened her lips ever so slightly, and his tongue skimmed the inside of her mouth. He widened the kiss, and their tongues entwined. Wrapping her arms around his neck, she pressed her body into his, feeling his arousal, which heightened her own.

His five-o'clock shadow tickled her chin, firing her up as if he'd struck a match inside her. Moaning, she whispered his name, and the bulge nudging her stomach grew harder and bigger.

He pulled his mouth from hers. "Is that a yes?"

"I don't want us to regret this," she whispered.

"There's no way in the world I'd ever regret making love to you, Patti. Since we started working together, I've fallen in love with you all over again."

Glancing at a point in the middle of his chest, she shook her head.

He lifted her chin with his finger. "You're shaking your head no. And that's okay, Patti. But please don't be afraid of me. I won't hurt you."

She looked him in the eyes. "It's more than that, Robert. I don't want to get hurt again. I tried for two years, *two years*, to wipe you out of my heart."

"And did it work?"

"No, it did not."

He smiled. "You still have feelings for me, don't you?"

"Against all odds, yes, I do."

He took her face in his hands, kissing her almost breathless.

She pulled away, her breathing rapid.

"It's different this time," he said. "I want us to see where this leads. I don't want to just fool around."

"Neither do I. I'm pregnant. The last thing I need is the stress of my heart breaking while a baby's growing inside me."

"I have no intention of breaking your heart this time. I promise you that. We were good before I left you. We can be good again. And I'm not going anywhere."

"Neither am I." She paused, pressing her lips together tightly.

He wrapped a stray lock of hair around her ear, smiling down at her. "Let's try to be us again. I want that. Do you?"

"God help me, I do." She reached up, cradled his face in her hands. "But, Robert, I'm pregnant. With another man's child. A child that's a product of a grossly violent act by a man who's an awful human being. Do you really want to be a part of that?"

He gently lifted her mouth up to meet his, slipping his tongue inside. After several seconds, he pulled back slowly. "I want to be a part of your life, Patti. I love you. And I'll love your baby. It's not your child's fault how she or he was conceived. When your baby's born, it will still be a miracle. I want to be a part of that miracle."

She felt her heart slowly melting at his words. He didn't know how very much she needed to hear them said out loud. "Oh, Robert," she whispered. "I love you, too."

"We can go as slow as you like," he murmured against her mouth. "I want you to feel comfortable. I understand after what you went through with Charlie that—"

She gently placed her finger on his lips. "Shh." She intertwined her fingers with his and pulled him behind her through the front room and up the stairs.

When they reached the second floor, he slipped his hands under her thighs, lifted her gently, as if she were made of hand-blown glass, and carried her into his bedroom, then set her on top of the comforter.

Their lovemaking had always been one of the best qualities of their relationship, and if anything, she blossomed with his matured adeptness and heightened attention to her needs. Afterward, with their legs entwined and her cheek nestled on his chest, their breathing slowed, and they smiled at each other.

"I love you so much, Patti," he whispered on a sigh."More than you'll ever know."

"And I love you, Robert," she answered as her eyelids slid closed.

# Chapter Thirty-Four

With no little amount of restraint, Patti and Robert managed to return to their normal work relationship back at the office. They didn't kiss each other hello or goodbye. They agreed to keep the workplace free of romantic gestures.

Although that wasn't easy, Patti appreciated the separation of work and romance. Besides, she wanted to take it slow with Robert. When he invited her to his house in the evening after they finished work, she explained she was exhausted from the pregnancy, and they should reserve their get-togethers for the weekends. They agreed their romantic endeavors would stay at his house and, if in public, only when they were alone. Plus, she enjoyed coming home after work and talking to Kathy. And always in her thoughts was saving up enough money to buy her own house.

In late August, a month after Patti and Robert's afternoon liaison at his house and after a three-hour lunch and an even longer dinner, Patti took an Uber home, dropped her briefcase at the front door, and trudged to the couch to join her sister.

"Have you forgotten you're going to have a baby in January?" Kathy said.

Patti leaned her head back on the couch pillow, her hands over her swollen abdomen, and sighed. "And you're due in December, girlfriend. So what's your excuse for working five days a week and sometimes Saturdays? And in this heat. Is August always this hot?"

Kathy muted the television and, sitting cross-legged, turned to her sister. "I know. It's almost eighty degrees, but there's a breeze coming in through the window. It feels so good." She paused. "I have some news that could possibly be really good news."

Patti slapped her sister's knee. "I can hardly keep my eyes open. I'm exhausted. This heat is killing me. What's the possibly really good news?"

Kathy inhaled a deep breath. "I may have a company interested in my video game." She bobbed up and down on the couch cushion.

Patti pushed herself to an upright position, her mouth agape. "Are you freaking serious? Oh, my God!"

Kathy's smile stretched from one side of her face to the other. "I'm trying not to get too excited in case it falls through, but—"

"What happened? Tell me everything."

"Okay, okay. You remember I told you about that guy I work with who plays all the levels of my games after I finish them? Mark?" Patti nodded. "His uncle works at this company that distributes video games, right? So Mark's uncle was talking to the owner of the company at a party one night, and his uncle mentioned that his nephew, Mark, knows this woman, that would be me, who created this bad-ass, his words, video game that would appeal to teens as well as adults. So his uncle set up a meeting between me and the owner of the company he works for. It's this Friday. I'm so nervous, I feel like I'm coming out of my skin."

"This is absolutely phenomenal, Kath." Patti walked into the kitchen and returned with a bottle of sparkling apple cider and two flutes. "This calls for a clean and sober celebration. Cold cider tastes so good on a hot day."

Kathy held her flute while Patti poured, then they clinked glasses.

"To my amazing sister, that would be you, Kathy, whose future in the video game world is going to be oh-so-impressive. I just know it. I wish you more luck than I can express. In fewer than a hundred words, you go, girl."

Kathy pushed herself off the couch and began to pace, gesturing wildly. "If this company buys my game, I could earn a ton of money. Usually, you get a set amount when signing a contract, then a portion of each game sold. I could stop work and take care of my baby, or hire a nanny so I can work at home on another video game." She turned to Patti and grinned. "You and your baby can still live here. That doesn't have to change, Patti. The nanny could take care of two kids. Then you wouldn't have to quit work or spend extra money for a sitter."

Patti laughed out loud. "Hey, don't worry about me. This is your future we're talking about, and it's so bright, I've gotta wear shades, man."

Kathy plopped back down on the couch. "I love that line. I don't remember who sings the song."

Patti smiled. "You really want to know?"

Kathy nodded.

"For the people in the eighties, the future was very bright, and everybody needed their Ray-Ban sunglasses. So there was this group, Timbuk3, who wrote the song, but it's actually a criticism of society and the impending nuclear holocaust."

Kathy pulled her head back. "Are you kidding me?"

Patti shook her head.

"Where do you get this kind of trivia, Patti?"

Patti shrugged. "Inquiring minds," she said with a smirk.

"Well, anyway, I hope this happens. I'll be so disappointed if it doesn't."

Patti wagged her finger at her sister. "Stop being negative. You know, I'm not familiar with the business, or how this sort of thing works, but if they want you to make changes, is that something you do, or they do, or do they have to get your okay to make changes or what?"

"From what I've heard, the video game company would have a boilerplate contract that I can then request changes to. Personally, I'd change anything if they're willing to buy it. Heck, this is my future and my baby's future we're talking about."

"Wow. I'm nervous for you. But I have a good feeling about this, Qui-Gon."

"*Star Wars*?"

"Well, sort of. Though the line was actually, 'I have a *bad* feeling about this, Qui-Gon.' When's the meeting again?"

"This Friday." Kathy scooched into the corner of the couch. "I have to buy a very conservative suit. That's what Mark told me anyway."

"I'll help you with that. We can go shopping tomorrow night. I'll tell Robert I have to leave early."

"What's going on with you two?"

Patti grinned. "I was going to talk to you about it, but it's only been a month, so—"

"Enough with the prologue, Patti. So you've been waiting since July to tell me something scandalous?"

"No, it's not like that at all. I just wanted to make sure it wasn't a one-off. You know, a one-night stand. Or in this case, a one-afternoon stand."

Kathy bounced up and down on the couch cushions. "Tell me. Tell me."

Patti waved her hand side to side. "We made love for the first time that day I told you we had lunch at his house. Remember?"

Kathy nodded. "Uh-huh. Go on."

"Anyway, we're taking it slow, just like I told you I wanted. He agrees. He's not pushing me to do anything I don't feel comfortable with. He knows I feel tentative, given the fact he pretty much walked out on me before. So there's a bit of a trust issue."

"I haven't met him yet." Kathy cocked an eyebrow. "Why is that?"

"I wanted to wait to see how this all shakes down, like I just told you. I was a bit, or actually a lot, gun-shy, you know? After what happened the first time with him. You get my drift." Patti leaned back into the cushions of the couch. "But Labor Day's coming up. We could visit Dad and Sharon at the ranch… and Helen, of course. Last time I talked to Sharon she didn't mention her. I'm assuming she's back and being…"

"Helen!" they both said, then laughed.

"I'll invite Robert and perhaps your can ask you friend from work, Mark?"

"Sounds good to me. Have you talked to Dad about it yet?"

The landline rang, and Patti reached for the receiver. "Hello?" She turned to Kathy. "Oh, my God, it's Sharon." She told her, "I'm putting you on speaker. Kathy and I were just talking about you." She placed the phone on the coffee table in front of them.

"Hey, Kathy. December twentieth is getting closer. And Patti? It's January twenty-third, right?"

Patti laughed. "We're starting birthing classes soon. Dr. Holmer said to begin them during the third trimester, so we're going in September—a bit early for me, but perfect for Kathy."

"How're you doing, Share?" Kathy asked.

"It's sort of strange with only Dad and me here. Quiet, you know?"

Kathy's eyes widened. "Helen didn't come back? I assumed—"

"You never mentioned anything, Share," Patti interrupted with a frown. "I just assumed she was back, too, being her normal Helen self."

Kathy sighed. "We all know what assuming makes us, right?"

"You two were here in June," Sharon said. "It's August. She's been gone a little over two months." She paused. "I didn't say anything because I thought she'd return any day. Then we got super busy, and time just flew by. Dad wasn't worried. He said she's a big girl and she'd be back soon enough."

"Sounds fishy to me," Patti said. "I would have thought—"

"He talked to her," Sharon interjected.

"He did?" Kathy and Patti said together.

"That's why I wasn't worried. What you don't know is…"

"What aren't you telling us, Sharon?" Patti said, sharing a look with Kathy.

They heard Sharon let out a long breath. "Helen's a bit, you know… an odd bird. Anyway, sometimes she just leaves. The longest she's ever been gone, though, was a month. This is the longest she's spent away from the ranch. It makes me so mad, because it leaves Dad and me with a lot more work. More work than he should be taking on at this time of his life."

"And that's why you didn't say anything," Kathy said in a monotone.

"Yes," Sharon answered. "It's not that unusual."

Kathy shook her head. "I wonder where she is. Did she tell Dad?"

"No," Sharon answered. "All she ever says is that she's in LA and she's working on her acting career. Whatever *that* means."

Kathy lifted an eyebrow. "I've heard of struggling actresses being coerced into working in porn when they're desperate for work."

"That could very well be the case, Kathy, but I don't know," Sharon said.

"She left because of me," Kathy added. "When Dad said he wanted to start a college fund for my baby, Helen went ballistic, remember?"

"Oh, come on, Kathy. Helen's a big girl," Patti added. "Just wait until Dad finds out about *my* baby. Then he'll tell Helen, and… I can't imagine what she'll say, but I know it'll upset him."

"I want you to know," Sharon went on, "I have no problem with Dad setting up college funds for your children, or whatever he wants to do with his money. It's none of my business what he chooses to do. I don't have the sense of entitlement that I believe consumes Helen, you know what I mean?"

"I agree with you about the whole entitlement thing," Patti said.

"I will never understand why she turned out so different from the rest of us," Kathy said.

"Daddy's worked hard for everything he has," Sharon said, "and it's not our right to tell him how to spend his money. He and his attorney met soon after you two left in June, so I'm sure Daddy's already taken care of any changes he wanted to make to the will."

"So what's going on at the ranch?" Patti said.

"Daddy and I would like to invite you to our annual Labor Day barbecue. It's become something of a tradition here. End of summer and all that. Do you think you could make it? And you both can bring a friend."

Patti and Kathy laughed out loud.

"Is that a no?" Sharon asked.

"Not at all," Patti answered. "Kathy and I were just talking about that. I think it would also be a good time for me to make my announcement to Dad about being pregnant."

"That's great," Sharon said. "Are you both bringing guests, then?"

"I'll invite Robert," Patti said, turning to Kathy. "And you're going to invite Mark, right?"

"I know who Robert is," Sharon said. "He's the guy you used to go out with when you lived in Alameda, and now he's your boss. Right, Patti?"

"Yes," Patti said. "He left me to pursue a career here in the San Diego area, and I work with him now."

"And who's this Mark guy, Kathy?" Sharon asked.

"Mark's a guy at work who's helping me with the development of that video game I told you about, Sharon."

"Okay," Sharon said. "I hope he can come, then."

Kathy smiled. "I'll see what he says."

"Is this Mark a new love interest?" Sharon said.

Kathy blushed. "I never thought of him that way, but he *is* cute and has a, uh, different personality."

"What does *different* mean? Or should I wait to meet him?" Sharon said.

"I haven't met him either, Sharon," Patti said. "This should be an intriguing barbecue."

"Come on, you guys," Kathy said. "Gimme a break. He probably has plans anyway."

"Don't kid yourself, buster," Patti said. "I always loved it when Dad would say that."

"Who's Buster anyway?" Kathy said.

Patti slapped Kathy's knee. "It's just a humorous way of addressing someone, not an actual person."

"Hey, you two, I gotta go," Sharon said.

"We'll get back to you in a day or two about our flight plans, okay?" Patti said.

"Thanks. Call me. Bye," Sharon said.

Patti leaned back into the couch cushions and stared at the ceiling.

"This'll be fun, getting together for Labor Day," Kathy said.

"And all the rest of the stuff that goes along with it." Patti sighed.

"Whaddaya mean by that?" Kathy said.

"There's always some drama at the ranch, wouldn't you agree?"

Kathy smiled. "I hope Helen's okay."

"Maybe she'll show up for the barbecue, especially since it's obviously an annual celebration at the ranch."

"Well, weirder things have happened." Patti chuckled. "But, seriously, I don't want to spend the weekend arguing with Helen. It would upset Dad. It'll be upsetting enough when I tell him how I got pregnant."

"I know. Hey, you think Robert will go with you?"

Patti shrugged. "I don't know. His mom and sister live in this area, and he might already have plans. A lot of people have barbecues or watch the parade or whatnot."

Kathy tapped a finger to her lips. "Mark might be so surprised at my asking, he'll automatically say no and stutter out some excuse. Maybe I won't ask him. It might make things awkward at work."

"Says the woman who agreed with Robert that my having a romantic relationship with my boss is completely acceptable because we're mature adults."

Kathy rolled her eyes. "Mark has never shown any romantic interest in me, ever. He'd assume I'm asking him as a friend. So, maybe he *will* accept my invitation, then."

"What's this guy look like?"

Kathy's lips quirked up, and she looked at the dark television. "Kind of nerdy, but really cute."

"Kind of nerdy? You mean like big black glasses with thick lenses and a ponytail, flood-water polyester pants, black Converse tennies?"

Kathy laughed out loud. "He wears normal glasses with black frames, just like mine. Short, dark hair that's kind of curly but not like a 'fro or anything. He's tall, maybe a little over six feet." She looked at the ceiling. "Um, he's actually really nice-looking, but it seems he doesn't give a crap about what he's wearing.

"He comes into work, and I swear he looks like he just got out of bed. His pants are that pajama type, and they're all wrinkled. His shirts look like they've been rolled up in a ball and stuffed in a corner for ten years. Usually plaid or something, and they totally clash with the patterned pajama pants. But, seriously, if he cleaned up, as Dad would say, he'd have potential."

"Potential to be a model on the cover of *GQ* or more the back of a catalog like JCPenney?"

Kathy clapped her hands. "You can be hysterical, you know that? Not exactly *GQ* but no way JCPenney. Maybe Nordstrom?"

Patti sat up straight. "Seriously? You go, girl."

Kathy grinned. "I was kidding."

"I'll bet he accepts your invite, Kath. You better ask him right away so no one else gets him before you."

"Don't worry your pretty little blonde head about it, Sis. I'll do it tomorrow when I get to work… a little earlier than usual, of course."

# Chapter Thirty-Five

The next night, Patti fixed spaghetti, hot French bread, and a salad for dinner. When Kathy arrived home after work, she sniffed the air. "Something smells really good in here."

Patti rounded the corner and placed two plates on the coffee table. "Wash up, little sister. Dinner is served."

"What's the occasion?" Kathy said.

Patti stretched her closed hand toward her sister, and they bumped fists.

"Mark said yes, didn't he?" Patti asked.

Kathy's eyebrows raised toward her hairline. "How did you know?"

"I have this gut feeling that you have no idea this guy has the hots for you. You're always telling me how he offers to help out with your video game development, and you're a beautiful woman, so hey, do the math, sistuh."

Kathy shook her head. "And Robert?"

Patti nodded. "I hardly got the words out of my mouth, and he said he'd love to join us. Now I just have to make plane reservations."

"Mark said he'd gladly accept my gracious offer. No one but someone like him says gracious. But he insists on paying my airfare, since my family's hosting dinner."

Patti dabbed at her lips with a napkin, chuckling. "Robert said the same thing. I think you and I are the ones making out on this deal. Free airfare? That'll save us some major bank."

"Are you planning on sleeping in separate rooms at the ranch?" Kathy asked.

"If Dad feels more comfortable, we can have separate rooms, but that most definitely doesn't mean separate beds."

"Oh, I see how it is. Well, Mark and I are just friends, so I won't have to discuss the matter with Dad."

Patti winked. "Maybe next year."

The two couples had to sit in separate sections of the plane in order to get a direct flight—Patti and Robert in business class and Kathy and Mark in coach. Total flight time was a bit more than seventy minutes from San Diego to Reno, Nevada. Then they rented a car and drove to Quincy in an hour and a half. On the way to the ranch, the conversation flowed from work to photography to video games. As they drove under the Fabulous Friesians sign at the entrance to the ranch, Mark brought up the weather.

"I hate to admit it," Mark said to Kathy in the backseat, "but I had no idea it would be so hot here. It was seventy-five in San Diego when we departed, and it's eighty-eight here."

Kathy patted his knee. "Not to worry. You can easily fit into a pair of my dad's shorts or something, if you didn't bring any. He's about your height and weight."

Patti turned around in the passenger seat and shook her head at Kathy. "Oh, yeah, Mark. You'll look sharp in a pair of our eighty-three-year-old father's baggy, old shorts from 1950."

Mark's eyebrows flipped upward into his shock of dark brown hair. "I brought lightweight pants. They'll be fine."

Kathy laughed out loud. "That's too formal. You have no idea how laidback life is at the ranch. Unless it's changed in the ten years since I've been home for Labor Day weekend."

"Yeah," Patti added. "You're talking cutoff jeans and T-shirts. You brought those, didn't you?"

Mark nodded. "I'm wearing my jeans, and they're not cut off, but I know how to use a pair of scissors. And I brought some T-shirts I've gotten at various concerts."

"We can fix your shorts if you want, Mark," Kathy said. "Dad has a sewing machine. What bands have you seen?"

"I went with my dad to Black Sabbath's The End concert in San Diego," Mark said. "It was the last time they played together."

"I love Ozzy Osbourne," Robert interjected. "I saw him at Oracle Arena in Oakland way back in the eighties."

"I didn't know you liked them," Patti said. "I still want to see Drake in concert. Maybe he'll play at San Diego's Viejas Arena someday."

Robert glanced at her for a second. "You're into rap?"

Patti rested a hand on his forearm. "Who knew, right? And yes, not only is the guy a total fox, but I love his music. You know his song that goes, 'Club goin' up on a Tuesday'?" she sang.

"Oh, is that Drake?" Mark asked. "I've heard that genre of music before."

"Okay, everyone," Robert interrupted, "here's the ranch, and the thermometer in the car reads ninety-two degrees. Mark may want to take a cold shower."

"You'll be fine, Mark," Patti said, turning around and smiling at him.

Robert parked the car, and as all four doors swung outward, the house's screen door flew open, and their father walked onto the porch in a pair of cowboy boots, jeans, and a wife-beater shirt.

"What'd I tell you, Mark?" Kathy said. "Look what my dad's wearing."

Mark let out a breath. "Good, because I really didn't want to make a bad impression on your father."

Patti grinned at Kathy, who smiled back at her sister.

The guys grabbed their suitcases and satchels from the trunk and met Sharon and their father on the porch for introductions. Then they all shuffled into the foyer.

Sharon showed the four of them to their individual rooms, where they dropped off their suitcases, then they met in the front room shortly thereafter.

"Sit down, boys," Bill said. "I'd like to get to know the men in my daughters' lives."

Kathy's face turned as red as a robin's breast. "Mark and I are work buddies, Dad."

"Doesn't mean he doesn't have intentions of which you aren't aware," Bill said.

Kathy choked on her sparkling water, almost spewing it onto the Persian rug in front of the couch.

Mark looked straight into Bill's eyes. "I don't think she's aware yet, Mr. Michaels."

At that point, Kathy took a giant sip of water and closed her eyes. "Oh… my… God. Dad, could we talk about something else? How's business?"

Her father turned in her direction. "I know when I should zip my mouth, so I will. Uh, people are already gearing up for the winter. Friesians love the cold, and they're wonderful to ride in the snow. So, clients begin their searches now. We're pretty darn busy. But I'll tell ya, riding with chaps in this weather is not my idea of keeping cool." He chuckled.

Mark glanced around the room. "What are chaps, Mr. Michaels?"

"Mark," Kathy interjected, "everyone calls him Bill, and I'm sure he's okay with your doing so."

Bill nodded. "She's right, son. And chaps are leather covers for your legs. You see cowboys wearing them in Western movies, sometimes with tassels dangling off the sides."

Mark nodded. "Oh, right. Yes, sir, I've seen them. Thank you for explaining."

Patti and Kathy again shared a glance and a grin.

"And you, Robert," Bill said, "you're the one who broke my little girl's heart several years back. Isn't that right?"

Patti let out a huge sigh. "Dad, I explained all that on the phone last time I talked to you, remember?"

"Yes, you did." Bill pursed his lips, then said, "I'd like to know what his current intentions are, Patti."

Robert smiled. "My intentions, Bill, are entirely honorable. Not that they were dishonorable the first time your daughter and I were together. But I've matured a great deal since moving to San Diego. As I'm sure Patti's told you, we work with very wealthy clients, and it's serious business. La Jolla Photography and Media is a very well-known company. I feel good about my life now. And I can surely offer your daughter a more comfortable life than I would have before now… if we end up marrying down the road."

Patti turned to Robert, eyes wide.

Robert patted her on the knee. "Don't look at me that way. When I pop the question, I don't want you to be totally surprised."

She shook her head, staring into his eyes. "We'll talk about this later."

"I'm sure we will," Robert agreed, grinning.

Patti shared a quizzical look with Kathy, then glanced at Sharon and shrugged.

"So," Sharon said, "I'll be waking up very early tomorrow morning to start making potato salad, macaroni salad, several pies, a cake. Then there's the barbecued chicken Daddy loves so much. If anyone wants to help, I'd gladly accept it."

Everyone except Bill answered with a resounding, "Sure."

"It's late," Bill said. "Think I'll hit the hay. Nice to meet you, boys. I'll see you tomorrow."

Robert and Mark stood, then plopped back down on the couch after Bill left the room.

"He's a real piece of work," Robert said. "In a good way. I like his directness."

"A bit too direct at times," Kathy said, her face still pink.

Mark's eyebrows drew together. "I find him exquisitely forthright."

Robert chuckled. "Why don't you just say he's outspoken, Mark?"

Mark turned to Robert. "My mind extracts the simplest adjective to reflect the situation at hand."

Robert shook his head and smiled.

Kathy stood. "I think I'll go to bed, too. I want to help Sharon in the morning."

"Me, too," Patti said. "She shouldn't have to do all the work. See you tomorrow, guys." She winked at Robert and walked behind Kathy up the stairs to their bedrooms.

"Told you," Patti whispered. "Mark has *intentions*."

"Who knew?" Kathy whispered in return.

"Me," Patti said.

Kathy smiled and turned toward her room. Patti swatted her sister on the backside and ran into the bathroom.


"Why is it that it's the twenty-first century, and the women are still the ones in the kitchen, while the men are," Patti looked from left to right, "not?"

Kathy shoved Patti aside with her butt and poured the macaroni noodles into a pot of boiling water for the salad. "Because Dad wanted to be with the guys."

Sharon tsk-tsked. "You two aren't being fair. Daddy wanted to show off the barn and the horses, then take them for a ride around the ranch in the ATV. It's not like he's trying to keep them from helping us with dinner."

"You're right," Patti said. "I'm actually glad they're doing their male-bonding thing, getting to know each other. By the way, Kathy, I really like Mark. He's kind of a serious guy, so I get what you were saying about him being sort of a nerd. I love the Elvis Costello glasses."

"I'm glad he said what he did last night to Dad about his intentions," Kathy said. "I never would have known, otherwise."

"And you never know what other secrets are being revealed at this moment," Sharon added.

"When do you think I should have my little talk with Dad about being pregnant?" Patti asked.

"Daddy'll take it in stride," Sharon said. "I just hope his blood pressure doesn't shoot sky-high, because he'll definitely want to kill Charlie for what he did to you."

"Sharon, when are you going to bring home your man, so Dad can grill him about his intentions?" Patti said.

Sharon opened the oven to check on the pies.

"Sharon?" Patti repeated.

Sharon closed the oven door, straightened her posture, then glanced from Kathy to Patti. "I'm gay."

"Wh-what did you say?" Patti stuttered.

"You heard me," Sharon said. "I took after Mom in many ways, but this is the one thing I feel I should come out and tell you right here, right now." Her eyes shone with unshed tears. "Before I get any older and your questions escalate about when I'm getting married to a man."

Kathy dropped the towel she was holding and grabbed Sharon's hands. "You can still get married, you know. And Patti and I would still like to be your bridesmaids. Right, Patti?"

Patti put her arm around Sharon's shoulders and hugged her tightly. "I'd love to be part of your wedding party. Are you seeing anyone special?"

Sharon nodded, her bottom lip trembling. "I told Dad about a month ago. He said Maggie could move in, help with the horses, and he'd even pay her a salary, too."

"Why are you crying, honey?" Patti asked.

"Because I wasn't entirely sure how you two would respond to my announcement. I don't want there to be any weirdness between us."

Kathy frowned. "You mean like Patti or I would feel uncomfortable around you?"

Sharon shrugged. "I don't know. Sometimes people get weird when they find out I'm gay. I didn't want you to feel awkward."

Patti grasped Sharon by the shoulders and faced her dead-on.

"I'm sorry Mom felt she had to hide it from us for all those years. How painful that must have been for her! I would have loved her then, just as much as I love her now. Her being gay would never change that. And we are not just any people, Sharon. We're your sisters, and nothing's going to change. We love you." She glanced at Kathy, who walked over and stood next to Patti. "I speak for both of us. Right, Kathy?"

Kathy nodded. "Most definitely. When can we meet Maggie? Can she come to dinner today?"

"She's on call today. She's a veterinarian. That's how we met. She takes care of all our horses. Because she's on call, she might not be able to stop by."

"How did Dad react?" Patti asked.

"That's the unbelievable part. When I told Daddy, he said he already knew."

Patti pulled her head back. "About you? How is that possible?"

"Yeah," Kathy said, "how the heck would he know that?"

Sharon smiled. "Daddy said he'd seen the way Maggie and I interacted in the barn. I guess he's pretty intuitive."

"Good old Dad." Patti grinned. "Who'd a'thunk Daddy-O would be so open-minded, right? But after he went through finding out Mom was gay, it shouldn't be too surprising. He loved Mom to the very end."

"Girls! Is dinner almost ready?"

The three sisters looked at each other. "Yes, Dad," they said in unison, then burst out laughing.

"What in hell's bells is so funny?" their father said, striding into the kitchen, followed by Mark, then Robert.

"Why don't you wash up and sit down, Daddy? Kathy and Patti and I will put the dishes on the table in a moment."

"Fine by me," he answered.

"I'll pull the chicken off the barbecue," Robert said.

"I'm quite capable of assisting you with that, Robert," Mark said.

Robert chuckled. "Sure."

Patti and Kathy shared a look, both smiling.

Robert gave Patti a peck on the cheek on his way outside, and Mark followed him.

# Chapter Thirty-Six

Ten minutes later, everyone was seated at the table, flutes of champagne and sparkling apple cider raised.

"I propose a toast," Bill announced. "To my daughters, Sharon, Kathy, and Patti, who are all gathered here today—inside, because that's where the air conditioning is—to celebrate family, our family. And to our guests," he nodded to Mark and Robert, "who graciously accepted our invitation to join us today. And to Maggie," he winked at Sharon, "who would be here but for her dedication to all animals great and small." He raised his glass higher. "And to Barbara, who is with us here today in spirit. I love you, Bobbi, now and forever."

Everyone clinked glasses, and there was a comforting murmuring and smiling before Sharon interrupted. "Let's eat this feast."

"I take great delight in eating barbecued chicken," Mark said.

"Me, too," Robert added with a smile.

"What a cozy little family scene."

All heads turned with a collective gasp.

In the foyer, Helen leaned against the doorjamb, hair shorn to within an inch of her scalp, wearing ripped jeans and a USC sweatshirt, mascara drooling down her cheeks.

Sharon slowly lifted out of her chair. "Helen. My God, where have you been?" She took two steps toward her sister.

Helen raised her hand, palm outward. "Don't. Just don't, Sharon." She shook her head.

The sisters knew she loved her Scotch on the rocks a little too much. An odor wafted toward the table, a combination of alcohol, bad breath, and dirty clothes emanating from their normally perfectly coiffed sister.

"I didn't hear my name mentioned in your toast, Dad."

Bill, who sat at the head of the table facing the foyer, pushed his chair back and stood, knuckles leaning on the tabletop. "You didn't think you owed me the courtesy of telling me where you've been? I've been worried sick about you."

"Oh, yeah, right. I can tell. I coulda been found, Dad. You got 'nough money to sic your private investigator on me," she slurred. "Guess I wasn't worth it." She paused, drew in a deep breath. "Or do ya plan to spend all your money on Kathy's bastard kid?"

Kathy stood. "Helen, what is your problem?"

"Kathy!" Bill's voice echoed through the dining room. "I'll take care of this."

Kathy sat down.

Bill dropped back into his chair, then took a sip of champagne. "This will always be your home, Helen, and you're welcome to return at any time." He held up a finger. "On one condition. You will either accept the fact I will spend my money however I want, *and* you will be respectful to your sisters as well as any kids that have yet to be conceived, who also will forever be a part of this family." He stared at Helen, unblinking. "Or you can leave right this minute."

Through the silence, the grandfather clock ticked off the seconds. No one spoke. No one moved.

"Before she answers, Dad, I want to share something with you," Patti interrupted.

"It can't wait?" her father asked.

Patti shook her head. "No, I'm sorry, it can't. And it's pertinent to this conversation. I may as well get it over with now. I know it may seem inappropriate, but time keeps zooming by, and it's easy to put off because I don't live here. But I need to say this in person." She glanced at Robert, who nodded for her to continue.

"Go on," her father said.

She closed her eyes momentarily and breathed in, letting it out slowly. "I went to talk to Charlie. Kathy's Charlie?"

Her father nodded.

"I wanted to get the truth out of him, so Kathy would know why he dumped her. Give her some closure? I never got a chance to tell him that, or discuss anything for that matter, because he served me a drink and drugged me. Then he raped me and told me I'd come on to him and it was consensual sex. I found out I was pregnant while I was in the hospital in Quincy after our accident. I'm due in January."

If looks could kill, Helen wanted Patti dead.

Tears rolled down Patti's cheeks. "I'm sorry, Dad."

"What the hell do you have to be sorry for?" he said, his face reddening.

Sharon pushed back her chair. "Daddy, you have to watch your blood pressure. Please don't get upset."

"What the Sam Hill do you want me to do, Sharon?" He stood. "I'd like to kill that son of a bitch."

Helen laughed out loud, and within seconds, the laugh turned into outright cackles, which segued into a wracking cough before she doubled over and slumped to the ground.

Sharon rushed over and knelt next to her, putting her arm around Helen's shoulders, bringing her close and hugging her. "Shhh."

Helen shook Sharon off like a dog fresh from a swim and stood. Stumbling into the dining room, she walked around the table while she talked. "So now we have two, everybody, two bastard kids. Both from the same daddy. Kinda like two, two, two mints in one." She laughed uproariously. "Who's next? Sharon? Certainly not me. When I have my kid, I'll be legally married." She gestured toward the table. "Not like these two. Ever heard of birth control, Kathy? Or you, Patti. Ever heard of abortion?"

Bill remained standing, but his breathing appeared labored, and with one arm extended, he leaned heavily on the table. "Get out, Helen." He rocked slightly back and forth.

Sharon ran toward him. Patti and Kathy stood abruptly. "Dad," they shouted in unison.

He wobbled and fell to the floor, pulling the tablecloth and various plates and silverware down with him.

Mark rushed to their father's side and began CPR immediately.

"I'm calling 911," Robert announced, grabbing his phone out of his pocket.

Kathy knelt next to her father's head, while Mark continued compressions on Bill's chest. Patti knelt on the other side, holding her father's hand. Sharon stood nearby, hand covering her mouth, tears rolling down her face.

Within ten minutes, an ambulance pulled up outside the house. Robert opened the front door, and the EMTs rushed in.

Mark made room for the EMTs, while the girls tried to make sense of the medical chatter going on in front of them.

"Grab Patti and Kathy's purses, guys," Sharon cried. "We'll follow the ambulance to the hospital."

Mark and Robert ran upstairs for the women's purses and cell phones, then followed them out the front door behind the EMTs carrying the gurney.

Robert insisted on driving, and they all piled into the SUV. He followed behind the ambulance to Quincy General. They were quiet during the drive, still in shock over Helen's appearance and behavior, as well as the sickly look on their father's face before he'd fallen to the floor.

"Here we go again," Sharon said. "But this time I have a horrible feeling Daddy really did have another heart attack. This whole thing with Helen bothered him a lot more than he let on. She was gone longer than she'd ever been before."

"Of course it bothered him," Patti agreed. "And I didn't help matters with my story about Charlie. It's all my fault. I shouldn't have ever said anything, dammit."

"So, what, you'd just show up at the ranch one day with your newborn and yell, 'Surprise, Dad'?" Kathy said.

"Patti, for goodness sake," Sharon interjected, "of course Daddy was upset about Charlie, but the way Helen is acting… I don't think he ever really knew how awful she can be."

"You may be right," Patti answered, holding back the tears.

"It's terribly disappointing for Daddy," Sharon said. "He loves her."

Patti nodded. "And when I have my child, I'm sure I'll love him or her, no matter how poorly she or he behaves, too."

"Ditto," Kathy added.

Robert parked, and they scrambled out, then ran through the sliding doors into the waiting room. Sharon filled out the paperwork to admit their father, then joined the rest of the group.

"The admitting nurse said she'll give us an update on Daddy's condition as soon as she knows anything," Sharon told them.

"Has Helen always upset your father like that?" Robert asked.

"Recently, yes." Patti took his hand in hers. "When Kathy told Dad about her baby, Helen went ballistic about Kathy's bastard child taking away our inheritance, blah, blah, blah. Dad was upset and put Helen in her place. She has this whole entitlement thing going on.

She seems to think our parents' money should be hers and definitely not be distributed to his grandchildren."

Mark shook his head slowly. "I'm so very sorry that happened to you, Patti. I didn't know, of course. It wasn't Kathy's place to tell me. So those of you who have children will ipso facto inherit more money than Helen? It appears very problematic for her."

Kathy nodded. "Problematic can't begin to describe how Helen feels about *any* of Dad's money going to *any* of us, our children included. She thinks she's entitled to it all, I swear to God."

"But Dad said it would be a college fund," Patti added, "which is different than just handing over money to a kid to spend on whatever he or she wants."

"Sufficiently wise," Mark said.

"I'm sorry you had to witness that family debacle, Mark," Patti said.

"Please do not feel any obligation to apologize for familial controversies," Mark answered. "We all have them."

At that moment, the wide metal doors swooshed open, and a young man wearing green scrubs, a stethoscope hanging around his neck, walked straight toward them.

"Are you the daughters of William Michaels?"

"Yes, we are, Doctor. How's our father?" Patti said.

"The good news is he didn't have a heart attack. It was an anxiety attack brought on by stress."

"No surprise there," Kathy added. "You said that's the good news, doctor. Is there bad news?"

His eyes moved from one sister to the next. "Someone has to monitor him closely. No more family arguments. I know that may sound impossible, but I don't want to see him in here for this at his age, since he did suffer a heart attack several years ago. He might not come out alive next time if he goes into cardiac arrest."

"I live with Daddy," Sharon said. "I'll take care of him."

"Good to know," the doctor said. "He can go home tomorrow. I'd like to monitor him for the night. I'll call you tomorrow."

"Can we see him?" Kathy asked.

"I gave him something to relax him, and he's asleep. Why don't you come back tomorrow? That would be my advice."

"I need to stay," Sharon spoke up, "in case he needs me."

The doctor faced Sharon. "He will be asleep until morning, Ms. Michaels, and I need you to be rested tomorrow and ready to take care of anything he may need. So please, go home and get a good night's sleep. Come back in the morning, or call us, to make sure he's ready to go home." He nodded, turned, and walked away.

"How do you know Helen won't return after we leave the ranch? She could be there now," Robert said.

"We don't," Patti answered.

"What're you going to do, Sharon?" Kathy said. "Maybe Patti or I should stay here with you for a few days, just to make sure."

Sharon shut her eyes for a second. "I have her cell number. I'll call her tomorrow and explain the situation. I've called her many times in the last two months, but maybe she'll answer this time. You could be waiting here for weeks to see if she turns up, and neither of you can do that. You have full-time jobs.

"Believe me, it wouldn't make a difference if you stayed. Maybe when I get in touch with her, she'll have sobered up and be willing to have a mature discussion about Daddy's condition. I'm hoping she'll do as the doctor asked and stay away until she can abide by his wishes."

Kathy snickered. "Or one day, out of the blue, she'll show up pregnant just to spite us all."

Patti rolled her eyes. "Wouldn't put it past her. Then she'd think she'd be guaranteed a bigger chunk of the money, even though her kid would be getting a college fund like ours. Good God!"

"Please don't think I'm being too analytical," Sharon said, "but should we maybe discuss whether Helen needs help? You saw how unkempt she was, which is very unlike her. That seems like a red flag that she's in distress."

"I agree," Patti said, glancing at Kathy.

"Me, three," Kathy added.

"Why don't we all go home and eat first?" Sharon interjected. "The barbecued chicken's just sitting on the table getting cold. We can talk about Helen later, perhaps."

"Or it's on the floor, along with the macaroni salad and potato salad," Kathy added.

"I don't think *all* the food was pulled off the table," Patti said.

"Unless you have a cat or dog that's eaten it already, I'm hungry enough to partake of leftovers, no matter where they are, table or floor," Robert said, chuckling.

Mark rubbed his hands together. "I concur. I'm feeling quite peckish."

Robert patted Mark on the back. "You are one helluva piece of work, my man."

Mark glanced at Robert, looking confused. "What did I say?"

# Chapter Thirty-Seven

Mark pushed his chair away from the dining table and leaned back. "I feel rather stuffed. I ate an inordinate amount of food."

"I don't think I've ever heard someone say they ate an inordinate amount of anything," Robert said, laughing.

"You understood me, though, right?" Mark asked seriously.

"Since spending a few hours with you eating dinner, I have to say, Mark, your vocabulary is voluminous."

Mark squinted at Robert. "A voluminous vocabulary, Robert? Who talks like *that*?"

Robert smiled. "My point exactly. Hey, are you from California, by any chance?"

Mark quirked up an eyebrow. "I grew up in Berkeley. Received my doctorate from Cal. Don't tell me. You graduated from Harvard."

"Hah-vud?" Patti interrupted. "Robert and I both got our MFAs in photography while in San Francisco."

"Master of fine arts," Mark said.

Robert tipped his champagne flute at Mark. "The Institute of Photography in San Francisco. That's where Patti and I met."

"And you've been friends ever since," Mark added.

"Not exactly," Patti said, glancing at Robert. "Let's just say Robert moved down to La Jolla to pursue a career. We re-established our friendship when I moved in with Kathy."

"You continue to reside here on the farm, Sharon?" Mark said.

Sharon grinned. "Yes, I do, Mark. However, we call it a ranch. We don't raise cows or pigs or chickens. We import Friesian horses from Holland and sell them to clients from all around the United States."

"Sharon's very good at it," Patti said. "Dad told me the business has made more money in the last year than ever before."

"We're not in a recession any longer," Sharon added.

"The ranch has been in business for more than a decade," Patti replied, "and we haven't been in a recession for years, Sharon. You're just being modest."

"Helen helped Daddy for most of those years, and I watched her grow the business," Sharon said.

"Some people are better at sales and PR than others," Robert said.

Sharon stood and picked up her plate. "I love meeting people and talking about the horses, but that was always Helen's forte."

"In what facet of the business do you excel, Sharon?" Mark said.

"I enjoy training the horses. Riding them to at least the first dressage level."

"Dressage?" Robert asked.

Mark leaned forward. "The highest expression of horse training. Where horse and rider are expected to perform from memory a series of predetermined movements."

The three sisters and Robert were quiet for several seconds, mouths half open.

Kathy patted Mark's forearm. "It's hard being a genius."

Sharon stood. "Dessert, anyone?"

They all groaned.

"I'll take that to mean you're all too full. We can save it for later," Sharon said, moving toward the kitchen.

"I'm going to call the hospital and check on Dad," Kathy said. "BRB."

Mark shook his head. "I do not understand this current need to communicate in acronyms. Why doesn't she just say the words 'be right back' without succumbing to our societal need to diminish speech to the least amount of syllables with the intention of saving a millisecond of time? Words are precious commodities meant for our personal use to enhance the flavor of our interactional dialogue."

Robert groaned again.

Mark frowned. "I continue to irritate you with my vocabulary, Robert. My sincere apologies."

Robert waved his hand, chuckling. "You most definitely do not irritate me, Mark. I'm being exposed to a quality of the English language that has been missing for decades." He stood and followed Sharon into the kitchen.

Kathy returned and grabbed her plate. "The doctor and I had a discussion. He wanted to know if we were all staying at the house and for how long. I told him we planned to leave Sunday morning. He thought it would be less stressful if Dad stayed one extra day and came home Sunday afternoon, after we're gone. He's very concerned about sending him home too early, especially with a house full of people."

Patti frowned. "We're not just people. We're his family. But I do understand. If Helen sobers up and decides to make an appearance, though, that could be disastrous."

Kathy walked to the kitchen. "I agree with the doctor."

"We'll spend our last day at the ranch just relaxing, then?" Mark asked.

Patti patted him on the back as she walked by. "Yeah, right."

Mark frowned.

"You'll see," Patti replied at the confused look on his face. She passed Kathy and Robert as they exited the kitchen.

Sharon sat at the kitchen table, her head in her hands.

"What is it, Share?" Patti asked.

"How the heck am I going to run this ranch without Dad?"

Patti sat next to Sharon and took both of Sharon's hands in hers, looking her straight in the eyes. "Look at me, Sharon."

Sharon twisted in her chair to face Patti.

"Share, you don't have to do this alone. Granted, I can't stay at the ranch for too long because I don't make enough money yet to take time off and pay rent and all that, without using up the rest of my savings. Kathy's probably in the same position." Patti put her index finger up. "But Dad is not poor. He can afford to hire help until he gets on his feet and is feeling like his usual spunky self."

Sharon nodded slowly. "You're right. I'm just feeling a bit overwhelmed right now."

"And I get that. I would, too. Do you have anyone you can call who could recommend someone to help you out here at the ranch?"

Sharon leaned back in her chair and stared at the ceiling for several seconds. "I do, as a matter of fact," she said, standing. "I'm going to call Sam, who owns a ranch down the way. He always has extra hands working for him year-round, instead of hiring and letting workers go every few months. He might loan me some of his guys."

Patti stood. "So there ya go. Why don't you go into Dad's office and take care of business?"

Sharon hugged Patti. "Thanks for understanding. In case you don't already know, I would never expect either you or Kathy to stay here and help out at the ranch. You have lives that don't involve this business. This is Daddy's thing, and I'm just helping out, but at the same time, I'm getting paid for something I absolutely love doing. So I consider myself one of the luckiest people in the world."

Patti kissed Sharon on the cheek. "That is something that very few people have, Sharon—a job they love doing every single day. Fortunately, I like my boss and am treated very, very well. And if Kathy's video game is purchased by that company, she'll be a very happy camper as well."

"I hope that happens for her. I really do." Sharon paused, frowning. "Now if only Helen could find something that would make her happy. She can't be content working here, especially when she's just doing it for the money she'll inherit after Daddy dies. He could live until he's a hundred years old."

Patti nodded. "And that's a very long time to wait. Helen needs to get a life." Patti sat down and pulled Sharon toward her. "Can you stay for a few extra minutes before you call Sam? I have something I want to talk to you about."

Sharon dropped into the chair next to her sister. "Of course. What's wrong?"

Patti let out a long breath. "I feel like I'm going to have an anxiety attack like Dad. If Helen shows up unexpectedly and gets into another argument with Dad, I swear she'll send him right back to the hospital. I'm worried she's not finished with him. That she's going to cause more trouble. It was relaxing the last time we were here, but I'm so worried about him. And now, you'll be the only buffer between Dad and Helen. Are you sure you can be as aggressive and, let's just say, ballsy to go up against Helen at her worst?"

Sharon laughed. "You know, you and Kathy have this impression of me as always sweet and laid-back, almost shy. But you don't live here. Helen and I have had our battles, and you know what? I've won almost every one of them." She paused. "The ones I choose to fight, that is. I let her have her way when Daddy insists his sweet little girl has to get what she wants, which almost always involves material things she just has to have. You know what I mean—a new car or SUV for the farm, new bling for the horses to entice customers to buy them—that sort of thing. I go along with that because it's not worth fighting about.

"But in this case, where we know how destructive Helen can be to Daddy's mental and physical health… believe me, Patti, I'll win this one. Don't you worry your pretty little head about it, to coin one of Daddy's favorite phrases."

"That makes me feel much better, Share. I'll talk to Kathy about this, too, if you don't mind. She's worried about us leaving you here alone at the ranch while Helen is God knows where and might return at any time."

Sharon smiled. "Tell Kathy I won't let Helen put Daddy back into the hospital. She won't get within three feet of him—at least, not over my dead body." She chuckled.

"Don't let it come to that, please," Patti said. "Dad does have guns here, and I wouldn't want to have to fly up for another funeral."

Sharon swatted at Patti. "Oh, stop. Helen's not violent, and neither am I. In fact, neither of us has ever even shot a gun. Daddy has them for protection and to scare off wild animals who make their way onto the ranch. Even then, he shoots into the air. He doesn't aim to kill the coyotes or mountain lions."

"Good to hear," Patti said. "That would scare the crap out of me, if I ran into a mountain lion at night… or during the day."

"Generally, what happens is we hear the horses making a ruckus. Then Daddy takes his gun and scares away any predators."

"So you'll have access to a gun, in case you have to scare Helen away from Dad?" Patti asked, smirking.

"Helen definitely has a predatory nature when it comes to preying on Daddy's wallet. But in this case, we're not talking about Helen's relentless requests for Daddy to spend his money. We're talking about Helen fighting over Daddy's will and how he decides his money is to be allocated *after* he dies. But as you well know, Daddy's very stubborn when it comes to what he and Mom decided in his will. He'll discuss it with his attorney, but he doesn't ask us for advice. He and Mom decided what was best, and Daddy's determined to keep his word."

"You're right," Patti said. "Dad's a man of his word. And he was pretty closemouthed when we talked to him about whether he'd changed the will for Helen's benefit. You noticed he didn't elaborate. We still don't know how it's designed. Then again, I don't care. I just don't like the fact Helen tried to coerce him into changing it. It rubs me the wrong way."

"Me, too," Sharon said and stood. "I'm glad we were able to talk to Daddy about it."

"Wait a sec." Patti gently grasped Sharon's forearm, guiding her back down into the chair.

"What is it now, Patticake?"

"I just want to thank you for being here for Dad. I know it can't be fun living with Helen. And I know I speak for Kathy, too, when I say we both appreciate all you do here at the ranch. And we both think you should be compensated for it in the end."

"And you? What about everything you did for Mom for ten years while she battled cancer?"

Patti shrugged. "It was a time when Mom and I bonded. We became so close. It was all worth it."

Sharon's eyebrows rose, wrinkling her forehead. "That's how I feel about all the time I've been able to spend with Daddy."

"But I know it must be hard watching how he mollycoddles Helen and sticks up for her all the time."

"It can be," she said with a smile. "But I know he's just being a good father. He doesn't want to foment discord between Helen and me."

Patti laughed. "Foment? I think you've been hanging around Mark too much."

"Indubitably," Sharon replied.

Patti shook her head. "Oh, brother."

They spent the following day grooming the horses, mucking out stalls, and eating leftovers, of course. Early Sunday morning, they all went to the hospital, where they said goodbye to their father and Sharon, then sped off to the airport just in time to catch their flight.

They took an Uber to Kathy's place, arriving at eight o'clock. The guys picked up their vehicles and said goodbye.

Patti and Kathy dropped their suitcases.

Patti let out a deep sigh. "I think I'm at the point where I'm craving—"

"Please don't talk about food. I'm still stuffed from our eat-a-thon." Kathy rubbed her stomach. "I gained more weight. Dr. Holmer's going to be mad at me."

"If you hadn't interrupted me, I was going to say I'm craving boring."

Kathy's eyebrows twitched upward. "Huh?"

Patti sat on the couch. "Well, it wasn't exactly a relaxing vacation after Helen showed up and sent Dad to the hospital. But I do feel good about my talk with Sharon that I told you about."

Kathy joined her sister on the couch. "I was surprised to hear Sharon has an assertive side to her. Now I won't worry as much about Helen showing up and causing trouble."

"Speaking of causing trouble," Patti said, "let's talk about causing Charlie some trouble."

Kathy shook her head. "Thank you anyway. I'd rather not."

Patti rested a hand on Kathy's thigh. "I want to do this thing. Soon."

"So you *really* want to jeopardize your future by taking a loaded gun and doing a home invasion?"

"Oh, my God, Kathy. How many times do I have to tell you that you don't have to do this? I've devoted a ton of hours thinking and plotting. I bought everything we could possibly need after we enter his house. My plan's foolproof. All you have to do is follow my instructions without asking any questions, and we'll pull it off without a hitch."

"Ugh! I was hoping you'd forgotten," Kathy said.

"Not on your life. Or the lives of Charlie's two babies. He's going to pay for what he did, Kath."

"Even if it means we both go to jail?"

"I can't promise you anything, but I'm betting my next paycheck he'll let us in his home voluntarily. All we're going to do is make him listen to what we have to say and force him to admit he raped me. Then we're outta there."

"And if he doesn't?"

"I already told you. If he refuses to admit he raped me, it'll be enough for me that he finds out how it feels *not* to be in control. And since you said he's afraid of guns, that will make it even more fun. He'll probably pee his pants when he sees the .357 Magnum. Then we leave him there, tied up." She raised her index finger. "With a phone close at hand, so he can call for help, mind you." She chuckled. "But once again, he won't be in control. See how he likes it, the bastard."

Kathy chewed at her bottom lip. "You do make it sound pretty easy. It's like we're pulling a prank."

"Exactly," Patti said. "He invites us inside, we put on gloves so our fingerprints won't be on anything in his house, we force him to sit in a chair and duct-tape his legs and arms. And his mouth if he starts yelling or screaming. We don't want to alert the neighbors. We make him listen to what we have to say. Wait to see if he'll nod and agree to talk to us without raising his voice. He'll either talk to us or he won't, but he sure as hell won't enjoy us having the upper hand.

"Either way, we leave him tied up, split, and drive home. He won't die. We can leave a pair of scissors near, so he can free himself once we're gone, and his phone, so he can call the police if he chooses." She paused. "He may be too humiliated to use the phone and call for help. He wouldn't want anyone to find out two chicks pulled a home invasion on big old manly Charlie." Patti laughed out loud.

Kathy grinned. "You've thought of everything, haven't you?"

"I think I have."

"You know what they say about best-laid plans."

Patti let out a loud sigh. "Don't worry so much." She stood. "I'm doing this thing with or without you, Kathy, and I'm tired. Let's do the couch-potato thing and watch TV and eat popcorn. Tomorrow's Monday." She flicked up one eyebrow. "A good day for a home invasion."

"Can't we spend tomorrow evening watching *Monday Night Football*?"

Patti's eyes widened. "Didn't you tell me once that Charlie always watches *Monday Night Football*?"

"I did. Probably with a bunch of dudes."

Patti walked into the kitchen. "They won't be spending the night, will they?"

"Noooo, probably not."

Patti poured the kernels into the pan and added a bit of oil. "If it doesn't work out tomorrow night, we'll shoot for another time."

"Don't say the word shoot, okay?" Kathy rubbed her temples with her fingers. "At this point, I just want to get it over with."

"I promise not to be mad if you want to back out. This is my thing, not yours."

Kathy joined her sister at the stove. "He was my boyfriend, and he raped you. That makes it my business, too."

Patti turned and hugged Kathy. "Together forever."

Kathy stuck out her baby finger. "It'll be our secret. Pinkie promise."

They hooked pinkie fingers and smiled at each other.

# Chapter Thirty-Eight

The next day, Patti and Kathy lounged around the house, computers perennially on their laps. Patti got up to speed on new clients and talked to Robert on the phone. Kathy fine-tuned her video game, often with Mark on the line. They ate dinner in front of the TV, watching football.

When the game ended at eight o'clock, Patti turned to her sister. "It's time."

Kathy pulled her feet off the coffee table. "Let's do this and get it over with. I hope I don't puke, because this makes me really nervous."

Patti stood in front of her sister, blocking the television. "Last chance, Kath. You're pregnant. You don't need any additional stress. You do not have to do this."

Kathy stood and faced her sister. "You're pregnant, too, you dork. And I won't let you do this alone. It's only for a short time, so the stress will pass. We won't be there long, will we?"

"I'm hoping not, but you can always leave or wait in the car. I'll be safe. I'm the one with the gun. And I'll be armed with rolls and rolls of duct tape." She grinned.

"Should I dress in all black and wear a baseball cap?"

Patti gave it some thought. "We don't want to look suspicious. Wear something dark. No white anything. Put your hair up or something, so you look different than usual. We don't want to be recognized, but we also don't want to look like burglars in a *Lifetime* movie. I'll wear black leggings as I often do, along with a dark T-shirt."

"You and your *Lifetime* movies." Kathy laughed. "I'll go change."

Moments later, they met back in the front room. Patti carried a midsize black satchel slung over her shoulder.

"I don't even want to know what's inside that thing," Kathy said.

"Well, I'm not going to put on a holster and carry the gun at my hip, for God's sake." She grinned. "Take it easy there, pilgrim," Patti said in a deep voice. "This ain't the Wild Wild West, ya know."

"John Wayne?"

Patti gave her sister a thumbs-up.

"I guess it wouldn't be a good idea to wear a holster, then," Kathy said.

"Anyway. We'll drive your car. Park several blocks away from his house. That way, when we leave, none of his immediate neighbors will be able to identify our car."

"Wow. You're really good at this stuff, you know that?" Kathy said.

"I don't want to get caught any more than you do."

Thirty minutes later, Kathy was driving down Charlie's street, then around the corner and down two blocks, parking where there was no street lamp in front of a home with no lights on. "Is this okay?"

"Perfect," Patti said, pulling the satchel out of the backseat. "Turn off the car's interior lights before opening your door."

"Yes, ma'am."

"Don't be snarky. I told you, I've thought of everything. Just do what I tell you, and we'll get through this thing. Unscathed and unharmed."

"I swear, you've got a real flare for this criminal stuff," Kathy said.

"Oh, for God's sake, Kathy. I wouldn't exactly call *us* the ones who are the criminals here."

"I know, and I'm sorry. Charlie's the criminal who'll never spend one night in the slammer for raping you. I get it."

"Leave the car unlocked. This is a safe area, and it'll make for a quicker getaway. Oh, and keep the keys in your front pocket for easy access. No fumbling around."

"Roger that," Kathy replied.

Patti laughed under her breath. "Now you're getting the hang of it. Just do as you're told and don't talk much. Leave it to me. I'll take care of everything. Just follow my directions."

They walked at a normal pace and stopped two houses from Charlie's. Lights were on in the front bay window. They listened for any shouting or talking. None. No cars were in the driveway or parked in front of his house.

"Does he park in the garage, or do you think he's gone?" Patti asked.

"There's a small window that runs across the garage door. I'll look inside."

They walked up to his house, and Kathy cupped her hands against the glass and looked through the window into the garage. "His car's here," she whispered.

Patti nodded, then tiptoed up the walkway to the front door. "Here goes." She knocked on the door.

In less than five seconds, it opened. Charlie switched on the porch light and squinted. "What the hell are you doing here?"

"We wanted to talk to you, Charlie," Patti said politely. "It'll only take a moment. May we come in?"

"I don't have anything to say to either of you, so no, you can't come in." He started to push the door closed.

Patti stuck her black boot out, stopping the door. "Five minutes, Charlie. What're you afraid of? We just want to talk. Clear the air."

He screwed up his lips, nostrils flaring. "Five minutes, then you're outta here. I told you, I have nothing to say to either of you." He opened the door wide.

Patti and Kathy slipped past him and stood in the foyer.

"Can we at least sit down?" Patti asked, looking him in the eyes.

He walked into the front room, and they followed him.

Patti dropped the satchel onto the wood coffee table in front of the couch and sat down. Kathy sat next to her, balancing on the edge of the cushion.

Charlie sat across from them in a Barcalounger.

Patti leaned over, stuck her hand into the satchel, and switched on the small voice recorder she'd placed inside.

"What's in that thing?" Charlie said.

"A recorder."

"What for? This isn't a police station, Patti. I don't have to talk to you about anything."

She pulled out two pairs of surgical gloves and tossed a pair to Kathy.

"What the hell are you doing?" he said, rising from the lounger.

Patti stuffed her hands inside the gloves, then extracted the .357 Magnum, holding it securely in one hand, cupping the hand holding the gun with her other hand, and pointed it straight at him.

Charlie jumped back in his chair, both hands stuck out, palms facing outward. "Whoa, whoa, whoa!"

"I want to ask you a question, Charlie. And I just want to make sure you answer honestly," Patti said.

"What're you gonna do, Patti? Kill me?"

"Don't be ridiculous, Charlie. I have no intention of killing you. Though after I left the yacht that day, I felt like murdering you."

"You and I had a good time that day," he said, quirking up an eyebrow.

"You may have had a good time, Charlie, but I don't remember a single thing, because you drugged me. What did you put in my drink? Some sort of date-rape drug?"

He glanced to the side. "Don't know what you're talking about."

"Oh, yes, you do. And we're not leaving until you own up to what you did to me."

He turned to Kathy. "Why're you here?"

"Backup," Kathy said as she pulled on the gloves.

He turned to Patti. "I'm not saying a thing to either of you about that day. You and I spent an afternoon together in bed. That's the end of it."

Patti shook her head slowly and smiled. "Guess we'll need something to help you remember, Charlie." She nodded at Kathy.

Kathy stood, reached into the satchel, and took out a large roll of duct tape.

Charlie raised his butt out of the chair several inches.

Patti stood and pointed the gun squarely at him. "Do. Not. Move."

"You're not going to shoot me, Patti, so I'm hardly afraid for my life."

She let off the safety with a click. "Don't kid yourself, buster. I am dead serious."

He slowly lowered his butt into the chair, his face beet red.

She knew he was taking her seriously. And he was mad as hell.

"I won't kill you, but I will hurt you, Charlie. Have you ever been shot? They say it hurts like hell, especially in the arm or the leg. And you usually don't pass out. You remain awake, praying for the pain to go away."

"The neighbors will hear," he replied.

"Then Kathy will just have to turn on the television. Really, really loud."

"I never do that. They'll know something's up," he said.

"Well, then." Patti stretched out her hand toward Kathy. Her eyes remained unblinkingly on Charlie, and the gun never shifted position.

Kathy handed her the roll of duct tape.

"You're not serious," Charlie said. "Are you two nuts?"

"On second thought, Kathy, will you do the honors?" Patti handed Kathy the duct tape, eyes never leaving Charlie. "I don't want to be distracted. I need to keep this gun aimed at him at all times. And if you're going to make noise, Charlie, then I have no alternative."

Kathy picked at the edge of the roll of duct tape until it started to unwind. She yanked harder, and almost two feet ripped off. "Shit!"

"That's okay." Patti flipped her chin toward Charlie. "Mouth."

Kathy took a step toward Charlie.

"Hey!" he shouted.

Kathy's eyes bulged, and she froze in mid-stride.

"Hurry up," Patti said.

"Wait!" he yelled.

Kathy lunged toward him, smashing the tape against his lips.

He grabbed both her arms, swinging her away from him onto the floor, then pulled the duct tape from his mouth.

Patti aimed the gun at the side of the Barcalounger and fired.

The sound reverberated off the walls, sounding like a minor sonic boom.

Charlie froze.

Kathy rolled to her back and sat up, covering her mouth with both hands.

Patti smiled. "Huh! Not as loud as I thought it would be. But we better hurry this little discussion along in case I've disturbed any of your neighbors, Charlie." She aimed the gun at him again. "I'm only going to say this once, Charlie. Keep quiet, or I'll wrap this duct tape around your mouth so tightly, when you pull it off, it'll rip your skin off. Understood?"

Charlie nodded. "I'll be quiet."

"Thank you, Charlie," Patti said in a sickeningly sweet tone of voice. "Now, Kathy? Stand up and give Charlie the duct tape, please."

Kathy reached out and handed him the roll.

His hand shook so badly, he dropped it on the floor, then picked it up.

"Charlie, I want you to wrap your ankles together. Make it tight. I'll be watching every freaking move you make. And after you do that, I want you to duct-tape your knees together." She motioned with the gun. "Kathy, when he's finished, he's going to hand you the tape. Then I want you to put the handcuffs on him. Do you understand me?"

Kathy nodded, reached in the satchel, and pulled out the handcuffs.

"You know what to do," Patti urged.

Kathy glanced at Patti, then down at the handcuffs, looking at them as if they were moon rocks.

Patti took a step toward Charlie and pointed the gun at his legs, moving it from side to side. "Get going, Charlie, or I'll shoot you in the leg. I swear to God."

He bent over and began wrapping the tape around his ankles.

"Put your feet closer together and wrap it tighter, and don't stop until I tell you."

He glanced up at her, eyes blazing, lips bunched so tightly it looked as if he'd been sucking on a lemon.

Silence hung in the air like a cloud while she watched him push his knees together firmly and wrap them with the tape.

"You can stop now," Patti said. "And don't do anything to her, Charlie. Don't you touch her. And don't make any quick moves, or I'll pull the trigger, and I may miss and hit you God knows where." She paused and watched as Kathy took the duct tape from Charlie's hand and stuffed it into the satchel.

"Handcuffs, Kathy," Patti said in a monotone.

Kathy stood, wobbling.

Patti frowned. "You all right, Kath?"

Kathy nodded while snapping the handcuffs on Charlie's wrists and squeezing them so they were tight.

"Since you pulled that little stunt with my sister, she's now going to tape your mouth shut."

"Please," he whispered.

"Please what, Charlie?"

"I feel sick to my stomach. If I puke, I'll die choking on my vomit."

"Then are you ready to talk?" Patti asked.

He nodded.

"I said, are you ready to talk? Say it."

"Yes, I'm ready to talk," he mumbled.

"I want you to tell me what happened the day I came to visit you at the yacht, Charlie. And you better tell the truth, or I'll aim this gun at your leg and pull the trigger."

"That would be murder."

"Oh, don't worry, Charlie. We'll call an ambulance on our way home." She cleared her throat. "Now. Back to the business at hand." She paused. "I went to the ER after you raped me. They examined me and collected evidence for a Sexual Assault Kit. Then I spoke with the police. But you already know that, because the sergeant told me what you said to them. That we had consensual sex over and over throughout that afternoon. That we both took drugs to enhance our sexual experience. That I was a jealous bitch who wanted you back from my sister. That I came to your house every day, begging for you to take me back.

"But they couldn't identify any known drug. The test was therefore what they call inconclusive. Lucky me." She sneered at him, her eyes never leaving his face. "So essentially it's your word against mine. The DA will never file charges against you. And if I hired an attorney, he or she would have a hard time proving you'd drugged me then raped me.

"But now, you know what, Charlie? Now you know what it feels like to be helpless. Just like you made me feel when I woke up in your bed on the yacht... after you drugged me and raped me. And you won't be able to prove we were ever here, or that I shot a bullet into your Barcalounger. This gun's not registered in my name. In fact, it's not registered at all. And the first thing I'll do is get rid of it. And my voice recorder? Believe me, I'll hide it where even I won't remember where it is. So if you try to accuse the two of us for assault? All I can say to that it," Patti giggled, " good luck Charlie! Even if the police got a search warrant, they won't find a dam thing. Plus, Kathy and I are both wearing surgical gloves, too. And you know where Kathy and I are? We're home, watching TV. And it's on really loud, so even my neighbors can hear it. Hey, Charlie. We were never here." Patti laughed out loud.

"Whaddaya want me to say?" he whispered.

"The truth, you bastard," she replied, taking a step closer and pointing the gun straight at his crotch.

His eyes began to water. "You said my leg."

"I'll reposition my aim as soon as you start talking."

"All right. I dropped a roofie into your champagne. Are you satisfied now?"

"As a matter of fact, no, I'm not satisfied. But *you* sure were after you raped me." She stepped a few inches closer, still aiming at his crotch. "What drug was it, Charlie? Where'd you get it?"

"I don't know what it was. I got it from a friend who bought it from someone who lives in Colombia."

"Thanks for the information, Charlie. That makes me feel a whole lot better. What did you do while I was drugged and not awake?"

"We had sex."

She cocked the gun. "I'll repeat this only once, Charlie. One. More. Time." She paused. "What happened while I was drugged out of my mind on the drug you put in my drink? Say it loud and clear so Kathy and I can hear you."

He stared at the tip of the gun. Wet ovals of sweat appeared on his T-shirt under his arms, and his thighs shook.

"I raped you, okay? I said what you wanted me to say. Now let me go."

"That's not what I want you to say, Charlie. I want you to tell me in your own words exactly what you did to me. A blow-by-blow description of exactly what happened that day." She waved the gun again and held the muzzle mere inches from his groin.

"All right. Just please don't shoot me in the balls," he pleaded. "I swear to God, I'll fucking kill you if you do."

"You'll probably die first, so I'm not really worried about that, Charlie." She flicked the gun again. "Now start talking, or I swear to God…"

"Okay!" he shouted, then took a deep breath. "I picked you up and took you into the bedroom and laid you on top of the bed."

"Nope, that's not true, Charlie. When I woke up, I was under the sheets. How did I get there? I told you, give me a blow-by-blow account or else."

"All right! I already had the sheets pulled back before I took you to the bedroom."

"What great planning, Charlie. Continue, please. Then what happened?"

"I put you on the bed and took off your clothes and—"

"Exactly what clothes did you start with? Tell me exactly which clothes you removed, Charlie."

He huffed out a breath. "I pulled off your shorts first, then I unbuttoned your blouse."

"What color were my shorts, Charlie?"

"Huh?"

"I said, what color were my shorts?"

He closed his eyes for a second. "Some sort of brownish yellow, like khaki."

"And my blouse?"

"White."

"Go on. What did you remove next?"

"Your panties. White panties, kind of like a thong."

"Next?"

"Bra."

"What color?"

"White with lace on the outside of the cups."

"Oh, you're getting your memory back, Charlie. Good for you."

Silence.

"Then what did you do?"

"What do you want me to say? That I had sex with you? Okay, I did."

Patti shook her head. "Not good enough, Charlie. I want you to tell me exactly which parts of my body you touched with what parts of your body."

"You've gotta be kidding me." He glanced at Kathy.

"My sister is intimately aware of how you made love to her, Charlie, so don't be embarrassed. Now you're going to tell me exactly what you did to *me*."

His nostrils flared, and he blew out a puff of air through his nose. "I went down on you."

"You mean, you made oral contact with my vaginal area and my clitoris with your mouth and tongue?"

"Jesus, Patti." He paused.

She stared him down, unblinking.

"Yes, I licked your vaginal area." He paused. "And I rubbed your breasts with my hands at the same time."

"Did that feel good, Charlie? Did it give you an erection?"

"Fuck." He paused. "Yes, I got an erection."

"Then what did you do?"

"You moaned, and I thought you were enjoying it."

"You asshole. I was completely out of it. I don't remember a thing. You drugged me!"

"I know. I'm sorry, okay?"

"Not good enough, Charlie. What did you do next?"

"I laid on top of you, and… and—"

"And? Come on and say it, Charlie. Did you stick your penis in my vagina?"

"Yes, I did."

"You told me I put the condom on you."

"I didn't wear a condom," he whispered.

"You didn't wear a condom," she said. "So you lied to me about that?"

He nodded.

"I asked you a question, Charlie. Did you lie to me about my putting the condom on your erect penis?"

"Yes, I lied. I didn't wear a condom."

"How long did it take for you, once you entered my vagina, to ejaculate? How long were you pumping your penis into my vagina before you came?"

"Hell, I don't remember! Jesus Christ!"

"When a man does what you did to me, Charlie, what would you call that act? You know, sticking your penis in my vagina without my consent?"

He mumbled something unintelligible.

She stepped closer to him and brought the muzzle of the gun to within an inch of the zipper of his pants.

He sucked in his abdomen. "Rape," he said, his voice shaking. "I raped you."

She shuffled backward and sat on the couch, then placed the gun on the table close to her within easy reach. She clapped her hands together lightly, then stronger and louder until the sound echoed throughout the front room.

"Good for you, Charlie," she said, "for admitting what you did to me. You really manned up. I'm proud of you."

He stared into her eyes. "You can't use that recording as evidence, you know. You coerced me into saying what you wanted to hear."

She stood and picked up the gun, then glanced at Kathy.

"Tape his mouth."

"No!" he yelled.

Patti lifted an eyebrow. "What are you scared of, Charlie? I was never going to shoot you, and you know it. But your version of what happened that night is the truth, isn't it?" She glared at him, shaking the gun back and forth next to her upper thigh.

His eyes widened. He looked terrified as he nodded.

"I can't hear you, Charlie," Patti said loudly.

"Yes. It's true what I told you." He hesitated, staring at Patti's hand holding the gun as she patted it against her thigh.

"I raped you that night," he said, his voice shaking. "I'm sorry!"

Patti nodded at her sister. "Do it, Kathy. Tape him up. There's a pair of scissors in a plastic bag in the satchel. Remove the plastic bag and leave them on the table over here next to me, after you've taped his mouth shut. And put the phone on the table next to the Barcalounger in case Charlie wants to call 911. Then we're leaving."

"You can't do this," he said. "You can't leave me tied—"

Kathy stuck the duct tape over his lips, silencing his words mid-sentence.

After wrapping the tape around his mouth and head twice, she glanced at Patti. Patti nodded, and Kathy cut the tape, then smoothed the end down near his ear. She placed the scissors on the table, then swung around, grabbed the phone, and set it next to the scissors.

"Oh, wait," Patti said. "Charlie, stand up."

His eyebrows drew together, and he didn't move.

Patti grabbed the handcuffs and yanked. "I said, stand the fuck up!"

Charlie stood, and Patti pushed the Barcalounger to the side with her foot.

"Kathy, get the scissors and dig the bullet out of the side of the Barcalounger. You can see where it is, on the inside of the right armrest."

Kathy took the scissors and dug the bullet out of the side of the ragged-looking Barcalounger, making a hole the size of a marshmallow. She handed the bullet to Patti.

"Sorry about the Barcalounger, Charlie," Patti said, "but I don't think anyone will notice. It's not in the best condition."

Patti threw the bullet in the satchel, placed the gun inside as well, then picked up the satchel, nodded at her sister, and they walked into the foyer, opened the front door, and left.

Charlie's grunts could be heard from the doorstep, but the sounds faded as the women walked down the path to the sidewalk.

Patti pulled off her gloves and rummaged in the satchel while they walked slowly to the car. She grabbed the recorder and pressed rewind, then play, and they listened to Charlie's voice saying, "You can't leave me tied—" before Kathy taped his mouth shut.

Patti grinned, turned to Kathy, and Kathy smiled back as she handed her gloves to Patti.

When they reached the car, Kathy slipped behind the wheel, started the car, and they drove home in silence. It wasn't until Patti dropped the satchel on the coffee table at home that she exhaled one long, deep breath.

Patti lowered the volume on the TV. "I feel good."

"Never thought I'd say it, but revenge really is sweet," Kathy replied.

"And none of his neighbors called the cops." Patti smiled. "I guess luck was on our side tonight."

They plopped down onto the couch, reached toward each other, and held hands.

After several silent moments, Patti said, "I'm going to change into something more comfortable. Let's meet back here and watch some TV." She stood, grabbing the duffel bag on her way out of the room.

Kathy yawned. "I'll put a bag of popcorn in the microwave, then put on my jammies. BRB."

# Chapter Thirty-Nine

Kathy stared at the television, remote in hand, changing channels. "I'm worried there's going to be a knock on our front door, and it'll be the cops. I'm so stressed out right now."

"What proof would Charlie have, Kath?"

"I don't know." Kathy shrugged. "Fingerprints?"

Patti laughed out loud. "You watch too much *Forensic Files*. We both had gloves on, remember?"

"You're right. I forgot."

"I put both pairs back under the kitchen sink where they belong. I took everything out of the duffel bag when we got home and put the bag back in the attic. If the cops were to come to our door right now, I wouldn't deny we were at Charlie's house. We've known him since high school. We were visiting him. We talked. We left. That's it."

"And the duct tape we used?"

"For one, it's my duct tape, but hey, I loaned it to Charlie. We've all been friends for years. Two, I hid the gun in that special place under the stairs you showed me when I moved in, so we don't have to worry about that. What's he got on us?"

Kathy held up her index finger. "The bullet from your gun is… oh, that's right. I took it out of the Barcalounger." Kathy held up her finger again. "Wait! You can clearly hear the gun go off in the recording."

"No one is going to hear that recording, Kathy. So listen to me. I don't own a real gun. If someone were to ask you about a gun, you say you don't know anything about a gun. Deny. Deny. Deny. I'm telling you, Charlie can't prove a thing." Patti shrugged. "I can always say he made up the entire story because he was pissed off I wouldn't go out with him. He was your boyfriend for more than a year, and I wasn't interested, blah, blah, blah. It's the whole jilted-love interest thing, okay? So that's what we'll say if it ever comes to that. Ya got it?"

"Okay. Okay. We just have to get our stories straight in case the cops *do* come knocking at our door."

"You really are paranoid, Kath. If for some reason, though I have no idea what that reason would be, we got arrested, though I really don't see how the hell that could happen either, then we could always play the recording of Charlie admitting he raped me."

"And the gun? It's obvious on the recording you were holding a gun, Patti, and that you shot it. They can hear it on the recording."

"He admitted he raped me *after* I shot the gun, Kathy. So I delete that part of the recording and let the police listen to it. And even if the recording isn't acceptable evidence in court, because we coerced his confession from him, I doubt a judge or jury would give either of us a lengthy sentence. If we got any sentence at all. We can say yes, we tied him up with duct tape. Kind of like a prank."

"Even if you deleted the part of the recording where you can hear the gun go off, Patti, you still mention the gun again and again after you shoot it. Like when Charlie said something about not shooting him in the balls. It's right there in the recording."

Patti let out a sigh. "Listen, Kathy. All I'd have to say is that I had a toy gun that looked very real, and I pretended I was going to use it. Charlie didn't know the difference, and it worked. Afterward, I threw the gun into the recycling bin, since I'd had it since I was a kid." She paused. "You really are making this more difficult than it needs to be."

"Okay, I'm sorry. It's just, we have to think of all the things the police might ask us if they came to our door right now. We have to get our stories straight."

"You're right, Kathy, and I'm sorry. I said you were being difficult, and you really aren't. You are completely correct. I was wrong for not making sure we sit down and talk this out completely. I'm glad we're doing that now."

"I just want to cover all our bases. Just in case."

"And you are totally right. I should have thought of that, and I didn't. I'm an idiot."

"But, Patti—"

"Yeah?"

"We really don't need the recording, then. It sounds to me like Charlie can't prove a damn thing if there's no bullet, no gun, no fingerprints. There's no proof that anything went on tonight except what's on that recording. And if we're never going to really use it, then why don't we throw it away?"

Patti shrugged. "Good point. And you know what? I could throw the damn thing away, because I got what I wanted. I got the confession I needed. But I'm not a genius, Kath. I can't predict the future. What if for some reason we can't possibly know right now, they bring us in for questioning, and we need to explain why we were there at Charlie's house or something? I don't know what it could be, but—"

"Just in case, right? I get it. Let's keep the recording then. I'd feel better having it for backup. We aren't attorneys, and there could be some reason we can't think of right now where we'll need it. I agree with you."

Patti sighed. "I'm exhausted."

"What if the police get a warrant to search this house and find the gun under the stairs?"

"If it'll make you feel better," Patti said, smiling, "I can throw the damn thing in the middle of the ocean. Robert's always asking me if I want to go sailing. It's the perfect venue for getting rid of a gun. I promise I'll do that."

"When?" Kathy asked.

Patti rolled her eyes. "Will you just chill? I said I'll do it, and I will. Don't worry your pretty little head about it."

Kathy rolled her eyes, mimicking her sister. "I'm just making sure we've thought of literally everything. Everything. But, okay, just get rid of the gun as soon as you can, and I'll shut up now."

Kathy and Patti fell asleep on the couch. Kathy woke up at midnight and trudged upstairs to bed. She tossed and turned for hours, worrying the San Diego police would show up at their door. As long as that gun was still under the stairs, she was going to continue to worry. Every wisp of air through the curtains, every creak in the house caused Kathy to cringe, afraid she and Patti would be arrested.

Finally, at six o'clock in the morning, she got out of bed, showered, and dressed, then went downstairs to eat breakfast.

She found Patti sitting at the kitchen table.

"What are you doing up?" Kathy asked.

"Couldn't sleep. I was so amped after last night, I couldn't calm down."

Kathy blurted out, "Is it harmful to smoke weed when you're pregnant?"

Patti jerked her head back. "You smoke weed?"

"I did before I found out I was pregnant. Now I'm worried about its effects on the baby, so I stopped."

"From what I've read, if marijuana is smoked or ingested by a pregnant woman, THC might cross the placenta and enter the fetus' bloodstream. So it could be harmful."

Kathy tilted her head. "Why'd you look it up in the first place?"

"Same reason as you. I've been smoking it since I was a teenager. Off and on, that is. Only recreational. Maybe four or five times a year."

"Same for me. I'd hardly call myself a pothead."

"How'd we get on this subject?" Patti asked.

"I asked you if weed's harmful to the baby."

Patti frowned. "Why'd you ask?"

"I tossed and turned all night, worrying the cops were going to knock on our door." Kathy stood. "I almost wish I could have a shot of whiskey right now. But I can't drink. I can't smoke. So I better fix some chamomile tea or something. But I hate chamomile tea."

"What are you going to do when you go to work? You'll see Mark. You can't tell him about any of this," Patti said.

Kathy waved away her sister. "I'm not telling him a thing about last night. Are you telling Robert?"

"Never," Patti said. "He'd be angry I took the matter into my own hands and left him out. I promised him I'd think about letting him participate."

"You did think about it and decided against exacting revenge," Kathy replied.

"Egg-zactly." Patti grinned, then turned toward the stairs.

"Wait," Kathy said.

Patti faced her sister.

"Do you think Charlie will call the police?"

Patti laughed out loud. "You are relentless, Kath. Obviously, he hasn't called them yet, 'cause no police have shown their faces at our door, have they? So I highly doubt it. Hey, I've gotta get to work."

"And the gun?"

Patti rolled her eyes. "I promise to ask Robert if we can go sailing this weekend. And I'll take it with me and throw it overboard when he's not looking. Okay? Satisfied?"

"Just covering our bases." Kathy grinned.

They didn't hear from Charlie or the cops that day nor the weeks following. After spending Halloween night handing out candy, they both plopped down on the couch and sighed.

"That was exhausting," Kathy said.

Patti leaned her head back and shut her eyes. "I want to just veg out and watch a movie. How 'bout you?"

"We could watch *Halloween* one, two, three, four—"

Patti bolted upright. "Hey, you know what? All's quiet on the Western front."

"Never saw that movie," Kathy replied.

"Ernest Borgnine, Donald Pleasence, Richard Thomas." Patti slapped at her sister's arm. "But that's not what I'm talking about."

Kathy frowned. "What?"

"We haven't heard anything since that night with Charlie."

Kathy let out a huge sigh. "You're right."

"Have you finally settled down and stopped fretting about what happened, Kath?"

"Ever since you threw the gun in the ocean, I've felt better, yes," Kathy said. "I'm not so paranoid any longer that anything's going to happen to us if the cops come to our door. Plus, if I were Mom or Sharon, I'd say Charlie's the type of guy who'd be too humiliated to admit that two, quote unquote, *women* got the better of him. Two *women* busted into his house, overpowered him, tied him up, and scared the crap out of him. He wouldn't want anyone to know that. Ever.

"He might also be afraid you'd press charges for drugging and raping you. He knows you went to the ER and got the test results, and though they were inconclusive, that doesn't mean you couldn't still take him to court, right? He might be shaking in his boots right now, as Dad would say. I'm sure he wouldn't want to take the chance of ruining his reputation at his very upscale yacht business to accuse us of an unprovable home invasion."

Patti pointed at her sister. "Sounds to me as if this time *you've* got it all figured out."

# Chapter Forty

And suddenly it was Thanksgiving. It had been several months since the Labor Day debacle. Sharon and Dad had hired extra help to make sure everything worked smoothly on the ranch. Sharon said their father was feeling like his "old*er* self," his words. Everyone decided to spend Thanksgiving Day at the ranch. Kathy, Mark, Patti, and Robert rented a Mercedes SUV and took two days to drive to Quincy.

They visited San Francisco and took a boat ride around the island of Alcatraz, wine-tasted in the Sonoma Valley, and arrived at the ranch Thanksgiving Day morning.

Dad walked from the barn, leading one of the horses, and waved to them as he approached.

"Happy Turkey Day to y'all." He hugged the two women and shook hands with Mark and Robert. "Sharon and I are so happy you all decided to spend the holiday with us. There will be some good eatin', too. Sharon baked a twenty-pound turkey, and we've got green bean casserole and scalloped potatoes and pies. She even made fudge."

Kathy groaned. "And when I get home, Dr. Holmer is going to be very angry at all the extra weight I gained."

Mark put his arm around her shoulders, bringing her in closer, and kissed her forehead. "Hate to be cliché, but hey, more of you to love."

"Oh, there's plenty of me, all right. I'm due in one month. I'm the size of a hot-air balloon."

Bill laughed and glanced at Mark, giving him a thumbs-up.

"Speaking of more to love," Robert added, leaning over and kissing Patti on the cheek.

She slapped him away, giving him a dirty look. "I cannot wait for January to come. By then, I'll be as big as a horse." She stepped next to her father and looked into the big, black Friesian's eyes. "Who is this big guy, Dad? I'm almost as big as he is."

Her dad chuckled. "Just arrived yesterday. Sharon has a client who's already paid forty grand for this stallion."

"And he's a beauty. I'd love to ride him," she said.

"Do you think that's a good idea, honey?" Robert asked.

Patti shook her head. "No. Especially since the doctor said the baby could come earlier. I wouldn't want to risk it since I haven't ridden in quite a while."

"Why don't you all go inside?" Bill said. "Sharon's in the kitchen, cooking up a storm."

Robert gestured toward the driveway. "Wonder whose car that is?"

"Maybe Maggie's," Kathy replied. "Sharon wants us to meet her."

"It's Helen's car," Bill said.

Patti stopped in her tracks.

Kathy's mouth dropped half open.

"Why's *she* here?" Patti asked.

Her father squared his shoulders and looked into Patti's eyes. "Because she's family, that's why."

Patti stared at her father, unblinking. He was right. It was all about family, and if Helen abided by Dad's rules, she was welcome at the ranch. Dad had said as much before Helen left. "Okay."

Kathy touched Patti on the forearm. "He's right, you know. This is still Helen's home."

Bill led the stallion back to the barn. Mark and Robert retrieved their suitcases and satchels from the back of the SUV and walked up the pathway.

The two couples traipsed up the stairs to the porch. Patti reached the porch first, followed by Kathy, then Robert and Mark.

The front door opened.

"Hey," Helen said, lifting her hand in a gentle wave.

"The prodigal daughter returns," Patti said. "How long have you been back?"

Helen held the front door open. "Got here yesterday."

Patti walked past Helen into the foyer.

Kathy stopped in front of Helen, looking into her eyes. "I hope your visit isn't going to upset Dad. You know what his doctor told him about stress."

Helen met her sister's gaze full-on. "I'm aware of that, Kathy. And I want to apologize for what I said. For everything I said to you and Patti and Sharon and Dad about your babies."

Patti grasped Kathy's arm, staring at Helen. "What's with the big turnaround, Helen? You haven't suddenly seen the light at the end of the tunnel of the Lord or something, have you?"

Helen sucked in her lips, her eyes shiny with tears. "I've been in therapy since the last time I saw you. And rehab. I know I'm going to have to prove to Dad, to all of you, that I've changed."

"What happened?" Patti said. "We've had bets on whether you'd come back to the ranch pregnant. Just to make sure you got as much money as the rest of us."

"Patti, don't," Kathy interjected.

"Don't what?" Patti said, staring into Helen's face. "Answer me, Helen. Is that what's going on here?"

"Peter and I are having a baby, yes."

"Who the hell is Peter?" Patti said.

"He and I have been seeing each other since October. I just found out I was pregnant last week."

"How very convenient," Patti said. "I'm sure it was a planned pregnancy. Unlike Kathy and me. Charlie dumped Kathy, thank God, since he turned out to be a rapist anyway. But you remember that story, don't you, Helen?"

"I know it's going to take a while for you to see that I've changed, Patti." Helen faced Kathy. "I'm sorry for what happened between you and Charlie." She turned to Patti. "And I think he's a real shit for what he did to you." She paused. "I don't think either of you could hate me more than I hate myself. What I said to you, calling your babies bastards... I was a real bitch."

Sharon entered the foyer. "Hey, everybody. Why don't you shut the door? You're letting all the warm air out."

Mark and Robert walked through the doorway and shut the door behind them. "Hey, Sharon," they said.

"You can talk in the front room," Sharon said.

"I don't think there's much to discuss," Patti said, shifting her eyes to Helen, then Kathy.

"I apologized to Patti and Kathy, but Patti doesn't want to believe I've changed." Helen shrugged. "And I don't have much time to prove myself, do I? You guys are leaving on Sunday."

"Maybe you can come visit us in San Diego for a weekend," Kathy said.

Patti shook her head. "Get real, Kath. A leopard doesn't change its spots overnight."

Helen touched Kathy's arm. "She's right, Kathy. I don't expect either of you to suddenly believe in me. I'm a work in progress. But I'm getting there."

"So," Patti added, "your deep sense of entitlement just vanished into thin air practically overnight? Because you're now seeing a counselor? Sounds like you found quite the therapist. Or should we call him or her a miracle worker?"

Helen sucked in a breath. "I deserve that. And more. I just hope it doesn't take forever for you to love me again. I want us to be sisters."

Kathy hugged Helen. "We'll always be sisters. And we never stopped loving you, Helen. You're our sister, right?" Kathy turned to Patti and Sharon, who both nodded slowly. "I want you to come down for a visit, okay? I think it would go a long way to making us all feel comfortable and help us get to know the new Helen."

Robert came up behind Patti and wrapped his arms around her waist. "Holding in all this negativity can be damaging to you and our baby, right, Sharon? You have to try to let it go, babe. Give your sister a chance to prove herself." He looked over Patti's head into Helen's eyes.

Helen tilted her head. "*Your* baby?"

Kathy and Sharon moved closer to Patti and Robert.

Patti stepped to the side, bringing Robert in next to her. She stuck her left arm into the middle of their little circle and wiggled her fingers. "We're getting married after Kathy has her baby in December."

Kathy squealed. "How long has that been on your finger?"

Patti grinned. "I hid it in may purse until just now."

Kathy enveloped Patti in a hug, then turned and hugged Robert. "Congratulations, you guys! That's wonderful."

Robert beamed. "Our ceremony will be after Kathy and Mark's wedding."

Patti shifted her eyes to Kathy. "You and Mark are engaged… and you knew, Robert?"

"We'll get married after I have the baby," Kathy said.

Sharon looked at Patti, then Kathy. "Are we all invited to your wedding? Helen, too?"

Patti glanced down, took a deep breath, and met Helen's gaze. "Yes, Helen, too."

Kathy smiled. "Ditto."

"Maybe you should have a dual wedding ceremony," Sharon added.

Everyone laughed.

"We'll have to talk about that," Patti said.

Kathy nodded with a smile spread across her face.

Helen reached out with both hands and took hold of Patti's and Kathy's. "You'll see, Patti, Kathy. I've really changed." She glanced at Sharon.

Sharon looked Helen in the eyes. "I believe you have, Helen."

Patti nodded.

Kathy grasped Patti's other hand, then hitched her chin toward Sharon. Sharon moved next to Helen and joined the circle.

"Family," Kathy said, looking from one sister to the next.

"Family," they all chimed together, laughing.

"And fences can be mended," Sharon added.

# About the Author

Born and raised in the San Francisco Bay Area, Patricia attended St. Mary's College, studied her junior year at the University of Madrid, received a B.A. in Spanish at UC Santa Barbara then went on to get a Master's degree in Education at Oregon State University. She lives with her husband and two teenage children in Alameda, across the bay from San Francisco, along with two very large chocolate labs, Annabella and Jack. Her Friesian horse Maximus lives in the Oakland hills in a stall with a million dollar view.